SANTORIN

CRETE
ARABIAN TUNNEL

CRESPO

TROPIC OF CANCER

HAWAII

PACIFIC OCEAN

EQUATOR

NUKAHIVA

TIMOR
TORRES ST. VANIKORO SAMOA

KEELING CORAL COOK TAHITI
SEA FIJI CLERMONT-
TONNERRE

CAPRICORN

PAPUA

TORRES STRAIT CUEBOROAR I.
MURRAY
MULGRAVE I.
GREAT BARRIER REEF

CORAL
SEA

MAP OF THE VOYAGE MADE
20,000 LEAGUES
UNDER THE SEAS

– – – – TRACK OF THE ABRAHAM LINCOLN
——— TRACK OF THE NAUTILUS

ANTARCTIC CIRCLE

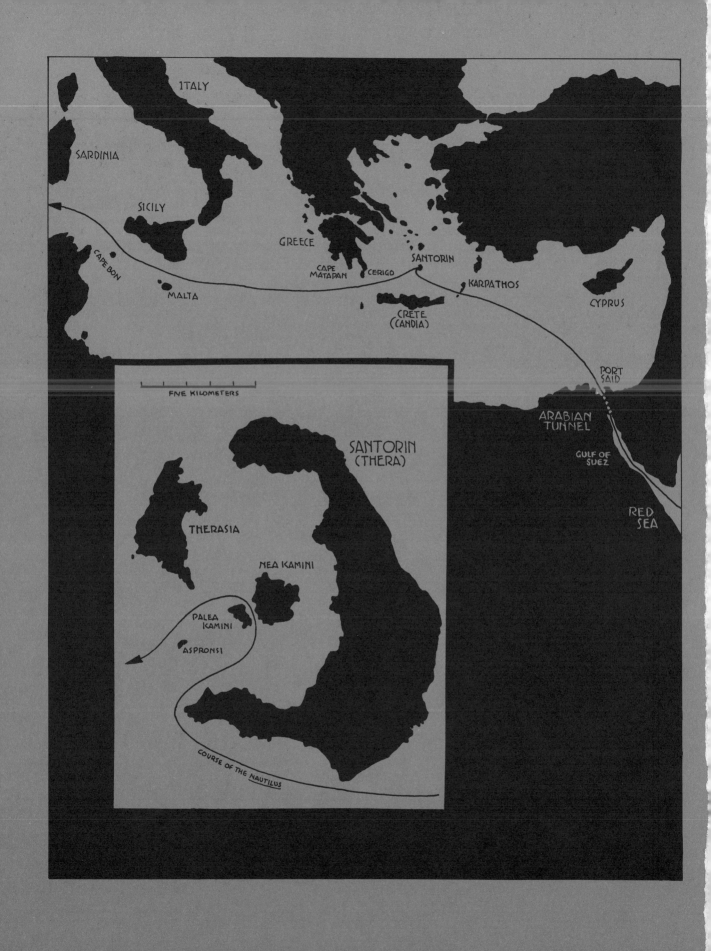

TWENTY THOUSAND LEAGUES UNDER the SEAS

TRANSLATOR'S NOTE

Twenty Thousand Leagues Under the Seas has only been translated into English about half a dozen times since it was originally published as *Vingt milles lieues sous les Mers.* The first time was in 1871 by Lewis Mercier. Five years later, another one appeared, translated by Henry Frith. Not for nearly a century was *Twenty Thousand Leagues* translated anew, this time by Anthony Bonner in 1962. It was followed by Walter Miller in 1965 and one by Mendor Brunetti in 1969.

Mercier's translation has become the "standard" English version because for ninety years it was the main English translation, and thus, was the first edition to enter the public domain. Today, there are scores of editions of the Mercier translation available, as opposed to those of Brunetti, Bonner or Walter Miller, as Mercier's is copyright-free. In the past century, there have been literally hundreds of reprints of the "standard" translation. It has become so ubiquitous, in fact, that many people believe that Verne wrote in English! This misconception is bolstered by the fact that many publishers leave off the name of the old translator.

Mercier, a Protestant minister and theological writer, had little background for translating a book full of scientific, technical, and nautical details. Very often, things were translated incorrectly. For example, at one point Mercier has Nemo explain that iron is lighter than water! Unfortunately, Verne was blamed for these errors. Additionally, Mercier cut the text wherever he did not understand Verne's science, or did not agree with Verne's politics or religion. Ultimately, Mercier cut more than twenty percent of the text! Hundreds of paragraphs of action, narration, and important character development are gone from Mercier's edition. In one case, an entire chapter is missing. It is little wonder, then, that for generations, readers of *Twenty Thousand Leagues Under the Seas* have often found themselves confused about what was going on!

Bonner's translation was a great improvement; his language and style are close to Verne's own. Unfortunately, there are still some things missing, and many of Mercier's old mistakes are re-made. Brunetti's is extremely accurate so far as content is concerned, but he has heavily rewritten Verne; the style is very much Brunetti's own. Miller's is good, but I find it compressed; narration and dialogue are often paragraphed. Miller also edited the *Annotated Jules Verne: Twenty Thousand Leagues Under the Sea* in which he explains in detail the problems with the "standard" translation, and undertakes to reprint it with the reinstated passages. However, man of Mercier's translating errors are left unexplained, and many of the missing parts are still missing.

So now we arrive at the book you have in your hands. It has at its core the old Mercier translation. I started with this because Mercier translated Verne very literally, changing word order only to the degree dictated by the differences in grammar. As a result, the style is very true to Verne's own. Beginning with this edition, I started making corrections. Errors in translation and scientific errors (Mercier's, not Verne's; any mistakes Verne himself made were left unchanged) were all fixed. This amounted to literally several thousand corrections. The style and wording was made as true as possible to the original. An example is the title: literal translation from the original French makes "Seas" plural. This is actually more accurate than "Sea" (singular), but the singular version is the most familiar.

Next, the missing text was replaced. More than three hundred passages were restored, ranging from individual paragraphs to several pages. Eventually, the finished manuscript was more than one-fifth longer than the "standard" text!

The same care was taken with the art. Each illustration, map and chart was as meticulously researched as Verne's original text. Every character, device, plant, animal and landscape, as well as the *Nautilus*, were made as true to the book as possible, and they are enhanced by full-color reproductions.

What you are about to read is probably the most complete, accurate version of *Twenty Thousand Leagues* available in the English language. As a great fan of Jules Verne, I tried to make this American edition as true to the thrust of Verne's scientific knowledge, political ideas, and vivid imagination as originally expressed in the original French edition.

Ron Miller
Fredericksburg, Virginia

December, 1987

TWENTY THOUSAND LEAGUES UNDER the SEAS

Illustrated by
RON MILLER
Story by Jules Verne

Translated by Ron Miller

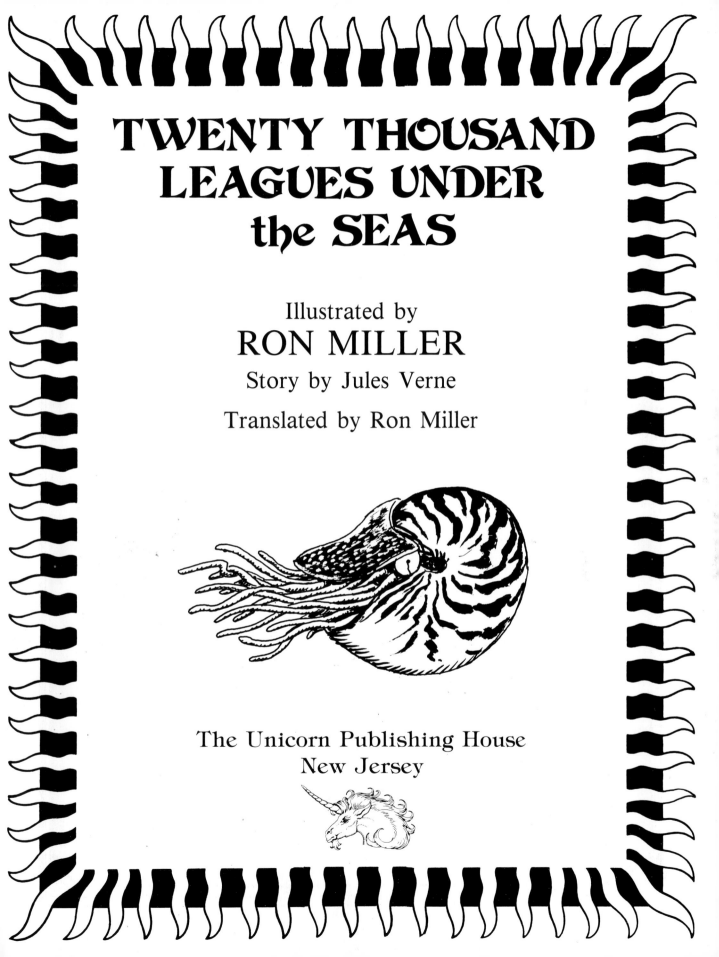

The Unicorn Publishing House
New Jersey

Designed and edited by Jean L. Scrocco
Associate Juvenile Editor: Heidi K.L. Corso
Printed in Singapore by Singapore National Printers Ltd
through Palace Press, San Francisco, CA.
Typography by Straight Creek Company, Denver, CO
Reproduction Photography by The Color Wheel, New York, NY

◆ ◆ ◆ ◆ ◆

◆ ◆ ◆ ◆ ◆

Distributed in Canada to the book trade by Doubleday Canada, Ltd., Toronto, ON
M5B 1Y3, Canada

◆ ◆ ◆ ◆ ◆

Special thanks to the entire Unicorn staff

◆ ◆ ◆ ◆ ◆

Printing History 15   14   13   12   11   10   9   8   7   6   5   4   3   2   1

◆ ◆ ◆ ◆ ◆

Library of Congress Cataloging-in-Publication Data

Verne, Jules, 1828-1905.
[Vingt mille lieues sous les mers. English]
20,000 leagues under the seas / by Jules Verne; illustrated by Ron Miller.
p.   cm.
Translation of: Vingt mille lieues sous les mers.
Summary: A nineteenth-century science fiction tale of an electric submarine, its
eccentric captain, and undersea world, which anticipated many of the scientific
achievements of the twentieth century.
ISBN 0-88101-085-5: $19.95
[1. Submarines—Fiction.   2. Sea stories.   3. Science fiction.]   I. Miller, Ron,
1947-   ill. II. Title.   III. Title: Twenty thousand leagues under the seas.
PZ.V594Tw   1988
[Fic]--dc19   88-10190
                                            CIP
                                            AC

Additional Classic and Contemporary Editions
Richly Illustrated in
This Unicorn Heirloom Collection:

PHANTOM OF THE OPERA
DAVY AND THE GOBLIN
AESOP'S FABLES
POLLYANNA
PETER PAN
PINOCCHIO
POE
THE WIZARD OF OZ
DRACULA
HEIDI
ANTIQUE FAIRY TALES
FROM TOLKIEN TO OZ
PETER COTTONTAIL'S SURPRISE
TREASURES OF CHANUKAH
A CHRISTMAS TREASURY

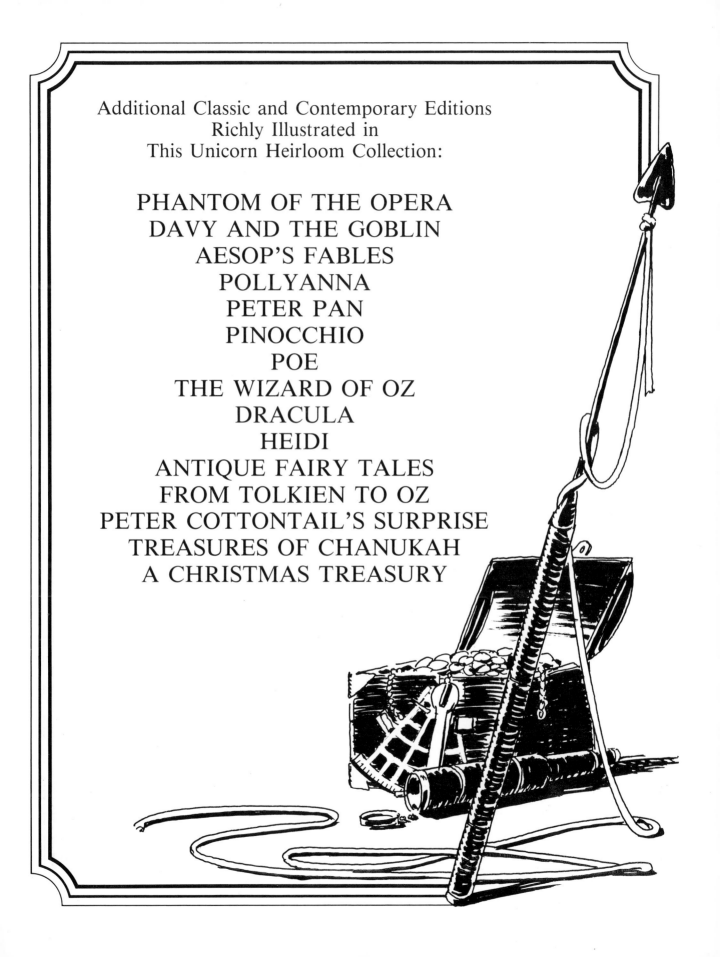

CAST OF CHARACTERS

David Reynolds—Captain Nemo
Tony Hardy—Conseil
Robb Kneebone—Ned Land

The likeness of Jules Verne was used for the character of
Professor Aronnax. Ron Miller posed for the scenes.

A sincere thank you to my friends
who posed for the unknown characters
in this edition of
Twenty Thousand Leagues Under the Seas

The Natives
The Crew of the Nautilus
The Crowd at the Brooklyn Pier

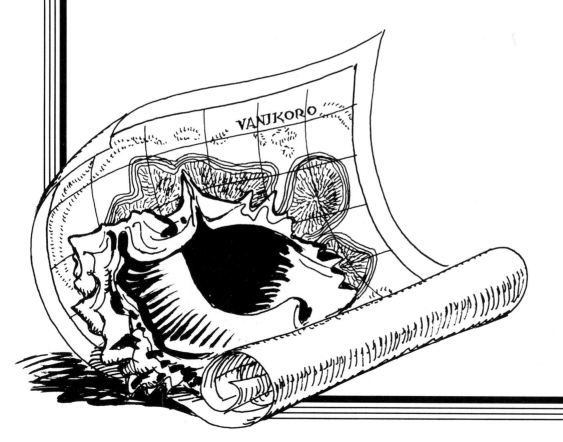

LIST OF ILLUSTRATIONS

LIST OF CHAPTERS

PART I

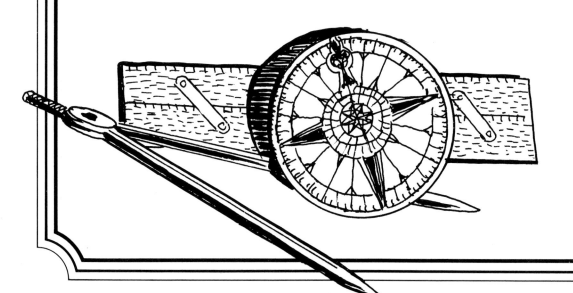

PART II

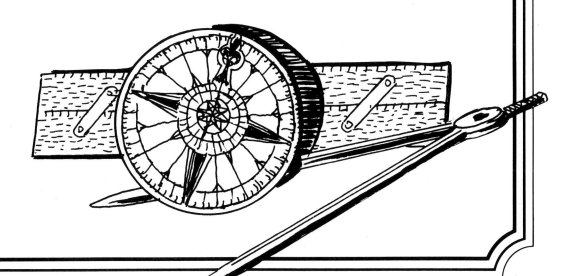

This book is dedicated to
fellow Vernians
Larry Knight, Tom Scherman, and
the late I.O. Evans

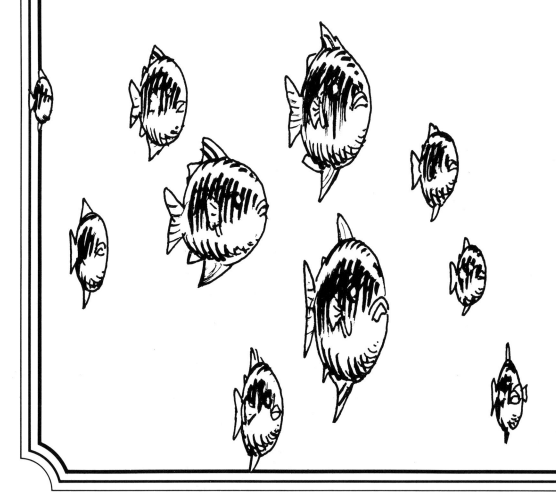

PART I

· THE SCOTIA ·

◄ CHAPTER I ►

A SHIFTING REEF

The year 1866 was signalized by a bizarre incident, a mysterious and inexplicable phenomenon, which doubtless no one has yet forgotten. Not to mention rumors which agitated the maritime population and excited the public mind, even in the interior of continents, seafaring men were particularly excited. Merchants, common sailors, captains of vessels, skippers and masters both of Europe and America, naval officers of all countries, and the Governments of several states on the two continents, were deeply interested in the matter.

For some time past, vessels had been met by "an enormous thing," a long object, spindle-shaped, occasionally phosphorescent, and infinitely larger and more rapid in its movements than a whale.

The facts relating to this apparition, entered in various log books, agreed in most respects as to the shape of the object or creature in question, the untiring rapidity of its movements, its surprising power of locomotion, and the peculiar life with which it seemed endowed. If is was a cetacean, it surpassed in size all those hitherto classified in science. Neither Cuvier, Lacédède, Dumeril nor de Quatrefayes would have admitted the existence of such a monster—unless they had seen it with their own scientists' eyes.

Taking the average of observations made at different times,—rejecting the timid estimate of those who assigned to this object a length of two hundred feet, equally with the exaggerated opinions which set it down as a mile in width and three in length,—we might fairly conclude that this mysterious being surpassed greatly all dimensions admitted by the ichthyologists of the day, if it existed at all.

But that it *did* exist was an undeniable fact; and, with that tendency which disposes the human mind in favor of the marvelous, we can understand the excitement produced in the entire world by this supernatural apparition. As to classing it in the list of fables, the idea was out of the question.

On the 20th of July 1866, the steamer *Governor Higginson,* of the Calcutta and Burnach Steam Navigation Company, had met this moving mass five miles off the east coast of Australia. Captain Baker thought at first that he was in the presence of an unknown reef; he even prepared to determine its exact position, when two columns of water, projected by the inexplicable object, shot with a hissing noise a hundred and fifty feet up into the air. Now, unless the reef had been submitted to the intermittent eruption of a geyser, the *Governor Higginson* had to do neither more nor less than with an aquatic mammal, unknown till then, which threw up from its blow-holes columns of water mixed with air and vapor.

Similar facts were observed on the 23rd of July in the same year, in the Pacific Ocean, by the *Cristobal Colon,* of the West India and Pacific Steam Navigation Company. Apparently this extraordinary cetaceous creature could transport itself from one place to another with surprising velocity; as, in an interval of three days, the *Governor Higginson* and the *Cristobal Colon* had observed it at two different points of the chart, separated by a distance of more than seven hundred nautical leagues.[1]

Fifteen days later, two thousand miles farther off, the *Helvetia,* of the Compagnie-Nationale, and the *Shannon,* of the Royal Mail, passing in opposite directions in that portion of the Atlantic lying between the United States and Europe, respectively signalled to one another that the monster had been seen in 42° 15′ N. lat. and 60° 35′ W. long. In these simultaneous observations, they thought themselves justified in estimating the minimum length of the mammal at more than three hundred and fifty feet,[2] as the *Shannon* and *Helvetia* were of smaller dimensions than it, though they both measured three hundred feet overall. Now the largest whales, those which frequent those parts of the sea round the Aleutian, Kulammak, and Umgullich islands, have never exceeded the length of fifty-six meters, if they attain that.

The reports arriving one after the other, with fresh observations made on board the transatlantic ship, *Le Pereire,* a collision which occurred between the *Etna* of the Inman line and the monster, an official memorandum directed by the officers of the French frigate *Normandie,* a very accurate survey made by the staff of Commodore Fitz-James on board the *Lord Clyde,* greatly influenced public opinion. Light-thinking people jested upon the phenomenon, but grave practical countries, such as England, America, and Germany, treated the matter more seriously.

In all the great capitals the monster was the fashion. They sang of it in the cafés, ridiculed it in the papers, and represented it on the stage. All kinds of stories were circulated regarding it. There appeared in the papers—otherwise short of copy—caricatures of every gigantic and imaginary creature, from the white whale, the terrible "Moby Dick" of hyperborean regions, to the immense kraken whose tentacles could entangle a ship of five hundred tons, and hurry it into the abyss of the ocean. The legends of ancient times were even resuscitated, and the opinions of Aristotle and Pliny revived, who admitted the existence of these monsters, as well as the Norwegian tales of Bishop Pontoppidan, the accounts of Paul Heggede, and, last of all, the reports of Mr. Harrington (whose good faith no one could suspect), who affirmed that, being on board the *Castillan,* in 1857, he had seen this enormous serpent, which had never until that time frequented any other seas but those once "navigated" by the now-defunct newspaper, *"Constitutionel."*

Then burst forth the interminable controversy between the credulous and the incredulous in the societies of savants and scientific journals. The "question of the monster" inflamed all minds. Editors of scientific journals, quarrelling with believers in the supernatural, spilled seas of ink during this memorable campaign, some even drawing blood; for, from talking about the sea-serpent, they turned all too easily to direct personalities.

For six months war was waged with various fortune. To leading articles by the geographical Institution of Brazil, the Royal Academy of Science of Berlin, the British Association, the Smithsonian Institution of Washington; to the discussions in the *Indian Archipelago,* in the *Cosmos* of the Abbé Moigno, in the *Mittheilungen* of Petermann; to the scientific chronicles of the great journals of France and other countries, the cheaper journals replied keenly and with inexhaustible zest. These satirical writers parodied a remark of Linnaeus, quoted by the adversaries of the monster, maintaining "that nature did not make fools," and adjured their contemporaries not to give the lie to nature by admitting the existence of krakens, sea-serpents, "Moby Dicks," and other lucubrations of delirious sailors. At length an article in a well-known satirical journal by a favorite contributor, the chief of the staff, settled the monster, like Hippolytus, giving it the death-blow amidst a universal burst of laughter. Wit had conquered science.

During the first months of the year 1867, the question seemed buried, never to revive, when new facts were brought before the public. It was then no longer a scientific problem to be solved, but a real danger seriously to be avoided. The question took quite another shape. The monster became again a small island, a rock, a reef, but a reef of indefinite and shifting proportions.

On the 5th of March, 1867, the *Moravian,* of the Montreal Ocean Company, finding herself during the night in 27° 30′ lat. and 72° 15′ long., struck on her starboard quarter a rock, marked in no chart for that part of the sea. Under the combined efforts of the wind and its four hundred horsepower, it was going at a rate of thirteen knots. Had it not been for the superior strength of the hull of the *Moravian,* she would have been broken by the shock, and gone down with the 237 passengers she was bringing home from Canada.

The accident happened about five o'clock in the morning, as the day was breaking. The officers of the watch hurried to the after-part of the vessel. They examined the sea with the most scrupulous attention. They saw nothing but a strong eddy about three cables' length distant, as if the smooth surface had been violently agitated. The bearings of the place were taken exactly, and the *Moravian* continued its route without apparent damage. Had it struck on a submerged rock, or on an enormous wreck? They could not tell; but on examination of the ship's bottom when undergoing repairs, it was found that part of her keel was broken.

This fact, so grave in itself, might perhaps have been forgotten like many others, if, three weeks after, it had not been re-enacted under similar circumstances. But, thanks to the nationality of the victim of the shock, thanks to the reputation of the company to which the vessel belonged, the circumstances became extensively circulated.

Everyone knows the name of the celebrated British shipowners, Cunard and Co. This intelligent company founded, in 1840, a postal service between Liverpool and Halifax, with three wooden vessels with engines of 400 horsepower, and a capacity of 1,162 tons. Eight years afterwards the stock of the company increased to four vessels of 650 horsepower and 1,820 tons, and two years later they had two more boats, superior in power and tonnage. In 1853 the Cunard Company, whose privilege of carrying the mails had just been renewed, added successively to their stock the *Arabia, Persia, China, Scotia, Java,* and *Russia,* all vessels of first-rate speed, and the largest which, next to the *Great Eastern,* had ever ploughed the seas. Thus, then, in 1867 the company possessed twelve vessels, eight with paddles and four with screws.

I give these brief details to show the importance of this maritime transport company, known to the entire world by its intelligent administration. No enterprise of transoceanic navigation has been conducted with more skill; no business affair has been crowned with more success. During the last twenty-six years the Cunard vessels have crossed the Atlantic more than two thousand times, and no voyage has ever failed, no letter, man, nor vessel has ever been lost. Notwithstanding the powerful competition of France, passengers still chose the Cunard route in preference to every other, as is apparent from an examination of the official documents of late years. This understood, no one will be astonished at the commotion caused by the accident that happened to one of its finest steamers.

The 13th of April 1867, the sea being beautiful, the breeze favorable, the *Scotia* found herself in 15° 12′ long. and 45° 37′ lat., driven by her 1000-horsepower engines. She was going at the speed of thirteen and a half knots. Her paddlewheels beat the sea with perfect regularity. She drew 6.7 meters and displaced 6,624 cubic meters.

At seventeen minutes past four in the afternoon, whilst the passengers were assembled at lunch in the great salon, a slight shock was felt on the hull of the *Scotia,* on the side, a little aft of the port-paddle.

The *Scotia* had not struck, but she had *been* struck, and seemingly by something rather sharp and penetrating than blunt. The shock had been so slight that no one had been alarmed, had it not been for the shouts of the stokers who rushed on to the bridge exclaiming, "We are sinking! We are sinking!"

At first the passengers were much frightened, but Captain Anderson hastened to reassure them. The danger could not be imminent. The *Scotia,* divided into seven compartments by watertight bulkheads, could brave with impunity any leak.

Captain Anderson went down immediately into the hold. He found that the sea was pouring into the fifth compartment; and the rapidity of the influx proved that the size of the leak was considerable. Fortunately this compartment did not hold the boilers, or the fires would have been immediately extinguished.

Captain Anderson ordered the engines to be stopped at once, and one of the men went down to ascertain the extent of the injury. Some minutes afterwards they discovered the existence of a large hole, two meters wide,[3] in the ship's bottom. Such a leak could not be patched;

and the *Scotia,* her paddles half submerged, was obliged to continue her course. She was then three hundred miles from Cape Clear, and after three days' delay, which caused great uneasiness in Liverpool, she entered the shipyards of the company.

The engineers visited the *Scotia,* which was put in dry dock. They could scarcely believe their eyes: at two and a half meters below the water-line was a regular rent, in the form of an isosceles triangle. The broken place in the iron plates was so perfectly defined, that it could not have been more neatly done by a punch. It was clear, then, that the instrument producing the perforation was not of a common stamp! And after having been driven with prodigious strength, piercing an iron plate 4 cm. (1½ inches) thick, had withdrawn itself by a retrograde motion truly inexplicable.

This latest incident resulted in exciting once more the torrent of public opinion. From this moment all unlucky casualties which could not be otherwise accounted for were put down to the monster. Upon this imaginary creature rested the responsibility of all these shipwrecks, which unfortunately were considerable; for of three thousand ships whose loss was annually recorded at the Bureau Veritas, the number of sailing and steam ships supposed to be totally lost, from the absence of all news, amounted to not less than two hundred!

Now, it was the "monster" who, justly or unjustly, was accused of their disappearance, and, thanks to it, communication between the different continents became more and more dangerous. The public demanded peremptorily that the seas should, at any price, be relieved from this formidable cetacean.

---

[1]A league is equal to a little more than 2.16 miles (in the Nineteenth century). R.M.

[2]About 106 meters. An English foot equals 30.4 cm. J.V.

[3]A meter equals 3.28 feet. A kilometer equals about 0.6 mile, or about 3,280 feet. R.M.

◄ **CHAPTER II** ►

PRO AND CON

t the period when these events took place, I had just returned from a scientific expedition in the Badlands of Nebraska, in the United States. In my capacity as Assistant Professor in the Museum of Natural History in Paris, the French Government had attached me to that expedition. After six months in Nebraska, I arrived in New York towards the end of March, laden with a precious collection. My departure for France was fixed for the first days in May. Meanwhile, I was occupying myself in classifying my mineralogical, botanical, and zoological riches, when the accident happened to the *Scotia.*

I was perfectly up in the subject which was the question of the day. How could I be otherwise? I had read and re-read all the American and European papers without being any nearer a conclusion. This mystery puzzled me. Under the impossibility of forming an opinion, I jumped from one extreme to the other. That there really was something could not be doubted, and the incredulous were invited to put their finger on the wound of the *Scotia.*

On my arrival at New York, the question was at its height. The hypothesis of the floating

island, and the unapproachable reef, supported by minds little competent to form a judgment, was abandoned. And, indeed, unless this shoal had a machine in its stomach, how could it change its position with such astonishing rapidity?

From the same cause, the idea of a floating hull of an enormous wreck was quickly given up.

There remained then only two possible solutions of the question, which created two distinct parties: on one side, those who were for a monster of colossal strength; on the other, those who were for a "submarine" vessel of enormous motive power.

But this last hypothesis, plausible as it was, could not stand against inquiries made in both the Old and New Worlds. That a private gentleman should have such a machine at his command was not likely. Where, when, and how was it built? And how could its construction have been kept secret? Only a Government might possess such a destructive machine. And in these disastrous times, when the ingenuity of man is daily multiplying the power of weapons of war, it was possible that, without the knowledge of others, a state might try to work such a formidable engine. After the Chassepot rifles came the torpedoes, after the torpedoes the submarine rams, then—the reaction. At least, I hope so.

But the hypothesis of a war machine fell before the denials of all the Governments. As public interest was in question, and transatlantic communications suffered, their veracity could not be doubted, And, how could the construction of this submarine boat escape the public eye? For a private gentleman to keep the secret under such circumstances would be very difficult, and for a State whose every act is persistently watched by powerful rivals, certainly impossible.

After inquiries made in England, France, Russia, Prussia, Spain, Italy, and America, even in Turkey, the hypothesis of a submarine *Monitor* was definitely rejected. The "monster" therefore resurfaced, in spite of the incessant jokes made by the popular press. Their imaginations soon allowed the most absurd ichthyological fantasies to be printed.

Upon my arrival in New York several persons did me the honor of consulting me on the phenomenon in question. I had published in France a work in quarto, in two volumes, entitled, *Mysteries of the Great Submarine Depths.* This book, highly approved of in the learned world, gained for me a special reputation in this rather obscure branch of Natural History. My advice was asked. As long as I could ignore the facts, I confined myself to a decided skepticism. But soon finding myself driven into a corner, I was obliged to explain myself categorically. And even "the Honorable Pierre Aronnax, Professor at the Museum of Paris," was called upon by the *New York Herald* to express a definite opinion of some sort.

I did something. I spoke, for want of power to hold my tongue. I discussed the question in all its forms, politically and scientifically; and I give here an extract from a carefully-studied article which I published in the number of the 30th of April. It ran as follows:—

"After examining one by one the different hypotheses, rejecting all other suggestions, it becomes necessary to admit the existence of a marine animal of enormous power.

"The great depths of the ocean are entirely unknown to us. Soundings cannot reach them. What passes in those remote depths—what beings live, or can live, twelve or fifteen miles beneath the surface of the waters—what is the organization of these animals, we can scarcely conjecture. However, the solution of the problem submitted to me is affected by the form of the dilemma. Either we do know all the varieties of creatures which inhabit our planet, or we do not. If we do *not* know them all—if Nature has still secrets in ichthyology for us, nothing is more conformable to reason than to admit the existence of fishes or cetaceans, or even of new species of an organization formed to inhabit the most inaccessible depths, and which an accident of some sort, either fantastical or capricious, has brought at long intervals to the upper level of the ocean.

"If, on the contrary, we *do* know all living kinds, we must necessarily seek for the animal in question amongst those marine beings already classed; and, in that case, I should be disposed to admit the existence of a *gigantic narwhal.*

"The common narwhal, or sea-unicorn, often attains a length of sixty feet. Increase its size five-fold or ten-fold, give it strength proportionate to its size, enlarge its destructive weapons, and you obtain the animal required. It will have the proportions determined by the officers of the *Shannon,* the instrument required for the perforation of the *Scotia,* and the power necessary to pierce the hull of a steamer.

"Indeed the narwhal is armed with a sort of ivory sword, or halberd, according to the expression of certain naturalists. The principal tusk has the hardness of steel. Some of these tusks have been found buried in the bodies of other whales, which the sea-unicorn always attacks with success. Others have been drawn out, not without trouble, from the bottoms of ships, which they had pierced completely through, as a gimlet pierces a barrel. The Museum of the Faculty of Medicine of Paris possesses one of these defensive weapons, 2.25 meters long and 48 cm. in diameter at the base.

"Very well! Suppose this weapon to be ten times stronger, and the animal ten times more powerful; launch it at the rate of twenty miles an hour, its mass multiplied by the square of its speed, and you obtain a shock capable of producing the catastrophe required.

"Until further information, therefore, I shall maintain it to be a sea-unicorn of colossal dimensions, armed, not with a halberd, but with a real spur, as the armoured frigates, or the "rams" of war, whose massiveness and motive power it would possess at the same time.

"Thus may this inexplicable phenomenon be explained, unless there be something over and above all that one has ever conjectured, seen, perceived, or experienced; which is just within the bounds of possibility."

These last words were cowardly on my part; but, up to a certain point, I wished to shelter my dignity as Professor, and not give too much cause for laughter to the Americans, who laugh well when they do laugh. I reserved for myself a way of escape. In effect, however, I admitted the existence of the "monster."

My article was hotly discussed, which procured it a high reputation. It rallied round it a certain number of partisans. The solution it proposed gave, at least, full liberty to the imagination. The human mind delights in grand conceptions of supernatural beings. And the sea is precisely their best vehicle, the only medium through which these giants (against which terrestrial animals, such as elephants or rhinoceroses, are as nothing), can be produced or developed. The liquid masses transport the largest known species of mammals and they perhaps contain mollusks of enormous size, crustaceans frightful to contemplate, such as lobsters more than a hundred meters long, or crabs weighing two hundred tons! Why should it not be so? Formerly, terrestrial animals, contemporaries of the geological epochs, quadrupeds, quadrumanes, reptiles, and birds, were constructed in a gigantic scale. The Creator had thrown them into a colossal mold which time has gradually lessened. Why should not the sea in its unknown depths have kept there vast specimens of the life of another age—the sea which never changes, while the earth changes incessantly? Why should it not hide in its bosom the last varieties of these Titanic species, whose years are centuries, and whose centuries are millenniums?

But I am letting myself be carried away by reveries which are no longer such to me. Enough of chimeras which time has changed for me into terrible realities. I repeat, opinion was then made up as to the nature of the phenomenon, and the public admitted without contestation the existence of the prodigious animal which had nothing in common with the fabulous sea serpents.

But if some people saw in this nothing but a purely scientific problem to solve, others more positive, especially in America and England, were of an opinion to purge the ocean of this formidable monster, in order to reassure transoceanic communications.

The industrial and commercial papers treated the question chiefly from this point of view. The *Shipping and Mercantile Gazette,* the *Lloyds' List,* the *Paquebot,* and the *Revue Maritime et Coloniale,* all papers devoted to insurance companies which threatened to raise their rates of premium, were unanimous on this point.

Public opinion had spoken. The United States were the first in the field; and in New York they made preparations for an expedition destined to pursue this narwhal. A frigate of great speed, the *Abraham Lincoln,* was put in commission as soon as possible. The arsenals were opened to Commander Farragut, who hastened the arming of his frigate.

But, as it always happens, the moment it was decided to pursue the monster, the monster did not appear. For two months no one heard it spoken of. No ship met with it. It seemed as if this sea-unicorn knew of the plots weaving around it. It had been so much talked of, even through the Atlantic cable, that jesters pretended that this intelligent creature had intercepted a telegram on its passage, and was making the most of it.

So when the frigate had been armed for a long campaign, and provided with formidable fishing apparatus, no one could tell what course to pursue. Impatience grew apace, when, on the 3rd of July, they learned that a steamer of the San Francisco to Shanghai line, had seen the animal three weeks before in the North Pacific Ocean.

The excitement caused by this news was extreme. Captain Farragut was granted but twenty-four hours before he was to sail. The ship was revictualled and well stocked with coal. The crew were there to a man, and there was nothing to do but to light the fires, stoke up and weigh anchor! There would be no excuse for even half a day's delay. All Captain Farragut demanded was the order to depart.

Three hours before the *Abraham Lincoln* left Brooklyn pier, I received a letter worded as follows:

"To M. Aronnax, Professor at the Museum of Paris,
    Fifth Avenue Hotel, New York.

"Sir,—If you will consent to join the *Abraham Lincoln* in this expedition, the Government of the United States will with pleasure see France represented in the enterprise. Commander Farragut has a cabin at your disposal.
"Very cordially yours,

J. B. Hobson,
Secretary of the Navy"

◄ CHAPTER III ►

WHATEVER PLEASES MONSIEUR

hree seconds before the arrival of J. B. Hobson's letter, I no more thought of pursuing the sea-unicorn than of attempting the Northwest Passage. Three seconds after reading the letter of the honorable Secretary of the Navy, I felt that my true vocation, the sole end of my life, was to chase this disturbing monster, and purge it from the world.

But I had just returned from a fatiguing journey, weary and longing for rest. I aspired to nothing more than again seeing my country, my friends, my little lodging by the Jardin des

Plantes, and my dear and precious collections. But nothing could keep me back! I forgot all—fatigue, friends, and collections—and accepted without hesitation the offer of the American Government.

"Besides," thought I, "all roads lead back to Europe; and the sea-unicorn may be amiable enough to hurry me towards the coast of France! This worthy animal may allow itself to be caught in the seas of Europe—for my personal benefit—and I will not bring back less than half a meter of his ivory halberd to the Museum of Natural History."

But in the meanwhile I must seek this narwhal in the North Pacific Ocean, which, to return to France, was taking a road via the Antipodes.

"Conseil," I called, in an impatient voice.

Conseil was my servant, a true, devoted Flemish boy, who had accompanied me in all my travels. I liked him, and he returned the liking well. He was phlegmatic by nature, punctual on principle, zealous from habit, evincing little disturbance at the different surprises of life, very quick with his hands, and apt at any service required of him; and, despite his name, never giving advice—even when asked for it.[1]

Rubbing shoulders with scientists in our little world of the Jardin des Plantes, Conseil had picked up some odd bits of learning. In him I had a specialist, very well versed in the classification of natural history. With all the agility of an acrobat, he could run up and down the ladder of branches, groups, classes, sub-classes, orders, families, genera, sub-genera, species and varieties. But his science stopped there. Classification was his life, he knew nothing else. Very learned in the theory of classification he was, but in things practical, I do not believe that he could distinguish between a cachalot[2] and a baleen whale. But in all, what a fine, dignified fellow!

Conseil had followed me for the last ten years wherever science led. Never once did he complain of the length or fatigue of a journey, never did he make an objection to packing his valise for whatever country it might be, or however far away, whether China or the Congo. He would go anywhere without questioning the reason. Besides all this, he had good health, which defied all sickness, solid muscles and no nerves, not even the appearance of nerves; and he was very moral, of course.

This boy was thirty years old, and his age to that of his master was as fifteen to twenty. May I be excused for this roundabout way of admitting that I was forty years old?

But Conseil had one fault: he was formal to a fault, and would never speak to me but in the third person, which was sometimes provoking.

"Conseil," said I again, beginning with feverish hands to make preparations for my departure.

Certainly I was sure of this devoted boy. As a rule, I never asked him if it were convenient for him or not to follow me in my travels; but this time the expedition in question might be prolonged, and the enterprise might be hazardous in pursuit of an animal capable of sinking a frigate as easily as a nutshell. Here there was matter for reflection even to the most impassive man in the world. What would Conseil say?

"Conseil," I called a third time.

Conseil appeared.

"Did monsieur call?" said he, entering.

"Yes, my boy; make preparations for me and yourself too. We leave in two hours."

"As monsieur pleases," replied Conseil tranquilly.

"Not an instant to lose;—lock in my trunk all travelling utensils, coats, shirts, and stockings—without counting, as many as you can, and make haste."

"And monsieur's collections?" observed Conseil.

"We will think of them by and by."

"What! the archiotherium, the hyracotherium, the oreodons, the cheropotamus, and monsieur's other specimens?"

"They will keep them at the hotel."

"And monsieur's live babiroussa?"

"They will feed it during our absence; besides, I will give orders to forward our menagerie to France."

"We are not returning to Paris, then?" asked Conseil.

"Oh! Certainly," I answered, evasively, "by making a detour."

"Whatever detour pleases monsieur."

"Oh! it will be nothing! Not quite so direct a road, that is all. We take our passage in the *Abraham Lincoln.*"

"As monsieur thinks proper," coolly replied Conseil.

"You see, my friend, it has to do with the monster—the famous narwhal. We are going to purge it from the seas! The author of a work in quarto, in two volumes, on the *Mysteries of the Great Ocean Depths* cannot forbear embarking with Commander Farragut. A glorious mission, but a dangerous one! We cannot tell where we may go; these animals can be very capricious. But we will go whether or no! We have got a captain who is pretty wide-awake."

"As monsieur does, I will do," answered Conseil.

"But think, for I will hide nothing from you. It is one of those voyages from which people do not always come back!"

"As monsieur pleases."

A quarter of an hour afterwards our trunks were ready. Conseil had packed them by sleight of hand, and I was sure nothing would be missing, for the fellow classified shirts and clothes as well as he did birds or mammals.

The hotel lift deposited us in the large vestibule of the first floor. I went down the few stairs that led to the ground floor. I paid my bill at the vast counter, always besieged by a considerable crowd. I gave the order to send my cases of stuffed animals and dried plants to Paris. I opened a sufficient credit for the babiroussa, and, Conseil following me, I sprang into a cab.

The cab, at twenty francs the course, descended Broadway as far as Union Square, went along Fourth Avenue to its junction with Bowery Street, then along Katrin Street, and stopped at the thirty-fourth pier. There the Katrin ferry-boat transported us, men, horses and vehicle, to Brooklyn, the great annex of New York, situated on the left bank of East River, and in a few minutes we arrived at the quay opposite which the *Abraham Lincoln* was pouring forth clouds of black smoke from her two funnels.

Our luggage was transported to the deck of the frigate immediately. I hastened on board and asked for Commander Farragut. One of the sailors conducted me to the poop, where I found myself in the presence of a good-looking officer, who held out his hand to me.

"Monsieur Pierre Aronnax?" said he.

"Himself," replied I; "Commander Farragut?"

"In person. You are welcome, Professor; your cabin is ready for you."

I bowed, and desired to be conducted to the cabin destined for me.

The *Abraham Lincoln* had been well chosen and equipped for her new destination. She was a frigate of great speed, fitted with high-pressure engines which generated a pressure of seven atmospheres. Under this the *Abraham Lincoln* attained the mean speed of nearly eighteen and a third knots—a considerable speed, but, nevertheless, insufficient to grapple with the gigantic cetacean.

The interior arrangements of the frigate corresponded to its nautical qualities. I was well satisfied with my cabin, which was in the after part, opening upon the officers' quarters.

"We shall be well off here," said I to Conseil.

"As well, if monsieur will permit me to say so, as a hermit-crab in the shell of a whelk," said Conseil.

I left Conseil to stow our trunks conveniently away, and remounted the poop in order to survey the preparations for departure.

At that moment Commander Farragut was ordering the last moorings to be cast loose which held the *Abraham Lincoln* to the Brooklyn pier. So in a quarter of an hour, perhaps less, the frigate would have sailed without me. I should have missed this extraordinary, supernatural, and incredible expedition, the recital of which may well meet with incredulity.

For Commander Farragut would not lose a day nor an hour in scouring the seas in which the animal had been sighted. He sent for the engineer.

"Is the steam full on?" asked he.

"Yes, sir," replied the engineer.

"Go ahead," cried Commander Farragut.

At his order, transmitted by means of a compressed-air machine, the engineers put the starting-wheel into motion. Steam hissed through the half-open valves. Long horizontal pistons groaned and pushed the rods and drive-shaft. The blades of the propeller struck the water with increasing rapidity, and the *Abraham Lincoln* advanced majestically in the midst of a hundred ferry-boats and tenders, crowded with spectators, which made a real parade.

The quay of Brooklyn, and all that part of New York bordering on the East River, was crowded with spectators. Three hurrahs burst successively from five hundred thousand throats; thousands of handkerchiefs were waved above the heads of the crowded mass, saluting the *Abraham Lincoln,* until she reached the waters of the Hudson, at the point of that elongated peninsula which forms the city of New York. Then the frigate, following the coast of New Jersey along the right bank of the beautiful river, covered with villas, passed between the forts, which saluted her with their heaviest guns. The *Abraham Lincoln* answered by hoisting the American colors three times, whose thirty-nine stars[3] shone resplendent from the mizzen-peak; then modifying its speed to take the narrow channel marked by buoys placed in the inner bay formed by Sandy Hook Point, it coasted the long sandy beach, where some thousands of spectators gave it one final cheer. The escort of boats and tenders still followed the frigate, and did not leave her until they came abreast of the lightship, whose two lights marked the entrance of New York Harbor. Three o'clock was signalled, the pilot got into his boat, and rejoined the little schooner which was waiting under our lee, the fires were stoked, the screw beat the waves more rapidly, the frigate skirted the low yellow coast of Long Island; and at eight o'clock, after having lost sight in the north-west of the lights of Fire Island, she ran at full steam on to the dark waters of the Atlantic.

---

[1] Jacques-Francois Conseil was the inventor of a steam-powered submarine, whom Verne met in about 1865. R.M.

[2] Sperm whale—R.M.

[3] In 1867 the U.S. flag had only 37 stars. It did not have 39 stars until 1889. R.M.

◄ **CHAPTER IV** ►

NED LAND

 aptain Farragut was a good seaman, worthy of the frigate he commanded. His vessel and he were one. He was the soul of it. On the question of the cetacean there was no doubt in his mind, and he would not allow the existence of the animal to be disputed on board. He believed in it, as certain good women believed in the Leviathan,—by faith, not by reason. The monster did exist, and he had sworn to rid the seas of it. He was a kind of Knight of Rhodes, a second Dieudonné de Gozon, going to meet the serpent which desolated the island. Either Captain Farragut would kill the narwhal, or the narwhal would kill the captain. There was no third course.

The officers on board shared the opinion of their chief. They were ever chatting, discussing, and calculating the various chances of a meeting, watching narrowly the vast surface of the ocean. More than one took up his quarters voluntarily in the cross-trees, who would have cursed such a berth under any other circumstances. As long as the sun described its daily course, the rigging was crowded with sailors, whose feet were burnt to such an extent by the heat of the deck as to render it unbearable; still the *Abraham Lincoln* had not yet breasted the suspected waters of the Pacific.

As to the ship's company, they desired nothing better than to meet the sea-unicorn, to harpoon it, hoist it on board, and despatch it. They watched the sea with eager attention. Besides, Captain Farragut had spoken of a certain sum of two thousand dollars, set apart for whoever should first sight the monster, were he cabinboy, common seaman, or officer. I leave you to judge how eyes were used on board the *Abraham Lincoln*.

For my own part, I was not behind the others, and left to no one my share of daily observations. The frigate might have been called the *Argus,* for a hundred reasons.[1] Only one among us, Conseil, seemed to protest by his indifference against the question which so interested us all, and seemed to be out of keeping with the general enthusiasm on board.

I have said that Captain Farragut had carefully provided his ship with every apparatus for catching the gigantic cetacean. No whaler had ever been better armed. We possessed every known engine, from the harpoon thrown by the hand to the barbed arrows of the blunderbuss, and the explosive balls of the duck-gun. On the forecastle lay the perfection of a breech-loading gun, very thick at the breech, and very narrow in the bore, the model of which had been in the Universal Exhibition of 1867. This precious weapon of American origin could throw with ease a conical projectile of four kilograms, or nine pounds, to a mean distance of sixteen kilometers.

Thus the *Abraham Lincoln* lacked no methods of destruction; and, what was better still, she had on board Ned Land, the prince of harpooners.

Ned Land was a Canadian, with an uncommon quickness of hand, and who knew no equal in his dangerous occupation. Skill, coolness, audacity, and cunning, he possessed in a superior degree, and it must be a cunning whale or a singularly shrewd cachalot to escape the blow of his harpoon.

Ned Land was about forty years of age; he was a tall man—more than six feet high—strongly built, grave and taciturn, occasionally violent, and very passionate when contradicted. His person attracted attention, but above all the boldness of his look, which gave a singular emphasis to his face.

I believe that Captain Farragut had done wisely in engaging this man. He was worth all the rest of the ship's company as far as his eye and arm went. I could only compare him to a powerful telescope, which could also serve as a cannon primed to fire.

Who calls himself Canadian calls himself French; and as uncommunicative as Ned Land was, I must admit that he took a certain liking for me. My nationality drew him to me, no doubt. It was an opportunity for him to speak, and for me to hear, that old language of Rabelais, which is still in use in some Canadian provinces. The harpooner's family was originally from Quebec, and was already a tribe of hardy fishermen when this town still belonged to France.

Little by little, Ned Land acquired a taste for chatting, and I loved to hear the recital of his adventures in the polar seas. He related his fishing, and his combats, with natural poetry of expression; his recital took the form of an epic poem, and I seemed to be listening to a Canadian Homer singing the Iliad of the regions of the North.

I am portraying this hardy companion as I really knew him. We are old friends now, united in that unchangeable friendship which is born and cemented amidst extreme dangers. Ah, brave Ned! I ask no more than to live a hundred years longer, that I may have more time to dwell the longer on your memory.

Now, what was Ned Land's opinion upon the question of the marine monster? I must admit that he did not believe in the giant sea-unicorn, and was the only one on board who did not share that universal conviction. He even avoided the subject, which I one day thought it my duty to press upon him.

One magnificent evening, the 25th of June—that is to say, three weeks after our departure—the frigate was abreast of Cape Blanc, thirty miles to leeward of the coast of Patagonia. We had crossed the tropic of Capricorn, and the Straits of Magellan opened less than seven hundred miles to the south. Before eight days were over, the *Abraham Lincoln* would be ploughing the waters of the Pacific.

Seated on the poop, Ned Land and I were chatting of one thing and another as we looked at this mysterious sea, whose great depths had up to this time been inaccessible to the eye of man. I naturally led up the conversation to the giant sea-unicorn, and examined the various chances of success or failure of the expedition. But seeing that Ned Land let me speak without saying too much himself, I pressed him more closely.

"Well, Ned," said I, "is it possible that you are not convinced of the existence of this cetacean that we are following? Have you any particular reason for being so incredulous?"

The harpooner looked at me fixedly for some moments before answering, struck his broad forehead with his hand (a habit of his), closed his eyes as if to collect himself, and said at last, "Perhaps I have, Monsieur Aronnax."

"But, Ned, you, a whaler by profession, familiar with all the great marine mammals—you, whose imagination might easily accept the hypothesis of enormous cetaceans, *you* ought to be the last to doubt under such circumstances!"

"That is just what deceives you, Professor," replied Ned. "That the vulgar should believe in extraordinary comets traversing space, and in the existence of antediluvian monsters in the heart of the globe, may well be; but neither astronomers nor geologists believe in such chimeras.[2] As a whaler, I have followed many a cetacean, harpooned a great number, and killed several; but, however strong or well-armed they may have been, neither their tails nor their weapons would have been able even to scratch the iron plates of a steamer."

"But, Ned, they tell of ships which the tusk of the narwhal has pierced right through."

"Wooden ships—that is possible," replied the Canadian; "But I have never seen it done; and, until further proof, I deny that whales, cachalots, or narwhals could ever produce the effect you describe."

"Listen to me, Ned . . ."

"No, Professor, no. Anything you want but that. A gigantic octopus, perhaps . . . ?"

"Even less likely, Ned. The octopus is only a mollusk, and even its name indicates the softness of its flesh—since it comes from the Latin *mollis,* soft. Even if one were 500 feet long, this octopus—which is not a member of the vertebrate branch—would be completely inoffensive to ships like the *Scotia* or the *Abraham Lincoln.* We must reject the kind of fables that tell of the prowess of the krakens or other monsters of that species.''

"So, Monsieur le Naturaliste,'' replied Ned, in a sly tone, "you persist in admitting the existence of a huge whale . . .?''

"Well, Ned, I repeat it with a conviction resting on the logic of facts. I believe in the existence of a mammal powerfully organized, belonging to the branch of vertebrates like the whales, the cachalots, or the dolphins, and furnished with a defensive horn of great penetrating power.''

"Hum!'' said the harpooner, shaking his head with the air of a man who would not be convinced.

"Notice one thing, my worthy Canadian,'' I resumed. "If such an animal is in existence, if it inhabits the depths of the ocean, and if it frequents the strata lying miles below the surface of the water, it must necessarily possess an organization the strength of which would defy all comparison.''

"And why this powerful organization?'' demanded Ned.

"Because it requires incalculable strength to keep one's self in these strata and resist their pressure.''

"Truly?'' replied Ned, winking at me.

"Truly; and a few figures will prove it without difficulty.''

"Oh, figures!'' replied Ned, "they can prove anything!''

"That may be true in business, but not in mathematics. Listen to me. Let us admit that the pressure of the atmosphere is represented by the weight of a column of water thirty-two feet high. In reality the column of water would be shorter, as we are speaking of sea water, the density of which is greater than that of fresh water. Well then, when you dive, Ned, as many times thirty-two feet of water as there are above you, so many times does your body bear a pressure equal to that of the atmosphere, that is to say, 15 pounds for each square inch of its surface. It follows then, that at 320 feet this pressure equals that of 10 atmospheres, 100 atmospheres at 3200 feet, and of 1000 atmospheres at 32,000 feet, that is, more than two leagues or about 6 miles. This is equivalent to saying that, if you could attain this depth in the ocean, each square inch of the surface of your body would bear a pressure of 15,000 pounds. Ah! my brave Ned, do you know how many square inches are on the surface of your body?''

"I have no idea, Monsieur Aronnax.''

"About 2600.''

"As much as that?''

"And, as in reality the atmospheric pressure is about 15 pounds to the square inch, your 2600 square inches bear at this moment a pressure of 39,000 pounds.''

"Without my perceiving it?''

"Without your perceiving it. And if you are not crushed by such a pressure, it is because the air penetrates the interior of your body with equal pressure. Hence perfect equilibrium between the interior and exterior pressure, which thus neutralize each other, and which allows you to bear it without inconvenience. But in the water it is another thing.''

"Yes, I understand,'' replied Ned, becoming more attentive; "because the water surrounds me, but does not penetrate.''

"Precisely, Ned. So that at 32 feet beneath the surface of the sea you would undergo a pressure of 39,000 pounds; at 320 feet, ten times that pressure; at 3200 feet, a hundred times that pressure; lastly, at 32,000 feet, a thousand times that pressure would be 39,000,000 pounds—that is to say, that you would be flattened as if you had been taken from the plates of a hydraulic press!''

"The devil!" exclaimed Ned.

"Very well then, my worthy harpooner, if some vertebrate, several hundred meters long, and large in proportion, can maintain itself in such depths—whose bodily surface is represented by millions of square inches, that is by tens of millions of pounds, we must estimate the pressure they undergo. Consider, then, what must be the resistance of their bony structure, and the strength of their organization to withstand such pressure!"

"Why!" exclaimed Ned Land, "they must be made of iron plates eight inches thick, like the armored frigates."

"As you say, Ned. And think what destruction such a mass would cause, if hurled with the speed of an express train against the hull of a vessel."

"Yes—certainly—perhaps," replied the Canadian, shaken by these figures, but not yet willing to give in.

"Well, have I convinced you?"

"You have convinced me of one thing, Monsieur Le Naturaliste, which is that, if such animals do exist at the bottom of the seas, they must necessarily be as strong as you say."

"But if they do not exist, my obstinate harpooner, how explain the accident to the *Scotia?*"

"Because it is . . ." began Ned hesitatingly.

"Go on!"

"Because . . . it is not true!" answered the Canadian, repeating without knowing it, the celebrated answer of Arago.

But this answer proved the obstinacy of the harpooner and nothing else. That day I did not press him further. The accident to the *Scotia* was undeniable. The hole existed so truly that they were obliged to stop it up, and I do not think that the existency of a hole can be more categorically demonstrated. Now the hole had not made itself, and since it had not been done by submarine rocks or submarine machines, it was certainly due to the perforating tool of an animal.

Now, in my opinion, and for all the reasons previously deduced, this animal belonged to the branch of Vertebrata, to the class of mammals, to the group of pisciforms, and finally to the order of cetaceans. As to the family in which it took rank, whale, cachalot, or dolphin, as to the genus of which it formed a part, as to the species in which it would be convenient to put it, that was a question to be elucidated subsequently. In order to solve it the unknown monster must be dissected: to dissect it, it must be taken, to take it, it must be harpooned—which was Ned Land's business—to harpoon it, it must be seen—which was the crew's business—and to see it, it must be encountered—which was the business of chance.

---

[1] The Argus was a mythical beast with a hundred eyes. R.M.

[2] Verne may have been poking fun at himself here. *Journey to the Center of the Earth* (1864) described just such monsters. R.M.

◄ CHAPTER V ►

ON AN ADVENTURE!

 he voyage of the *Abraham Lincoln* was for a long time marked by no special incident. But one circumstance happened which showed the wonderful dexterity of Ned Land, and proved what confidence we might place in him.

The 30th of June, the frigate hailed some American whalers near the Falkland Islands, from whom we learned that they knew nothing about the narwhal. But one of them, the captain of the *Monroe,* knowing that Ned Land had shipped on board the *Abraham Lincoln,* begged for his help in chasing a whale they had in sight. Commander Farragut, desirous of seeing Ned Land at work, gave him permission to go on board the *Monroe.* And fate served our Canadian so well that, instead of one whale, he harpooned two in succession, striking one straight to the heart and catching the other after only a few minutes' pursuit.[1]

Decidedly, if the monster ever has to deal with Ned Land's harpoon, I would not bet in its favor.

The frigate skirted the southeast coast of America with great rapidity. The 3rd of July we were at the opening of the Straits of Magellan, off Cape Vierges. But Commander Farragut would not take such a tortuous passage, and doubled Cape Horn, instead.

The ship's crew agreed with him. And certainly it was not likely that they might meet the narwhal in that narrow channel. Many of the sailors affirmed that the monster could not pass there, "that he was too big for that!"

The 6th of July, about three o'clock in the afternoon, the *Abraham Lincoln,* fifteen miles further to the south, doubled the solitary island, this lost rock at the extremity of the American continent, to which some Dutch sailors gave the name of their native town, Cape Horn. The course was taken towards the northwest, and the next day the screw of the frigate was at last beating the waters of the Pacific.

"Keep your eyes open! Keep your eyes open!" called out the sailors of the *Abraham Lincoln.*

And they were opened widely. Both eyes and telescopes, a little dazzled, it is true, by the prospect of two thousand dollars, had not an instant's repose. Day and night they watched the surface of the ocean, and even nyctalopes, whose faculty of seeing in the darkness multiplies their chances a hundredfold, would have had enough to do to gain the prize.

I myself, for whom money had no charms, was not the least attentive on board. Giving but few minutes to my meals, but a few hours to sleep, indifferent to either rain or sunshine, I did not leave the poop of the vessel. Now leaning on the netting of the forecastle, now on the taffrail, I devoured with eagerness the soft foam which whitened the sea as far as the eye could reach; and how often have I shared the emotion of the majority of the crew, when some capricious whale raised its black back above the waves! The poop of the vessel was crowded in a moment. The cabins poured forth a torrent of sailors and officers, each with heaving breast and troubled eye watching the course of the cetacean. I looked, and looked, till I was nearly blind, while Conseil, always phlegmatic, kept repeating in a calm voice:

"If monsieur would not squint so much he would see better!"

But vain excitement! The *Abraham Lincoln* changed its course and made for the animal sighted, a simple whale, or common cachalot, which soon disappeared amidst a storm of curses.

But the weather was good. The voyage was being accomplished under the most favorable auspices. It was then the bad season in the Southern Hemisphere, the July of that zone corresponding to our January in Europe; but the sea was beautiful and easily scanned round a vast circumference.

Ned Land always showed the most tenacious incredulity; he even affected not to examine the seas except during his watch, unless a whale was in sight; and yet his marvelous power of vision might have been of great service. But eight hours out of the twelve the obstinate Canadian read or slept in his cabin.

"Bah!" he would answer; "there is nothing, Monsieur Aronnax; and even if there is an animal, what chance have we of seeing it? Are we not going about at random? I will admit that the beast has been seen again in the North Pacific, but two months have already gone by since that meeting, and according to the temperament of your narwhal it does not like to stop long in place. It is endowed with a prodigious faculty of moving about. Now, you know as well as I do, Professor, that Nature makes nothing inconsistent, and would not give a slow animal the faculty of moving rapidly if it did not want to use it. Therefore, if the beast exists, it is far enough off now."

I did not know what to answer to that. We were evidently going along blindly. But how were we to do otherwise? Our chances, too, were very limited. In the meantime no one yet doubted our eventual success, and there was not a sailor on board who would have bet against the narwhal and against its early apparition.

And nothing! Nothing was seen but the immense waste of waters—nothing that resembled a gigantic narwhal, nor a submarine islet, nor a wreck, nor a floating reef, nor anything at all supernatural!

The reaction, therefore, began. Discouragement at first took possession of all minds, and opened a breach for incredulity. A new sentiment was experienced on board, composed of three tenths of shame and seven tenths of rage. They called themselves fools for being taken in by a chimera, and were still more furious at it. The mountains of arguments piled up for a year fell down all at once, and all everyone thought of was to make up the hours of meals and sleep which they had so foolishly sacrificed.

With the mobility natural to the human mind, they threw themselves from one excess into another. The warmest partisans of the enterprise became finally its most ardent detractors.

On the 20th of July, the tropic of Capricorn was crossed at 105° longitude, and on the 27th of the same month we crossed the equator at the 110th meridian.[1] This passed, the frigate took a more decided westerly direction, and scoured the central waters of the Pacific. Commander Farragut thought, and with reason, that it was better to remain in deep water, and keep clear of continents or islands, which the beast itself seemed to shun. "Perhaps because there was not enough water for him!" suggested the greater part of the crew. The frigate steamed past the Tuamotu Islands, the Marquesas, and the Sandwich Islands, crossed the tropic of Cancer at 132°, and made for the seas of China.

We were in the theat of the last appearances of the monster! And, to say truth, we no longer lived normally on board. Hearts palpitated, fearfully preparing themselves for future incurable aneurisms. The entire ship's crew were undergoing a nervous excitement, of which I can give no idea: they could not eat, they could not sleep. Twenty times a day, a misconception or an optical illusion of some sailor seated on the taffrail, would cause dreadful perspirations, and these emotions, twenty times repeated, kept us in a state of excitement so violent that a reaction was unavoidable.

And truly, reaction was not slow in showing itself. For three months, three months during which each day seemed an age, the *Abraham Lincoln* furrowed all the waters of the Northern Pacific, running at whales, making sharp deviations from her course, veering suddenly from one tack to another, stopping suddenly, putting on steam, and backing ever and anon at the risk of deranging her machinery; and not one point between the Japanese or American coasts was left unexplored.

Reaction mounted from the crew to the captain himself, and certainly, had it not been for resolute determination on the part of Captain Farragut, the frigate would have headed due southward.

This useless search could not last much longer. The *Abraham Lincoln* had nothing to reproach herself with, she had done her best to succeed. Never had an American ship's crew shown more zeal or patience; its failure could not be held against them—there remained nothing but to return.

This was made clear to the commander. Captain Farragut held his ground. The sailors could not hide their discontent, and their work suffered. I will not say there was a mutiny on board, but after a reasonable period of obstinacy, Captain Farragut (as Columbus did) asked for three days' patience. If in three days the monster did not appear, the man at the helm should give three turns of the wheel, and the *Abraham Lincoln* would make for the European seas.

This promise was made on the 2nd of November. It had the effect of rallying the ship's crew. The ocean was watched with renewed attention. Each one wished for a last glance in which to sum up his remembrance. Telescopes were used with feverish activity. It was a grand defiance given to the giant narwhal, and he could scarcely fail to answer the summons "Appear!"

Two days passed. The *Abraham Lincoln's* steam was at half pressure. A thousand schemes were tried to attract the attention and stimulate the apathy of the animal in case it should be met in those parts. Large quantities of bacon were trailed in the wake of the ship, to the great satisfaction (I must say) of the sharks. Small craft radiated in all directions round the *Abraham Lincoln* as she lay to, and did not leave a spot of the sea unexplored. But the night of the 4th of November arrived without the unveiling of this submarine mystery.

The next day, the 5th of November, at noon, the delay would expire as promised. After that time, Commander Farragut, faithful to his word was to turn the course to the southeast and abandon forever the northern regions of the Pacific.

The frigate was then in 31° 15′ north latitude and 136° 42′ east longitude. The coast of Japan still remained less than two hundred miles to leeward. Night was approaching. They had just struck eight bells. Large clouds veiled the disk of the moon, then in its first quarter. The sea undulated peaceably under the bow of the vessel.

At that moment I was leaning forward on the starboard netting. Conseil, standing near me, was looking straight before him. The crew, perched in the ratlines, examined the horizon, which contracted and darkened little by little. Officers with their night glasses scoured the growing darkness. Sometimes the ocean sparkled under the rays of the moon, which darted between two clouds. Then all trace of light was lost in the darkness.

In observing Conseil, I could see that the brave lad was undergoing a little of the general influence. At least I thought so. Perhaps for the first time his nerves vibrated to a sentiment of curiosity.

"Come, Conseil," said I, "this is the last chance of pocketing the two thousand dollars."

"May monsieur permit me to say," replied Conseil, "that I never reckoned on getting the prize; and, had the government of the Union offered a hundred thousand dollars, it would have been none the poorer."

"You are right, Conseil. It is a foolish affair after all, and one upon which we entered too lightly. What time lost, what useless emotions! We should have been back in France six months ago."

"In monsieur's apartment," replied Conseil, "and in his museum; and I should have already classified all of monsieur's fossils! And the babiroussa would have been installed in its cage in the Jardin des Plantes, and have attracted all the curious people of the capital!"

"As you say, Conseil. I fancy we shall run a fair chance of being laughed at for our pains."

"That's tolerably certain," replied Conseil, quietly. "I think they will make fun of monsieur. And, must I say it!"

"Go on, my good friend."

"Well, monsieur will only get what he deserves."

"Indeed!"

"When one has the honor of being a savant as monsieur is, one should not expose one's self to . . ."

Conseil had not time to finish his compliment. In the midst of general silence a voice had just been heard. It was the voice of Ned Land shouting—

"Ahoy! it's the thing we're looking for, to leeward, a ship's-length away!"

[1]Aronnax measures longitude from the meridian of Paris, which is 2° east of the meridian of Greenwich, which is the zero meridian we use today. The map included with this book uses Aronnax's figures. R.M.

◄ CHAPTER VI ►

AT FULL STEAM

 t this cry the whole ship's crew hurried towards the harpooner,—commander, officers, masters, sailors, cabin boys; even the engineers left their engines, and the stokers their furnaces. The order to stop her had been given, and the frigate now simply went on by her own momentum.

The darkness was then profound, and however good the Canadian's eyes were, I asked myself how he had managed to see, and what he had been able to see. My heart beat as if it would break.

But Ned Land was not mistaken, and we all perceived the object he pointed to.

At two cables' lengths[1] from the *Abraham Lincoln,* on the starboard quarter, the sea seemed to be illuminated all over. It was not a mere phosphorescent phenomenon. The monster was submerged some fathoms below the surface, and radiated that very intense but inexplicable light mentioned in the report of several captains. This magnificent radiation must have been produced by an agent of great illuminating power. The luminous area made on the sea an immense oval, much elongated, the center of which was intense and whose overpowering brilliancy died out by successive gradations.

"It is only an agglomeration of phosphorescent organisms," cried one of the officers.

"No, sir, certainly not," I replied with conviction. "Never did pholades or salpae produce such a powerful light. That brightness is of an essentially electrical nature. . . . Besides, see, see! It moves! It is moving forwards, backwards! It is darting towards us!"

A general cry rose from the frigate.

"Silence!" said the captain; "helm alee, reverse the engines."

The sailors worked at the wheel, the engineers at their machines. The steam was immediately reversed, and the *Abraham Lincoln,* beating to port, described a semicircle.

"Right helm, go ahead," cried the captain.

These orders were executed, and the frigate moved rapidly from the intense light.

I was mistaken. We tried to sheer off, but the supernatural animal approached with a velocity double our own.

We gasped for breath. Stupefaction more than fear made us silent and motionless. The animal gained on us, sporting with the waves. It made the round of the frigate, which was then making fourteen knots, and enveloped it with its electric rings like luminous dust. Then it moved away two or three miles, leaving a phosphorescent track, like those volumes of steam that express trains leave behind. All at once from the dark line of the horizon where it had retired to regain its momentum, the monster rushed suddenly towards the *Abraham Lincoln* with alarming rapidity, stopped suddenly about twenty feet from the hull, and died out,—not diving under the water, for its brilliance did not abate,—but suddenly, and as if the source of this brilliant emanation was exhausted. Then it reappeared on the other side of the vessel, as if it had turned and slid under the hull. Any moment a collision might have occurred which would have been fatal to us.

However, I was astonished at the maneuvers of the frigate. She fled and did not attack. She was no longer the pursuer: she was the pursued. On the captain's face, generally so impassive, was an expression of unaccountable astonishment.

"Mr. Aronnax," he said, "I do not know with what formidable being I have to deal, and I will not imprudently risk my frigate in the midst of this darkness. Besides, how attack this unknown thing, how defend one's self from it? Wait for daylight, and the scene will change."

"You have no further doubt, Captain, of the nature of the animal?"

"No, sir; it is evidently a gigantic narwhal, and an electric one."

"Perhaps," added I, "one can get no closer to it than one can to an electric eel."

"Undoubtedly," replied the captain, "if it possesses such dreadful power, it is the most terrible animal that ever was created. That is why, sir, I must be on my guard."

The crew were on their feet all night. No one thought of sleep. The *Abraham Lincoln,* not being able to struggle with such velocity, had moderated its pace, and sailed at half speed. For its part, the narwhal, imitating the frigate, let the waves rock it at will, and seemed decided not to leave the scene of the struggle.

Towards midnight, however, it disappeared, or, to use a more appropriate term, it was extinguished like a large glow-worm. Had it fled? One could only fear, not hope it. But at seven minutes to one o'clock in the morning a deafening whistling was heard, like that produced by a column of water rushing with great violence.

The captain, Ned Land, and I, were then on the poop, eagerly peering through the profound darkness.

"Ned Land," asked the commander, "you have often heard the roaring of whales?"

"Often, sir; but never such whales the sight of which brought me in two thousand dollars."

"True, you have a right to the prize, but tell me, is it the same noise whales make when they vent water?"

"The same noise, sir; but this one is incomparably louder. It is not to be mistaken. It is certainly a cetacean there in our seas. With your permission, sir," added the harpooner "we will have a few words with him at daybreak."

"If he is in a humor to hear them, Mr. Land," said I, in an unconvinced tone.

"If I can only approach within four harpoon lengths of it!"

"But to approach it," said the commander, "I ought to put a whaler at your disposal?"

"Certainly, sir."

"That will be trifling with the lives of my men."

"And mine too," responded the harpooner simply.

Towards two o'clock in the morning, the burning light reappeared, not less intense, about five miles to windward of the *Abraham Lincoln.* Notwithstanding the distance, and the noise of the wind and sea, one heard distinctly the loud strokes of the animal's tail, and even its panting breath. It seemed that, at the moment that the enormous narwhal had come to take breath at the surface of the water, the air was engulfed in its lungs, like the steam in the vast cylinders of a machine of two thousand horsepower.

"Hum!" thought I, "a whale with the strength of a cavalry regiment would be a pretty whale!"

We were on the *qui vive* till daylight, and began preparing for the combat. The fishing implements were laid along the lockers. The second lieutenant loaded the guns, which could throw harpoons to the distance of a mile, and long duck-guns, with explosive bullets, which inflicted mortal wounds even to the strongest animals. Ned Land contented himself with sharpening his harpoon—a fearsome weapon in his hands.

At six o'clock, day began to break; and with the first glimmer of light, the electric light of the narwhal disappeared. At seven o'clock the day was sufficiently advanced, but a very thick sea fog obscured our view, and the best spyglasses could not pierce it. That caused disappointment and anger.

I climbed the mizzen-mast. Some officers were already perched on the mast heads.

At eight o'clock the fog lay heavily on the waves, and its thick scrolls rose little by little. The horizon grew wider and clearer at the same time.

Suddenly, just as on the day before, Ned Land's voice was heard:

"The thing itself on the port quarter!" cried the harpooner.

Every eye was turned towards the point indicated. There, a mile and a half from the frigate, a long blackish body emerged a meter above the waves. Its tail, violently agitated, produced a considerable eddy. Never did a caudal appendage beat the sea with such violence. An immense track, of a dazzling whiteness, marked the passage of the animal, and described a long curve.

The frigate approached the cetacean. I examined it thoroughly. The reports of the *Shannon* and of the *Helvetia* had rather exaggerated its size, and I estimated its length at only two hundred and fifty feet. As to its width, this was difficult to estimate, though I judged that the animal was admirably proportioned in all three dimensions.

While I watched this phenomenon, two jets of steam and water were ejected from its vents, and rose to the height of 40 meters. Thus I ascertained its way of breathing. I concluded definitely that it belonged to the vertebrate branch, class mammalia, sub-class of monodelphians, group of pisciforms, order of cetaceans, family of . . . what, I could not say. The order of cetaceans is composed of three families: the baleens, the cachalots and the dolphins. It is to this last that the narwhals belong. Each of these families is divided into several genera, each genus into species, each species into varieties. Variety, specie, genus and family I was still missing, but I did not doubt that I would soon complete the classification with the help of heaven and Captain Farragut.

The crew waited impatiently for their chief's orders. The latter, after having observed the animal attentively, called for the engineer. The engineer ran to him.

"Sir," said the commander, "you have steam up?"

"Yes, sir" answered the engineer.

"Good. Stoke up your fires and put on all steam!"

Three hurrahs greeted this order. The time for the struggle had arrived. Some moments after, the two funnels of the frigate vomited torrents of black smoke, and the bridge quaked under the trembling of the boilers.

The *Abraham Lincoln,* propelled by her powerful screw, went straight at the animal. The latter indifferently allowed it to come within half a cable's length; then, as if disdaining to dive, it took a little turn, and stopped a short distance off.

This pursuit lasted nearly three-quarters of an hour, without the frigate gaining two fathoms on the cetacean.[2] It was quite evident that at that rate we should never catch up with it.

Captain Farragut was outraged and tugged at the tuft of hair under his chin.

"Ned Land!" he called.

Ned responded to the order.

"Well, Mr. Land," asked the captain, "do you advise me to put the boats out to sea?"

"No, sir," replied Ned Land; "because we shall not take that beast easily."

"What shall we do then?"

"Put on more steam if you can, sir. With your leave, I mean to post myself under the bowsprit, and if we get within harpooning distance, I shall throw my harpoon."

"Go, Ned," said the captain. "Engineer, put on more pressure."

Ned Land went to his post. The fires were increased; the screw revolved forty-three times a minute, and the steam poured out of the valves. We heaved the log, and calculated that the *Abraham Lincoln* was going at the rate of 18½ miles an hour.

But the accursed animal swam too at the rate of 18½ miles an hour.

For a whole hour, the frigate kept up this pace, without gaining a fathom. It was humiliating for one of the swiftest ships in the American navy. A stubborn anger seized the crew. The sailors abused the monster, who, as before, disdained to answer them. The captain no longer contented himself with twisting his beard—he gnawed at it.

The engineer was again called.

"You have reached maximum pressure?"

"Yes sir," replied the engineer.

"And your valves are under what pressure . . . ?"

"Six and a half atmospheres."

"Charge them to ten atmospheres."

There was an American order for certain. I felt as though I were in a steamboat race on the Mississippi River!

"Conseil," I said to my brave servant, standing beside me, "you know that we will probably be blown up?"

"Whatever pleases monsieur!" he replied. Well! I admit that I was willing to take that risk.

The valves were charged. The coal was engulfed by the furnace. The ventilators carried torrents of air to the flames.

The speed of the *Abraham Lincoln* increased. Its masts trembled down to their stepping-holes, and the clouds of smoke could hardly find a way out of the funnels quickly enough.

They heaved the log a second time.

"Well, helmsman?" asked the captain of the man at the wheel.

"Nineteen and 3/10 miles an hour, sir."

"Clap on more steam."

The engineer obeyed. The manometer showed ten atmospheres of pressure. But the cetacean "got up steam" itself, no doubt for, without straining itself, it made 19-3/10 miles an hour.

What a pursuit! No, I cannot describe the motion that vibrated through me. Ned Land kept his post, harpoon in hand. Several times the animal let us gain upon it.

"We shall catch it! we shall catch it!" cried the Canadian.

But just as he was going to strike, the cetacean stole away with a rapidity that could not be estimated at less than 30 miles an hour. Even during our maximum speed, it bullied the frigate, going round and round it! A cry of fury broke from everyone!

At noon we were no further advanced than at eight o'clock in the morning.

The captain then decided to take more direct means.

"Ah!" said he, "that animal goes quicker than the *Abraham Lincoln!* Very well! we will see whether it will escape these conical bullets. Send your men to the forecastle, sir."

The forecastle gun was immediately loaded and slewed round. But the shot passed some feet above the cetacean, which was half a mile off.

"A better gunner!" cried the commander, "and five hundred dollars to whoever will hit that infernal beast!"

An old gunner with a grey beard—that I can see now—with steady eye and grave face, went up to the gun and took careful aim. A loud explosion was heard, with which were mingled the cheers of the crew.

The bullet did its work; it hit the animal, but not fatally, and sliding off the rounded surface, was lost two miles away.

"Ah!" cried the old gunner in his rage, "the thing must be covered in six-inch plates!"

"Curse the thing!" replied Captain Farragut.

The chase began again, and the captain, leaning towards me, said—

"I will pursue that beast till my frigate explodes."

"Yes," answered I; "and you will be quite right to do it!"

I wished the beast would exhaust itself, and not be insensible to fatigue like a steam engine! But it was of no use. Hours passed, without its showing any signs of exhaustion.

However, it must be said in praise of the *Abraham Lincoln,* that she struggled on with indefatigable tenacity. I cannot reckon she made less than five hundred kilometers during this unlucky day, November the 6th. But night came and enveloped the heaving ocean.

Now I thought our expedition was at an end, and that we should never again see the extraordinary animal. I was mistaken.

At ten minutes to eleven in the evening, the electric light reappeared three miles to windward of the frigate, as pure, as intense as during the preceding night.

The narwhal seemed motionless. Perhaps tired with its day's work, it slept, letting itself float with the undulation of the waves. Now was a chance of which the captain resolved to take advantage.

He gave his orders. The *Abraham Lincoln* kept up half steam, and advanced cautiously so as not to awake its adversary. It is no rare thing to meet in the middle of the ocean whales so sound asleep that they can be successfully attacked, and Ned Land had harpooned more than one during its sleep. The Canadian went to take his place again under the bowsprit.

The frigate approached noiselessly, stopped at two cables' lengths from the animal, and drifted forward. No one breathed; a deep silence reigned on the bridge. We were not a hundred feet from the burning focus, the light of which increased and dazzled our eyes.

At this moment, leaning on the forecastle bulwark, I saw below me Ned Land grappling the martingale in one hand, brandishing his terrible harpoon in the other, scarcely twenty feet from the motionless animal.

Suddenly his arm straightened, and the harpoon was thrown, I heard the sonorous blow of the weapon, which seemed to have struck a hard body.

The electric light went out suddenly, and two enormous waterspouts broke over the bridge of the frigate, rushing in a torrent from stem to stern, overthrowing men, and breaking the lashings of the spars. A fearful shock followed, and, thrown over the rail without having time to stop myself, I fell into the sea.

---

[1]A cable is equal to about 600 feet. R.M.

[2]A fathom = 6 feet. R.M.

◄ CHAPTER VII ►

AN UNKNOWN SPECIES OF WHALE

his unexpected fall so stunned me that I have no clear recollection of my sensations at the time. I was at first drawn down to a depth of about twenty feet. I am a good swimmer, though without pretending to rival Byron or Edgar Poe, who were masters of the art, and in that plunge I did not lose my presence of mind. Two vigorous strokes brought me to the surface of the water.

My first care was to look for the frigate. Had the crew seen me disappear? Had the *Abraham Lincoln* veered round? Would the captain put out a boat? Might I hope to be saved?

The darkness was profound. I caught a glimpse of a black mass disappearing in the east, its beacon lights dying out in the distance. It was the frigate! I was lost.

"Help, Help!" I shouted, swimming towards the *Abraham Lincoln* in desperation.

My clothes encumbered me; they seemed glued to my body, and paralyzed my movements. I was sinking! I was suffocating!

"Help!"

This was my last cry. My mouth filled with water; I struggled against being drawn down the abyss. . . .

Suddenly my clothes were seized by a strong hand, and I felt myself quickly drawn up to the surface of the sea; and I heard, yes, I heard these words pronounced in my ear—

"If monsieur would be so good as to lean on my shoulder, monsieur would swim with much greater ease."

I seized with one hand my faithful Conseil's arm.

"Is it you?" said I, "you?"

"Myself," answered Conseil; "and waiting for monsieur's orders."

"That shock threw you as well as me into the sea?"

"No; but being in monsieur's service, I followed him."

The worthy fellow thought that was but natural!

"And the frigate?" I asked.

"The frigate?" replied Conseil, turning on his back; "I think that monsieur had better not count too much on her!"

"You think so?"

"I say that, at the time I threw myself into the sea, I heard the men at the wheel say, 'The screw and the rudder are broken. . . .'"

"Broken?"

"Yes, broken by the monster's tusk. It is the only injury the *Abraham Lincoln* has sustained. But it is a bad outlook for us—she no longer answers her helm."

"Then we are lost!"

"Perhaps so," calmly answered Conseil. "However, we have still several hours before us, and one can do a good deal in some hours."

Conseil's imperturbable coolness set me up again. I swam more vigorously; but, cramped by my clothes, which stuck to me like a leaden weight, I felt great difficulty in bearing up. Conseil saw this.

"Will monsieur let me make a cut?" said he, and slipping an open knife under my clothes, he ripped them up from top to bottom very rapidly. Then he cleverly slipped them off me, while I swam for both of us.

Then I did the same for Conseil, and we continued to ''navigate'' near to each other.

Nevertheless, our situation was no less terrible. Perhaps our disappearance had not been noticed; and if it had been, the frigate could not tack to leeward, being without its rudder. Our only chance for safety lay in the ship's boats.

Conseil considered this, and laid his plans accordingly. What an amazing personality! This phlegmatic boy was perfectly self-possessed.[1]

We then decided that, as our only chance of safety was being picked up by the *Abraham Lincoln's* boats, we ought to manage so as to wait for them as long as possible. I resolved then to save our strength, so that both should not be exhausted at the same time; and this is how we managed: while one of us lay on our back, quite still, with arms crossed, and legs stretched out, the other would swim and push the other on in front. This towing business was not to last more than ten minutes each; and working in relays thus, we could swim on for some hours, perhaps till daybreak.

Poor chance! but hope is so firmly rooted in the heart of man! Moreover, there were two of us. Indeed I declare (though it may seem improbable) that I tried to destroy all hope,— but if I wished to despair, I could not.

The collision of the frigate with the cetacean had occurred about eleven o'clock the evening before. I reckoned then we should have eight hours to swim before sunrise, an operation quite practicable if we relieved each other. The sea, very calm, was in our favor. Sometimes I tried to see into the intense darkness that was only dispelled by the phosphorescence caused by our movements. I watched the luminous waves that broke over my hand, whose mirror-like surface was speckled with silvery patches. One might have thought that we were in a bath of quicksilver.

Near one o'clock in the morning, I was seized with dreadful fatigue. My limbs stiffened under the strain of violent cramp. Conseil was obliged to keep me up, and our preservation devolved on him alone. I heard the poor boy pant; his breathing became short and hurried. I found that he could not keep up much longer.

''Leave me! leave me!'' I said to him.

''Leave monsieur? never!'' replied he. ''I would drown first.''

Just then the moon appeared through the fringes of a thick cloud that the wind was driving to the east. The surface of the sea glittered with its rays. This kindly light reanimated us. My head got better again. I looked at all the points of the horizon. I saw the frigate! She was five miles from us, and looked like a dark mass, hardly discernible. But no boats!

I would have cried out. But what good would it have been at such a distance! My swollen lips could utter no sounds. Conseil could articulate some words, and I heard him repeat at intervals, ''Help! help!''

Our movements were suspended for an instant; we listened. It might be only a singing in the ear, but it seemed to me as if a cry answered the cry from Conseil.

''Did you hear?'' I murmured.

''Yes! yes!''

And Conseil gave one more despairing call.

This time there was no mistake! A human voice responded to ours! Was it the voice of another unfortunate creature, abandoned in the middle of the ocean, some other victim of the shock sustained by the vessel? Or rather was it a boat from the frigate, that was hailing us in the darkness?

Conseil made a last effort, and leaning on my shoulder, while I struck out in a despairing effort, he raised himself half out of the water, then fell back exhausted.

''What did you see?''

''I saw . . .'' murmured he; ''I saw . . . but do not talk . . . reserve all your strength! . . .''

What had he seen? Then, I know not why, the thought of the monster came into my head for the first time! But that voice? The time is past for Jonahs to take refuge in whales' bellies!

However, Conseil was towing me again. He raised his head sometimes, looked before us, and uttered a cry of recognition, which was responded to by a voice that came nearer and nearer. I scarcely heard it. My strength was exhausted; my fingers stiffened; my hand afforded me support no longer; my mouth, convulsively opening, filled with salt water. Cold crept over me. I raised my head for the last time, then I sank. . . .

At this moment a hard body struck me. I clung to it. Then I felt that I was being drawn up, that I was brought to the surface of the water, that my chest collapsed—I fainted. . . .

It is certain that I soon came to, thanks to the vigorous body rubbings that I received. I half opened my eyes.

"Conseil!" I murmured.

"Did monsieur call for me?" asked Conseil.

Just then, by the waning light of the moon, which was sinking down to the horizon, I saw a face which was not Conseil's, and which I immediately recognized.

"Ned!" I cried.

"The same, sir, who is seeking his prize!" replied the Canadian.

"Were you also thrown into the sea by the collision?"

"Yes, Professor; but more fortunate than you, I was able to find a footing almost immediately upon a floating island."

"An island?"

"Or, more correctly speaking, on our gigantic narwhal."

"Explain yourself, Ned!"

"Only I soon found out why my harpoon had not entered its skin and was blunted."

"Why, Ned, why?"

"Because, Professor, that beast is made of sheet iron!"

The Canadian's last words produced a sudden revolution in my brain. I wriggled myself quickly to the top of the creature, or object, half out of the water, which served us for a refuge. I kicked it. It was evidently a hard impenetrable body, and not the soft substance that forms the bodies of the great marine mammalia. But this hard body might be a bony carapace, like that of the antediluvian animals; and I should be free to class this monster among amphibious reptiles, such as tortoises or alligators.

Well, no! the blackish back that supported me was smooth, polished, without scales. The blow produced a metallic sound; and incredible though it may be, it seemed, I might say, as if it was made of riveted plates.

There was no doubt about it! This animal, this monster, this natural phenomenon that had puzzled the learned world, and overthrown and misled the imagination of seamen of both hemispheres, was, it must be admitted, a still more astonishing phenomenon, inasmuch as it was a simply human construction.

The discovery of the existence of the most fabulous mythological being could not have astonished me more. It had always seemed to me quite simple that anything prodigious should come from the hand of the creator. To find the impossible realized by the hand of man was enough to confound the imagination!

We had no time to lose, however. We were lying upon the back of a sort of submarine boat, which appeared (as far as I could judge) like a huge fish of steel. Ned Land's mind was made up on this point. Conseil and I could only agree with him.

"But then," I said, "this apparatus must have some mechanism of locomotion, and a crew to operate it."

"Evidently," answered the harpooner, "but all the same, in the three hours that I have inhabited this floating island, I have not seen a single sign of life."

"This boat has not moved?"

"No, Monsieur Aronnax. It just lies here, rocked by the waves, but has not budged."

"We know, beyond doubt, that it is capable of great speed. Therefore, since a machine is required to produce this speed, a mechanic is required to work the machine, I can only conclude . . . that we have been saved."

"Hum!" said Ned Land, reservedly.

Just then a bubbling began at the back of this strange thing, which was evidently propelled by a screw, and it began to move. We had only just time to seize hold of the upper part, which rose eighty centimeters or about three feet out of the water. Happily its speed was not great.

"As long as it sails horizontally," muttered Ned Land, "I do not mind; but if it takes a fancy to dive, I would not give two dollars for my skin."

The Canadian might have quoted still less. It became really necessary to communicate with the beings, whatever they were, shut up inside the machine. I searched all over the outside for an aperture, a panel, or a "man hole," to use a technical expression; but the lines of the iron rivets, solidly driven into the joints of the iron plates, were clear and uniform. Besides, the moon disappeared then, and left us in total darkness.

We had to wait for daylight before we could find some way to penetrate to the interior of the submarine boat.

Therefore, our safety depended entirely upon the whims of the mysterious steersman who directed this apparatus, for, if he decided to dive, we were lost! This case excepted, I did not doubt the possibility of entering into communication with him. Moreover, if they did not create their own air, it must be necessary to revisit from time to time the surface of the ocean to renew their supply of respirable molecules. So, there must necessarily be some opening that put the interior of the boat in touch with the atmosphere.

As for our hopes of being saved by Captain Farragut, we had to abandon that completely. We were drifting off to the west, and I estimated that our speed was relatively moderate, perhaps twelve miles an hour. The propellor beat the water with mathematical regularity, sometimes emerging and throwing phosphorescent spray to a great height.

At four in the morning, the speed of the apparatus increased. It was difficult to hold on at the dizzying speed, and with the waves pounding against us. Fortunately, Ned found under his hand a large mooring-ring attached to the upper part of the iron shell and we managed to get a solid hold onto that.

At last this long night passed. My indistinct remembrance prevents my describing all the impressions it made. I can only recall one circumstance. During some lulls of the wind and sea, I fancied I heard several times vague sounds, a sort of fugitive harmony produced by distant music. What was then the mystery of this submarine craft, of which the whole world vainly sought an explanation? What kind of beings existed in this strange boat? What mechanical agent caused its prodigious speed?

Daybreak appeared. The morning mists surrounded us, but they soon cleared off. I was about to examine the hull, which formed on its upper part a kind of horizontal platform or decks, when I felt it gradually sinking.

"Oh! a thousand devils!" cried Ned Land, kicking the resounding plate; "open, you inhospitable rascals!" It was difficult to make one's self heard above the noise of the screw.

Happily the sinking movement ceased. Suddenly a noise, like iron bolts violently pushed aside, came from the interior of the boat. One iron plate moved, a man appeared, uttered an odd cry, and disappeared immediately.

Some moments after, eight strong men, with masked faces, appeared noiselessly, and drew us down into their formidable machine.

◄ CHAPTER VIII ►

MOBILIS IN MOBILI

his forcible abduction, so roughly carried out, was accomplished with the rapidity of lightning. My friends and I did not have time to realize where we were being taken. My skin was cold and I shivered violently. Whom had we to deal with? No doubt some new sort of pirates, who exploited the sea in their own way.

Hardly had the narrow panel closed upon me, when I was enveloped in darkness. My eyes, dazzled from the outer light, could distinguish nothing. I felt my naked feet cling to the rungs of an iron ladder. Ned Land and Conseil, firmly seized, followed me. At the bottom of the ladder, a door opened, and shut after us immediately with a bang.

We were alone. Where? I could not say, could hardly imagine. All was black, and such a dense black that, after some minutes, my eyes had not been able to discern even those faintest glimmers one imagines one sees on the blackest of nights.

Meanwhile, Ned Land, furious at these proceedings, gave free vent to his indignation.

"A thousand devils!" cried he, "here are people who equal Scotch for hospitality. They only just miss being cannibals. I should not be surprised at it, but I declare that they shall not eat me without my protesting!"

"Calm yourself, friend Ned, calm yourself," replied Conseil, quietly. "Do not cry out before you are hurt. We are not in a pot yet."

"Not in a pot," sharply replied the Canadian, "but in an oven, at all events. Things look black. Happily, I still have my bowie-knife,[1] and I can always see well enough to use it. The first of these pirates who lays a hand on me . . ."

"Do not excite yourself, Ned," I said to the harpooner, "and do not compromise us by useless violence. Who knows that they will not listen to us? Let us rather try to find out where we are."

I groped about. In five steps I came to an iron wall, made of plates bolted together. Then turning back I struck against a wooden table, near which were ranged several stools. The boards of this prison were concealed under a thick mat of phormium, which deadened the noise of the feet. The bare walls revealed no trace of window or door. Conseil, going round the reverse way, met me, and we went back to the middle of the cabin, which measured about twenty feet by ten. As to its height, Ned Land, in spite of his own great height, could not measure it.

Half an hour had already passed without our situation being bettered, when the dense darkness suddenly gave way to extreme light. Our prison was suddenly lighted, that is to say, it became filled with a luminous matter, so strong that I could not bear it at first. In its whiteness and intensity I recognized that electric light which played round the submarine boat like a magnificent phenomenon of phosphorescence. After shutting my eyes involuntarily, I opened them and saw that this luminous agent came from a translucent half-globe, unpolished, placed in the roof of the cabin.

"At last one can see," cried Ned Land, who, knife in hand, stood on the defensive.

"Yes," said I, chancing a play on words; "but we are still in the dark about ourselves."

"Monsieur must have patience," said the imperturbable Conseil.

The sudden lighting of the cabin enabled me to examine it minutely. It only contained a table and five stools. The invisible door might be hermetically sealed. No noise was heard. All seemed dead in the interior of this boat. Did it move, did it float on the surface of the ocean, or did it dive into its depths? I could not guess.

However, the luminous globe was not lighted without a reason. I had hoped that the men of the crew would soon show themselves, and my hope was well founded. If you want to forget about people, you don't light up their prisons.

A noise of bolts was now heard, the door opened, and two men appeared.

One was short, very muscular, broad-shouldered, with robust limbs, strong head, an abundance of black hair, thick moustache, a quick penetrating look, and the vivacity which characterizes the population of Southern France. Diderot has maintained, with much justification, that a man's gestures are metaphoric, and this little man was certainly living proof. One could sense that his ordinary speech was spiced with quantities of prosopopeia, metynomy and hypallage. But this I was not able to verify, because he always used in my presence a singular and absolutely incomprehensible language.

The second stranger merits a more detailed description. A disciple of Gratiolet or Engel would have read his face like an open book. I made out his prevailing qualities directly:—self-confidence,—because his head was nobly set on the arc formed by the line of his shoulders, and his black eyes looked around with cold assurance; calmness,—for his skin, rather pale, showed his coolness of blood; energy,—evinced by the rapid contraction of his lofty brows; and courage,—because his deep breathing denoted great power of lungs.

I added that this man was proud. His firm, calm gaze seemed to reflect lofty thoughts; his whole being—the homogenity of expression and gesture of body and face, according to the observations of the physiognomists, indicated a man of great candor and openness.

I felt involuntarily reassured in his presence; it augured well for our interview.

Whether this person was thirty-five or fifty years of age, I could not say. He was tall, had a large forehead, straight nose, a clearly cut mouth, beautiful teeth, with fine tapered hands,—eminently "psychical," to use a word from palmistry—indicative of a passionate temperament. This man was certainly the most admirable specimen I had ever met. One remarkable feature was his eyes, rather far from each other, and which could take in nearly a quarter of the horizon at once. This faculty—which I verified later—gave him a range of vision far superior to Ned Land's. When this stranger fixed upon an object, his eyebrows met, his large eyelids closed around the pupils so as to contract the range of his vision, and then he would look. And what a look! He looked as if he magnified distant objects. His gaze penetrated one's very soul! As if he pierced those sheets of water so opaque to our eyes, and as if he read the very depths of the seas! . . .

The two strangers, with caps made from the fur of the sea otter, and shod with sea boots of seals' skin, were dressed in clothes of a peculiar texture, which allowed free movement of the limbs. The taller of the two, evidently the captain, examined us with great attention, without saying a word. Then, turning to his companion, talked with him in an unknown tongue. It was a sonorous, harmonious, and flexible dialect, the vowels seeming to admit of very varied accentuation.

The other replied by a shake of the head, and added two or three perfectly incomprehensible words. Then he seemed to question me by a look.

I replied in good French that I did not know his language; but he seemed not to understand me, and my situation became more embarrassing.

"If monsieur were to tell our story," said Conseil, "perhaps these gentlemen may understand some words."

I began to tell our adventures, articulating each syllable clearly, and without omitting one single detail. I announced our names and rank, introducing in person Professor Aronnax, his servant Conseil, and master Ned Land, the harpooner.

The man with the soft calm eyes listened to me quietly, even politely, and with extreme attention; but nothing in his countenance indicated that he had understood my story. When I finished, he said not a word.

There remained one resource, to speak English. Perhaps they would know this almost universal language. I knew it, as well as the German language,—well enough to read it fluently, but not to speak it correctly. But, we had to try to make ourselves understood.

"It's your turn," I said to the harpooner, "speak the best English ever spoken by an Anglo-Saxon, and try to do better than I."

Ned did not beg off, and recommenced our story. The main story was the same, but the form differed. The Canadian, true to his character, spoke with great animation. He complained violently about being imprisoned without regard to people's rights, demanded to know under what law he was being detained, invoked *habeas corpus,* threatened to take to court anyone who held him without due cause, raged, gestured, shouted, and finally, by a very comprehensive sign indicated that we were starving to death.

This was perfectly true, though we had almost forgotten about it.

To his great disgust, the harpooner did not seem to have made himself more intelligible than I had. Our visitors did not stir. They evidently understood neither the language of Arago nor of Faraday.

Very much embarrassed, after having vainly exhausted our philological resources, I knew not what action to take, when Conseil said—

"If monsieur will permit me, I will relate it in German."

"What! You speak German?" I cried.

"Because I'm Flemish, if it pleases monsieur."

"On the contrary, I'm very pleased. Go ahead, my boy."

And Conseil, for the third time, recounted the various perils of our story.

But in spite of the elegant turns and good accent of the narrator, the German language had no success. At last, nonplussed, I tried to remember my first lessons, and to narrate our adventures in Latin. Cicero would have stopped up his ears and sent me to the kitchen, but I tried anyway. The result was negative. This last attempt being of no avail, the two strangers exchanged some words in their unknown language, and without even a gesture of reassurance, as could have been easy in any language, retired. The door shut.

"This is infamous!" cried Ned Land, who broke out for the twentieth time; "Indeed, we speak to those rogues in French, English, German, and Latin, and not one of them has the politeness to answer!"

"Calm yourself," I said to the furious harpooner, "anger will do no good."

"But do you see, Professor," replied our irascible companion, "that we shall absolutely die of hunger in this iron cage?"

"Bah," said Conseil, philosophically; "we can hold out some time yet."

"My friends," I said, "we must not despair. We have been worse off than this. Do me the favor to wait a little before forming an opinion upon the commander and crew of this boat."

"My opinion is formed," replied Ned Land, sharply. "They are rogues."

"Good! And from what country?"

"From the Land of Rogues!"

"My brave Ned, that country is not clearly indicated on the map of the world; but I admit that the nationality of the two strangers is hard to determine. Neither English, French, nor German, that is quite certain. However, I am inclined to think that the commander and his companion were born in low latitudes. There is southern blood in them. But I cannot decide by their appearance whether they are Spaniards, Turks, Arabians, or Indians. As to their language, it is quite incomprehensible."

"There is the disadvantage of not knowing all languages," said Conseil, "or the disadvantage of not having one universal language."[2]

"That would be of no use," answered Ned Land. "Do you not see that those fellows have a language of their own—a language invented to make honest men who want their dinners despair? But in every country in the world, to open your mouth, move your jaws, snap your teeth and lips, is understood. Does it not mean in Québec as well as Pomotou, in Paris as well as the antipodes, 'I am hungry! Give me something to eat!'"

"Oh," said Conseil, "there are people so unintelligent . . ."

As he said these words, the door opened. A steward entered. He brought us clothes, coats and trousers, made of a stuff I did not know. I hastened to dress myself, and my companions followed my example.

During that time, the steward—mute, perhaps deaf—had arranged the table, and laid three plates.

"This is something like," said Conseil. "It looks promising!"

"Bah," said the rancorous harpooner, "what do you suppose they eat here? Tortoise liver, filleted shark, and beefsteaks from seadogs!"

"We shall see," said Conseil.

The dishes, with silver covers, were placed symmetrically on the table, and we took our places. Undoubtedly we had to do with civilized people, and had it not been for the electric light which flooded us, I could have fancied I was in the dining room of the Adelphi Hotel at Liverpool, or at the Grand Hotel in Paris. I must say, however, that there was neither bread nor wine. The water was fresh and clear, but it was water, and did not suit Ned Land's taste. Among the dishes which were brought to us, I recognized several fish delicately dressed; but of other dishes, although excellent, I could give no opinion, neither could I tell to what kingdom they belonged, whether animal or vegetable. As to the dinner service, it was elegant, and in perfect taste. Each utensil, spoon, fork, knife, plate, had a letter engraved on it, with a motto around it, of which this is an exact facsimile:

Mobile within a mobile element! An appropriate motto for this submarine craft—on condition that the preposition *in* is translated as *within* and not *on*. The letter *N* was no doubt the initial of the name of the enigmatical person, who commanded at the bottom of the seas.

Ned and Conseil did not reflect much. They devoured the food, and I did likewise. I was, besides, reassured as to our fate; and it seemed evident that our hosts would not let us die of want.

However, everything has an end, everything passes away, even the hunger of people who have not eaten for fifteen hours. Our appetites satisfied, we felt overcome with sleep. A natural reaction, after the fatigues of a long night struggling against death.

"Faith! I shall sleep well," said Conseil.

"So shall I," replied Ned Land.

My two companions stretched themselves on the cabin carpet, and were soon sound asleep.

For my own part I did not succumb so easily to sleep. Too many thoughts crowded my brain, too many insoluble questions pressed upon me, too many fancies kept my eyes half open. Where were we? What strange power carried us on? I felt—or rather fancied I felt—the machine sinking down to the lowest depths of the sea. Dreadful nightmares beset me; I saw in these mysterious asylums a world of unknown animals, among which this submarine boat seemed to be of the same kind, living, moving, and formidable as they! Then my brain grew calmer, my imagination wandered into vague unconsciousness, and I soon fell into a deep sleep.

---

[1]A knife with a broad blade that Americans carry with them wherever they go. J.V.

[2]Verne had a great interest in artificial languages, and once planned a novel to be written in Esperanto. R.M.

◄ CHAPTER IX ►
NED LAND'S TEMPER

How long we slept I do not know; but our sleep must have lasted long, for it rested us completely from our fatigues. I woke first. My companions had not moved, and were still stretched in their corner, a pair of inert masses.

Hardly roused from my somewhat hard couch, I felt my brain freed, my mind clear. I then began an attentive examination of our cell.

Nothing was changed inside. The prison was still a prison,—the prisoners, prisoners. However, the steward, during our sleep, had cleared the table. There was nothing to indicate an approaching change in our situation. I asked myself seriously if we might be destined to live indefinitely in this cage.

This prospect seemed to me even more painful because, though my head was clear of obsessions, still I felt a singular oppression on my chest. I breathed with difficulty. The heavy air seemed to oppress my lungs. Although the cell was large, we had evidently consumed a great part of the oxygen that it contained. Indeed, each man consumes, in one hour, the oxygen contained in more than one hundred liters of air, and when this air becomes charged with a nearly equal quantity of carbon dioxide, it becomes unbreathable.

It became necessary to renew the atmosphere of our prison, and no doubt that of the submarine boat as well. That gave rise to a question in my mind. How would the commander of this floating dwelling-place proceed? Would he obtain air by chemical means, in getting by heat the oxygen contained in chlorate of potash, and in absorbing carbon dioxide by caustic potash? If that was the case, he must maintain contact with land in order to obtain the necessary chemicals. Or did he confine himself to simply storing air under great pressure in reservoirs, releasing it as needed by himself and his crew? Possibly. Or, a more convenient, economical, and consequently more probable alternative, would he be satisfied to rise and take breath at the surface of the water, like a cetacean, and so renew for twenty-four hours the atmospheric provision? Whatever method he used, it seemed to me prudent to employ it without delay.

In fact, I was already obliged to increase my respirations to eke out of this cell the little oxygen it contained, when suddenly I was refreshed by a current of pure air, perfumed with the smell of salt. It was an invigorating sea breeze, charged with iodine! I opened my mouth wide, and my lungs saturated themselves with fresh molecules. At the same time I felt the boat rolling. Not violently, but still noticeably. The iron-plated monster had evidently just risen to the surface of the ocean to breathe, after the fashion of whales. I found out from that the mode of ventilating the boat.

When I had inhaled this air freely, I sought the conduit, the ''air pipe,'' which conveyed to us the beneficial breeze, and I was not long in finding it. Above the door was a ventilator, through which volumes of fresh air renewed the impoverished atmosphere of the cell.

I was making my observations, when Ned and Conseil awoke almost at the same time, under the influence of this reviving air. They rubbed their eyes, stretched themselves, and were on their feet in an instant.

"Did monsieur sleep well?" asked Conseil, with his usual politeness.

"Very well, my brave boy. And you, Mr. Ned Land?"

"Soundly, Professor. But if I am not mistaken, I seem to be breathing sea breeze!"

A seaman could not be mistaken, and I told the Canadian all that had passed during his sleep.

"Good!" said he; "that accounts for those roarings we heard, when the supposed narwhal sighted the *Abraham Lincoln.*"

"Quite so, Master Land; it was taking a breath."

"Only, Mr. Aronnax, I have no idea what hour it is, unless it is dinner-time?"

"Dinner-time, my good fellow? Say rather breakfast-time, for we certainly have begun another day."

"So," said Conseil, "we have slept twenty-four hours?"

"That is my opinion."

"I will not contradict you," replied Ned Land. "But dinner or breakfast, the steward will be welcome, whichever he brings."

"The one and the other," said Conseil.

"Certainly," answered the Canadian, "we have a right to two meals, and, for my own part, I shall do honor to both."

"Well, Ned, we must wait," I answered. "It is evident that those two men had no intention of leaving us to die of hunger, for in that case there would have been no reason to give us dinner yesterday."

"Unless it is to fatten us!" answered Ned.

"I protest," I answered. "We have not fallen into the hands of cannibals!"

"One swallow does not make a summer," answered the Canadian seriously. "Who knows if those fellows have not been deprived of fresh meat, and in that case these healthy and well-constituted individuals like the Professor, his servant, and me . . ."

"Drive away such ideas, Mr. Land," I answered, "and above all do not act upon them to get into a rage with our hosts, for that would only make the situation worse."

"Anyway," said the harpooner, "I am devilishly hungry, and, dinner or breakfast, the meal does not arrive!"

"Mr. Land," I replied, "we must conform to the rule of the vessel, and I suppose that our stomachs are in advance of the steward's bell."

"Well then, we'll just have to fix his clock!" responded Conseil calmly.

"That is just like you, friend Conseil," said Ned, impatiently. "You are never out of temper! always calm! you would say grace before receiving your blessings, and die of hunger rather than complain!"

"What is the use of complaining?" asked Conseil.

"It does one good to complain! It is something. And if these pirates—I say pirates not to vex the Professor, who does not like to hear them called cannibals—and if these pirates think that they are going to keep me in this cage where I am stifled without hearing how I can swear, they are mistaken! Come, Monsieur Aronnax, speak frankly. Do you think they will keep us long in this iron box?"

"To tell you the truth I know no more about it than you, friend Land."

"But what do you think about it?"

"I think that chance has made us masters of an important secret. If it is in the interest of the crew of this submarine vessel to keep it, and if this interest is of more consequence than the life of three men, I believe our existence to be in great danger. In the contrary case, on the first opportunity, the monster who has swallowed us will send us back to the world inhabited by our fellow men."

"Unless he enrolls us among his crew," said Conseil, "and keeps us thus. . . ."

"Until some frigate," replied Ned Land, "more rapid or more skilful than the *Abraham Lincoln,* masters this nest of plunderers, and sends its crew and us to breathe our last at the end of his mainyard."

"Well reasoned, Mr. Land," I replied. "But I believe no proposition of the sort has yet been made to us, so it is useless to discuss what we should do in that case. I repeat, we must wait, take counsel of circumstances, and do nothing, as there is nothing to do."

"On the contrary, Mr. Professor," answered the harpooner, who would not give up his point, "we must do something."

"What, then?"

"Escape."

"To escape from a terrestrial prison is often difficult, but from a submarine prison, that seems to me quite impracticable."

"Come, friend Ned," said Conseil, "what have you to say to monsieur's objection? I do not believe an American is ever at the end of his resources."

The harpooner, visibly embarrassed, was silent, a flight under the conditions chance had imposed upon us was absolutely impossible. But a Canadian is half a Frenchman, and Ned Land showed it by his answer.

"Then, Monsieur Aronnax," he said, after some minutes' reflection, "you do not guess what men ought to do who cannot escape from prison?"

"No, my friend."

"It is very simple; they must make their arrangements to stay in it."

"I should think so," said Conseil; "it is much better to be inside than on the top or underneath."

"But after you have thrown your jailers, turnkeys and keepers out?" added Ned Land.

"What, Ned? You seriously think of seizing this vessel?"

"Quite seriously," answered the Canadian.

"It is impossible."

"How so, sir? A favorable chance may occur, and I do not see what could prevent us profiting by it. If there are twenty men on board this machine they will not frighten two Frenchmen and a Canadian, I suppose."

It was better to admit the proposition of the harpooner than to discuss it. So I contented myself with answering—

"Let such circumstances come, Mr. Land, and we will see. But until they do I beg you to contain your impatience. We can only act by stratagem, and you will not make yourself master of favorable chances by getting in a rage. Promise me, therefore, that you will accept the situation without too much anger."

"I promise you, Professor," answered Ned Land in a not very assuring tone. "Not a violent word shall leave my mouth, not an angry movement shall betray me, even if we are not waited upon at table with desirable regularity."

"I have your word, Ned," I answered.

Then the conversation was suspended, and each of us began to reflect on his own account. I acknowledge that, for my own part, and notwithstanding the assurance of the harpooner, I was under no illusion. I did not admit the probability of the favorable occasions of which Ned Land had spoken. To be so well worked the submarine boat must have a numerous crew, and consequently, in case of a struggle, we should have to deal with numbers too great. Besides, before aught else we must be free, and we were not. I did not even see any means of leaving this iron cell so hermetically closed. And should the strange commander of the boat have a secret to keep—which appeared at least probable—he would not allow us freedom of movement on board. Now, would he get rid of us by violence, or would he throw us upon some corner of the earth? All that was the unknown. All these hypotheses seemed to be extremely plausible, and one must be a harpooner to hope to conquer liberty again.

I understood, though, that Ned Land should get more exasperated with the thoughts that took possession of his brain. I heard him swearing in a gruff undertone, and saw his looks again become threatening. He rose, moved about like a wild beast in a cage, and struck the wall with his fist and foot.

Time was getting on, and we were fearfully hungry; and this time the steward did not appear. It was rather too long to leave us. If they really had good intentions towards us they had too long forgotten our shipwrecked conditions.

Ned Land, tormented by the cravings of his robust stomach, got still more angry; and, notwithstanding his promise, I dreaded an explosion when he found himself finally in the presence of one of the crew.

For two hours more, Ned Land's temper increased; he cried, he shouted, but in vain. The iron walls were deaf. There was no sound to be heard in the boat: all was still as death. It did not move, for I should have felt the trembling motion of the hull under the influence of the screw. Plunged in the depths of the waters, it belonged to earth:—the silence was dreadful.

I dare no longer think how long our abandonment and isolation in this cell might last. The hopes that I had conceived after our interview with the commander of the vessel vanished one by one. The gentle look of the man, the generous expression of his face, nobility of his carriage, all disappeared from my memory. I again saw this enigmatical personage such as he must necessarily be: pitiless and cruel. I felt him to be outside the pale of humanity, inaccessible to all sentiment of pity, the implacable enemy of his fellow men, to whom he had vowed imperishable hatred!

But was the man going, then, to let us perish from inanition, shut up in this narrow prison, given up to the horrible temptations to which ferocious famine leads? This frightful thought took a terrible intensity in my mind, and imagination helping, I felt myself invaded by unreasoning fear.

Conseil remained calm, Ned Land roared.

Just then a noise was heard outside. Steps sounded on the metal floor. The locks were turned, the door opened, and the steward appeared.

Before I could rush forward to stop him, the Canadian had thrown the unlucky man down, and held him by the throat. The steward was choking under the grip of Ned's powerful hand.

Conseil was already trying to unclasp the harpooner's hand from his half-suffocated victim, and I was going to fly to the rescue, when suddenly I was nailed to the spot by hearing these words in French—

"Be quiet, Master Land; and you, Professor, you be so good as to listen to me!"

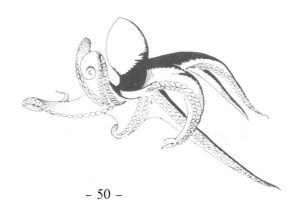

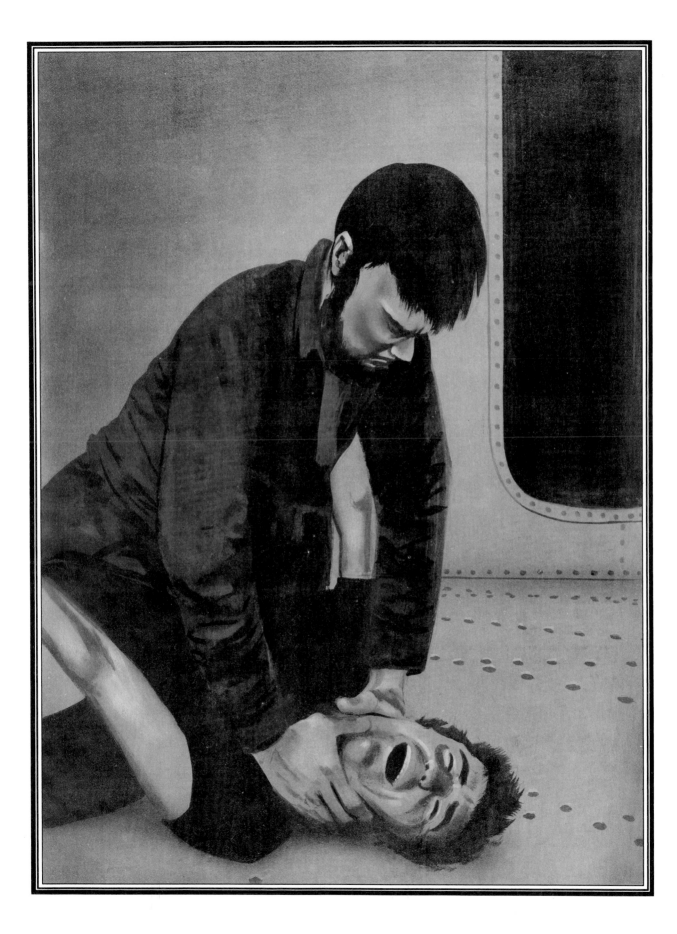

◄ **CHAPTER X** ►

THE MAN OF THE SEAS

t was the commander of the vessel who had spoken.

At these words, Ned Land rose suddenly. The steward, nearly strangled, tottered out on a sign from his master; but such was the power of the commander on board, that not a gesture betrayed the resentment which this man must have felt towards the Canadian. Conseil interested in spite of himself, and I stupefied, awaited in silence the result of this scene.

The commander, leaning against a corner of the table with his arms folded, scanned us with profound attention. Did he hesitate to speak? Did he regret the words which he had just spoken in French? One might almost think so.

After some moments of silence, which not one of us dreamed of breaking, "Gentlemen," said he, in a calm and penetrating voice, "I speak French, English, German, and Latin equally well. I could, therefore, have answered you at our first interview, but I wished to know you first, then to reflect. The story told by each one, entirely agreeing in the main points, convinced me of your identity. I know now that chance has brought before me Monsieur Pierre Aronnax, Professor of Natural History at the Museum of Paris, entrusted with a scientific mission abroad, Conseil his servant, and Ned Land, of Canadian origin, harpooner on board the frigate *Abraham Lincoln* of the navy of the United States of America."

I bowed assent. It was not a question that the commander put to me. Therefore there was no answer to be made. This man expressed himself with perfect ease, without any accent. His sentences were well turned, his words clear, and his fluency of speech remarkable. Yet, I did not recognize in him a fellow countryman.

He continued the conversation in these terms:

"You have doubtless thought, sir, that I have delayed too long in paying you this second visit. The reason is that, your identity recognized, I wished to ponder what part to act towards you. I have hesitated much. Most annoying circumstances have brought you into the presence of a man who has broken all the ties of humanity. You have come to trouble my existence. . . ."

"Unintentionally!" said I.

"Unintentionally?" replied the stranger, raising his voice a little; "was it unintentionally that the *Abraham Lincoln* pursued me all over the seas? Was it unintentionally that you took passage in this frigate? Was it unintentionally that your cannon balls rebounded off the plating of my vessel? Was it unintentionally that Mr. Ned Land struck me with his harpoon?"

I detected a restrained irritation in these words. But to these recriminations I had a very natural answer to make, and I made it.

"Sir," said I, "no doubt you are ignorant of the discussions which have taken place concerning you in America and Europe. You do not know that various accidents, caused by collisions with your submarine machine, have excited public opinion on the two continents. I won't mention the hypotheses without number by which it was sought to explain the inexplicable phenomenon of which you alone possess the secret. But you must understand that, in pursuing you over the high seas of the Pacific, the *Abraham Lincoln* believed itself to be chasing some powerful sea monster, of which it was necessary to rid the ocean at any price."

A half-smile curled the lips of the commander: then, in a calmer tone—

"Monsieur Aronnax," he replied, "dare you claim that your frigate would not as soon have pursued and cannonaded a submarine boat as a monster?"

This question embarrassed me, for certainly Captain Farragut might not have hesitated. He might have thought it his duty to destroy a contrivance of this kind, as he would a gigantic narwhal.

"You understand then, sir," continued the stranger, "that I have the right to treat you as enemies?"

I answered nothing, purposely. For what good would it be to discuss such a proposition, when force could destroy the best arguments?

"I have hesitated for some time," continued the commander; "nothing obliged me to show you hospitality. If I chose to separate myself from you, I should have no interest in seeing you again; I could place you upon the deck of this vessel which has served you as a refuge, I could sink beneath the waters, and forget that you had ever existed. Would not that be my right?"

"It might be the right of a savage," I answered, "but not that of a civilized man."

"Professor," replied the commander quickly. "I am not what you call a civilized man! I have done with society entirely, for reasons which I alone have the right of appreciating. I do not therefore obey its laws, and I desire you never to allude to them before me again!"

This was said plainly. A flash of anger and disdain kindled in the eyes of the stranger, and I had a glimpse of a terrible past in the life of this man. Not only had he put himself beyond the pale of human laws, but he had made himself independent of them, free in the strictest acceptation of the word, quite beyond their reach! Who then would dare to pursue him at the bottom of the sea, when, on its surface, he defied all attempts made against him! What vessel could resist the shock of his submarine *Monitor*? What armor, however thick, could withstand the blows of his lance? No man could demand from him an account of his actions; God, if he believed in one—his conscience, if he had one,—were the sole judges to whom he was answerable.

These reflections crossed my mind rapidly, while the strange personage was silent, absorbed, and withdrawn into himself. I regarded him with fear mingled with interest, as, doubtless, Œdipus regarded the Sphinx.

After rather a long silence, the commander resumed the conversation.

"I have hesitated," said he, "but I have thought that my interest might be reconciled with that pity to which every human being has a right. You will remain on board my vessel, since fate has cast you here. You will be free; and in exchange for this liberty, I shall only impose one single condition. Your word of honor to submit to it will suffice."

"Speak, sir," I answered. "I suppose this condition is one which a man of honor may accept?"

"Yes, sir; it is this. It is possible that certain events, unforeseen, may oblige me to consign you to your cabins for some hours or some days, as the case may be. As I desire never to use violence, I expect from you, more than all the others, a passive obedience. In thus acting, I take all the responsibility: I acquit you entirely, for I make it an impossibility for you to see what ought not to be seen. Do you accept this condition?"

Then things took place on board which, to say the least, were singular, and which ought not to be seen by people who were not placed beyond the pale of laws of society. Among the surprises which the future was preparing for me, this might not be the least.

"We accept," I answered; "only I will ask your permission, sir, to address one question to you—one only."

"Speak, sir."

"You said that we should be free on board."

"Entirely."

"I ask you, then, what you mean by this liberty?"

"Just the liberty to go, to come, to see, to observe even all that passes here,—save under rare circumstances,—the liberty, in short, which we enjoy ourselves, my companions and I.''

It was evident that we did not understand one another.

"Pardon me, sir," I resumed, "but this liberty is only what every prisoner has of pacing his prison! It cannot suffice us."

"It must suffice you, however."

"What! we must renounce forever seeing our country, our friends, our relations again?"

"Yes, sir. But to renounce that unendurable worldly yoke which men believe to be liberty, is not perhaps so painful as you think."

"Well," exclaimed Ned Land, "never will I give my word of honor not to try to escape."

"I did not ask you for your word of honor, Master Land," answered the commander, coldly.

"Sir," I replied, beginning to get angry in spite of myself, "you abuse your situation towards us. It is cruelty."

"No, sir, it is clemency! You are my prisoners of war. I keep you here, when I could by a word plunge you into the depths of the ocean! You attacked me! You stumbled upon a secret which no man in the world must penetrate,—the secret of my whole existence. And you think that I am going to send you back to that world which must know me no more? Never! In retaining you, it is not you whom I guard—it is myself."

These words indicated a resolution taken on the part of the commander, against which no arguments would prevail.

"So, sir," I rejoined, "you give us simply the choice between life and death?"

"Simply."

"My friends," said I, "to a question thus put, there is nothing to answer. But no word of honor binds us to the master of this vessel."

"None, sir," answered the Unknown.

Then, in a gentler tone, he continued—

"Now, permit me to finish what I have to say to you. I know you, Monsieur Aronnax. You and your companions will not, perhaps, have so much to complain of in the chance which has bound you to my fate. You will find among the books which are my favorite study the work which you have published on the great depths of the sea. I have often read it. You have carried your work as far as terrestrial science permitted you. But you do not know all—you have not seen all. Let me tell you then, Professor, that you will not regret the time passed on board my vessel. You are going to visit the land of marvels.

"Astonishment and stupefaction will probably become a normal state of mind. You will not be easily bored by the incessant spectacle I will offer your eyes. I am planning a new tour of the submarine world—who knows? it could be my last—and will revisit everything that I have so far studied in the depths of the sea, and you will be my fellow student. From this day, you will enter into a new element. You will be seeing what no man—and I and my men longer count—has seen before. Our planet, thanks to me, will reveal to you its last secrets."

These words of the commander had a great effect upon me. I cannot deny it. My weak point was touched; and I forgot, for a moment, that the contemplation of these sublime subjects was not worth the loss of liberty. Besides, I trusted to the future to decide this grave question. So I contented myself with saying—

"Sir, even if you have broken with humanity, I cannot believe that you have repudiated all human sentiment. We are the survivors of a shipwreck, charitably received on board, and we cannot forget that. As for me, I won't deny it, my interest in science overpowers my need for liberty. The promise of our association offers much compensation."

I thought that the captain would offer me his hand, to seal our bargain. He did nothing. I was sorry for him.

"By what name ought I to address you?"

"Sir," replied the commander, "I am nothing to you but Captain Nemo; and you and your companions are nothing to me but the passengers of the *Nautilus*,"

Captain Nemo called. A steward appeared. The captain gave him his orders in that strange language which I did not understand. Then, turning towards the Canadian and Conseil—

"A repast awaits you in your cabin," said he. "Be so good as to follow this man."

"I won't refuse that!" exclaimed the harpooner, and he and Conseil were led from the cell that had been their prison for more than thirty hours.

"And now, Monsieur Aronnax, our luncheon is ready. Permit me to lead the way."

"I am at your service, captain."

I followed Captain Nemo; and as soon as I had passed through the door, I found myself in a kind of passage lighted by electricity, similar to a corridor in a ship. After we had proceeded a dozen meters, a second door opened before me.

I then entered a dining-room, decorated and furnished in severe taste. High oaken sideboards, inlaid with ebony, stood at the two extremities of the room, and upon their scallop-edged shelves glittered china, porcelain, and glass of inestimable value. The plate on the table sparkled in the rays which the luminous ceiling lamps shed, while the light was tempered and softened by exquisite paintings.

In the center of the room was a table richly laid out. Captain Nemo indicated the place I was to occupy.

"Please be seated," invited the captain, "and eat like a man who must be starving."

The luncheon consisted of a certain number of dishes, the contents of which were furnished by the sea alone; and I was ignorant of the nature and mode of preparation of some of them. I acknowledged that they were good, but they had a peculiar flavor, which I easily became accustomed to. These different aliments appeared to me to be rich in phosphorus, and I thought they must have a marine origin.

Captain Nemo looked at me. I asked him no questions, but he guessed my thoughts, and answered of his own accord the questions which I was burning to address to him.

"The greater part of these dishes are unknown to you," he said to me. "However, you may partake of them without fear. They are wholesome and nourishing. For a long time I have renounced the food of the earth, and I am never ill now. My crew, who are healthy, are fed on the same food."

"So," said I, "all these eatables are the produce of the sea?"

"Yes, Professor, the sea supplies all my wants. Sometimes I cast my nets in tow, and when I draw them in they are ready to burst. Sometimes I hunt in the depths of the sea, which appears to be inaccessible to man, and quarry the game which dwells in my submarine forests. My flocks, like those of the shepherd Neptune, graze fearlessly in the immense prairies of the ocean. I have a vast domain there, which I cultivate myself, and which is constantly stocked by the hand of the Creator of all things."

I regarded the captain with some astonishment, then answered:

"I can understand perfectly, sir, that your nets furnish excellent fish for your table; I understand less how you hunt aquatic game in your submarine forests; but I cannot understand at all how a particle of meat, no matter how small, can figure in your bill of fare."

"Professor," responded Captain Nemo, "I never use the flesh of terrestrial animals."

"Then what is this?" I asked, indicating a plate that appeared to still hold some filleted meat.

"This, which you believe to be meat, Professor, is nothing else than fillet of sea tortoise. Here are also some dolphin's livers, which you take to be ragout of pork. My cook is a clever fellow, who excels in dressing these various products of the ocean. Taste all these dishes. Here is a preserve of holothuria,[1] which a Malay would declare to be unrivalled in the world; here is a cream, of which the milk has been furnished by the whales, and the sugar by the great fucus of the North Sea; and lastly, permit me to offer you some preserve of anemones, which is equal to that of the most delicious fruits."

I tasted, more from curiosity than as a gourmet, while Captain Nemo enchanted me with his extraordinary stories.

"But this sea, Monsieur Aronnax," he said to me, "this great provider, inexhaustible, not only nourishes me. She clothes me as well. That material which you are wearing is woven from the fibers of certain shellfish, and is dyed with the purple of the ancients and shaded with violet extracted from the Mediterranean seahare. The perfumes that you will find at the toilet in your cabin are the product of distillation from marine plants. Your bed is made from the softest sea-grass in the ocean. Your pen is made from the bone of the baleen whale, your ink is a liquor secreted by the cuttlefish or squid. I get everything from the sea, and someday I will return to it!"

"You love the sea, Captain?"

"Yes; I love it! The sea is everything! It covers seven-tenths of the terrestrial globe. Its breath is pure and healthy. It is an immense desert, where man in never lonely, for he feels life stirring on all sides. The sea is the embodiment of a supernatural and wonderful existence. It is nothing but love and emotion; it is the "living infinite," as one of your poets has said. In fact, Professor, Nature is manifested in it by her three kingdoms, mineral, vegetable, and animal. The last is the largest, represented by four groups of zoöphytes, by three classes of articulata, by five classes of mollusks, by three classes of vertebrates—mammals, reptiles and innumerable legions of fish; an infinite order of animals which total more than 13,000 species, only one-tenth of which belong to fresh water. The sea is the vast reservoir of Nature. The globe began with sea, so to speak; and who knows if it will not end with it? It is supreme tranquillity. The sea does not belong to despots. Upon its surface men can still exercise unjust laws, fight, tear one another to pieces, and be carried away with terrestrial horrors. But at thirty feet below its level, their reign ceases, their influence is quenched, and their power disappears. Ah! sir, live—live in the bosom of the waters! Only there is independence! There I recognize no masters! There I am free!"

Captain Nemo suddenly became silent in the midst of this enthusiasm, by which he was quite carried away. Had he inadvertently allowed himself to exceed his habitual reserve? Had he said too much? For a few moments he paced up and down, much agitated. Then he became more calm, regained his accustomed coldness of expression, and turning towards me—

"Now, Professor," said he, "if you wish to visit the *Nautilus,* I am at your service."

---

[1]Holothurians are simple animals that include the sea-cucumber and the sea-slug. R.M.

◄ CHAPTER XI ►

THE *NAUTILUS*

aptain Nemo rose. I followed him. A double door, contrived at the back of the dining-room, opened, and I entered a room equal in dimensions to that which I had just quitted.

It was a library. High pieces of furniture, of black rosewood inlaid with brass, supported upon their deep shelves a great number of books uniformly bound. They followed the shape of the room, terminating at the lower part in huge divans, covered with brown leather, which were curved, to afford the greatest comfort. Light moveable desks, made to slide in and out at will, allowed one to rest one's book while reading. In the center stood an immense table, covered with pamphlets, among which were some newspapers, already old. The electric light flooded this harmonious whole; it was shed from four translucent globes half sunk in the volutes of the ceiling. I looked with real admiration at this room, so ingeniously fitted up, and I could scarcely believe my eyes.

"Captain Nemo," said I to my host, who had just thrown himself on one of the divans, "this is a library which would do honor to more than one of the continental palaces, and I am absolutely astounded when I consider that it can follow you to the bottom of the seas."

"Where could one find greater solitude or silence, Professor?" replied Captain Nemo. "Did your study in the Museum afford you such perfect quiet?"

"No, sir; and I must confess that it is a very poor one after yours. You must have six or seven thousand volumes here."

"Twelve thousand, Monsieur Aronnax. These are the only ties which bind me to the earth. But I had done with the world on the day when my *Nautilus* plunged for the first time beneath the waters. That day I bought my last volumes, my last pamphlets, my last newspapers, and from that time I wish to think that men no longer think or write. These books, Professor, are at your service, and you can make use of them freely."

I thanked Captain Nemo, and went up to the shelves of the library. Works on science, ethics, and literature abounded in every language; but I did not see one single work on political economy; that subject appeared to be strictly proscribed. A curious detail was that all these books were irregularly classified, in whatever language they were written; and this medley proved that the captain of the *Nautilus* could read with no difficulty any book which he might take up by chance.

Among these works, I noticed classics by masters both ancient and modern, that is to say, the most beautiful writings man has produced on history, poetry, fiction and science; from Homer to Victor Hugo, from Xenophon to Michelet, from Rabelais to Mme. Sand.[1] But science, most especially, dominated this library. Books on mechanics, ballistics, hydrography, meteorology, geography, geology, etc. took up no less space than works on natural history. I realized that these formed the principal study of the captain. I saw all of Humboldt, all of Arago, the works of Foucault, d'Henri Sainte-Claire Deville, Chasles, Milne-Edwards, Quatrefayes, Tyndall, Faraday, Berthelot, the Abbé Secchi, Petermann, Commander Maury, d'Agassiz, etc.; the journals of the Academy of Sciences, bulletins of various geographic societies, etc,; and in the first row the two volumes which had perhaps won me this relatively charitable reception by Captain Nemo. Among the works of Joseph Bertrand was a book entitled *The Founders of Astronomy* that gave me an exact date. I knew that it had appeared in the course of 1865, so I could conclude that the launch of the *Nautilus* could not have taken place before this date. Therefore, three years earlier, no longer, Captain Nemo had commenced his underwater existence. Perhaps the dates of more recent works would allow me to fix a more precise period, but I had time for this research. Right now, I did not want to delay our tour of the wonders of the *Nautilus*.

"Sir," said I to the captain, "I thank you for having placed this library at my disposal. It contains some treasures of science, and I shall profit by them."

"This room is not only a library," said Captain Nemo, "it is also a smoking-room."

"A smoking-room!" I cried. "Then one may smoke on board?"

"Without doubt."

"Then, sir, I am forced to believe that you have kept up a communication with Havana."

"Not at all," answered the captain. "Accept this cigar, Monsieur Aronnax; and though it does not come from Havana, you will be pleased with it, if you are a connoisseur."

I took the cigar which was offered me; its shape recalled the London ones, but it seemed to be made of leaves of gold. I lighted it at a little brazier, which was supported upon an elegant bronze stand, and drew the first whiffs with the delight of a lover of smoking who has not smoked for two days.

"It is excellent," said I, "but it is not tobacco."

"No!" answered the captain, "this tobacco comes neither from Havana nor from the East. It is a kind of sea-weed, rich in nicotine, with which the sea provides me, but somewhat sparingly."

"Do you miss your Londons, sir?"

"Captain, from this day I will despise them."

"Smoke all you wish, and do not worry about their origin. They do not carry a tax stamp, but they are no less good for all that, I imagine."

"On the contrary!"

At that moment Captain Nemo opened a door which stood opposite to that by which I had entered the library, and I passed into an immense, splendidly-lighted drawing-room.

It was a vast, four-sided room, with canted walls, ten meters long, six wide, and five high. A luminous ceiling, decorated with graceful arabesques, shed a soft clear light over all the marvels accumulated in this museum. For it was in fact a museum, in which an intelligent and prodigal hand had gathered all the treasures of nature and art, with the artistic randomness which distinguishes a painter's studio.

Thirty first-rate pictures, uniformly framed, separated by bright drapery, ornamented the walls, which were hung with tapestry of severe design. I saw works of great value, many of which I had admired in the special collections of Europe, and in painting exhibitions. The various schools of the old masters were represented by a Madonna of Raphael, a Virgin of Leonardo da Vinci, a nymph of Corregio, a woman of Titian, an Adoration of Veronese, an Assumption of Murillo, a portrait by Holbein, a monk of Velasquez, a martyr of Ribera, a fair of Rubens, two Flemish landscapes of Teniers, three little "genre" pictures of Gérard Dow, Metsu, and Paul Potter, two specimens of Géricault and Prud' hon, and some sea pieces of Backhuysen and Vernet. Among the works of modern painters were pictures with the signatures of Delacroix, Ingres, Decamp, Troyon, Meissonnier, Daubigny, etc.; and some admirable reproductions of statues in marble and bronze, after the finest models of antiquity, stood upon pedestals in the corners of this magnificent museum. Amazement, as the Captain of the *Nautilus* had predicted, had already begun to take possession of me.

"Professor," said this strange man, "you must excuse the uceremonious way in which I receive you, and the disorder which reigns in this room."

"Sir," I answered, "without seeking to know who you are, may I recognize in you an artist?"

"An amateur, nothing more, sir. Formerly I loved to collect these beautiful works created by the hand of man. I sought them greedily, and ferreted them out indefatigably, and I have been able to bring together some objects of great value. These are my last souvenirs of that world which is dead to me. In my eyes, your modern artists are already old; they are two or three thousand years old; I confuse them in my own mind. Masters have no age.''

"And these musicians?" said I, pointing out some works of Weber, Rossini, Mozart, Beethoven, Haydn, Meyerbeer, Hérold, Wagner, Auber, Gounod, and a number of others, scattered over a large piano-organ which occupied one of the panels of the drawing-room.

"These musicians," replied Captain Nemo, "are the contemporaries of Orpheus; for in the memory of the dead all chronological differences are effaced; and I am dead, Professor; as much dead as those of your friends who are sleeping six feet under the earth!"

Captain Nemo was silent, and seemed lost in a profound reverie. I contemplated him with deep interest, analyzing in silence the strange expression on his countenance. Leaning on his elbow against an angle of a costly mosaic table, he no longer saw me,—he had forgotten my presence.

I did not disturb this reverie, and continued my observation of the curiosities which enriched this drawing room or salon. Next to the works of art, rarities of nature took the most important place. These consisted principally of plants, shells and other products of the ocean, collected entirely by the personal efforts of Captain Nemo. In the middle of the salon a jet of water, lit by electricity, fell back into a bowl made from a single giant clam. This shell was furnished by the largest of the acephalous mollusks, and measured about six meters in circumference around its delicately scalloped sides. It surpassed in grandeur the beautiful clamshells given to Francois I by the Republic of Venice, now in the church of Saint-Sulpice, in Paris, in the form of two gigantic holy-water fountains.

Under elegant glass cases, reinforced by copper bands, were classed and labelled the most precious productions of the sea which had ever been presented to the eye of a naturalist. My delight as a professor may be imagined.

The division containing the zoöphytes[2] presented the most curious specimens of the two groups of polyps and echinoderms. In the first group, the tubipores, were gorgones arranged like a fan, soft Syrian sponges, the isis of the Moluccas, pennatules, an admirable virgularia of the Norwegian seas, variegated umbellulairæ, alcyonariæ, a whole series of madrepores, which my teacher, Milne-Edwards, has so cleverly classified, among which I remarked some wonderful flabellinæ, oculinæ of the island of Bourbon, the "Neptune's Chariot" of the Antilles, superb varieties of corals, in short, every species of those curious polyps of which entire islands are formed, which will one day become continents. Of the echinoderms, remarkable for their coating of spines, were asteri, or starfish, pantacrinæ, comatules, astérophons, echini, or sea urchins, holothuri, etc., representing a complete collection of individuals from this group.

A somewhat nervous conchologist would certainly have fainted before other more numerous cases, in which were classified the specimens of mollusks. It was a collection of inestimable value, which time fails me to describe minutely. Among these specimens, I will quote from memory only the elegant royal hammer-fish of the Indian Ocean, whose regular white spots stood out brightly on a red and brown ground, an imperial spondyle, bright-colored, bristling with spines,—a rare specimen in the European museums (I estimated its value at not less than twenty thousand francs); a common hammer-fish of the seas of Australia, which is only procured with difficulty; exotic buccardia of Senegal—fragile white bivalve shells, which a breath might shatter like a soap bubble; several varieties of the aspirgillum of Java, a kind of calcareous tube, edged with leafy folds, and much prized by collectors; a whole series of trochi, some a greenish-yellow, found in the American seas, others a reddish-brown, natives of Australian waters; others from the Gulf of Mexico, remarkable for their imbricated shell; stellari found in the Southern Seas; and last, the rarest of all, the magnificent spur shell of New Zealand.

Around this bowl, there were also admirable sulfur tellins, precious specimens of cytherean and venus shells, a trellised sundial from the coasts of Tranquebar, a marble sabot with its resplendent pearlescence, green parrot-shells from the seas of China, the rare cone shell of the genus

Coenodulli, all the varieties of porcelaines that serve as money in India and Africa, the "Glory of the Sea"—the most precious shell of the East Indies, and finally the littorinae, the delphinulae, turritellae, janthinae, ovulae, volutes, olivae, mitrae, helmet shells, purpurae, whelks, harpae, rock shells, tritons, cerithidae, spindle shells, strombes, pterocerae, limpets, hyalinae, cleodorae—shells delicate and fragile that science has baptized with such charming names.

Apart, in separate compartments, were spread out chaplets of pearls of the greatest beauty, which reflected the electric light in little sparks of fire; pink pearls, torn from the pinnamarina of the Red Sea; green pearls of the haliotyde iris; yellow, blue, and black pearls, the curious productions of the various mollusks of every ocean, and certain mussels of the water courses of the North; lastly, several specimens of inestimable value which had been gathered from the rarest pintadines. Some of these pearls were larger than a pigeon's egg, and were worth as much, and more than the one which the traveller Tavernier sold to the Shah of Persia for three million francs, and surpassed the one in the possession of the Imam of Muscat, which I had believed to be unrivaled in the world.

Therefore, to estimate the value of this collection was simply impossible. Captain Nemo must have expended millions in the acquirement of these various specimens, and I was thinking what source he could have drawn from, to have been able thus to gratify his fancy for collecting, when I was interrupted by these words—

"You are examining my shells, Professor? Unquestionably they must be interesting to a naturalist; but for me they have a far greater charm, for I have collected them all with my own hand, and there is not a sea on the face of the globe which has escaped my researches."

"I can understand, Captain, the delight of wandering about in the midst of such riches. You are one of those who have collected their treasures themselves. No museum in Europe possesses such a collection of the produce of the ocean. But if I exhaust all my admiration upon it, I shall have none left for the vessel which carries it! I do not wish to pry into your secrets; but I must confess that this *Nautilus,* with the motive power which it contains, the contrivances which enable it to be worked, the powerful agent which propels it, all excite my curiosity to the highest pitch. I see suspended on the walls of this room instruments of whose use I am ignorant. They are . . . ? May I presume . . . ?"

"Monsieur Aronnax," Captain Nemo responded, "I have told you that you have complete liberty while on board; consequently, no part of the *Nautilus* is forbidden to you. You can examine it in detail, and it will be my pleasure to act as your guide."

"I don't know how to thank you, sir, but I don't want to abuse your kindness. I ask of you only what the uses are for these instruments. . . ."

"You will find these same instruments in my own room, Professor, where I shall have much pleasure in explaining their use to you. But first come and inspect the cabin which is set apart for your own use. You must see how you will be accommodated on board the *Nautilus.*"

I followed Captain Nemo, who, by one of the doors opening from each panel of the salon, regained the passage. He conducted me towards the bow, and there I found, not a cabin, but an elegant room, with a bed, a dressing-table, and several other pieces of furniture.

I could only thank my host.

"Your room adjoins mine," said he, opening a door, "and mine opens into the salon that we have just quitted."

I entered the captain's room: it had a severe, almost monastic aspect. A small iron bedstead, a work-table, some articles for the toilet; the whole lit very dimly. No comforts, the strictest necessaries only.

Captain Nemo pointed to a seat.

"Be so good as to sit down," he said.

I seated myself, and he began thus:

_____

[1]George Sand was the pseudonym of Aurore Dupin, a friend of Verne's. It has been suggested that she may have proposed the idea of an undersea adventure to him. R.M.

[2]Zoöphytes are animals that resemble plants, such as the sea anemone, and coral. R.M.

◄ CHAPTER XII ►
ALL BY ELECTRICITY

"ir," said Captain Nemo, showing me the instruments hanging on the walls of his room, "here are the devices required for the navigation of the _Nautilus_. Here, as in the salon, I have them always under my eyes, and they indicate my position and exact direction in the middle of the ocean. Some are known to you, such as the thermometer, which gives the internal temperature of the _Nautilus;_ the barometer, which indicates the weight of the air and foretells the changes of the weather; the storm-glass, the contents of which, by decomposing, announce the approach of tempests; the compass, which guides my course; the sextant, which shows the latitude by the altitude of the sun; chronometers, by which I calculate the longitude; and telescopes for day and night use, with which I examine every point on the horizon when the _Nautilus_ rises to the surface of the waves."

"These are the usual nautical instruments," I replied, "and I know the use of them. But these others, no doubt, answer to the particular requirements of the _Nautilus_. This dial with the moveable needle is a manometer, is it not?"

"It is a manometer. By communication with the water, whose external pressure it indicates, it gives our depth at the same time."

"And these are sounding-lines of a new kind?"

"They are thermometric, and give the temperature of the water at different depths."

"And these other instruments, whose use I cannot guess?"

"Here, Professor, I ought to give you some explanations. Will you be kind enough to listen to me?"

He was silent for a few moments, then he said—

"There is a powerful agent, obedient, rapid, easy to use, which conforms to every need, and reigns supreme on board my vessel. Everything is done by means of it. It lights my ship, warms it, and is the soul of my mechanical apparatus. This agent is electricity."

"Electricity?" I cried in surprise.

"Yes, sir."

"Nevertheless, Captain, you possess an extreme rapidity of movement, which does not agree well with the power of electricity. Until now, its dynamic force has remained under restraint, and has only been able to produce a small amount of power."

"Professor," said Captain Nemo, "my electricity is not that of the world's, and you will allow me to say no more about it."

"I will not insist, sir; I will content myself with being astonished at such wonderful results.

A single question, however, I will ask, which you need not answer if it is an indiscreet one. The elements which you employ to produce this marvellous agent must necessarily be soon consumed. The zinc, for instance, that you use—how do you obtain a fresh supply? You now have no communication with the land?"

"I will answer your question," replied Captain Nemo. "In the first place I must inform you that there exist, at the bottom of the sea, mines of zinc, iron, silver, and gold, the working of which would most certainly be practicable; but I am not indebted to any of these terrestrial metals. I was determined to seek from the sea alone the means of producing my electricity."

"From the sea?"

"Yes, Professor, and I was at no loss to find these means. It would have been possible, by establishing a circuit between two wires plunged to different depths, to obtain electricity by the difference of temperature to which they would have been exposed; but I preferred to employ a more practicable system."

"And what was that?"

"You know what sea water is composed of. In a thousand grams are found 96½ percent water, and about 2⅔ percent sodium chloride; then, in a smaller quantity, chlorides of magnesium and of potassium, bromide of magnesium, sulphate of magnesia, sulphate and carbonate of lime. You see, then, that sodium chloride forms a large part of it. So it is this sodium that I extract from sea water, and from which I create my electricity."

"Sodium?"

"Yes, Professor. Mixed with mercury it forms an amalgam that takes the place of zinc in the Bunsen pile. The mercury is never exhausted; only the sodium is consumed, and the sea itself gives me that. I must tell you that the sodium batteries are the most powerful, their electric power is double that of the zinc ones."

"I clearly understand, Captain, the convenience of sodium in the circumstances in which you are placed. The sea contains it. Good. But you still have to make it, to extract it in a word. And how do you do that? Your battery would evidently serve the purpose of extracting it; but unless I am mistaken, the consumption of sodium necessitated by the electrical apparatus would exceed the quantity extracted. The consequence would be that you would consume more of it than you would produce!"

"That is why I do not extract it with the batteries, my dear Professor. I employ nothing but the heat of coal."

"Coal from the earth?" I urged.

"We will call it sea-coal if you like," replied Captain Nemo.

"And you are able to work submarine coal mines?"

"You shall see me so employed, Monsieur Aronnax. I only ask you for a little patience; you have time to be patient here. I owe all to the ocean; it produces electricity, and electricity gives heat, light, motion: in a word, life to the *Nautilus.*"

"But not the air you breathe?"

"Oh! I could manufacture the air needed for my consumption, but it is not necessary, because I go up to the surface of the water when I please. However, if electricity does not furnish me with air to breathe, it works at least the powerful pumps that store it in spacious reservoirs, and which enable me to prolong at need, and as long as I will, my stay in the depths of the sea."

"Captain," I replied, "I can do nothing but admire. You have evidently discovered what mankind at large will, no doubt, one day discover: the true dynamic power of electricity."

"Whether they will discover it I do not know," replied Captain Nemo coldly, "however that may be, you now know the first application that I have made of this precious agent. It gives a uniform and uninterrittent light, which the sun does not. Now look at this clock; it is electrical, and goes with a regularity that defies the best chronometers. I have divided it into twenty-four hours, like the Italian clocks, because for me there is neither night nor day, sun nor moon, but only that artificial light that I take with me to the bottom of the sea. See! Just now, it is ten o'clock in the morning.''

''Exactly.''

''Here is another application of electricity. This dial hanging in front of us indicates the speed of the *Nautilus*. An electric wire puts it in communication with the screw, and the needle indicates the actual speed. Look! At this moment we are spinning along at a modest speed of fifteen miles an hour.''

''It is marvellous! And I see, Captain, you were right to make use of this agent that takes the place of wind, water, and steam.''

''We have not finished, Monsieur Aronnax,'' said Captain Nemo, rising; ''if you will follow me, we will examine the rear portion of the *Nautilus.*''

I knew already the forward part of this submarine boat, which, going from amidship toward the bow, was divided as follows: the dining-room, five meters long, separated from the library by a water-tight bulkhead; the library, five meters long; the large salon, ten meters long, separated from the captain's room by a second water-tight bulkhead; his room, five meters in length and mine, two and a half meters; and lastly, a reservoir of air, seven and a half meters, that extended to the bows. Total length thirty-five meters, or almost one hundred and fifteen feet. The bulkheads had doors that were shut hermetically by means of india-rubber seals, and they ensured the safety of the *Nautilus* in case of a leak.

I followed Captain Nemo through the passage, and arrived at the center of the boat. There was a sort of well that opened between two wells. An iron ladder, fastened with an iron hook to one well, led upwards. I asked the captain what the ladder was used for.

''It leads to the launch,'' he said.

''What! Have you a launch?'' I exclaimed, in surprise. ,

''Of course; an excellent vessel, light and insubmersible, that serves either as a fishing or as a pleasure boat.''

''But then, when you wish to embark, you are obliged to come to the surface of the water?''

''Not at all. The launch is attached to the upper part of the hull of the *Nautilus,* and occupies a cavity made for it. It is decked, quite water-tight and held together by solid bolts. This ladder leads to a manhole made in the hull of the *Nautilus,* that corresponds with a similar hole made in the side of the launch. By this double opening I get into the small vessel. My men shut the one belonging to the *Nautilus,* I shut the other by means of screw pressure. I undo the bolts, and the little boat goes up to the surface of the sea with prodigious rapidity. I then open the hatch in the deck, carefully shut till then; I mast it, hoist my sail, take my oars, and I'm off.''

''But how do you get back on board?''

''I do not come back, Monsieur Aronnax; the *Nautilus* comes to me.''

''By your orders?''

''By my orders. An electric wire connects us. I telegraph to it, and that is enough.''

''Really,'' I said, astonished at these marvels, ''nothing can be more simple!''

After having passed by the cage of the staircase that led to the platform, I saw a cabin two meters long, in which Conseil and Ned Land, enchanted with their repast, were devouring it with avidity. Then a door opened into a kitchen three meters long, situated between large storerooms. There electricity, better than gas itself, did all the cooking. The wires under the furnaces gave to platinum sponges a heat which was regularly kept up and distributed. they also heated a distilling apparatus, which, by evaporation, furnished excellent drinking water. Near this kitchen was a bathroom comfortably furnished, with hot and cold water taps.

Next to the kitchen was the berth room of the vessel, five meters long. But the door was shut, and I could not see the arrangement of it, which might have given me an idea of the number of men employed on board the *Nautilus.*

At the far end was a fourth bulkhead that separated us from the engine room. A door opened, and I found myself in the compartment where Captain Nemo—certainly an engineer of a very high order—had arranged his locomotive machinery. This engine room, clearly lighted, did not measure less than twenty meters in length. It was divided into two parts; the first contained the materials for producing electricity, and the second held the machinery that connected with the screw. I was surprised at first by a smell *sui generis* which filled the compartment. The captain saw that I noticed it.

"It is only a slight escape of gas produced by the sodium. It is not more than an inconvenience since each morning we purify the air in the ship by ventilating it in the open."

I examined it with great interest, in order to understand the workings of the *Nautilus.*

"You see," said the captain, "I use Bunsen's contrivances, not Ruhmkorff's. Those would not have been powerful enough. Bunsen's are fewer in number, but strong and large, which experience proves to be the best. The electricity produced passes aft, where it works, by electromagnets of great size, on a system of levers and cog-wheels that transmit the movement to the propeller shaft. The screw, the diameter of which is six meters, and the pitch seven and a half meters, can perform up to about a hundred and twenty revolutions per second."[1]

"And you get then?"

"A speed of 50 miles an hour."

Here was a mystery, but I did not press for a solution. How could electricity act with so much power? Where did this almost unlimited force originate? Was it in the excessive tension obtained by some new kind of coil winding? Could a system of unknown levers infinitely increase its transmission? There was no way of knowing.

"Captain Nemo," I replied, "I recognize the results, and do not seek to explain them. I have seen the *Nautilus* maneuver around the *Abraham Lincoln,* and I have my own impression of its speed. But this is not enough. You must see where you go! You must be able to direct the *Nautilus* to the right, to the left, above, below. How do you get to the great depths, where you find increasing pressures, which are measured in hundreds of atmospheres? How do you return to the surface of the ocean? And how do you keep yourself at any required depth? Am I indiscreet in asking these questions?"

"Not at all, Professor," replied the captain, after a little hesitation; "since you may never leave this submarine boat. Come into the salon, it is our real study, and there you will learn all you want to know about the *Nautilus."*

---

[1] There has been talk about a discovery of this type, in which a new system of levers produces considerable force. Has the inventor interviewed Captain Nemo? J.V.

◄ CHAPTER XIII ►

SOME FIGURES

 moment later we were seated on a divan in the salon smoking. The captain showed me a drawing that gave the plan, section, and elevation of the *Nautilus*. Then he began his description in these words:—

"Here, Monsieur Aronnax, are the various dimensions of the boat you are in. It is an elongated cylinder with conical ends. It is very like a cigar in shape, a shape already adopted in London in several constructions of the same sort. The length of this cylinder, from stem to stern, is exactly 70 meters, or 228.9 feet, and its maximum breadth is 8 meters, or 26.16 feet. It is not built quite like your long-voyage steamers, in the ratio of ten to one, but its lines are sufficiently long, and its curves prolonged enough, to allow the water to slide past easily, and oppose no obstacle to its passage.

"These two dimensions enable you to obtain by a simple calculation the surface and volume of the *Nautilus*. Its area measures 1011.45 square meters; and its contents about 1500.2 cubic meters; that is to say, when completely immersed it displaces 1500.2 cubic meters of water, or 1,500.2 metric tons.

"When I made the plans for this submarine vessel, I meant that nine-tenths should be submerged when it is floating: consequently, it ought only to displace nine-tenths of its bulk. That is to say, it should only weigh 1356.48 metric tons. I ought not, therefore, to have exceeded that weight, constructing it in the aforesaid dimensions.

"The *Nautilus* is composed of two hulls, one inside, the other outside, joined by T-shaped irons, which render it extremely rigid. Indeed, owing to this cellular arrangement it resists like a block, as if it were solid. Its sides cannot yield; it resists spontaneously, and not by the closeness of its rivets; and the homogenity of its construction, due to the perfect union of the materials, enables it to defy the roughest seas.

"These two hulls are composed of iron plates, whose density is 7.8 times that of water. The first is not less that five centimeters thick, and weighs 394.96 tons. The second hull, which includes the keel—which is 50 centimeters high and 25 wide—alone weighs 62 tons. The engine, the ballast, the assorted accessories and apparatus, the braces and bulkheads, all add up to another 961.62 tons. This, plus 394.96 equals 1,356.68 tons. Almost exactly the weight I require. Do you follow all this?"

"I do."

"Then," continued the captain, "when the *Nautilus* is afloat under these circumstances, one-tenth is out of the water. Now, if I have made reservoirs of a volume equal to this tenth, or capable of holding 150.72 tons, and if I fill them with water, the boat, weighing then 1,507 tons, will be completely submerged. Which is what happens, Professor. These reservoirs are in the lower part of the *Nautilus*. I turn valves and they fill, and the vessel sinks until it is just level with the surface."

"Well, Captain, but now we come to the real difficulty. I can understand your rising to the surface; but diving below the surface, does not your submarine contrivance encounter a pressure, and consequently undergo an upward thrust of one atmosphere for every thirty feet of water, just about one kilogram for each square centimeter?"

"Just so, sir."

"Then, unless you quite fill the *Nautilus*, I do not see how you can draw it down to those depths."

"Professor, you must not confound statics with dynamics, or you will be exposed to grave errors. There is very little labor spent in attaining the lower regions of the ocean, for all bodies have a tendency to sink. Let us continue our reasoning."

"I am following you, captain."

"When I wanted to find out the necessary increase of weight required to sink the *Nautilus,* I had only to calculate the reduction of volume that sea water acquires according to the depth."

"That is evident."

"Now, if water is not absolutely incompressible, it is at least capable of very slight compression. Indeed after the most recent calculations this reduction in only .0000436 of an atmosphere for each thirty feet of depth. If we want to sink 1000 meters, I should take into account the reduction in volume of a column of water of a thousand meters deep, under a pressure of 100 atmospheres. This reduction would be .00436. I must increase the weight of the ship to 1513.77 tons instead of 1507.2 tons. The increase would consequently be 6.57 tons."

"That's all?"

"That's all, Monsieur Aronnax, and the calculation is easily verified. Now, I have supplementary reservoirs capable of holding a hundred tons. Therefore I can sink to a considerable depth. When I wish to rise to the level of the sea, I only let out the water; and if I empty all the reservoirs the *Nautilus* emerges above the water by 1/10 of its volume."

I could not object to these reasonings, based as they were on figures.

"I admit your calculations, Captain," I replied. "I should be wrong to dispute them since daily experience confirms them; but I foresee a real difficulty in the way."

"What, sir?"

"When you are about 1,000 meters deep, the walls of the *Nautilus* bear a pressure of 100 atmospheres. If, then, just now you were to empty the supplementary reservoirs, to lighten the vessel, and to go up to the surface, the pumps must overcome the pressure of 100 atmospheres, which is 100 kilograms on every square centimeter. That could require power . . ."

"That electricity alone can give," said the captain, quickly. "I repeat, sir, that the dynamic power of my engines is almost infinite. The pumps of the *Nautilus* have enormous force, as you must have observed when their jets of water burst like a torrent upon the *Abraham Lincoln.* Besides, I use subsidiary reservoirs only to attain a mean depth of 1500 to 2000 meters, and that with a view of saving my engines. Also, when I have a mind to visit the depths of the ocean five or six miles below the surface, I make use of slower but not less infallible means."

"What are they, Captain?"

"That involves my telling you how the *Nautilus* is steered."

"I am impatient to learn."

"To steer this boat to starboard or port, to turn, in a word, in a horizontal plane, I use an ordinary rudder fixed on the back of the stern-post, and with one wheel and some tackle to steer by. But I can also make the *Nautilus* rise and sink, and sink and rise, in the vertical plane, by means of two inclined planes fastened to its sides, opposite the center of flotation, planes that move in every direction, and that are worked by powerful levers from the interior. If the planes are kept parallel with the boat, it moves horizontally. If slanted, the *Nautilus,* according to this inclination, and under the influence of the screw, either sinks diagonally or raises diagonally as it suits me. And even if I wish to rise more quickly to the surface, I stop the screw, and the pressure of the water causes the *Nautilus* to rise vertically like a balloon filled with hydrogen."

"Bravo, Captain! But how can the steersman follow the route in the midst of the water?"

"The steersman is placed in a box with glass windows, that is raised above the hull of the *Nautilus.*

"Are these windows capable of resisting such pressure?"

"Perfectly. Glass, which breaks at a blow, is, nevertheless, capable of offering considerable resistance to pressure. During some experiments in fishing by electric light in 1864 in the northern seas, we saw plates less than seven millimeters thick resist a pressure of sixteen atmospheres and at the same time permit powerful heat rays to penetrate and be diffused by them. Now, the glass that I use is not less than thirty times thicker, or 21 centimeters through the center."

"Granted. But, after all, in order to see, the light must dispel the darkness, and in the midst of the darkest water, how can you see?"

"Behind the steersman's cage is placed a powerful electric reflector, the rays from which light up the sea for half a mile in front."

"Ah! bravo, three times bravo, Captain! Now I can account for the phosphorescence of the supposed narwhal that puzzled us scientists so. I now ask you if the collision of the *Nautilus* and of the *Scotia,* that has made such a stir, was the result of a chance encounter?"

"Quite accidental, sir. I was sailing only two meters below the surface of the water, when the shock came. It had no bad result?"

"None, sir. But now, about your encounter with the *Abraham Lincoln? . . .*"

"Professor, I am sorry for one of the best vessels in the American navy; but they attacked me, and I was bound to defend myself! I contented myself, however, with putting the frigate *hors de combat:* she will not have any difficulty in getting repaired at the next port."

"Ah, Captain!" I exclaimed with conviction, "your *Nautilus* is certainly a marvellous boat!"

"Yes, Professor," responded the captain with real emotion, "and I love it as if it were flesh of my flesh. Danger constantly threatens your vessels, subjected to the ocean, and the first impression is the feeling of an abyss below, in the words of the good Dutchman, Jansen. On the *Nautilus* men's hearts never fail them. No defects to be afraid of, for the double hull is as firm as iron; no rigging to attend to; no sails for the wind to carry away; no boilers to burst; no fire to fear, for the vessel is made of iron, not of wood; no coal to run short, for electricity is the only mechanical agent; no collision to fear, for it alone swims in these deep waters; no tempests to brave, for when it dives below the water, it reaches absolute tranquillity! There, sir! That is the perfect vessel! And if it is true that the engineer has more confidence in the vessel than the builder, and the builder than the captain himself, you understand the trust I repose in my *Nautilus;* for I am at once captain, builder, and engineer!"

Captain Nemo spoke with captivating eloquence. His fiery look and passionate gestures transfigured him. Yes! he did love his vessel like a father loves his child!

But a question, perhaps an indiscreet one, came up naturally, and I could not help asking it.

"Then you are an engineer, Captain Nemo?"

"Yes, Professor, I studied in London, Paris and New York when I was still an inhabitant of the world's continents."

"But how could you construct this wonderful *Nautilus* in secret?"

"Each separate portion, Monsieur Aronnax, was brought from different parts of the globe, reaching me at a disguised address. The keel was forged by Creusot, the shaft of the screw at Penn & Co., London; the iron plates of the hull at Laird's of Liverpool; the screw itself at Scott's at Glasgow. The reservoirs were made by Cail & Co. at Paris, the engine by Krupp in Prussia, the ram at Motala's workshop in Sweden, the precision instruments by Hart Brothers, of New York, etc.; and each of these people had my orders under different names."

"But these parts had to be put together and arranged?"

"Professor, I had set up my workshops upon a desert island in the ocean. There my workmen, that is to say, the brave men that I instructed and educated, and myself put together our *Nautilus.* Then, when the work was finished, fire destroyed all trace of our proceedings on this island, that I should have blown up if I could."

"Then the cost of this vessel is great?"

"Monsieur Aronnax, an iron vessel costs 1125 francs per ton. Now the *Nautilus* weighs

1,500 tons. It came therefore to 1,697,000 francs. Two million more if its fittings are included, and 4 or 5 million francs including the artwork and collections.''

"One last question, Captain Nemo.''

"Ask it, Professor.''

"You are rich?''

"Immensely rich, sir; and I could, without missing it, pay the 12 billion franc national debt of France!''

I stared at the singular person who spoke thus. Was he playing upon my credulity? The future would decide that.

◄ CHAPTER XIV ►

THE BLACK RIVER

The portion of the terrestrial globe which is covered by water is estimated at upwards of 94 billion acres, 3,832,558 myriameters or 148 million square miles. This fluid mass comprises two billion two hundred and fifty million cubic miles. It could form a sphere with a diameter of sixty leagues, or 2000 miles, the weight of which would be three quintillion tons. To comprehend the meaning of these figures, it is necessary to observe that a quintillion is to a billion as a billion is to one; in other words, there are as many billions in a quintillion as there are ones in a billion! This mass of fluid is equal to about the quantity of water which would be discharged by all the rivers of the earth in forty thousand years.

During the geological epochs, the igneous period was succeeded by the aqueous. The ocean prevailed everywhere. Then, little by little, in the Silurian period, the tops of the mountains began to appear, the islands emerged, then disappeared in partial deluges, reappeared, became settled, formed continents, till at length the earth became geographically arranged as we see in the present day. The solid had wrested from the liquid 37,657,000 square miles, equal to 12,916,000,000 hectares, or 24 billion acres.

The appearance of the continents divided the waters into five great portions: the Arctic, the Antarctic, the Indian, the Atlantic and the Pacific Oceans.

The Pacific Ocean extends from north to south between the two polar circles, and from east to west between Asia and America, over an extent of 145 degrees of longitude. It is the quietest of seas; its currents are broad and slow, it has medium tides, and abundant rain. Such was the ocean that my fate destined me first to travel upon under such strange conditions.

"Sir,'' said Captain Nemo, "we will, if you please, take our exact bearings and fix the starting point of this voyage. It is a quarter to twelve; I will go up again to the surface.''

The captain pressed an electric bell three times. The pumps began to drive the water from the tanks; the needle of the manometer indicated by a differing pressure the ascent of the *Nautilus*. Then is stopped.

"We have arrived,'' said the captain.

I went to the central staircase which opened onto the platform, clambered up the iron steps, passed through several hatches, and found myself on the upper part of the *Nautilus*.

The platform was only three feet out of water. The front and back of the *Nautilus* was of that spindle-shape which caused it justly to be compared to a cigar. I noticed that its iron plates, slightly overlaying each other, resembled the shell which clothes the bodies of large terrestrial reptiles. It explained to me how natural it was, in spite of all glasses, that this boat should have been taken for a marine animal.

Towards the middle of the platform the launch, half buried in the hull of the vessel, formed a slight excrescence. Fore and aft rose two cages of medium height with inclined sides, and partly closed by thick lenticular glasses; one destined for the steersman who directed the *Nautilus,* the other containing a brilliant and powerful electric lantern to give light on the road.

The sea was beautiful, the sky pure. Scarcely could the long vessel feel the broad swells of the ocean. A light breeze from the east rippled the surface of the water. The horizon, free from mist made observation easy.

Nothing was in sight. Not a reef, not an island. The *Abraham Lincoln* was nowhere to be seen. A vast desert.

Captain Nemo, by the help of his sextant, took the altitude of the sun, which ought also to give the latitude. He waited for some moments till the image of its disc appeared to touch the horizon. While taking observations not a muscle moved, the instrument could not have been more motionless in a hand of marble.

"Twelve o'clock, sir," said he. "When you are ready. . . ."

I cast a last look upon the sea, slightly yellow near the Japanese coast, and descended to the salon.

There the captain made his point, and calculated his longitude chronometrically, which he controlled by preceding observations of hourly angles. Then he said to me—

"Monsieur Aronnax, we are in west longitude 137° 15′."

"By what meridian?" I asked quickly, hoping that the captain's answer might indicate his nationality.

"Sir," he answered, "I have different chronometers regulated on the meridians of Paris, Greenwich and Washington. But, in your honor, I will use that of Paris."

This answer taught me nothing. I bowed, and the commander continued—

"Thirty-seven degrees and fifteen minutes longitude west of the Paris meridian, and thirty degrees and seven minutes north latitude—that is to say, about three hundred miles from the coast of Japan. Today, the 8th of November, at noon, our voyage of exploration under the waters begins."

"God preserve us!" I answered.

"And now, sir, I leave you to your studies," added the captain; "our course is E.N.E., our depth is fifty meters. Here are maps on a large scale by which you may follow it. The salon is at your disposal, and with your permission I will retire."

Captain Nemo bowed, and I remained alone, lost in thoughts all bearing on the commander of the *Nautilus.*

Should I ever know to what nation belonged the strange man who boasted of belonging to none? This hatred which he had vowed to humanity—this hatred which perhaps sought terrible means of revenge, what had provoked it? Was he one of those misjudged thinkers, a genius whom "the truth has made sorrowful," according to an expression of Conseil's; a modern Galileo, or one of those scientific men like the American Maury, whose career has been broken by political revolutions? I could not yet say. I, whom chance had just cast upon his vessel—I, whose life he held in his hands. He had received me coldly, but with hospitality. Only he had never taken the hand I had held out to him. He had never held his out to me.

For a whole hour I was deep in these reflections, seeking to pierce this mystery so interesting to me. Then my eyes fell upon the vast planisphere spread upon the table, and I placed my finger on the very spot where the given latitude and longitude crossed.

The sea like the continents has its large rivers. They are special currents known by their temperature and their color. The most remarkable of these is known by the name of the Gulf Stream. Science has decided on the globe the direction of five principal currents: one in the North Atlantic, a second in the South Atlantic, a third in the North Pacific, a fourth in the South Pacific, and a fifth in the Southern Indian Ocean. It is even probable that a sixth current existed at one time or another in the Northern Indian Ocean, when the Caspian and Aral seas formed but one vast sheet of water.

At this point indicated on the planisphere one of these currents was rolling, the Kuro-Sivo of the Japanese, the Black River, which, leaving the Gulf of Bengal where it is warmed by the perpendicular rays of a tropical sun, crosses the Straits of Malacca along the coast of Asia, curves into the North Pacific as far as the Aleutian Islands, carrying with it trunks of camphor trees and other indigenous products, and tinting the waves of the ocean with the pure indigo of its warm water. It was this current that the *Nautilus* was to follow. I followed it with my eye; saw it lose itself in the vastness of the Pacific, and felt myself drawn with it, when Ned Land and Conseil appeared at the door of the salon.

My two brave companions remained petrified at the sight of the wonders spread before their eyes.

"Where are we? Where are we?" exclaimed the Canadian. "In the museum at Quebec?"

"If monsieur will permit me to say so," spoke Conseil, "it appears more like the Hôtel du Sommerard!"

"My friends," I answered, making a sign for them to enter, "you are neither in Canada nor France, but on board the *Nautilus,* fifty meters below the level of the sea."

"We must believe what monsieur says," replied Conseil, "but frankly this salon is enough to astonish even a Flemishman like myself."

"Marvel and look, my friend, for there is enough for such a good classifier as you to do here."

There was no need for me to encourage Conseil. The worthy fellow, leaning over the cases, was already muttering words in the language of naturalists—class of gasteropods, family of buccinoides, genus of porcelaines, species of *Cypraea Madagascariensis,* etc.

During this time Ned Land, who was not much interested in conchology, questioned me about my interview with Captain Nemo. Had I discovered who he was, from whence he came, whither he was going, to what depths he was dragging us?—in short, a thousand questions, to which I had not time to answer.

I told him all I knew, or rather all I did not know, and I asked him what he had heard or seen on his side.

"I have seen nothing, heard nothing," answered the Canadian, "I have not even perceived the ship's crew. Is it by chance, or can they be electric too?"

"Electric!"

"On my word, anyone would think so."

"But, Monsieur Aronnax," demanded Ned Land, "can you tell me how many men there are on board? Ten, twenty, fifty, a hundred?"

"I cannot answer you, Mr. Land; it is better to abandon for a time all idea of seizing the *Nautilus* or escaping from it. This ship is a masterpiece of modern industry, and I should be sorry not to have seen it! Many people would accept the situation forced upon us, if only to move among such wonders. So be quiet and let us try and see what passes around us."

"See!" exclaimed the harpooner, "but we can see nothing in this iron prison! We are moving—we are sailing—blindly . . ."

Ned Land had scarcely pronounced these last words when it was suddenly dark. The luminous ceiling had gone out and so rapidly that my eyes received a painful sensation, analogous to that produced after passing from profound darkness into the most brilliant light.

We remained mute, not stirring, and not knowing what surprise awaited us, whether agreeable or disagreeable. A sliding noise was heard: one would have said that panels were moving in the sides of the *Nautilus*.

"It is the end of the end!" said Ned Land.

"Order of hydromedusas!" muttered Conseil.

Suddenly light broke at each side of the salon, through two oblong openings. The liquid mass appeared vividly lit up by the electric gleam. Two crystal plates separated us from the sea. At first I trembled at the thought that this frail partition might break, but strong bands of copper bound them, giving an almost infinite power of resistance.

The sea was distinctly visible for a mile radius all round the *Nautilus*. What a spectacle! What pen can describe it? Who could paint the effects of the light through those transparent sheets of water, and the softness of the successive gradations from the lower to the upper levels of the ocean?

The transparency of the sea is well known, and that its clearness is far beyond that of fresh water. The mineral and organic substances, which it holds in suspension heightens its transparency. In certain parts of the ocean, at the Antilles for example, under 145 meters of water, can be seen with surprising clearness a bed of sand. The penetrating power of the solar rays does not seem to cease until a depth of 300 meters. But in the midst of this fluid travelled by the *Nautilus,* the electric brightness was produced in the bosom of the waves. It was no longer luminous water, but liquid light.

If the hypothesis of Erhemberg, who believes in a phosphorescent illumination in the submarine depths, is admitted, Nature has certainly reserved to the inhabitants of the sea one of her most marvellous spectacles, and I could judge of it by the effects of the thousand rays of this light.

On each side a window opened into this unexplored abyss. The darkness within the salon showed to advantage the brightness outside, and we looked out as if this pure crystal had been the glass of an immense aquarium.

The *Nautilus* did not seem to be moving. It was because there were no landmarks. Sometimes, however, the lines of water, furrowed by her prow, flowed before our eyes with excessive speed.

Lost in wonder we stood before these windows, and none of had broken this silence of astonishment when Conseil said—

"You wished to see, friend Ned; well, you see now."

"Curious! Curious!" muttered the Canadian, who, forgetting his ill temper, seemed to submit to some irresistible attraction; "and one would come further than this to admire such a sight!"

"Ah!" thought I to myself, "I understand the life of this man; he has made a world apart for himself, in which he treasures all his greatest wonders."

"But the fish!" said the Canadian, "I don't see any fish!"

"What does it matter to you, friend Ned," answered Conseil, "since you know nothing about them."

"I! A fisherman?" cried Ned Land.

And thereupon a dispute arose between the two friends, for each had some knowledge of fish, though in very different ways.

Everyone knows that fish come from the fourth and last class of vertebrates. They have been rightly defined as "vertebrates with double circulation and cold blood, breathing through gills, and which live in water." They are composed of two distinct series: the series of bony fish—that is to say, those whose spines are made of bony vertebrae, and the series of cartilaginous fish—that is to say, those whose spines are made of cartilaginous vertebrae.

Perhaps the Canadian knew this distinction, but Conseil knew much more, and now that he had made friends with Ned, he could not allow himself to seem less learned than he. He accordingly said to him—

"Friend Ned, you are a killer of fish—a very skilful fisherman. You have taken a great number of these interesting animals. But I wager you do not know how they are classified!"

"Yes, I do," answered the harpooner seriously, "they are classified into fish that are good to eat and fish that are not!"

"That is the distinction of a gourmand," answered Conseil, "but do you know the difference between bony and cartilaginous fish?"

"Perhaps I do, Conseil."

"And the subdivision of these two large classes?"

"I daresay I do," answered the Canadian.

"Well, friend Ned, listen and remember! The bony fish are subdivided into six orders. Primo, the acanthopterygians, of which the upper jaw is complete, mobile and with gills in the form of a comb. This order comprises fifteen families—that is to say, three fourths of all known fish. Type: the common perch."

"Pretty good eating," answered Ned Land.

"Secundo," continued Conseil, "the abdominals, an order of fish whose ventral fins are placed behind the pectoral, without being attached to the shoulderbones—an order which is divided into five families, and comprises most fresh-water fish. Types: the carp, pike, etc."

"Peuh!" said the Canadian disdainfully, "fresh-water fish!"

"Tertio," said Conseil, "the sub-brachians, with ventral fins attached under the pectoral, and fastened to the shoulderbones. This order contains four families. Types: plaice, dabs, brills, soles, etc."

"Excellent—excellent!" cried the harpooner, who would only think of them from their edible point of view.

"Quarto," said Conseil, not at all confused, "the apodes, with long bodies and no ventral fins, covered with a thick and often sticky skin—an order that only comprises one family. Types: the ordinary eel and the gymnote, or electric eel."

"Middling!—only middling!" answered Ned Land.

"Quinto," said Conseil, "the lophobranchiates, whose jaw is complete and free, and the gills are formed into little tufts, arranged in pairs along the branchial arches. This order has only one family: seahorses and pipefish."

"Bad!—bad!" replied the harpooner.

"Secto, and lastly," said Conseil, "the plectognathes, which include those which have the maxillary bones attached firmly to the sides of the intermaxillaries, which form the jaws. The palantine arch is meshed by a suture to the skull, rendering it immobile. The order has no real ventral fins, and is composed of two families. Types: the sunfish and tetradons."

"Which any saucepan would be ashamed of!" cried the Canadian.

"Do you understand, friend Ned?" asked the learned Conseil.

"Not the least in the world, friend Conseil," answered the harpooner, "but go on, for you are very interesting."

"As to the cartilaginous fish," continued the imperturbable Conseil, "they only include three orders."

"So much the better," said Ned.

"Primo, the cyclostomes, with circular mouths and gills opening by numerous holes—an order including only one family. Type: the lamprey."

"You must get used to one to like it," answered Ned.

"Secundo, the selachines, with gills like the cyclostomes, but whose lower jaw is mobile.

This order, which is the most important of the class, includes two families. Types: rays and sharks.''

"What!" cried Ned, "Rays and sharks in the same order? Well, friend Conseil, I should not advise you to put them in the same fishbowl!"

"Tertio," answered Conseil, "the sturionians, with gills opened as usual by a single slit, furnished with an operaculum—an order which includes four genera. Type: the sturgeon."

"Well, friend Conseil, you have kept the best for the last—in my opinion, at least. Is that all?"

"Yes, Ned," answered Conseil, "and remember that even when you know that much you still know nothing, for the families are subdivided into genera, sub-genera, species, and varieties . . .''

"Well, friend Conseil," said the harpooner, leaning against the glass of the panel, "there are some varieties passing now!"

"Yes!—some fish," cried Conseil, "It is like being at an aquarium!"

"No," I answered, "for an aquarium is only a cage, and those fish are as free as birds in the air."

"Well, now, Conseil, tell me their names!—tell me their names!" said Ned Land.

"I?" answered Conseil, "I could not do it; that is my master's business."

And, in fact, the worthy fellow, though an enthusiastic classifier, was not a naturalist, and I do not know if he could have distinguished a tuna from a bonito. The Canadian, on the contrary, named them all without hesitation.

"A triggerfish," I said.

"And a Chinese triggerfish, at that," answered Ned Land.

"Genus of the balistes, family of the scleroderms, order of the plectognaths," muttered Conseil.

Decidedly, between them, Ned Land and Conseil would have made a distinguished naturalist.

The Canadian was not mistaken. A shoal of triggerfish with fat bodies, grained skins, and armed with a spur on their dorsal fins, were playing round the *Nautilus* and agitating the four rows of quills that bristled on either side of their tails. Nothing could be more admirable than their bodies: grey underneath, white stomachs, and gold spots that sparkled amid the somber eddies of the waves. Among them undulated skates like sheets abandoned to the winds, and with them I perceived, to my great joy, the Chinese skate, yellow above, pale pink underneath, with three darts behind each eye—a rare species, and even doubtful in the time of Lacepéde, who had never seen any except in a book of Japanese drawings.

For two whole hours an aquatic army escorted the *Nautilus*. During their games, their bounds, while rivaling each other in beauty, brightness, and speed, I distinguished the green labre; the banded mullet, marked by double stripes of black; the round-tailed goby, of a white color, with violet spots on the back; the Japanese scombrus, a beautiful mackerel of these seas, with a blue body and silvery head; the brilliant azures, whose name alone renders description unnecessary; some banded spares, with variegated fins of blue and yellow; striped giltheads, with a band of black across their caudal fins; the gilthead *zonephorus,* with an elegant corset of six stripes; some aulostones, with flute-like mouths, the woodcocks of the seas, some specimens of which attain a meter in length; Japanese salamanders, spiny lampreys, serpents six feet long, with eyes small and lively, and a huge mouth bristling with teeth; and many others.

Our imagination was kept at its height, interjections followed quickly on each other. Ned named the fish, and Conseil classified them. Myself, I was in ecstasies with the vivacity of their movements and the beauty of their forms. Never had it been given to me to see these animals, alive and at liberty, in their natural element.

I will not mention all the varieties which passed before my dazzled eyes, all the collection of the seas of China and Japan. These fish, more numerous than the birds of the air, came, attracted, no doubt, by the brilliant focus of the electric light.

Suddenly there was light in the salon, the iron panels closed again, and the enchanting vision disappeared. But for a long time I continued dreaming, till my eyes fell on the instruments hanging on the wall. The compass still showed the course to be N.N.E., the manometer indicated a pressure of five atmospheres, equivalent to a depth of fifty meters, and the electric log gave a speed of fifteen miles an hour. I expected Captain Nemo, but he did not appear. The clock marked the hour of five.

Ned Land and Conseil returned to their cabin, and I retired to my chamber. My dinner was ready. It was composed of turtle-soup made of the most delicate hawksbills, a sea tortoise, of a surmullet with white, flaky flesh, (the liver of which, prepared by itself, was most delicious), and fillets of the emperor–holocanthus, the flavor of which seemed to me superior even to salmon.

I passed the evening reading, writing, and thinking. Then sleep overpowered me, and I stretched myself on my couch of zostera, and slept profoundly, while the *Nautilus* was gliding rapidly through the current of the Black River.

◄ CHAPTER XV ►

A NOTE OF INVITATION

he next day, the 9th of November, I awoke after a sleep of twelve hours. Conseil came, according to custom, to know "how monsieur had passed the night," and to offer his services. He had left his friend the Canadian sleeping like a man who had never done anything else all his life.

I let the worthy fellow chatter fancifully, without caring to answer him. I was preoccupied by the absence of the captain during our experience of the day before, and was hoping to see him today.

I was soon clothed in my byssus garments. Their nature provoked many reflections from Conseil. I told him they were manufactured from the lustrous and silky filaments—the byssus—which fasten to the rocks a sort of shell, the "jambonneaux," that is very abundant on the shores of the Mediterranean. Formerly beautiful materials—stockings and gloves—were made from it, and they were very soft and very warm. The crew of the *Nautilus* could, therefore, be clothed at a cheap rate, without help of either cotton trees, sheep or silkworms of the earth.

As soon as I was dressed I went into the salon. It was deserted.

I plunged into the study of the conchological treasures hidden behind the glasses. I reveled also in great herbals filled with the rarest marine plants, which, although dried, retained their lovely colors. Among these precious hydrophytes I noticed some vorticellæ, pavonariæ, vine-leafed caulerpae, grainy callithamnion, delicate ceramies with scarlet tints, some fan-shaped agari, and some acetabularia like very flat mushrooms, which at one time used to be classed among the zoöphytes; in short, a complete series of algae.

The whole day passed without my being honored by a visit from Captain Nemo. The panels of the salon did not open. Perhaps he did not wish us to tire of such beautiful things.

The course of the *Nautilus* was E.N.E., her speed twelve knots, the depth below the surface between fifty and sixty meters.

The next day, 10th of November, the same desertion, the same solitude. I did not see one of the ship's crew: Ned and Conseil spent the greater part of the day with me. They were astonished at the inexplicable absence of the captain. Was this singular man ill? Had he altered his intentions with regard to us?

After all, as Conseil said, we enjoyed perfect liberty, we were delicately and abundantly fed. Our host kept to his terms of the treaty. We could not complain, and, indeed, the singularity of our fate held such wonderful compensation for us, that we had no right to complain about it as yet.

That day I commenced the journal of these adventures which has enabled me to relate them with more scrupulous exactitude and minute detail. I wrote it on paper made from the zostera marina.

On 11th of November, early in the morning, the fresh air spreading through the interior of the *Nautilus* told me that we had come to the surface of the ocean to renew our supply of oxygen. I directed my steps to the central staircase, and climbed to the platform.

It was six o'clock, the weather was cloudy, the sea grey but calm. Scarcely a billow. Captain Nemo, whom I hoped to meet, would he be there? I saw no one but the steersman imprisoned in his glass cage. Seated upon the projection formed by the hull of the launch, I inhaled the salt breeze with delight.

By degrees the fog disappeared under the action of the sun's rays. The radiant star rose from behind the eastern horizon. The sea flamed under its glance like a train of gunpowder. The clouds scattered in the heights were colored with lively tints of beautiful shades, and numerous "mare's tails,"[1] which betokened wind for that day.

But what was wind to this *Nautilus* which tempests could not frighten!

I was admiring this joyous rising of the sun, so gay, and so lifegiving, when I heard steps approaching the platform.

I was prepared to greet Captain Nemo, but it was his second-in-command (whom I had already seen on the captain's first visit) who appeared. He advanced on the platform not seeming to be aware of my presence. With his powerful telescope to his eye he scanned every point of the horizon with great attention. This examination over, he approached the hatch and pronounced a sentence in exactly these terms. I have remembered it, for every morning it was repeated under exactly the same conditions. It was thus worded—

"Nautron respoc lorni virch."

What it meant I could not say.

These words pronounced, the second-in-command descended. I thought that the *Nautilus* was about to return to its submarine navigation. I regained the hatch and returned to my chamber.

Five days sped thus, without any change in our situation. Every morning I mounted the platform. The same phrase was pronounced by the same individual. But Captain Nemo did not appear.

I had made up my mind that I should never see him again, when on the 16th of November, on returning to my room with Ned and Conseil, I found upon my table a note addressed to me.

I opened it impatiently. It was written in a bold, clear hand, recalling the Gothic style of the Germans.

The note was worded as follows:—

"To Professor Aronnax, on board the *Nautilus.*

"16th of *November* 1867.

"Captain Nemo invites Professor Aronnax to a hunting party, which will take place tomorrow morning in the forests of the island of Crespo. He hopes that nothing will prevent the Professor from being present, and he will with pleasure see him joined by his companions.

"Captain Nemo, Commander of the *Nautilus.*"

"A hunt!" exclaimed Ned.

"And in the forests of the island of Crespo!" added Conseil.

"Then he does go on land, this strange individual?" replied Ned Land.

"That seems to me to be clearly indicated," said I, reading the letter once more.

"Well, we must accept," said the Canadian. "But once more on dry ground, we can decide what to do. Indeed, I shall not be sorry to eat a piece of fresh venison."

Without seeking to reconcile what was contradictory between Captain Nemo's manifest aversion to islands and continents, and his invitation to hunt in a forest, I contented myself with replying—

"Let us first see where the island of Crespo is."

I consulted the planisphere, and in 32° 40′ north lat., and 167° 50′ west long., I found a small island, recognized in 1801 by Captain Crespo, and marked on ancient Spanish maps as Rocca de la Plata, which means "The Silver Rock." We were then about eighteen hundred miles from our starting-point, and the course of the *Nautilus,* a little changed, was bringing it back towards the southeast.

I showed to my companions this little rock lost in the midst of the North Pacific.

"If Captain Nemo does sometimes go on dry ground," said I, "he at least chooses islands absolutely deserted."

Ned Land shrugged his shoulders without speaking, and Conseil and he left me. After supper, which was served by the steward, silent and impassible, I went to bed, though not without some anxiety.

The next morning, the 17th of November, on awakening I felt that the *Nautilus* was perfectly still. I dressed quickly and entered the salon.

Captain Nemo was there, waiting for me. He rose, bowed, and asked me if it was convenient for me to accompany him.

As he made no allusion to his absence during the last eight days, I did not mention it, and simply answered that my companions and myself were ready to follow him.

"Only, sir," I said, "if you will permit me to ask one question."

"Ask, Monsieur Aronnax, and, if I can answer, I will."

"Well then, Captain, how is it that, if you have cut off all relations with the earth, you possess forests on the island of Crespo?"

"Professor," answered the captain, "the forests that I possess do not ask the sun for light or heat. There are no lions, tigers, panthers, no any other quadruped. It is known only to myself. It grows only for myself. These are not terrestrial forests, but submarine forests."

"A submarine forest!" I cried.

"Yes, Professor."

"And you offer to take me there? On foot?"

"And on dry foot."

"And hunting?"

"Hunting."

"With guns?"

"With guns."

I looked at the commander of the *Nautilus* with an air that would not have flattered anyone.

"Surely, he is mad," I thought, "It must be an attack that has lasted eight days, and it is still upon him. Too bad! I liked him better strange than foolish!"

These thoughts must have shown clearly on my face, but Captain Nemo was content to invite me to follow him, and I followed, resigned to anything.

We entered the dining room, where breakfast was served.

"Monsieur Aronnax," said the captain, "pray, share my informal breakfast; we will chat as we eat. For though I promised you a walk in the forest, I did not promise to find restaurants there. So eat as a man who will most likely not have his dinner till very late."

I did honor to the repast. It was composed of several kinds of fish, and slices of holothurian (excellent zoöphytes), and spiced with tasty seaweeds, such as *Porphyria laciniata* and *Laurentia primafetida*. Our drink consisted of pure water, to which the captain added some drops of a fermented liquor, extracted by the Kamschatcha method from a seaweed known under the name of *Rhodomenia palmata*. Captain Nemo ate at first without saying a word. Then he began—

"Professor, when I proposed a hunt in the forest of Crespo, you thought that I was contradicting myself. When I told you that these forests were underwater, you thought me mad. Professor, you must not judge any man so lightly."

"But, Captain, believe me"—

"Be kind enough to listen, and you will then see whether you have any cause to accuse me of folly or contradiction."

"I listen."

"You know as well as I do, Professor, that man can live underwater, providing he carries with him a sufficient supply of breathable air. In working underwater, the workman, clad in a waterproof outfit, with his head in a metal helmet, receives air from above by means of forcing pumps and regulators."

"That is a diving apparatus," said I.

"Just so, but under these conditions the man is not at liberty; he is attached to the pump which sends him air through an india-rubber tube, and if we were obliged to be thus held to the *Nautilus,* we could not go far."

"And the means of getting free?" I asked.

"It is to use the Rouquayrol-Denzyrouze apparatus, invented by two of your own countrymen, which I have brought to perfection for my own use, and which will allow you to risk yourself under these new physiological conditions, without any organic damage whatever. It consists of a reservoir of thick iron plates, in which I store the air under a pressure of fifty atmospheres. This reservoir is fixed on the back by means of braces, like a soldier's knapsack. Its upper part forms a box in which the air is kept by means of a bellows-like mechanism, and therefore cannot escape unless at its normal pressure. In the Rouquayrol apparatus such as was originally used, two india-rubber pipes left this box and joined a sort of mask which covered the operator's nose and mouth; one to introduce fresh air, the other to let out the foul. The tongue closed one or the other according to the wants of the diver. But I, in encountering great pressures at the bottom of the sea, was obliged to shut my head, like that of a diver, in a ball of copper; and it is to this ball of copper that the two pipes, the inspirator and the expirator, open."

"I understand perfectly, Captain Nemo; but the air that you carry with you must soon be used; when it contains less than fifteen percent oxygen, it is no longer fit to breathe."

"Without doubt! But I told you, Monsieur Aronnax, that the pumps of the *Nautilus* allow me to store air under considerable pressure, and under those conditions, the reservoir of the apparatus can furnish breathable air for nine or ten hours."

"I have no further objections to make," I answered; "I will only ask you one thing, Captain—how can you light your way at the bottom of the sea?"

"With the Ruhmkorff apparatus, Monsieur Aronnax; one part of which is carried on the back, the other part is fastened at the waist. It is composed of a Bunsen pile, which I do not work with bichromate of potash, but with sodium. A wire is introduced which collects the electricity produced, and directs it towards a specially made lantern. In this lantern is a spiral glass tube which contains a small quantity of carbon dioxide gas. When the apparatus is at work this gas becomes luminous, giving out a white and continuous light. Thus provided, I can breathe and I can see.''

"Captain Nemo, to all my objections you make such crushing answers, that I dare no longer doubt. But if I am forced to admit the Rouquayrol and Ruhmkorff apparatus, I must be allowed some reservations with regard to the gun I am to carry.''

"But it is not a gun that uses powder," answered the Captain.

"Then it is an air gun?''

"Doubtless! How would you have me manufacture gunpowder on board, without either saltpetre, sulphur, or charcoal?''

"Besides," I added, "to fire underwater in a medium fifty five times denser than the air, you must overcome very considerable resistance.

"That would be no difficulty. There exist guns, invented by Fulton, perfected in England by Philip Coles and Burley, in France by Furcy, and in Italy by Landi, which are furnished with a watertight system of closing, which can fire under these conditions. But I repeat, having no powder, I use air under great pressure, which the pumps of the *Nautilus* furnish abundantly.''

"But this air must be rapidly used up?''

"Well, have I not my Rouquayrol reservoir, which can furnish it at need? A tap is all that is required. Besides, Monsieur Aronnax, you will see for yourself that, during our submarine hunt, we spend but little air and but few balls.''

"But it seems to me that in this half-light, and in the midst of this fluid, which is very dense compared with the atmosphere, shots could not go far, nor easily prove deadly.''

"Sir, on the contrary, with this gun every blow is mortal; and however lightly the animal is touched, it falls as if struck by a thunderbolt.''

"Why?''

"Because the balls sent by this gun are not ordinary balls, but little capsules of glass— invented by Leniebroek, an Austrian chemist—of which I have a large supply. These capsules are covered with a case of steel, and weighted with a pellet of lead; they are real Leyden jars, into which a powerful charge of electricity is forced. With the slightest shock they are discharged, and the animal, however strong it may be, falls dead. I must tell you that these capsules are size number four, and that an ordinary gun could hold ten.''

"I will argue no longer," I replied, rising from the table; "the only thing left for me is to take up my gun. At all events, I will go where you go.''

Captain Nemo then led me aft; and is passing Ned and Conseil's cabin, I called to my two companions, who followed immediately. We then came to a kind of cell near the engine room, in which we were to put on our diving-dress.

---

[1]Small white clouds, light, with indented edges. J.V.

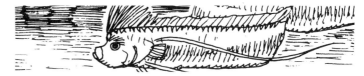

◄ **CHAPTER XVI** ►

A WALK ON THE BOTTOM OF THE SEA

his cell was, to speak correctly, the arsenal and dressing room of the *Nautilus*. A dozen diving apparatuses hung from the wall waiting our use.

Ned Land, on seeing them, showed evident repugnance to dress himself in one.

"But, my worthy Ned, the forests of the Island of Crespo are nothing but submarine forests!"

"Good!" said the disappointed harpooner sarcastically who saw his dreams of fresh meat fade away. "And you, Monsieur Aronnax, are you going to dress yourself in those clothes?"

"There is no alternative, Master Ned."

"As you please, sir," replied the harpooner, shrugging his shoulders; "but as for me, unless I am forced, I will never get into one."

"No one will force you, Master Ned," said Captain Nemo.

"Is Conseil going to risk it?" asked Ned.

"I follow monsieur wherever he goes," replied Conseil.

At the captain's call two of the ship's crew came to help us to dress in these heavy and impervious clothes, made of seamless india-rubber and constructed expressly to resist considerable pressure. One would have thought it a suit of armor, both supple and resisting. This suit formed trousers and tunic. The trousers were finished off with thick boots, weighted with heavy lead soles. The material of the tunic was held together by bands of copper, which crossed the chest, protecting it from the great pressure of the water, and leaving the lungs free to act; the sleeves ended in gloves, which in no way restrained the movement of the hands.

There was a vast difference noticeable between these perfected apparatuses and the old cork breastplates, jackets, and other contrivances in vogue during the eighteenth century.

Captain Nemo and one of his companions (a sort of Hercules, who must have possessed great strength), Conseil, and myself, were soon enveloped in our suits. There remained nothing more to be done but to enclose our heads in the spherical metal helmets. But before proceeding to this operation, I asked the captain's permission to examine the guns we were to carry.

One of the *Nautilus'* men gave me a simple gun, the butt end of which, made of steel and hollow in the center, was rather large. This served as a reservoir for compressed air, which a valve, worked by a spring, allowed to escape into a tubular metal chamber. A box of projectiles, set in a groove in the thickness of the butt end, contained about twenty of these electric balls, which, by means of a spring, were forced into the barrel of the gun. As soon as one shot was fired, another was ready.

"Captain Nemo," said I, "this weapon is perfect, and easily handled; I only ask to be allowed to try it. But how shall we gain the bottom of the sea?"

"At this moment, Professor, the *Nautilus* is laying on the bottom in ten meters of water, and we have nothing to do but to start."

"But how shall we get out?"

"You shall see."

Captain Nemo thrust his head into the helmet, Conseil and I did the same, not without hearing an ironical "Good hunting!" from the Canadian. The upper part of our suit terminated in a copper collar, upon which was screwed the metal helmet. Three holes, protected by thick glass, allowed us to see in all directions, by simply turning our head in the interior of the headdress. As soon as it was in position, the Rouquayrol apparatus on our backs began to act; and, for my part, I could breathe with ease.

With the Ruhmkorff lamp hanging from my belt, and the gun in my hand, I was ready to set out. But to speak the truth, imprisoned in these heavy garments, and glued to the deck by my leaden soles, it was impossible for me to take a step.

But this state of things was provided for. I felt myself being pushed into a little room contiguous to the wardrobe-room. My companions followed, towed along in the same way. I heard a water-tight door, furnished with stopper plates, close upon us, and we were wrapped in profound darkness.

After some minutes, a loud hissing was heard. I felt an impression of cold mount from my feet to my chest. Evidently from some part of the vessel they had, by means of a tap, given entrance to the water, which was invading us, and with which the room was soon filled. A second door, in the side of the *Nautilus,* then opened. We saw a faint light. In another instant our feet trod the bottom of the sea.

And now, how can I retrace the impression left upon me by that walk under the waters? Words are impotent to relate such wonders! If an artist's brush cannot reproduce the miraculous effects of the deep sea, how can my pen?

Captain Nemo walked in front, his companion followed some steps behind. Conseil and I remained near each other, as if an exchange of words had been possible through our metallic helmets. I no longer felt the weight of my clothing, or of my shoes, of my reservoir of air, or my thick round helmet, in the midst of which my head rattled like an almond in its shell. All objects, when immersed in water, lose that part of their weight equal to the weight of the liquid displaced. I appreciated this discovery of Archimedes. I was no longer an inert mass, but could now move with relative liberty.

The light, which lit the soil thirty feet below the surface of the ocean, astonished me by its power. The solar rays shone through the watery mass easily, and dissipated its color. I clearly distinguished objects at a distance of a hundred meters. Beyond that the tints darkened into fine gradations of ultramarine, turned blue in the distance, and faded into vague obscurity. Truly this water which surrounded me was but another air denser than the terrestrial atmosphere, but almost as transparent. Above me was the calm surface of the sea.

We were walking on fine sand, not wrinkled, as on a flat shore, which retains the impression of the billows. This dazzling carpet, like a mirror, reflected the rays of the sun with wonderful intensity. This accounted for the brilliant light, which penetrated every atom of liquid. Shall I be believed when I say that, at that depth of thirty feet, I could see as if I was in broad daylight?

For a quarter of an hour I trod on this sand, sown with the impalpable dust of shells. The hull of the *Nautilus,* resembling a long shoal, disappeared by degrees; but its lantern, when darkness should overtake us in the waters, would help to guide our return by its distinct rays. This effect is difficult to imagine for anyone who has only seen the whitish beams that are so prominent on land. There the dust with which the air is saturated gives the rays the appearance of a luminous fog; but on the sea, and under the sea, these electric beams are transmitted with incomparable purity.

We continued walking; the vast sandy plain seemed without limits. My hands seemed to be parting liquid curtains, that closed behind me, and all trace of my footsteps were effaced under the pressure of the water.

Soon forms of objects outlined in the distance were discernible. I recognized magnificent rocks, hung with a tapestry of zoöphytes of the most beautiful kind, and I was at first struck by the peculiar effect of this medium.

It was then ten in the morning; the rays of the sun struck the surface of the waves at an oblique angle, and were refracted as if through a prism. Flowers, rocks, plants, shells, and

polyps were shaded by the seven colors of the solar spectrum. It was marvellous, a feast for the eyes, this complication of colored tints, a perfect kaleidoscope of green, yellow, orange, violet, indigo, and blue; in one word, the whole palette of an enthusiastic colorist! Why could I not communicate to Conseil the lively sensations which were mounting to my brain, and rival him in expressions of admiration? For aught I knew, Captain Nemo and his companion might be able to exchange thoughts by means of signs previously agreed upon. So, for want of better, I talked to myself; I declaimed in the copper box which covered my head, thereby expending more air in vain words than was perhaps expedient.

Before this splendid spectacle, Conseil and I stopped. Evidently, this worthy lad, in the presence of such samples of zoöphytes and mollusks was classifying! Always classifying! Polyps and echinoderms covered the soil. Various kinds of isis, clusters of pure tuft-coral, isolated cornulaires, clusters of virginal uculines, once called by the name "white coral," prickly fungi that resembled mushrooms, and anemones, adhering with their muscular discs, formed a brilliant garden of flowers, enameled with porphitæ, decked with their collarettes of blue tentacles, sea-stars studding the sandy bottom, together with warty asterophytons, like fine lace embroidered by the hands of na°ads, whose festoons were waved by the gentle undulations caused by our walk. It was a real grief to me to crush under my feet the brilliant specimens of mollusks which strewed the ground by thousands: concentric combshells; hammerheads; donaciæ, veritable jumping shells; troques; red helmet-shells; angel-winged strombes; aphasmidia, and many others produced by this inexhaustible ocean. But we were bound to walk, so we went on, while above our heads waved shoals of physalides leaving their ultramarine tentacles to float in their train, jellyfish whose umbrellas of opal or rose-pink, festooned with a border of blue, sheltered us from the rays of the sun; and fiery pelagiæ, which, if it had been dark would have strewn our path with phosphorescent light.

All these wonders I saw in the space of a quarter of a mile, scarcely stopping, and following Captain Nemo, who beckoned me on by signs. Soon the nature of the soil changed; the sandy plain succeeded to an extent of viscous mud, which the Americans call "ooze," composed of equal part of silicious and calcareous shells. We then travelled over a plain of algae and deep sea vegetation. This had not been disturbed by the water and grew in profusion. This lawn was as thick as in a greenhouse and soft to the feet, rivaled the softest carpet woven by the hand of man. But while verdure was spread at our feet, it did not abandon our heads. A light network of marine plants, of that inexhaustible family of seaweeds of which more than two thousand kinds are known, grew on the surface of the water. I saw long ribbons of fucus floating, some globular, others tube-shaped; laurenciæ and cladostephi with the most delicate foliage, and some *Rhodemeniæ* palmatæ, resembling the fan of a cactus. I noticed that the green plants kept nearer the top of the sea, while the red were at a greater depth, leaving to the black or brown hydrophytes the care of forming gardens and flower beds in the very remote depths of the ocean.

These algae are truly a prodigy of creation, one of the marvels of the floral universe. This family produces, at the same time, both the largest and smallest plants in the world. On one hand it has been possible to count forty thousand of these almost imperceptible plants in the space of five cubic centimeters; on the other we can find fucus whose length exceeds five hundred meters.

We had been away from the *Nautilus* about an hour and a half. It was near noon; I knew by the perpendicularity of the sun's rays, which were no longer refracted. The magical colors disappeared by degrees, and the shades of emerald and sapphire were gone from our "sky." We walked with a regular step, which rang upon the ground with astonishing intensity. The slightest noise was transmitted with a quickness to which the ear is unaccustomed on the earth. Indeed, water is a better conductor of sound than air, in the ratio of four to one.

At this point the earth sloped downwards; the light took a uniform tint. We were at a depth of a hundred meters, undergoing a pressure of ten atmospheres.

But my diving-suit was so well made for these conditions that I did not suffer at all from the pressure. I only experienced a certain discomfort in moving my fingers, but even this disappeared. As for the fatigue I should have felt after walking for two hours in such an unfamiliar harness, I felt none. My movements, aided by the water, were produced with surprising ease.

At the depth of three hundred feet I could still see the rays of the sun, though feebly; to their intense brilliancy had succeeded a reddish twilight, halfway between day and night. But we could still see well enough; it was not necessary to resort to the Ruhmkorff apparatus as yet.

At this moment Captain Nemo stopped; he waited till I joined him and then pointed to an obscure mass, looming in the shadow, at a short distance.

"It is the forest of the Island of Crespo," I thought; and I was not mistaken.

◄ CHAPTER XVII ►

A SUBMARINE FOREST

e had at last arrived on the borders of this forest, doubtless one of the most beautiful of Captain Nemo's immense domains. He looked upon it as his own, and considered he had the same right over it that the first men had in the first days of the world. And, indeed, who would have disputed with him the possession of this submarine property? What other hardier pioneer would come, hatchet in hand, to cut down the dark copses?

This forest was composed of large tree-like plants; and the moment we penetrated under its vast arcades, I was struck by the singular position of their branches, an effect I had not before observed.

Not an herb which carpeted the ground, not a branch which clothed the trees, was either dropping or bent, or extended horizontally. All stretched up to the surface of the ocean. Not a filament, not a ribbon, however thin they might be, that did not keep straight as a rod of iron. The fuci and lianas grew in rigid perpendicular lines, commanded by the density of the element which had produced them. Motionless, yet, when bent to one side by my hand, they directly resumed their former position. Truly it was the region of perpendicularity!

I soon accustomed myself to this fantastic effect, as well as to the comparative darkness which surrounded us. The soil of the forest seemed covered with sharp blocks, difficult to avoid. The submarine flora struck me as being very perfect, and richer even than it would have been in the arctic or tropical zones, where these productions are not so plentiful. But for some minutes I involuntarily confused the genera, taking zoöphytes for hydrophytes, animals for plants; and who would not have been mistaken? The fauna and the flora are too closely allied in this submarine world!

I observed that all of these productions of the vegetable kingdom were attached to the soil only by the most superficial footing. Without roots, they needed solid ground, sand, shells or pebbles only for support, not for nourishment.

These plants are self-propagated and their existence depends upon the water, which supports and nourishes them. The greater number, instead of leaves, shoot forth blades of capricious shapes, shaded within a limited scale of colors,—pink, carmine, green, olive, fawn, and brown. I saw there (but not dried up, as our specimens of the *Nautilus* are) pavonari spread like a fan, as if to catch the breeze; scarlet ceramies; laminaries, which extended their young edible shoots; fern-shaped nereocysti, which when blossoming, grow to a height of fifteen meters; bouquets of acetabuli, whose stems increase in size upwards; and numbers of other marine plants, all devoid of flowers! "Curious anomaly, fantastic element!" said an ingenious naturalist, "in which the animal kingdom blossoms, and the vegetable does not!"

Under these numerous shrubs, as large as trees of the temperate zone, and under their damp shadow, were massed together real bushes of living flowers, hedges of zoöphytes, on which blossomed some zebra-meandrines with crooked grooves, some yellow caryophylliæ with diaphanous tentacles; grassy tufts of zoantharia; and, to complete the illusion, the fish-flies flew from branch to branch like a swarm of hummingbirds, while yellow lepisacanthi, with bristling jaws and sharp scales, dactylopteri, and monocentrides rose at our feet like a flight of woodcocks.

At about one o'clock Captain Nemo gave the signal to halt. I, for my part, was not sorry, and we stretched ourselves under an arbor of alariæ, the long thin blades of which stood up like arrows.

This short rest seemed delicious to me; there was nothing wanting but the charm of conversation. But it was impossible to speak, impossible to answer. I put my great copper head to Conseil's. I saw the worthy fellow's eyes glistening with delight, and to show his satisfaction, he shook himself in his breastplate of air, in the most comical way in the world.

After four hours of walking I was surprised not to find myself dreadfully hungry. How to account for this state of the stomach I could not tell. But instead I felt an insurmountable desire to sleep, which happens to all divers. And my eyes soon closed behind the thick glass ports, and I fell into a heavy slumber, which movement alone had prevented before. Captain Nemo and his robust companion, stretched in the clear crystal, set us the example.

How long I remained buried in this drowsiness, I cannot judge; but, when I woke, the sun seemed sinking towards the horizon. Captain Nemo had already risen, and I was beginning to stretch my limbs, when an unexpected apparition brought me briskly to my feet.

A few steps off, a monstrous sea spider, about a meter high, was watching with squinting eyes, ready to spring upon me. Though my diver's dress was thick enough to defend me from the bite of this animal, I could not help shuddering with horror. Conseil and the sailor of the *Nautilus* awoke at this moment. Captain Nemo pointed out the hideous crustacean, which a blow from the butt end of the gun knocked over, and I saw the horrible claws of the monster writhe in terrible convulsions. This encounter reminded me that other animals more to be feared might haunt these obscure depths, against whose attacks my diving-dress would not protect me. I had never thought of it before, but I now resolved to be upon my guard. Indeed, I thought that this halt would mark the termination of our walk; but I was mistaken, for, instead of returning to the *Nautilus,* Captain Nemo continued his bold excursion.

The ground was still on the incline, its slope seemed to be getting steeper, and to be leading us to greater depths. It must have been about three o'clock when we reached a narrow valley, between high perpendicular walls, situated about one hundred and fifty meters deep. Thanks to the perfection of our apparatus, we were ninety meters below the limit which nature seems to have imposed on man's submarine excursions.

I say one hundred and fifty, though I had no instrument by which to judge the distance. But I knew that even in the clearest waters, the solar rays could not penetrate further. And accordingly the darkness deepened. At ten paces not an object was visible. I was groping my way, when I suddenly saw a brilliant white light. Captain Nemo had just put his electric apparatus into use; his companion did the same, and Conseil and I followed their example. By turning a screw I established a communication between the wire and the spiral glass, and the sea, lit by our four lanterns, was illuminated for a radius of twenty five meters.

Captain Nemo was still plunging into the dark depths of the forest, whose trees were getting scarcer at every step. I noticed that vegetable life disappeared sooner than animal life. The marine plants had already abandoned the arid soil, from which a great number of animals, zoöphytes, articulata, mollusks, and fishes, still obtained sustenance.

As we walked, I thought the light of our Ruhmkorff apparatus could not fail to draw some inhabitant from its dark hiding place. But if they did approach us, they at least kept at a respectful distance from the hunters. Several times I saw Captain Nemo stop, put his gun to his shoulder, and after some moments drop it and walk on.

At last, at about four o'clock, this marvellous excursion came to an end. A wall of superb rocks, in an imposing mass, rose before us, a heap of gigantic blocks, an enormous steep granite shore, forming dark grottos, but which presented no practicable slope. It was the base of the Island of Crespo. It was the earth!

Captain Nemo stopped suddenly. A gesture of his brought us all to a halt; and however desirous I might be to scale the wall, I was obliged to stop. Here ended Captain Nemo's domains. And he would not go beyond them. Further on was a portion of the globe he might not trample upon.

The return began. Captain Nemo had returned to the head of his little band, directing our course without hesitation. I thought we were not following the same route to return to the *Nautilus*. The new path was very steep, and consequently very painful. We approached the surface of the sea rapidly. But this return to the upper strata was not so sudden as to cause decompression too rapidly, which might have produced serious injury to our bodies of the kind so fatal to divers. Very soon light reappeared and grew, and the sun again being low on the horizon, the refraction of its light haloed the different objects with the colors of the spectrum.

At a depth of ten meters, we walked amidst a shoal of little fishes of all kinds, more numerous than the birds of the air, and also more agile: but no aquatic game worthy of a shot had as yet met our gaze. At that moment I saw the captain shoulder his gun quickly, and follow a moving object into the shrubs. He fired—I heard a slight hissing, and a creature fell stunned at some distance from us.

It was a magnificent sea otter, an enhydrus, the only exclusively marine quadruped. This otter was one and a half meters long, and must have been very valuable. Its skin, chestnut brown above, and silvery underneath, would have made one of those beautiful furs so sought after in the Russian and Chinese markets; the fineness and the luster of its coat would certainly fetch 2000 francs. I admired this curious mammal, with its rounded head ornamented with short ears, its round eyes, and white whiskers like those of a cat, with webbed feet and claws, and tufted tail. This precious animal, hunted and tracked by fishermen, has now become very rare, and taken refuge chiefly in the northern parts of the Pacific, or probably its species would soon become extinct.

Captain Nemo's companion took the beast, threw it over his shoulder, and we continued our journey. For one hour a plain of sand lay stretched before us. Sometimes it rose to within two meters of the surface of the water. I then saw our image clearly reflected on the undersurface of the waves, and above us appeared an identical group reflecting our movements and our actions; in a word, like us in every point, except that they walked with their heads downward and their feet in the air.

Another effect I noticed was the passage of thick clouds which formed and vanished rapidly; but on reflection I understood that these seeming clouds were due to the varying depth of the water as the waves passed over us, and I could even see the fleecy foam which their broken tops multiplied on the water, and the shadows of large birds passing above our heads, whose rapid flight I could follow on the surface of the sea.

On this occasion, I was witness to one of the finest gun-shots which ever thrilled the nerves of a hunter. A large bird of great breadth of wing, clearly visible, approached and hovered over us. Captain Nemo's companion shouldered his gun and fired when it was only a few meters above the waves. The creature fell stunned, and the force of its fall brought it within the reach of the dexterous hunter's grasp. It was an albatross of the finest kind.

Our march had not been interrupted by this incident. For two more hours we followed these sandy plains, then fields of seaweed very disagreeable to cross. Candidly, I could go no further when I saw a glimmer of light, which, for a half mile, broke the darkness of the waters. It was the lantern of the *Nautilus.* Before twenty minutes were over we should be on board, and I should be able to breathe with ease, for it seemed that my reservoir supplied air very deficient in oxygen. But I made my calculation not reckoning on an accidental meeting, which delayed our arrival for some time.

I had remained about twenty steps behind, when I saw Captain Nemo coming hurriedly towards me. With his strong hand he bent me to the ground, his companion doing the same to Conseil. At first I knew not what to think of this sudden attack, but I was soon reassured by seeing the Captain lie down beside me, and remain immovable.

I was stretched on the ground, just under shelter of a bush of seaweed when raising my head, I saw a pair of enormous masses, casting phosphorescent gleams, pass blusteringly by.

My blood froze in my veins as I recognized two formidable sharks which threatened us! It was a couple of tintoreas, terrible creatures, with enormous tails and a dull glassy stare, the phosphorescent matter ejected from holes pierced around the muzzle. Monstrous brutes! which would crush a whole man in their iron jaws. I did not know whether Conseil stopped to classify them; for my part, I noticed their silver bellies, and their huge mouths bristling with teeth, from a very unscientific point of view, more as a possible victim than as a naturalist.

Happily the voracious creatures do not see well. They passed without seeing us, brushing us with their brownish fins, and we escaped by a miracle from a danger certainly greater than meeting a tiger full face in the forest.

Half an hour later, guided by the electric light, we reached the *Nautilus.* The outside hatch had been left open, and Captain Nemo closed it as soon as we had entered the first cell. He then pressed a knob. I heard the pumps working in the midst of the vessel, I felt the water sinking from around me, and in a few moments the cell was entirely empty. The inside door then opened, and we entered the dressing room.

There our diving-dress was taken off, not without some trouble; and, fairly worn out from want of food and sleep, I returned to my room, in great wonder at this surprising excursion at the bottom of the sea.

◄ CHAPTER XVIII ►

FOUR THOUSAND LEAGUES UNDER THE PACIFIC

he next morning, the 18th of November, I had quite recovered from my fatigues of the day before, and I went up on to the platform, just as the second-in-command was uttering his daily phrase. It then came into my mind that it had to do with the state of the sea, and that it signified "there is nothing in sight."

And, in fact, the ocean was quite clear. There was not a sail on the horizon. The heights of Crespo had disappeared during the night. The sea, absorbing the colors of the prism, with the exception of the blue rays, reflected them in every direction, and was of an admirable indigo shade. The silky sea was imprinted with broad streaks, regularly printed on its undulating surface.

I was admiring the magnificent aspect of the ocean when Captain Nemo appeared. He did not seem to be aware of my presence, and began a series of astronomical observations. Then, when he had finished, he went and leaned on the cage of the lantern, and gazed upon the ocean.

In the meantime, twenty sailors of the *Nautilus,* all strong and healthy men, had come up on to the platform. They came to draw up the nets that had been laid all night. These sailors were evidently of different nations, although the European type was visible in all of them. I recognized some unmistakable Irishmen, Frenchmen, some Slavs, and a Greek or a Cretan. They were men of few words, and only used that odd language among themselves, the origin of which I could not guess. Nor could I question them.

The nets were hauled in. They were a large kind of "chaluts," like those on the Normandy coasts, great pockets that a floating yard and a chain threaded through the lower meshes kept open. These pockets, drawn by iron poles, swept through the water, and gathered in everything in the way. That day they brought up curious specimens from those productive coasts,—angler-fish that, from their comical movements, have acquired the name of buffoons; black commersons, furnished with antennæ; trigger-fish, encircled with red bands; orthragorisci, with very subtle venom; some olive-colored lampreys; macrorhynci, covered with silvery scales; trichiuri, the electric power of which is equal to that of the electric eel and cramp-fish; scaly notopteri, with transverse brown bands; greenish cod; several varieties of gobies, etc. Also some larger fish; a caranx with a prominent head a meter long; several fine bonitos, streaked with blue and silver; and three splendid tunas, which, in spite of the swiftness of their motion, had not escaped the net.

I reckoned that the haul had brought in more than a thousand pounds of fish. It was a fine haul, but not to be wondered at. Indeed, the nets are let down for several hours, and enclose in there an entire aquatic world. We had no lack of excellent food, and the rapidity of the *Nautilus* and the attraction of the electric light could always renew our supply.

These many products of the sea were immediately lowered through the hatch to the steward's room, some to be eaten fresh, and others preserved.

The fishing ended, the provision of air renewed, I thought that the *Nautilus* was about to continue its submarine excursion, and was preparing to return to my room, when, without further preamble, the captain turned to me, saying—

"Professor, is not this ocean gifted with real life? Has it not its tempers and its gentle moods? Yesterday it slept as we did, and now it has woke after a quiet night."

Neither "Good morning" nor "Good evening!" It was as though this strange person was continuing a conversation we had already commenced.

"Look!" he continued, "it wakes under the caresses of the sun! It is going to renew its diurnal existence. It is an interesting study to watch the play of its organism. It has a pulse, arteries, spasms; and I agree with the learned Maury, who discovered in it a circulation as real as the circulation of blood in animals.

It was certain that Captain Nemo expected no answer from me, and it appeared useless to keep saying "evidently," or "you are right," or "it must be so." He was instead speaking to himself, taking some time between each sentence. He was meditating aloud.

"Yes, the ocean has indeed circulation, and to promote it, the Creator has caused things to multiply in it—caloric, salt, and animalculæ. Heat creates the different densities, the cause of currents and undercurrents. Evaporation, which does not go on at all in hyperborean regions, and is very active in the equatorial zones, constitutes a permanent exchange between tropical and polar water. Besides, I have felt the perpendicular currents, moving from high to low, low to high, which form the real respiration of the ocean. I have seen a molecule of sea water warmed on the surface, re-descend to the depths, reach its maximum density at two degrees below zero, then, cooling again, become lighter, and re-ascend. You will see at the poles the consequences of this phenomenon, and you will understand why, according to the law of provident Nature, freezing can never take place except on the surface of the water!"

While Captain Nemo was finishing his sentence I said to myself, "The Pole! Does the daring man intend to take us as far as that?"

In the meantime the captain had stopped talking, and was contemplating the element he so incessantly studied. Then he resumed.

"The salts," he said, "exist in a considerable quantity in the sea, Professor, and if you were to take out all it contains in solution, you would make a mass of four and a half million cubic leagues. Which, spread over the globe, would form a layer more than ten meters thick. And do not think that the presence of this salt is due to a caprice of Nature. No. It makes sea water less capable of evaporation, and prevents the wind taking off too great a quantity of water vapor, which, when it condensed, would submerge the temperate zones. It has a great balancing part to play in the general economy of the globe!"

Captain Nemo stopped, rose, took several steps on the platform, and came back towards me.

"As to the infusoria, as to the hundred of millions of tiny animals which exist in a drop of water, and of which it takes 800,000 to weigh a milligram, their part is no less important. They absorb the marine salts, they assimilate the solid elements of water, and, veritable manufacturers of calcareous continents, they make coral and madrepores! And then the drop of water, deprived of its mineral element, is lightened, mounts to the surface, absorbs there the salt left by evaporation, is weighted, sinks again, and takes back to the animalculæ new elements to absorb. Hence a double current, ascending and descending, always movement and always life!—life more intense than that of continents, more exuberant, more infinite, flourishing in every part of this ocean, an element of death to man, they say, an element of life to myriads of animals—and to me!"[1]

When Captain Nemo spoke thus, he seemed altogether changed, and aroused an extraordinary emotion in me.

"Also," he added, "true existence is there! I can imagine the foundations of nautical towns, clusters of submarine houses, which, like the *Nautilus,* would ascend every morning to breathe at the surface of the water, free towns, independent cities. Yet who knows whether some despot. . . ."

Captain Nemo finished his sentence with a violent gesture. Then, addressing me as if to chase away some sorrowful thought—

"Monsieur Aronnax," he asked, "do you know the depth of the ocean?"

"I only know, Captain, what the principal soundings have taught us."

"Could you tell me them, so that I can verify them if necessary?"

"These are some," I replied, "that I remember. If I am not mistaken, an average depth of 8,200 meters has been found in the North Atlantic, and 2,500 meters in the Mediterranean. The most remarkable soundings have been made in the South Atlantic, near the 35th parallel, and they gave 12,000 meters, 14,081 meters, and 15,149 meters. So sum up all, it is reckoned that if the bottom of the sea were levelled, its mean depth would be about seven kilometers."

"Well, Professor," replied the captain, "we shall show you better than that I hope. As to the mean depth of this part of the Pacific, I can tell you it is only 4000 meters."

Having said this, Captain Nemo went towards the hatch, and disappeared down the ladder. I followed him, and went into the large salon. The screw was immediately put in motion, and the log indicated twenty miles an hour.

During the days and weeks that passed, Captain Nemo was very sparing of his visits. I seldom saw him. The lieutenant pricked the ship's course regularly on the chart, so I could always tell exactly the route of the *Nautilus*.

Conseil and Land passed long hours with me. Conseil had related to his friend the marvels of our excursion, and the Canadian regretted not having joined us. But I hoped that another occasion would present itself for a visit to the undersea forest.

Nearly every day, for some time, the panels of the salon were opened, and we were never tired of penetrating the mysteries of the submarine world.

The general direction of the *Nautilus* was southeast, and it kept between 100 and 150 meters of depth. One day, however, I do not know why, being drawn diagonally down by means of the inclined planes, it touched the bed of the sea at a depth of 2000 meters. The thermometer indicated a temperature of 4.25° centigrade; a temperature that at this depth seemed common to all latitudes.

At three o'clock in the morning of the 26th of November, the *Nautilus* crossed the tropic of Cancer at 172° longitude. On the 27th it sighted the Sandwich Islands, where Cook died, February 14, 1779. We had then gone 4,860 leagues from our starting point. In the morning, when I went on the platform, I saw, two miles to windward, Hawaii, the largest of the seven islands that form the group. I saw clearly the cultivated ranges, and the several mountain chains that run parallel with the side, and the volcanoes of which the highest is Mauna Kea, which rises five thousand meters above the level of the sea. Besides other things the nets brought up, were several peacock flabella, a graceful polyp, that are peculiar to that part of the ocean.

The direction of the *Nautilus* was still to the southeast. It crossed the equator December 1, in 142° longitude; and on the 4th of the same month, after crossing rapidly and without anything particular occurring, we sighted the Marquesas group. I saw, three miles off, at 8° 57′ latitude south, and 139° 32′ west longitude, Martin's Peak in Nouka-Hiva, the largest of the group that belongs to France. I only saw the woody mountains against the horizon, because Captain Nemo did not wish to bring the ship too near the land. There the nets brought up beautiful specimens of fish; choryphenes, with azure fins and tails like gold, the flesh of which is unrivaled; hologymnoses, nearly destitute of scales, but of exquisite flavor; ostorhynes, with bony jaws; and yellow-tinged thasards, as good as bonitos; all fish that would be of use to our table.

After leaving these charming islands which are protected by the French flag, from the 4th to the 11th of December the *Nautilus* sailed over about two thousand miles. This navigation was remarkable for the meeting with an immense shoal of calmars, a curious mollusk, near neighbors to the cuttlefish. The French fishermen call them *encornets*: they belong to the cephalopod class, and to the dibranchial family, that includes the cuttlefish and the argonauts. These animals were particularly studied by students of antiquity, and they furnished numerous metaphors for the orators of the Agoras, as well as excellent dishes for the tables of the rich citizens, if one can believe Athenæus, a Greek doctor, who lived before Galen.

It was during the night of the 9th or 10th of December that the *Nautilus* came across this shoal of mollusks, that are peculiarly nocturnal. One could count them by millions. They migrate from the temperate to the warmer zones, following the track of herrings and sardines. We watched them through the thick crystal panes, swimming backward with great rapidity, moving by means of their locomotive tube, pursuing fish and other mollusks, eating the little ones, eaten by the big ones, and tossing about in indescribable confusion the ten arms that nature has placed on their heads like a crest of pneumatic serpents. The *Nautilus,* in spite of its speed, sailed for several hours in the midst of these animals, and its nets brought in an enormous quantity, among which I recognized the nine species that D'Orbigny classified for the Pacific.

One saw while cruising that the sea displays the most wonderful sights. They were in endless variety. The scene changed continually, and we were called upon not only to contemplate the works of the Creator in the midst of the liquid element, but to penetrate the awful mysteries of the ocean.

During the day of the 11th of December, I was busy reading in the large salon. Ned Land and Conseil watched the luminous water through the half-open panels. The *Nautilus* was motionless. While its reservoirs were filled, it kept at a depth of 1,000 meters, a region little inhabited in the ocean, and in which large fish were seldom seen.

I was then reading a charming book by Jean Macé, *Les Serviteurs de l'estomac* (*The Slaves of the Stomach*), and I was learning some valuable lessons from it, when Conseil interrupted me.

"Will monsieur come here a moment?" he said, in a curious voice.

"What is the matter, Conseil?"

"I want monsieur to look."

I rose, went and leaned on my elbows before the pane and watched.

In the full electric light, an enormous black mass, unmoving, was suspended in the midst of the waters. I watched it attentively, seeking to find out the nature of this gigantic cetacean. But a sudden thought crossed my mind.

"A ship!" I said, half aloud.

"Yes," replied the Canadian, "a disabled ship that has sunk perpendicularly."

Ned Land was right; we were close to a vessel of which the tattered shrouds still hung from their chains. The hull seemed to be in good order, and it had been wrecked at most some few hours. Three stumps of masts, broken off about two feet above the bridge, showed that the vessel had had to sacrifice its masts. But, lying on its side, it had filled, and it was heeling over to port. This skeleton of what it had once been, was a sad spectacle as it lay lost under the waves, but sadder still was the sight of the bridge, where some corpses, bound with ropes, were still lying. I counted five;—four men, one of whom was standing at the helm, and a woman standing by the poop, holding an infant in her arms. She was quite young. By the brilliant light from the *Nautilus,* I could distinguish her features, which the water had not yet decomposed. In one despairing effort, she had raised her infant above her head, poor little thing! whose arms encircled its mother's neck. The attitude of the four sailors was frightful, distorted as they were by their convulsive movements, while making a last effort to free themselves from the cords that bound them to the vessel. The steersman alone, calm, with a grave, clear face, his grey hair glued to his forehead, and his hand clutching the wheel of the helm, seemed even then to be guiding the three-masted wreck through the depths of the ocean!

What a scene! We were silent; our hearts beat fast before this shipwreck, taken as it were from life, and photographed in its last moments. And I saw already, coming towards it with hungry eyes, enormous sharks, attracted by the human flesh.

The *Nautilus*, turning, went round the submerged vessel, and in one instant I read on the stern—"*Florida, Sunderland.*"

---

[1]Captain Nemo, in passages like this, can lay some claim to being one of the first ecologists. R.M.

◄ CHAPTER XIX ►
VANIKORO

his terrible spectacle was the forerunner of the series of maritime catastrophes that the *Nautilus* was destined to meet with in its course. As long as it went through more frequented waters, we often saw the hulls of shipwrecked vessels that were rotting in the depths, and deeper down, cannons, bullets, anchors, chains, and a thousand other iron materials eaten up by rust.

However, on the 11th of December, we sighted the Tuamotu Islands, the old "Dangerous Group" of Bougainville, that extend over a space of five hundred leagues from the E.S.E,. to W.N.W., between latitudes 13° 30′ and 23° 50′ South, and longitudes 125° 30′ and 151° 30′ East, from Ducie Island to Lazareff Island. This group covers an area of three hundred and seventy square leagues, and it is formed of sixty groups of islands, among which the Gambier group is remarkable, over which France exercises sway. These are coral islands, slowly but continuously raised, created by the daily work of polyps. At some future epoch this new island will be joined to the neighboring groups, and a fifth continent will stretch from New Zealand and New Caledonia, to the Marquesas.

One day, when I was suggesting this theory to Captain Nemo, he replied coldly—

"The earth does not need new continents, but new men."

The hazards of navigating the islands precisely had conducted the *Nautilus* towards the island of Clermont-Tonnerre, one of the most curious of the group, that was discovered in 1822 by Captain Bell of the *Minerva*. I could study now the madreporal system, to which the islands in this ocean are due.

Madrepores (which must not be mistaken for corals) have a tissue lined with a calcareous or limestone crust, and the modifications of its structure have induced Monsieur Milne-Edwards, my worthy master, to class them into five sections. The little animalculæ which these polyps secrete live by millions at the bottom of their cells. Their calcareous deposits become rocks, reefs, and large and small islands. Here they form a ring, surrounding a little lagoon, that communicates with the sea by means of gaps. There they make barriers of reefs like those on the coasts of New Caledonia and the various Tuamotu islands. In other places, like those at Réunion and at Maurice, they raise fringed reefs, high, straight walls, near which the depth of the ocean is considerable.

Some cable-lengths off the shores of the Island of Clermont-Tonnerre, I admired the gigantic work accomplished by these microscopical workers. These walls are specially the work of those madrepores known as milleporas, porites, meandrines, and astræas. These polyps are found particularly in those beds of the sea that are agitated by the rough waters of shallows, near the surface; and consequently it is from the upper part that they begin their operations in which they bury themselves by degrees with the débris of the secretions that support them. Such is, at least, Darwin's theory, who thus explains the formation of the *atolls*—a superior theory (to my mind) to that which holds that the madreporical works are begun atop summits of mountains or volcanoes, that are then gradually submerged some feet below the level of the sea.

I could observe closely these curious walls, our sounding line revealed that they were more than three hundred meters deep, and sheets of electric light illuminated this calcareous matter brilliantly. Replying to a question Conseil asked me as to the time these colossal barriers took to be raised, I astonished him much by telling him that learned men reckoned it about the eighth of an inch in an hundred years.

"To build these walls," he asked, "it must have taken. . . ."

"One hundred and ninety two thousand years, Conseil,[1] noticeably longer than the 'days' of the Bible. Besides, the formation of coal and the mineralizing of the forests buried by the deluge has taken a much longer time still. Therefore the days of creation in the Bible must refer to epochs, not to the intervals between the rising and setting of the sun. In fact, the Bible does not even date the sun from the first day of Creation!"

When the *Nautilus* returned to the surface of the ocean I could take in all the development of this low and wooded island of Clermont-Tonnerre. Its madreporal rocks were evidently fertilized by water-spouts and tempests. One day some grain, carried away from neighboring land by a tempest of wind, fell on these calcareous layers, mixed with the decomposed detritus of fish and marine plants which formed a vegetable soil. A coconut, pushed along by the waves, arrived on this new coast. The germ took root. The tree grew and held the water vapor. Streams were born, vegetation spread little by little. Animalculæ, worms, insects landed upon trunks of trees, torn away from other islands by the wind. Turtles came to lay their eggs. Birds built their nests in the young trees. In that manner animal life was developed, and attracted by the verdure and fertility, man appeared. Thus these islands, the immense works of microscopical animals, were formed.

Towards evening Clermont-Tonnerre was lost in the distance, and the route of the *Nautilus* was noticeably changed. After having crossed the tropic of Capricorn at 135° longitude, it sailed W.N.W., making again for the tropical zone. Although the summer sun was very strong, we did not suffer from heat, for at fifteen or twenty fathoms below the surface, the temperature did not rise above from ten to twelve degrees (Cent.).

On December 15, we left to the east the bewitching group of the Societies and the graceful Tahiti, queen of the Pacific. I saw in the morning, some miles to the windward, the elevated summits of the islands. These waters furnished our table with excellent fish, mackerel, bonitos, and albacores, and some varieties of a sea snake called munirophis, a kind of moray eel.

The *Nautilus* had come 8,100 miles; 9,720 miles were registered by the log as we passed through the archipelago of Tonga-Tabou, where perished the crews of the *Argo,* the *Port-au-Prince,* and the *Duke of Portland,* and the Navigator archipelago, where Captain Langle, the friend of La Pérouse, was killed. Then we sighted the archipelago Viti, where the natives massacred the crews of *L'Union* and Captain Burea, of Nantes, commander of *L'Aimable Josephine.*

This archipelago, which stretches over one hundred leagues from north to south, and ninety leagues from east to west, is comprised between 6° and 2° south latitude, and 179° west longitude. It is composed of a number of large and small islands and reefs, among which are the island of Viti-Levou, of Vanoua-Levou, and Kandubon.

It was Tasman who discovered this group in 1643, the same year that Torricelli invented the barometer and Louis XIV ascended the throne. I leave it to be imagined which of these facts was the more useful to humanity. Afterwards came Cook in 1714, d'Entrecasteaux in 1793, and lastly, Dumont d'Urville in 1827 unraveled all the geographical chaos of this archipelago. The *Nautilus* approached Waila Bay, the scene of the terrible adventures of Captain Dillon, who was the first to clear up the mystery of the shipwreck of La Pérouse.

This bay, after several draggings, furnished us with an abundance of excellent oysters. We ate them immoderately, opening them on our own table, according to the precept of Seneca. These mollusks belong to the species known under the name of *ostrea lamellosa,* which is very common in Corsica. This Waila bank must be considerable, and certainly without additional causes of destruction, the oysters would end up by filling up the bays, as each contains two million eggs.

If Ned Land had not to repent of his greediness in this case, it was because the oyster is the only dish which never provokes indigestion. In fact, it takes at least sixteen dozen of these acephalous mollusks to furnish the 315 grams of nitrogen necessary to the daily nutrition of one man.

On the 25th of December the *Nautilus* sailed into the midst of the New Hebrides, discovered by Quiros in 1606, and that Bougainville explored in 1768, and to which Cook gave its present name in 1773. This group is composed principally of nine large islands, that form a train one hundred and twenty leagues long, N.N.W. to S.S.E., between 15° and 2° south latitude, and 164° and 168° longitude. We passed tolerably near to the Island of Aurou, that at noon looked like a mass of green woods, surmounted by a peak of great height.

That day being Christmas Day, Ned Land seemed to regret sorely the non-celebration of "Christmas," the family *fête* of which Protestants are so fond.

I had not seen Captain Nemo for a week, when, on the morning of the 27th he came into the large salon, always acting as if he had seen you but five minutes before. I was busily tracing the route of the *Nautilus* on the planisphere. The captain came up to me, put his finger on one spot on the chart, and said this single word—

"Vanikoro."

The effect was magical! It was the name of the islands on which the ships of La Pérouse had been lost! I rose suddenly.

"The *Nautilus* has brought us to Vanikoro?" I asked.

"Yes, Professor," said the captain.

"And I can visit the celebrated islands where the *Boussole* and the *Astrolabe* were wrecked?"

"If you like, Professor."

"When shall we be there?"

"We are there now."

Followed by Captain Nemo, I went up on to the platform, and greedily scanned the horizon.

To the N.E. two volcanic islands of unequal size emerged, surrounded by a coral reef that measured forty miles in circumference. We were close to Vanikoro, the one to which Dumont d'Urville gave the name of de la Recherche, and exactly facing the little harbor of Vanou, situated in 16° 4′ south latitude, and 164° 32′ east longitude. The earth seemed covered with verdure from the shore to the summits in the interior, that were crowned by Mount Kapogo, 476 fathoms high.

The *Nautilus,* having passed the outer belt of rocks by a narrow strait, found itself among breakers where the sea was from thirty to forty fathoms deep. Under the verdant shade of some mangroves I perceived some savages, who appeared greatly surprised at our approach. In the long black body, moving between wind and water, did they not see some formidable cetacean that they regarded with suspicion?

Just then Captain Nemo asked me what I knew about the wreck of La Pérouse.

"Only what all the world knows, Captain," I replied.

"And could you tell me what all the world knows about it?" he inquired, ironically.

"Easily."

I related to him all that the last works of Dumont d'Urville had made known—works from which the following is a brief account.

La Pérouse, and his second-in-command, Captain de Langle, were sent by Louis XVI, in

1785, on a voyage of circumnavigation. They embarked in the corvettes the *Boussole* and the *Astrolabe,* neither of which were again heard of.

In 1791, the French Government, justly uneasy as to the fate of these two corvettes, manned two large merchantmen, the *Recherche* and the *Espérance,* which left Brest the 28th of September, under the command of Bruni d'Entrecasteaux.

Two months after, they learned from Bowen, commander of the *Albemarle,* that the débris of shipwrecked vessels had been seen on the coasts of New Georgia. But d'Entrecasteaux, ignoring this communication—rather uncertain, besides—directed his course towards the Admiralty Isles, mentioned in a report of Captain Hunter's as being the place where La Pérouse was wrecked.

They sought in vain. The *Espérance* and the *Recherche* passed by Vanikoro without stopping there, and in fact, this voyage was most disastrous, as it cost d'Entrecasteaux his life, and those of two of his lieutenants, besides several of his crew.

Captain Dillon, a shrewd old Pacific sailor, was the first to find unmistakable traces of the wrecks. On the 15th of May 1824, his vessel, the *St Patrick,* passed close to Tikopia, one of the New Hebrides. There a Lascar came alongside in a canoe, sold him the handle of a sword in silver, that bore the print of characters engraved on the hilt. The Lascar said that six years before, during a stay at Vanikoro, he had seen two Europeans that belonged to some vessels that had run aground on the reefs some years earlier.

Dillon guessed that he meant La Pérouse, whose disappearance had troubled the whole world. He tried to get on to Vanikoro, where, according to the Lascar, he would find numerous débris of the wreck, but winds and tide prevented him.

Dillon returned to Calcutta. There he interested the Asiatic Society and the East India Company in his discovery. A vessel, to which was given the name of the *Recherche,* was put at his disposal, and he set out, January 23, 1827, accompanied by a French agent.

The *Recherche,* after touching at several points in the Pacific, cast anchor before Vanikoro, July 7, 1827, in that same harbor of Vanou where the *Nautilus* was floating.

There Dillon collected numerous relics of the wreck—iron utensils, anchors, pulley-strops, swivel-guns, an 18 lb. shot, fragments of astronomical instruments, a piece of crown-work, and a bronze clock, bearing this inscription—*"Bazin m'a fait,"* the mark of the foundry of the arsenal at Brest about 1785. There could be no further doubt.

Dillon, having made all inquiries, stayed in the unlucky place till October. Then he quitted Vanikoro, and directed his course towards New Zealand; put into Calcutta, April 7, 1828, and returned to France, where he was warmly welcomed by Charles X.

But at the same time, without knowing Dillon's movements, Dumont d'Urville had already set out to find the scene of the wreck. And he had learned from a whaler that some medals and a cross of St Louis had been found in the hands of some savages of Louisiade and New Caledonia.

Dumont d'Urville, commander of the *Astrolabe,* had then sailed, and two months after Dillon had left Vanikoro, he put into Hobart Town. There he learned the results of Dillon's inquiries, and found that a certain James Hobbs, second lieutenant of the *Union* of Calcutta, after landing on an island situated 8° 18' south latitude, and 156° 30' east longitude, had seen some iron bars and red cloth used by the natives of these parts. Dumont d'Urville, much perplexed, and not knowing how to credit the reports of low-class newspapers, decided to follow Dillon's track.

On the 10th of February 1828, the *Astrolabe* appeared off Tikopia, and took as guide and interpreter a deserter found on the island; made his way to Vanikoro, sighted it on the 12th, lay among the reefs until the 14th and not until the 20th did he cast anchor within the barrier, in the harbor of Vanou.

On the 23rd, several officers went round the island, and brought back some unimportant trifles. The natives, adopting a system of denials and evasions, refused to take them to the unlucky place. This ambiguous conduct led them to believe that the natives had ill-treated the castaways, and indeed they seemed to fear that Dumont d'Urville had come to avenge La Pérouse and his unfortunate crew.

However, on the 26th, appeased by some presents, and understanding that they had no reprisals to fear, they lead Monsieur Jacquineot, the second-in-command, to the scene of the wreck.

There, in three or four fathoms of water, between the reefs of Pacou and Vanou, lay anchors, cannons, pigs of lead and iron, embedded in the limy concretions. The large boat and the whaler belonging to the *Astrolabe* were sent to this place, and, not without some difficulty, their crews hauled up an anchor weighing 1,800 lbs., a brass gun, some pigs of iron, and two copper swivel-guns.

Dumont d'Urville, questioning the natives, learned, too, that La Pérouse, after losing both his vessels on the reefs of this island, had constructed a smaller boat, only to be lost a second time. Where?—no one knew.

The commander of the *Astrolabe* then, under a thicket of mangroves, caused a cenotaph to be raised to the memory of the celebrated navigator and his companions. It was a simple quadrangular pyramid on a coral foundation, in which there was no iron to tempt the cupidity of the natives.

Then Dumont d'Urville wished to depart, but his crew were worn out by the fevers of those unhealthy shores, and he was so ill himself that he could not get under sail before the 17th of March.

But the French Government, fearing that Dumont d'Urville was not acquainted with Dillon's movements, had sent the corvette *Bayonnaise,* commanded by Legoarant de Tromelin, to Vanikoro, which had been stationed on the west coast of America. The *Bayonnaise* cast her anchor at Vanikoro some months after the departure of the *Astrolabe,* but found no new information; but reported that the savages had respected the monument to La Pérouse.

That is the substance of what I told to Captain Nemo.

"So," he said, "no one knows now where the third vessel perished that was constructed by the castaways on the island of Vanikoro?"

"No one knows."

Captain Nemo said nothing, but signed to me to follow him into the large salon. The *Nautilus* sank several meters below the waves, and the panels were opened.

I hastened to the window, and under the crustations of coral, covered with fungi, syphonules, alcyons, cariophylia, through myriads of charming fish—girelles, glyphisidons, pomphérides, diacopes, and holocentres—I recognized certain débris that the drags had not been able to tear up—iron stirrups, anchors, cannons, bullets, capstan fittings, the stem of a ship, all objects clearly proving the wreck of some vessel, and now carpeted with living flowers.

While I was looking on this desolate scene, Captain Nemo said, in a grave voice—

"Commander La Pérouse set out December 7, 1785, with his vessels *Boussole* and the *Astrolabe.* He first cast anchor at Botany Bay, visited the Friendly Isles, New Caledonia, then directed his course towards Santa Cruz, and put into Namouka, one of the Hapa° group. Then his vessels struck on the unknown reefs of Vanikoro. The *Boussole,* which went first, ran aground on the southerly coast. The *Astrolabe* went to its help, and ran aground too. The first vessel was destroyed almost immediately. The second, to windward, resisted some days. The natives made the castaways welcome. They installed themselves in the island, and constructed a smaller boat with the débris of the two large ones. Some sailors stayed willingly at Vanikoro; the others, weak and ill, set out with La Pérouse. They directed their course towards the Solomon Isles, and there perished, with everything, on the westerly coast of the chief island of the group, between Capes Deception and Satisfaction."

"How do you know that?" I exclaimed.

"By this, that I found on the spot where was the last wreck."

Captain Nemo showed me a tin-plate box, stamped with the French arms, and corroded by the salt water. He opened it, and I saw a bundle of papers, yellow but still readable.

They were the instructions of the naval minister to Commander La Pérouse, annotated in the margin in Louis XVI's handwriting!

"Ah! it is a fine death for a sailor!" said Captain Nemo, at last. It is a tranquil tomb that is a tomb of coral; and I trust that I and my comrades will find no other."

---

[1] Aronnax made an error in his calculations here. It would have taken nearly 9,600,000 years, according to the numbers he is using. R.M.

◄ CHAPTER XX ►

TORRES STRAITS

 uring the nights of the 27th and 28th of December, the *Nautilus* left the shores of Vanikoro with great speed. Her course was southwesterly, and in three days she had gone over the 750 leagues that separated La Pérouse's group from the southeast point of Papua.

Early on the 1st of January 1868, Conseil joined me on the platform.

"Will monsieur permit me to wish him a happy new year?"

"What! Conseil; exactly as if I was at Paris in my study at the Jardin des Plantes? Well, I accept your good wishes, and thank you for them. Only, I will ask you what you mean by a 'Happy New Year,' under our circumstances? Do you mean the year that will bring us to the end of our imprisonment, or the year that sees us continue this strange voyage?"

"Really, I do not know how to answer monsieur. We are sure to see curious things, and for the last two months we have not had time for boredom. The last marvel is always the most astonishing; and if this progression is maintained, I do not know how it will end. It is my opinion that we shall never again see the like."

"Never, Conseil."

"Besides, Captain Nemo, who well justifies his Latin name[1], is no more bother than if he really didn't exist. I think, then, with no offence to monsieur, that a happy year would be one in which we could see everything."

"To see everything, Conseil? That would perhaps take too long. But what does Ned Land think of it?"

"Ned thinks exactly the contrary to what I do," answered Conseil. "He has a positive mind and an imperious stomach. To look at fish, and to always eat them, does not satisfy him. The lack of wine, bread, and meat scarcely agrees with the worthy Saxon, to whom beefsteaks are familiar, and who is not frightened at brandy or gin, taken in moderation."

"For my own part, Conseil, it is not that which torments me, and I accommodate myself very well to the food on board."

"And so do I," answered Conseil, "and I think as much of staying as Land does of taking flight. Therefore, if the year that is beginning is not a happy one for me, it will be for him; or vice versa. By that means someone will be satisfied. In short, to conclude, I wish monsieur anything that would please him.''

"Thank you, Conseil; only I must ask you to put off the question of a New Year's present, and to accept provisionally a shake of the hand. That is all I have upon me.''

"Monsieur has never been so generous.''

And thereupon the worthy fellow went away.

On January 2, we had made 11,340 miles, or 5,250 French leagues since our starting point in the seas of Japan. Before the ship's spur stretched the dangerous shores of the Coral Sea, on the northeast coast of Australia. Our boat cruised along some miles from the dangerous bank on which Cook's vessel was almost lost, June 10, 1770. The boat which Cook was on struck on a rock, and if it did not sink, it was owing to a piece of the coral that was broken by the shock, and fixed itself in the broken keel.

I had wished to visit the reef, 360 leagues long, against which the sea, always rough, broke with great violence, with a noise like thunder. But just then the inclined planes drew the *Nautilus* down to a great depth, and I could see nothing of the high coral walls. I had to content myself with the different specimens of fish brought up by the nets. I noticed, among others, some germons, a species of mackerel as large as a tuna, with bluish sides, and striped with transverse bands, that disappear as the animal dies. These fish followed us in schools, and furnished us with very delicate food. We took also a large number of greenish giltheads, about five centimeters long, tasting like dorys; and flying pyrapeds like submarine swallows, which, in dark nights, light alternately the air and water with their phosphorescent light. Among the mollusks and zoöphytes, I found in the meshes of the net several species of alcyonarians, sea urchins, hammershells, spurshells, dials, cerites, and hyalleæ. The flora was represented by beautiful floating seaweeds, laminariæ, and macrocystes, impregnated with mucilage that seeps through their pores; and among which I gathered an admirable *Nemastoma geliniaroida*, that was classed among the natural curiosities of the museum.

Two days after crossing the Coral Sea, January 4, we sighted the Papuan coasts. On this occasion, Captain Nemo informed me that his intention was to get into the Indian Ocean by the Strait of Torres. His communication ended there. Ned saw with pleasure that this route would take him nearer to the seas of Europe.

The Torres Straits are considered to be no less dangerous on account of the reefs with which they bristle, than because of the savage inhabitants who frequent their shores. They separate Australia from the large island of Papua, also called New Guinea.

Papua is 400 leagues long and 130 leagues wide, with an area of 40,000 square leagues. It is situated between 0° 19' and 10° 2' south latitude, and between 128° 23' and 146° 15' east longitude. At noon, while the mate was taking the sun's altitude, I perceived the summits of the Arfalxs Mountains, rising by levels and terminating in sharp peaks.

This land, discovered in 1511 by the Portuguese Francisco Serrano, was successively visited by Don Jose de Meneses in 1526, by Grijalva in 1527, by the Spanish General Alvar de Saavedra in 1528, by Juigo Ortez in 1545, by the Dutchman Shouten in 1616, by Nicolas Sruick in 1753, by Tasman, Dampier, Fumel, Carteret, Edwards, Bougainville, Cook, Forrest, MacClure, by d'Entrecasteaux in 1792, by Duperrey in 1823, and by Dumont d'Urville in 1827. "It is the focus of the blacks who occupy all Malaysia,'' says Monsieur de Rienzi, and I little thought that the hazards of this navigation were going to bring me into the presence of the formidable Andamans.

The *Nautilus* then entered the most dangerous straits in the world, those that the boldest seamen dare scarcely cross, the straits of Louis Paz de Torres confronted when returning from the South Seas, and in which, in 1840, the stranded corvettes of Dumont d'Urville were on the point of being totally wrecked. The *Nautilus* itself, superior to all dangers of the sea, was going, however, to make the acquaintance of its coral reefs.

The Torres Straits are nearly thirty-four leagues wide; but they are obstructed by an innumerable quantity of islands, islets, breakers, and rocks, that make its navigation almost impracticable. In consequence, Captain Nemo took all needful precautions to cross them. The *Nautilus,* floating just beneath the surface, went at a moderate pace. Her screw, like a cetacean's tail, beat the waves slowly.

Profiting by this, I and my two companions went up on to the deserted platform. Before us was the steersman's cage, and I expected that Captain Nemo was there directing the course of the *Nautilus.*

I had before me the excellent charts of the Strait of Torres made out by the hydrographical engineer Vincendon Dumoulin, and the midshipman Coupvent Desbois—now an admiral—who made part of Dumont d'Urville's *état-major* during his last voyage around the world. These and Captain King's are the best charts that explain the intricacies of this strait, and I consulted them with scrupulous attention.

Round the *Nautilus* the sea dashed furiously. The course of the waves, that went from southeast to northwest at the rate of two and a half miles an hour, broke on the coral that showed itself here and there.

"This is a bad sea!" remarked Ned Land.

"Detestable indeed," I replied, "and one that does not suit a boat like the *Nautilus.*"

"The damned captain must be very sure of his route, for I see there pieces of coral that would break the keel into a thousand pieces if it only touched them slightly!"

Indeed the situation was dangerous, but the *Nautilus* seemed to slide like magic between these rocks. It did not follow the routes of the *Astrolabe* and the *Zélée* exactly, for they proved disastrous to Dumont d'Urville. It bore more northwards, coasted the Island of Murray, and came back to the southwest towards Cumberland Passage. I thought it was going to pass it by, when, going back to northwest, it went through a large quantity of islands and islets little known, towards the Tound Island and Mauvais Channel.

I wondered if Captain Nemo, foolishly imprudent, would steer his vessel into that pass where Dumont d'Urville's two corvettes grounded; when, turning again, and cutting straight through to the west, he steered for the Island of Gueboroar.

It was then three in the afternoon. The ebb tide was just beginning. The *Nautilus* approached the island, that I can still recall because of its remarkable border of screw pines. He stood off it at about two miles distant.

Suddenly a shock overthrew me. The *Nautilus* just touched a rock, and stayed immovable, listing lightly to port side.

When I rose, I perceived Captain Nemo and his second-in-command on the platform. They were examining the situation of the vessel, and exchanging words in their incomprehensible dialect.

This was the situation: Two miles, on the starboard side, appeared Gueboroar, stretching from north to west like an immense arm. Towards the south and east some heads of coral showed themselves, exposed by the ebb tide. We had run aground, and in one of these seas where the tides are middling—a sorry matter for the floating of the *Nautilus.* However, the vessel had not suffered, for her hull was solidly made. But if she could neither float off nor move, she ran the risk of being forever fastened to these rocks, and then Captain Nemo's submarine vessel would be done for.

I was reflecting thus, when the captain, cool and calm, always master of himself, appearing neither vexed nor moved, approached me.

"An accident?" I asked.

"No; an incident."

"But an incident that will oblige you perhaps to become an inhabitant of this land from which you flee!"

Captain Nemo looked at me curiously, and made a negative gesture, as much as to say that nothing would force him to set foot on *terra firma* again. Then he said—

"Monsieur Aronnax, the *Nautilus* is not lost; it will carry you yet into the midst of the marvels of the ocean. Our voyage is only begun, and I do not wish to be deprived so soon of the honor of your company."

"However, Captain Nemo," I replied, without noticing the ironical turn of his phrase, "the *Nautilus* ran aground in open sea. Now the tides are not strong in the Pacific; and if you cannot lighten the *Nautilus,* I do not see how it will be refloated."

"The tides are not strong in the Pacific: you are right there, Professor; but in Torres Straits, one finds still a difference of a meter and a half between the level of high and low seas. Today is January 4, and in five days the moon will be full. Now, I shall be very much astonished if that complaisant satellite does not raise these masses of water sufficiently, and render me a service that I should be indebted to her for."

Having said this, Captain Nemo, followed by his second-in-command re-descended to the interior of the *Nautilus.* As to the vessel, it moved not, and was immovable, as if the coralline polyps had already walled it up with their indestructible cement.

"Well, sir?" said Ned Land, who came up to me after the departure of the Captain.

"Well, friend Ned, we will wait patiently for the tide on the 9th; for it appears that the moon will have the goodness to set us afloat again."

"Really?"

"Really."

"And this captain is not going to weigh anchor at all, set his machines to work, or do anything at all?"

"The tide will suffice," answered Conseil, simply.

The Canadian looked at Conseil, then shrugged his shoulders. It was the seaman in him who was speaking.

"Sir, you may believe me when I tell you that this piece of iron will navigate neither on nor under the sea again; it is only fit to be sold for its weight. I think, therefore, that the time has come to part company with Captain Nemo."

"Friend Ned, I do not despair of this valiant *Nautilus,* as you do; and in four days we shall know what to think of the Pacific tides. Besides, flight might be possible if we were in sight of the English or Provençal coasts; but on the Papuan shores, it is another thing; and it will be time enough to come to that extremity if the *Nautilus* does not recover itself again, which I should look upon as a grave event."

"Can we not at least see how the land lays? There is an island; on that island there are trees; under those trees are terrestrial animals, bearers of cutlets and steaks, to which I would willingly get my teeth into!"

"In this, friend Ned is right," said Conseil, "and I agree with him. Could monsieur not obtain permission from his friend Captain Nemo to put us on land, if only so as not to lose the habit of treading on the solid parts of our planet?"

"I can ask him, but he will refuse."

"Will monsieur risk it?" asked Conseil, "and then we shall know how much to rely upon the captain's friendliness."

To my great surprise Captain Nemo gave me the permission I asked for, and he gave it very agreeably, without even exacting from me a promise to return to the vessel; but flight across New Guinea might be very perilous, and I should not have counseled Ned Land to attempt it. Better to be a prisoner on board the *Nautilus* than to fall into the hands of the natives of Papua.

The launch was put at our disposal the next morning. I did not seek to discover if Captain Nemo would accompany us. I even thought that no man of the crew would be sent with us, and that Ned Land alone would have the care of directing the boat. No matter: land was not more than two miles distant, and it was but play to the Canadian to conduct this light boat among the lines of reefs so fatal to larger ships.

The next day, January 5, the launch, its deck taken off, was lifted from its socket, and launched from the top of the platform. Two men sufficed for this operation. The oars were in the boat, and we only had to take our places.

At eight o'clock, armed with guns and hatchets, we got off the *Nautilus*. The sea was pretty calm; a slight breeze blew offshore. Conseil and I rowing, we sped along quickly, and Ned steered through the narrow passage between the breakers. The boat was easily handled, and moved rapidly.

Ned Land could not restrain his joy. He was like a prisoner that had escaped from prison, and knew not that it was necessary to re-enter it.

"Meat!" He repeated, "We are going to eat some meat; and what meat! Real game! There will still be no bread, though."

"I do not say that fish is not good; we must not abuse it; but a piece of fresh venison grilled on live coals, will agreeably vary our ordinary diet."

"Gourmand!" said Conseil, "he makes my mouth water."

"It remains to be seen," I said, "if these forests are full of game, and if the game is not such as will hunt the hunter himself."

"Well said, Monsieur Aronnax," replied the Canadian, whose teeth seemed sharpened like the edge of a hatchet; "but I will eat tiger—loin of tiger—if there is no other quadruped on this island."

"Friend Ned is making me uneasy about it," said Conseil.

"Whatever it may be," continued Ned Land, "every animal with four legs without feathers, or with two legs with feathers, will be saluted by my first shot."

"Good! Master Land is already becoming imprudent!"

"Never fear, Monsieur Aronnax," replied the Canadian; "keep rowing! I do not need twenty-five minutes to offer you a dish of my making."

At half past eight the *Nautilus'* boat ran softly aground, on a sand beach, after having happily passed the coral reef that surrounds the Island of Gueboroar.

---

[1]Nemo's name means "no one" in Latin. R.M.

◄ CHAPTER XXI ►

A FEW DAYS ON LAND

I was much impressed on touching land. Ned Land tried the soil with his feet, as if to take possession of it. Yet, it was only two months before that we had become, according to Captain Nemo, "passengers on board the *Nautilus*," but in reality, prisoners of its commander.

In a few minutes we were a gunshot from the beach. The soil was almost entirely madreporical, but certain beds of dried-up torrents, strewn with débris of granite, showed that this island was of primordial formation. The whole horizon was hidden behind a beautiful curtain of forests. Enormous trees, the trunks of which attained a height of two hundred feet, were tied to each other by garlands of vines, real natural hammocks, which a light breeze rocked. They were mimosas, ficuses, casuarinas, teaks, hibiscus, pedanus, and palm trees, mingled together in profusion; and under the shelter of their verdant vault, at the foot of their gigantic trunks, grew orchids, leguminous plants, and ferns.

But without noticing all these beautiful specimens of Papuan flora, the Canadian abandoned the agreeable for the useful. He discovered a coconut palm, beat down some of the fruit, broke them, and we drank the milk and ate the nutmeat, with a satisfaction that was a protest against the ordinary food on the *Nautilus.*

"Excellent!" said Ned Land.

"Exquisite!" replied Conseil.

"And I do not think," said the Canadian, "that Captain Nemo would object to our introducing a cargo of coconuts on board."

"I do not think he would, but he would not taste them."

"So much the worse for him," said Conseil.

"And so much the better for us," replied Ned Land. "There will be more for us."

"One word only, Master Land," I said to the harpooner, who was beginning to ravage another coconut tree. "Coconuts are good things, but before filling the launch with them, it would be wise to reconnoiter and see if the island does not produce some substance not less useful. Fresh vegetables would be welcome on board the *Nautilus.*"

"Monsieur is right," replied Conseil; "and I propose to reserve three places in our vessel, one for fruits, the other for vegetables, and the third for the venison, of which I have not yet seen the smallest specimen."

"Conseil, we must not despair," said the Canadian.

"Let us continue our excursion," I returned, "and lie in wait. Although the island seems uninhabited, it might still contain some individuals that would be easier to please than we on the nature of game."

"Ho! ho!" said Ned Land, moving his jaws significantly.

"Well, Ned!" cried Conseil.

"My word!" returned the Canadian, "I begin to understand the charms of cannibalism!"

"Ned! Ned! what are you saying?" replied Conseil, "you, a man-eater? I should not feel safe with you, especially as I share your cabin! Might I perhaps wake one day to find myself half devoured?"

"Friend Conseil, I like you much, but not enough to eat you unnecessarily."

"I would not trust you," replied Conseil. "Let's start. We must absolutely bring down some game to satisfy this cannibal, or else one of these fine mornings, monsieur will find only pieces of his servant to serve him."

While we were talking thus, we were penetrating the somber arches of the forest, and for two hours we surveyed it in all directions.

Chance rewarded our search for eatable vegetables, and one of the most useful products of the tropical zones furnished us with precious food that we missed on board. I would speak of the artocarpus: the breadfruit tree, very abundant on the island of Gueboroar; and I noticed chiefly the variety that is destitute of seeds, which bears in Malaya the name of "rima."

This tree was distinguished from others by its straight trunk, forty feet high; its summit, gracefully rounded and formed of large multi-lobed leaves, designated sufficiently to the eyes of a naturalist the artocarpus, or breadfruit, which has been very happily cultivated in the Mascarene Islands. From its mass of verdure stood out large globular fruit a decimeter wide, with a rough skin in a hexagonal pattern—a useful vegetable, with which Nature has graced the regions in which wheat is wanting, and which, without requiring any culture, gives fruit for eight months in the year.

Ned Land knew these fruits well. He had already eaten many during his numerous voyages, and he knew how to prepare its eatable part. Moreover, the sight of them excited his appetite, and he could contain himself no longer.

"Monsieur Aronnax," he said, "I shall die if I do not taste a little of this breadfruit pâte!"

"Taste it, friend Ned—taste it all you want. We are here to make experiments—make them."

"It won't take long," said the Canadian.

And provided with a lens, he lit a fire of dead wood, that crackled joyously. During this time, Conseil and I chose the best fruits of the artocarpus. Some had not then attained a sufficient degree of maturity and their skin covered a white but rather fibrous pulp. Others, the greater number yellow and gelatinous, waited only to be picked.

These fruits enclosed no kernel. Conseil brought a dozen to Ned Land, who placed them on a coal fire, after having cut them in thick slices, and while doing this kept saying—

"You will see, sir, how good this bread is."

"More so when one has been deprived of it so long," added Conseil.

"It is not even bread," Ned continued, "but a delicate pastry. You have never eaten any, Monsieur Aronnax?"

"No, Ned."

"Very well, prepare yourself for something succulent. If you do not come for more, I am no longer the king of harpooners!"

After some minutes, the part of the fruit that was exposed to the fire was completely roasted. The interior looked like a white pâte, a sort of soft crumb, the flavor of which was like that of an artichoke.

It must be confessed this bread was excellent, and I ate of it with great relish.

"Unfortunately," I said, "such paste will not keep fresh; and it appears useless to me to make any provision for the *Nautilus*."

"Why sir!" cried Ned Land, "you speak like a naturalist, but I am going to act like a baker. Gather some of the fruit, Conseil; we will take it on our return."

"And how do you prepare it?" I asked.

"By making a fermented paste with its pulp, which will keep any length of time without spoiling. When I wish to use it I will have it cooked in the kitchen on board; and, in spite of its slightly acid taste, you will find it excellent."

"Then, Ned, I see that nothing is needed except this bread."

"Yes, Professor," answered the Canadian, "we need fruit, or at least vegetables!"

"Then let us seek the fruit and vegetables."

When our gathering was over we set out to complete this "terrestrial" dinner.

Our search was not a vain one, and towards noon we had made an ample provision of bananas. These delicious products of the torrid zone ripen all through the year, and the Malaysians, who have given them the name of "pisang", eat them raw. With these bananas we gathered enormous "jaks" with a very decided taste, savory mangos, and pineapples of an incredible size. But this gathering took up a great deal of our time, which there was no cause to regret.

Conseil watched Ned continually. The harpooner marched on in front and during his walk across the forest he gathered with a sure hand the excellent fruit with which to complete his provisions.

"You do not want anything more, Ned, do you?"

"Hum!" said the Canadian.

"Why, what have you to complain of?"

"All these vegetables cannot constitute a meal," answered Ned. "They are the end of a meal, they are only dessert. But where is the soup? Where is the roast?"

"Yes," said I, "Ned had promised us cutlets, which seemed to me very problematic."

"Sir," answered the Canadian, "our sport is not only not ended, but it is not even begun. Patience! We shall end by meeting with some animal or bird, and if it is not in this place, it will be in another. . . ."

"And if it is not today, it will be tomorrow," added Conseil, "for we must not go too far away. I vote to go back to the launch now."

"What, already?" cried Ned.

"We must return before night," I said.

"What time is it now?" asked the Canadian.

"Two o'clock at least," replied Conseil.

"How time flies on firm ground!" sighed Ned Land, regretfully.

"Let us be off," replied Conseil.

We returned through the forest, and completed our collection by a raid upon the cabbage palms, that we gathered from the tops of the trees, little beans that I recognized as the "abrou" of the Malays, and yams of a superior quality.

We were overloaded when we reached the boat. But Ned Land did not find his provision sufficient. Fate, however, favored us. Just as we were pushing off, he perceived several trees, from twenty-five to thirty feet high, a species of palm tree. These trees, as valuable as the bread-fruit, justly are reckoned among the most useful products of Malaya.

There were sago trees, vegetables that grow without cultivation, and reproduce themselves like blackberries by their shoots and seeds.

Ned Land knew how to treat these trees. He took his hatchet, and using it vigorously, he soon brought two or three sago trees level with the ground, their ripeness being recognized by the white powder dusted over their branches.

I watched him more with the eyes of a naturalist than those of a famished man. He began by stripping the bark from each trunk, an inch thick, which covered a network of long fibers, forming inextricable knots, that a sort of gummy flour cemented. This flour was sago, an edible substance which forms the principal food of the Melanesian population.

Ned Land was content for the time being to cut these trunks in pieces, as he would have done for firewood, meaning to extract the flour later on, and to pass it through a cloth in order to separate it from its fibrous ligaments, to leave it to dry in the sun, and let it harden in molds.

At last, at five o'clock in the evening, loaded with all our riches, we quitted the shore, and half an hour later we hailed the *Nautilus*. No one appeared on our arrival. The enormous iron-plated cylinder seemed deserted. The provisions unloaded, I descended to my chamber. There I found my supper ready. I ate it and afterwards slept soundly.

The next day, January 6, nothing new on board. Not a sound inside, not a sign of life. The launch rested alongside, in the same place in which we had left it. We resolved to return to the island. Ned Land hoped to be more fortunate than on the day before with regard to the hunt, and wished to visit another part of the forest.

At sunrise we set off. The boat, carried on by the waves that flowed to shore, reached the island in a few minutes.

We landed, and thinking that it was better to give in to the Canadian, we followed Ned Land, whose long limbs threatened to distance us. He wound up the coast towards the west: then, fording some torrents, he gained a high plain that was bordered with admirable forests. Some kingfishers were prowling along the watercourses, but they would not let themselves be approached. Their circumspection proved to me that these birds knew what to expect from bipeds of our species, and I concluded that, if the island was not inhabited, at least human beings occasionally frequented it.

After crossing a rather large meadow, we arrived at the skirts of a little wood that was enlivened by the songs and flight of a large number of birds.

"There are only birds," said Conseil.

"But they are eatable!" replied the harpooner.

"No, friend Ned, for I see only simple parrots there."

"Friend Conseil," said Ned, gravely, "the parrot is like pheasant to those who have nothing else to eat."

"And," I added, "this bird, suitably prepared, is worth knife and fork."

Indeed, under the thick foliage of this wood, a world of parrots were flying from branch to branch, only needing a careful education to speak the human language. For the moment, they were chattering in company with parakeets of all colors, and grave cockatoos, who seemed to meditate upon some philosophical problem, while brilliant red lories passed like a piece of bunting carried away by the breeze; amidst the noisy flutter of kalaos and papuas, with the finest shades of azure, and in all a variety of winged things most charming to behold, but few eatable.

However, a bird peculiar to these lands, and which has never passed the limits of the Arrou and Papuan islands, was wanting in this collection. But fortune reserved me the pleasure of seeing it before long.

After passing through a moderately thick copse, we found a plain obstructed with bushes. I saw then those magnificent birds, whose long feathers oblige them to fly against the wind. Their undulating flight, graceful aerial curves, and the shading of their colors, attracted and charmed one's eyes. I had no trouble in recognizing them.

"Birds of paradise!" I exclaimed.

"Order of sparrows, section of clystornores," answered Conseil.

"Family of partridges?" asked Ned.

"I do not think so, Mr. Land. Nevertheless, I am counting on your skill to catch one of these charming products of tropical nature!"

"I will try, Professor, although I'm more used to handling a harpoon than a gun."

The Malays, who carry on a great trade in these birds with the Chinese, have several means that we could not employ for taking them. Sometimes they put snares at the top of high trees that the birds of paradise prefer to frequent. Sometimes they catch them with a tenacious glue that paralyzes their movements. They even go as far as to poison the fountains that the birds generally drink from. But we were obliged to fire at them during flight, which gave us few chances to bring them down; and indeed, we vainly exhausted part of our ammunition.

About eleven o'clock in the morning, the first ridge of mountains that form the center of the island was traversed, and we had killed nothing. Hunger drove us on. The hunters had relied on the products of the chase, and they were wrong. Happily Conseil, to his great surprise, made a double shot and secured breakfast. He brought down a white pigeon and a wood-pigeon, which, cleverly plucked and suspended from a skewer, was roasted before a red fire of dead wood. While these interesting birds were cooking, Ned prepared the fruit of the artocarpus. Then the pigeons were devoured to the bones, and declared excellent. The nutmeg, with which they are in the habit of stuffing their crops, flavors their flesh and renders it delicious eating.

"As good," declared Conseil, "as if they had been stuffed with truffles!"

"Now, Ned, what are you missing?"

"Some four-footed game, Mr. Aronnax. All these pigeons are only hors d'oeuvres, and trifles; and until I have killed an animal possessing cutlets, I shall not be content!"

"Nor I, Ned, if I do not catch a bird of paradise."

"Let us continue hunting," replied Conseil. "Let us go towards the sea. We have arrived at the first slopes of the mountains, and I think we had better regain the region of forests."

That was sensible advice, and was followed out. After walking for one hour, we had attained a forest of sago trees. Some inoffensive serpents glided away from us. The birds of paradise fled at our approach, and truly I despaired of getting near one, when Conseil, who was walking in front, suddenly bent down, uttered a triumphal cry, and came back to me bringing a magnificent specimen.

"Ah! bravo, Conseil!"

"Monsieur is very kind."

"No, my boy; you have made a master stroke. To take one of these living birds, and carry it in your hand!"

"If monsieur will examine it, he will see that I have not deserved great merit."

"Why, Conseil?"

"Because this bird is as drunk as a quail."

"Drunk?"

"Monsieur is correct; drunk with the nutmegs that it devoured under the nutmeg tree, under which I found it. See, friend Ned, see the monstrous effects of intemperance!"

"A thousand devils!" exclaimed the Canadian sarcastically, "considering I have drunk so much gin for two months, you have to reproach me!"

However, I examined the curious bird. Conseil was right. The bird, drunk with the juice, was quite powerless. It could not fly; it could hardly walk. But that did not bother me. I gave it time to recover from the effects of the nutmeg.

This bird belonged to the most beautiful of the eight species that are found in Papua and in the neighboring islands. It was a "large emerald," the most rare kind. It measured three decimeters in length, about one foot. Its head was comparatively small, its eyes placed near the opening of the beak, and also small. But its shades of color were beautiful: a yellow beak, brown feet and claws, nut-colored wings with purple tips, pale yellow at the back of the neck and head, and emerald color at the throat, chestnut on the breast and belly. Two horned downy plumes rose from below the tail, that consisted of long light feathers of admirable fineness. They completed the whole of this marvellous bird, that the natives have poetically named the "bird of the sun."

I much wished to be able to take this superb specimen back to Paris, in order that I might make a present of it to the Jardin des Plantes, which does not possess a single living one.

"Is it so rare, then?" asked the Canadian, in the tone of a hunter who does not care much for it as game, from the point of view of his art.

"Very rare, my brave companion, and, above all, very difficult to take alive, and even dead these birds are the object of an important traffic. Hence the imaginative natives fabricate them just as false pearls and diamonds are fabricated."

"What!" cried Conseil, "they make false birds of paradise?"

"Yes, Conseil."

"Does monsieur know how the natives set about it?"

"Perfectly. These birds, during the eastern monsoon, lose the magnificent feathers which surround their tails, which are called subulate feathers by naturalists. The counterfeiters gather up these feathers, which they skilfully fasten onto some poor parrot previously mutilated. Then they dye the sutures, varnish the bird, and send to the museums and collectors of Europe the product of their peculiar industry."

"Well!" said Ned Land, "if they don't have the bird they at least have its feathers, and as they don't want to eat it, I see no harm!"

But if my wishes were satisfied by the possession of the bird of paradise, the Canadian's were not yet. Happily about two o'clock Ned Land brought down a magnificent pig, of the kind the natives call "bari-outang." The animal came in time for us to procure real quadruped meat, and he was well received. Ned Land was very proud of his shot. The pig, hit by the electric ball, fell stone dead.

The Canadian skinned and cleaned it properly, after having taken half-a-dozen cutlets, destined to furnish us with a grilled repast in the evening. Then the hunt was resumed, which was again to be enlivened by Ned and Conseil's exploits.

Indeed, the two friends, beating the bushes, roused a herd of kangaroos, that fled and bounded along on their elastic paws. But these animals did not take flight so rapidly but what the electric capsule could stop their course.

"Ah, Professor!" cried Ned Land, who was carried away by the delights of the chase, "what excellent game, especially stewed! What a supply for the *Nautilus!* Two! Three! Five down! And to think that we shall eat that flesh, and that the idiots on board shall not have a crumb!"

I think that, in the excess of his joy, the Canadian, if he had not talked so much, would have killed them all! But he contented himself with single dozen of these interesting marsupials. "Which," said Conseil, "make up the first order of aplacental mammals."

These animals were small. They were a species of those "kangaroo rabbits" that live habitually in the hollows of trees, and whose speed is extreme; but they are moderately fat, and furnish, at least, estimable food. We were very satisfied with the results of the hunt. Happy Ned proposed to return to this enchanting island the next day, for he wished to depopulate it of all the eatable quadrupeds. But he reckoned without his host.

At six o'clock in the evening we had regained the shore, our boat was moored to the usual place. The *Nautilus,* like a long reef, emerged from the waves two miles from the beach. Ned Land, without waiting, occupied himself about the important business of dinner. He understood all about cooking well. The "bari-outang," grilled on the coals, soon scented the air with a delicious odor.

But here I perceived that I was walking in the footsteps of the Canadian. I, voicing ecstasy about freshly grilled pork! May I be pardoned as I pardon Master Land, and for the same reasons!

Indeed, the dinner was excellent. Two wood pigeons completed this extraordinary menu. The sago pâte, the breadfruit, some mangoes, half-a-dozen pineapples, and the liquor fermented from some coconuts, overjoyed us. I remember that my friends failed to express themselves with their usual directness.

"Suppose we do not return to the *Nautilus* this evening?" said Conseil.

"Suppose we never return?" added Ned Land.

Just then a stone fell at our feet, and cut short the harpooner's proposition.

◄ CHAPTER XXII ►

CAPTAIN NEMO'S THUNDERBOLT

We looked at the edge of the forest without rising, my hand stopping in the action of putting it to my mouth, Ned Land's, of course, completing its action.

"Stones do not fall from the sky," remarked Conseil, "or, when they do, they merit the name meteorite."

A second stone, carefully aimed, that made a savory pigeon's leg fall from Conseil's hand, gave still more weight to his observation. We all three arose, shouldered our guns, and were ready to reply to any attack.

"Are they apes?" cried Ned Land.

"Very nearly," replied Conseil, "they are savages."

"To the boat!" I said, hurrying to the sea.

It was indeed necessary to beat a retreat, for about twenty natives armed with bows and slings, appeared on the skirts of a copse that masked the horizon to the right, hardly a hundred steps from us.

Our boat was moored about ten fathoms from us. The savages approached us, not running, but making hostile demonstrations. Stones and arrows fell thickly.

Ned Land had not wished to leave his provisions; and, in spite of his imminent danger, carrying his pig on one side, and kangaroos on the other, he went tolerably fast. In two minutes we were on the shore. To load the boat with provisions and arms, to push it out to sea, and ship the oars, was the work of an instant. We had not gone two cables' lengths, when a hundred savages, howling and gesticulating, entered the water up to their waists. I watched to see if their appearance would attract some men from the *Nautilus* on to the platform. But no. The enormous machine, lying offshore, was absolutely deserted.

Twenty minutes later we were on board. The hatches were open. After making the boat fast, we entered into the interior of the *Nautilus.*

I descended to the salon, from whence I heard some chords of music. Captain Nemo was there, bending over his organ, and plunged into a musical ecstasy.

"Captain!"

He did not hear me.

"Captain!" I said again, touching his hand.

He shuddered, and turning round, said, "Ah! it is you, Professor? Well, have you had a good hunt, have you botanized successfully?"

"Yes, Captain; but we have also unfortunately brought a troop of bipeds with us, whose vicinity troubles me."

"What bipeds?"

"Savages."

"Savages!" he echoed, ironically. "So you are astonished, Professor, at having set foot on a strange land and finding savages? Savages! Where are there not any? Besides, are they worse than any others, these whom you call savages?"

"But, Captain. . . ."

"For my part, I have met with them everywhere."

"Well," I answered, "if you do not wish to receive any on board the *Nautilus,* you will do well to take some precautions."

"Calm yourself, Professor. There is nothing to worry about."

"But there are a large number of natives."

"How many have you counted?"

"A hundred at least."

"Monsieur Aronnax," replied Captain Nemo, placing his fingers on the organ keys, "if all the natives of Papua are assembled on that shore, the *Nautilus* would still have nothing to fear from their attacks!"

The Captain's fingers were then running over the keys of the instrument, and I noticed that he touched only the black keys, which gave to his melodies an essentially Scotch character. Soon he had forgotten my presence, and had plunged into another reverie that I did not seek to disturb.

I went up on to the platform:—night had already fallen; for, in this low latitude, the sun sets rapidly and without twilight. I could only see the island indistinctly; but the numerous fires, lighted on the beach, showed that the natives did not think of leaving it.

I was alone for several hours, sometimes thinking of the natives—but without any dread of them, for the imperturbable confidence of the Captain was catching—sometimes forgetting them to admire the splendors of the night in the tropics. My thoughts went to France, that these zodiacal stars would be shining over in some hours' time. The moon shone in the midst of the constellations of the zenith.

I then thought that this faithful and complaisant satellite would come back tomorrow to this same place, to attract the waves and tear the *Nautilus* away from its coral bed. About midnight, seeing that all was tranquil on the dark water, as well as under the trees on shore, I went down to my cabin and went peacefully to sleep.

The night slipped away without any mischance, the islanders frightened no doubt at the sight of a monster aground in the bay. The hatches were open, and would have offered an easy access to the interior of the *Nautilus*.

At six o'clock in the morning of the 8th of January, I went up on to the platform. The dawn was breaking. The island soon showed itself through the dissipating mists, first the shore, then the summits.

The natives were there, more numerous than on the day before—five or six hundred perhaps. Some of them, profiting by the low water, had come on to the coral heads, at less than two cable-lengths from the *Nautilus*. I distinguished them easily; they were true Papuans, with athletic figures, men of good race, large high foreheads, noses large, but not flat, and white teeth. Their woolly hair, with a reddish tinge, showed off on their black shining bodies like those of the Nubians. From the lobes of their ears, cut and distended, hung chaplets of bones. Most of these savages were naked. Among them I noticed some women, dressed from the hips to knees in a veritable crinoline of herbs, supported by a vegetable waistband. Some chiefs had ornamented their necks with a crescent and collars of glass beads, red and white. Nearly all were armed with bows, arrows, and shields, and carried on their shoulders a sort of net containing those round stones which they cast from their slings with great skill.

One of these chiefs, rather near to the *Nautilus,* examined it attentively. He was, perhaps, a "mado" of high rank, for he was draped in a mat of banana leaves, notched round the edges, and set off with brilliant colors.

I could easily have killed this native, who was within short range; but I thought it was better to wait for real hostile demonstrations. Between Europeans and savages, it is proper for Europeans to retaliate, but not to attack.

During low water the natives roamed about near the *Nautilus,* but were not troublesome; I heard them frequently repeat the word "assai," and by their gestures I understood that they invited me to go on land, an invitation that I declined.

So that, on that day, the launch did not push off, to the great displeasure of Master Land, who could not complete his provisions. This adroit Canadian instead employed his time in preparing the viands and meat that he had brought off the island. As for the savages, they returned to the shore about eleven o'clock in the morning, as soon as the coral tops began to disappear under the rising tide; but I saw their numbers had increased considerably on the shore. Probably they came from the neighboring islands, or very likely from the Papuan mainland. However, I had not seen a single native canoe.

Having nothing better to do, I thought of dragging these beautiful limpid waters, under which I saw a profusion of shells, zoöphytes, and marine plants. Moreover, it was the last day that the *Nautilus* would be in these parts, if the tide floated it the next day, according to Captain Nemo's promise.

I therefore called Conseil, who brought me a little drag net very like those for oyster fishing.

"What about these savages?" Conseil asked me. "If it does not displease monsieur for me to say so, they do not seem to be very cruel."

"They are cannibals, however, my boy."

"It is possible to be a cannibal and an honest man," answered Conseil, "as it is possible to be a gourmand and honest. One does not exclude the other."

"Good, Conseil! I grant you that there are honest cannibals, and that they honestly devour their prisoners. But as I do not care for being eaten, even honestly, I shall keep on my guard—even if the commander of the *Nautilus* does not appear to be taking any precautions. Now to work!"

For two hours we fished unceasingly, but without bringing up any rarities. The drag was filled with midas-ears, harps, melanias, and particularly the most beautiful hammershells I have ever seen. We also brought up some holothurians, pearl oysters, and a dozen little turtles, that were reserved for the pantry on board.

But just when I expected it least I put my hand on a wonder, I might say a natural deformity, very rarely met with. Conseil had just brought up the drag, and his net was filled with various ordinary shells, when, all at once, he saw me plunge my arm quickly into the net, to draw out a shell, and heard me utter a conchological cry, that is to say, the most piercing cry that human throat can utter.

"What is the matter with monsieur?" he asked, in surprise. "Has monsieur been bitten?"

"No, my boy; but I would willingly have given a finger for my discovery!"

"What discovery?"

"This shell," I said, holding up the object of my triumph.

"It is only an olive porphyry, genus olive, order of the pectinibranchidæ, class of gastropods, sub-class of mollusca . . . ."

"Yes, Conseil; but instead of spiralling from right to left, this olive turns from left to right."

"Is it possible?" cried Conseil.

"Yes, my boy; it is a left-handed shell!"

"A left-handed shell!" repeated Conseil, with a palpitating heart.

"Look at its spiral!"

"Ah, monsieur may believe me," said Conseil, taking the precious shell with a trembling hand, "I have never felt an emotion like this!"

And there was cause for emotion! It is well known, as the naturalists have caused to be remarked, that right-handedness is a Law of Nature. The stars and their satellites in their rotatory movements go from left to right. Man oftener uses his right than his left hand, and consequently his instruments, apparatus, staircases, locks, watchsprings, etc., are put together so as to be used from right to left. Nature has generally followed the same law in the spiral of its shells; they are all dexter, with rare exceptions, and when it happens that their spiral is sinister amateur collectors pay their weight in gold.

Conseil and I were absorbed in the contemplation of our treasure, and I was promising myself to enrich the museum with it, when a stone unfortunately thrown by a native, broke the precious object in Conseil's hand.

I uttered a cry of despair! Conseil took up his gun, and aimed at a savage who was poising his sling ten meters from him. I tried to stop him, but his blow took effect, and broke the bracelet of amulets which encircled the arm of the savage.

"Conseil!" I cried, "Conseil!"

"What? Does not monsieur see that the cannibal has commenced the attack?"

"A shell is not worth the life of a man," said I.

"Ah! the scoundrel!" cried Conseil, "I would rather he had broken my shoulder!"

Conseil was sincere, but I was not of his opinion. However the situation had changed some minutes before, and we had not noticed it. A score of canoes surrounded the *Nautilus*. These canoes, scooped out of the trunks of trees, long, narrow, well adapted for speed, were balanced by means of a long bamboo pontoon, which floated on the water. They were managed by skilful half-naked paddlers and I watched their advance with some uneasiness.

It was evident that these Papuans had already had dealings with Europeans, and knew their ships. But this long iron cylinder anchored in the bay, without masts or chimney, what could they think of it? Nothing good, for at first they kept at a respectful distance. However, seeing it motionless, by degrees they took courage, and sought to familiarize themselves with it. Now, this familiarity was precisely what it was necessary to avoid. Our arms which were noiseless, could only produce a moderate effect on the savages, who have little respect for aught but noisy things. The thunderbolt without the reverberations of thunder would frighten man but little, though the danger lies in the lightning, not in the noise.

At this moment the canoes approached the *Nautilus,* and a shower of arrows fell on her.

"The devil! It hails!" said Conseil, "and perhaps it is poisoned hail!"

"I must tell Captain Nemo," I said, going down through the hatch.

I went to the salon, but found no one there. I ventured to knock at the door that opened into the captain's room. "Come in," was the answer.

I entered, and found Captain Nemo deep in algebraical calculations in which X and other signs were not wanting.

"I am disturbing you?" said I, for courtesy sake.

"That is true, Monsieur Aronnax," replied the Captain; "but I think you have serious reasons for wishing to see me?"

"Very serious ones; the natives are surrounding us in their canoes, and in a few minutes we shall certainly be attacked by many hundreds of savages."

"Ah!" said Captain Nemo, quietly, "they are come with their canoes?"

"Yes, sir."

"Well, Professor, we must close the hatches."

"Exactly, and I came to say to you. . . ."

"Nothing can be more simple," said Captain Nemo. And pressing an electric button, he transmitted an order to the ship's crew.

"It is all done, sir" said he, after some moments. "The launch is secure, and the hatches are closed. You do not fear, I imagine, that these gentlemen could stave in walls on which the balls of your frigate have had no effect?"

"No, Captain; but a danger still exists."

"What is that, sir?"

"It is that tomorrow, at about this hour, we must open the hatches to renew the air of the *Nautilus.* . . ."

"Exactly, Professor, the *Nautilus* must breathe, like a whale."

"Now, if, at this moment, the Papuans should occupy the platform, I do not see how you could prevent them from entering."

"Then, sir, you suppose that they will board us?"

"I am certain of it."

"Well, sir, let them come. I see no reason for hindering them. After all, these Papuans are poor creatures, and I am unwilling that my visit to the Island of Gueboroar should cost the life of a single one of these wretches."

Upon that I was going away; but Captain Nemo detained me, and asked me to sit down by him. He questioned me with interest about our excursions on shore, and our hunting; and seemed not to understand the craving for meat that possessed the Canadian. Then the conversation turned on various subjects, and without being more communicative, Captain Nemo showed himself more amiable.

Among other things, we happened to speak of the situation of the *Nautilus,* run aground in exactly the same spot in the strait where Dumont d'Urville was nearly lost. Apropos of this—

"This d'Urville was one of your great sailors," said the Captain, to me, "one of your most intelligent navigators. He is the Captain Cook of you Frenchmen. Unfortunate man of science! After having braved the icebergs of the South Pole, the coral reefs of Oceania, the cannibals of the Pacific, to perish miserably in a railway accident! If this energetic man could have reflected during the last moments of his life, what must have been uppermost in his last thoughts, do you suppose?"

So speaking, Captain Nemo seemed moved, and his emotion gave me a better opinion of him. Then, chart in hand, we reviewed the travels of the French navigator, his voyages of circumnavigation, his double attempt at the South Pole, which led to the discovery of Adelaide Land and Louis Philippe Land, and fixing the hydrographical bearings of the principal islands of Oceania.

"That which your d'Urville has done on the surface of the seas," said Captain Nemo, "that have I done under them, and more easily, more completely than he. The *Astrolabe* and the *Zélée*, incessantly tossed about by the hurricanes, could not be worth the *Nautilus*, quiet laboratory that she is, motionless in the midst of the waters."

"However, Captain," I said, "there is one point of resemblance between the corvettes of Dumont d'Urville and the *Nautilus.*"

"What is that, sir?"

"Like them, the *Nautilus* is stranded."

"The *Nautilus* is not stranded," replied Captain Nemo coldly. "The *Nautilus* was built to lie on the sea floor, and the difficult work, the maneuver that d'Urville was obliged to have recourse to, to get his corvettes afloat again, I shall not have to undertake. The *Astrolabe* and the *Zélée* nearly perished, but the *Nautilus* runs no risk. Tomorrow, at the stated day and hour, the tide will quietly raise it, and it will recommence its navigation through the seas."

"Captain," I said, "I do not doubt. . . ."

"Tomorrow," added the captain, rising, "tomorrow, at twenty minutes to three P.M., the *Nautilus* shall float, and leave the Strait of Torres uninjured."

Having curtly pronounced these words, Captain Nemo bowed slightly. This was to dismiss me, and I went back to my room.

There I found Conseil, who wished to know the result of my interview with the Captain.

"My boy," said I, "when I feigned to believe that his *Nautilus* was threatened by the natives of Papua, the Captain answered me very sarcastically. I have but one thing to say to you: Have confidence in him, and go to sleep in peace."

"Has monsieur no need of my services?"

"No, my friend. What is Ned Land doing?"

"If monsieur will excuse me," answered Conseil, "friend Ned is busy making a kangaroo pâté, which will be a marvel."

I remained alone, and went to bed, but slept indifferently. I heard the noise of the savages, who stamped on the platform uttering deafening cries. The night passed thus, the crew maintaining their usual inertia. The presence of these cannibals affected them no more than the soldiers of a fortress care for the ants that crawl over its front.

At six in the morning I rose. The hatches had not been opened. The inner air was not renewed, but the reservoirs, filled ready for any emergency, were now resorted to, and discharged several cubic meters of oxygen into the exhausted atmosphere of the *Nautilus.*

I worked in my room till noon, without having seen Captain Nemo, even for an instant. On board no preparations for departure were visible.

I waited still some time, then went into the large salon. The clock marked half past two. In ten minutes it would be high tide: and, if Captain Nemo had not made a rash promise, the *Nautilus* would be immediately set free. If not, many months would pass before she could leave her bed of coral.

However, some warning vibrations began to be felt in the hull of the vessel. I heard its sides grating against the rough calcareous bottom of the coral reef.

At twenty-five minutes to three, Captain Nemo appeared in the salon.

"We are going to start," said he.

"Ah!" replied I.

"I have given the order to open the hatches."

"And the Papuans?"

"The Papuans?" answered Captain Nemo, slightly shrugging his shoulders.

"Will they not come inside the *Nautilus?*

"How?"

"Only by entering the hatches you have opened."

"Monsieur Aronnax," quietly answered Captain Nemo, "they will not enter the hatches of the *Nautilus* in that way, even if they were open."

I looked at the Captain.

"You do not understand?" said he.

"Hardly."

"Well, come and you will see."

I directed my steps towards the central staircase. There Ned Land and Conseil were watching with curiosity some of the ship's crew, who were opening the hatches, while cries of rage and fearful vociferations resounded outside.

The hatches were opened from the outside. Twenty horrible faces appeared. But the first native who placed his hand on the stair-rail was struck by some invisible force, I know not what, and fled, uttering the most fearful cries, and making the most extraordinary gambols.

Ten of his companions followed him. They met with the same fate.

Conseil was in ecstasy. Ned Land, carried away by his violent instincts, rushed on to the staircase. But the moment he seized the rail with both hands, he, in his turn, was overthrown.

"A thousand devils! I've been struck by lightning!" he cried.

This explained all. It was no rail, but a metallic cable, charged with electricity sent from the batteries, communicating with the platform. Whoever touched it felt a powerful shock—and this shock would have been mortal, if Captain Nemo had discharged into the conductor the whole force of the current. It might truly be said that between his assailants and himself he had stretched a barrier of electricity which none could pass with impunity.

Meanwhile, the exasperated Papuans had beaten a retreat, paralyzed with terror. As for us, half laughing, we consoled and rubbed the unfortunate Ned Land, who swore like one possessed.

But, at this moment, the *Nautilus,* raised by the last waves of the tide, left her coral bed exactly at the fortieth minute fixed by the captain. Her screw swept the waters slowly and majestically. Her speed increased gradually, and sailing on the surface of the ocean, she left safe and sound the dangerous passes of the Straits of Torres.

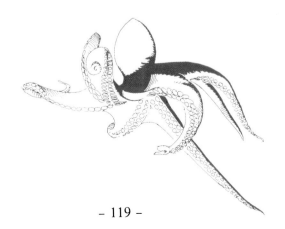

◄ **CHAPTER XXIII** ►

"AEGRI SOMNIA"—BITTER DREAMS

he following day, 10th of January, the *Nautilus* continued her underwater course, but with such remarkable speed that I could not estimate it at less that thirty-five miles an hour. The rapidity of her screw was such that I could neither follow nor count its revolutions. When I reflected that this marvellous electric agent, after having afforded motion, heat, and light to the *Nautilus,* still protected her from outward attack, and transformed her into an ark of safety, which no profane hand might touch without being thunderstricken, my admiration was unbounded, and that admiration extended from the structure to the engineer who had called it into existence.

Our course was directly to the west, and on the 11th of January we doubled Cape Wessel, situated in 135° longitude, and 10° north latitude, which forms the east point of the Gulf of Carpentaria. The reefs were still numerous, but not so close together, and marked on the chart with extreme precision. The *Nautilus* easily avoided the breakers of Money Reef to port, and the Victoria Reefs to starboard, at 130° longitude, and on the tenth parallel which we strictly followed.

On the 13th of January, Captain Nemo arrived in the Sea of Timor, and recognized the island of that name in 122° longitude. This island, the surface of which measures 1,625 square leagues, is governed by rajahs. These princes call themselves sons of crocodiles—that is to say, issues of the highest origin to which a human being can pretend. Their scaly ancestors swarm in the rivers of the islands, and are the objects of particular veneration. They are protected, spoiled, worshipped, fed; young girls are offered to them to graze upon, and woe to the stranger who lays hands on one of these sacred lizards.

But the *Nautilus* had nothing to do with these ugly animals. Timor was only visible for an instant at noon, while the first officer took our bearings. I likewise only caught a glimpse of Rotti Island, that forms a part of the group, and of which the women have a well-established reputation for beauty in Malaysian markets.

From this point, the direction of the *Nautilus* in latitude turned towards the southwest. Her bow was set for the Indian Ocean. Where would the fancy of Captain Nemo carry us next? Would he return to the coast or Asia? Or would he approach again the shores of Europe? Improbable conjectures both, for a man who fled from inhabited continents! Would he then descend to the south? Was he going to double the Cape of Good Hope, then Cape Horn, and finally go as far as the antarctic pole? Would he come back at last to the Pacific, where his *Nautilus* could sail free and independently? The future would show us.

After having skirted the reefs of Cartier, Hibernia, Seringapatam, and Scott, last efforts of the solid against the liquid element, on the 14th of January we lost sight of land altogether. The speed of the *Nautilus* was considerably abated, and, with irregular course, she sometimes swam in the depths of the waters, sometimes floated on the surface.

During this period of the voyage, Captain Nemo made some interesting experiments on the varied temperature of the sea, at different levels. Under ordinary conditions, these observations are made by means of rather complicated instruments, and with somewhat doubtful results, by means of thermometrical sounding-leads, the glasses often breaking under the pressure of the water. Or if an apparatus is based on the variations of the resistance of metals to electric current, the results so obtained could not be correctly controlled. On the contrary, Captain Nemo went himself to test the temperature in the depths of the sea, and his thermometer, placed in communication with the different levels of water, gave him the required information immediately and accurately.

It was thus that, either by flooding her reservoirs, or by descending obliquely by means of her inclined planes, the *Nautilus* successively attained the depth of three, four, five, seven, nine, and ten thousand meters, and the final result of this experience was that the sea at a depth of one thousand meters, preserved an average temperature of four and a half degrees (cent.) at all latitudes.

I followed these observations with the most lively interest. Captain Nemo studied them passionately. I often asked myself, to what purpose did he make these observations? Was it for the good of his fellow creatures? It was not probable, for one day his work must perish with him in some unknown sea, unless he destined the results of his experiments for me. But that was to admit that my strange voyage would have to end, and this end I did not yet perceive.

However that may be, Captain Nemo told me of different calculations obtained by him which established the relative density of water in the principal seas of the globe. From that communication I drew some personal information which was not at all scientific.

It was during the morning of the 15th of January. The captain, with whom I was walking on the platform, asked me if I knew the different densities of seawater. I answered in the negative, and added that rigorous observations were lacking to science on the subject.

"I have made those observations," he said to me, "and I can affirm that they are correct."

"That may be," I answered, "but the *Nautilus* is a world in itself, and the secrets of its scientists do not reach the earth."

"You are right, Professor," he answered after a short silence, "it is a world in itself. It is as much a stranger to the world as those planets that accompany this globe round the sun, and the world will never know the work of the scientists who live on Jupiter and Saturn. Still, as chance has united our two lives, I will give you the result of my observations."

"I shall be glad to hear it, Captain."

"You know, Professor, that seawater is denser than fresh water, but that its density is not uniform. In fact, if I represent by 1 the density of fresh water, I find a density of 1.028 for the waters of the Atlantic, 1.026 for those of the Pacific, 1.030 for those of the Mediterranean—"

"Ah!" I thought, "he does venture into the Mediterranean!"

"And 1.018 for the waters of the Ionian Sea, and 1.020 for those of the Adriatic."

Decidedly the *Nautilus* did not avoid the frequented seas of Europe, and I hence concluded that it would take us—perhaps before long—towards more civilized lands. I thought that Ned Land would learn this detail with very natural satisfaction.

We passed several days in making all sorts of experiments on the saltiness of the sea at different depths, on its electrical conductivity, color, transparency, and in all of them Captain Nemo displayed an ingenuity which was only equalled by his graciousness toward me. Then, for some days, I saw him no longer, and again remained isolated on board.

On the 16th of January, the *Nautilus* seemed becalmed, only a few meters beneath the surface of the waves. Her electric apparatus remained inactive, and her motionless screw left her to drift at the mercy of the currents. I supposed that the crew was occupied with interior repairs, rendered necessary by the violence of the mechanical movements of the machine.

My companions and I then witnessed a curious spectacle. The panels of the salon were open, and as the beacon light of the *Nautilus* was not in action, a dim obscurity reigned in the midst of the waters. A stormy sky that was obscured by dark clouds lent but a murky light to the depths. I observed the state of the sea under these conditions, and the largest fish appeared to me no more than scarcely defined shadows, when the *Nautilus* found herself suddenly transported into full light. I thought at first the beacon had been lighted, and was casting its electric radiance into the liquid mass. I was mistaken, and after a rapid survey, perceived my error.

The *Nautilus* floated in the midst of a phosphorescent bed, which, in this obscurity, became quite dazzling. It was produced by myriads of luminous animalculæ, whose brilliancy was increased as they glided over the metallic hull of the vessel. I was surprised by lightning in the midst of these luminous sheets, as though they had been rivulets of lead melted in an ardent furnace, or metallic masses brought to a white heat, so that, by force of contrast, certain portions of light appeared to cast a shadow in the midst of the general ignition, from which all shade seemed banished. No; this was not the calm radiation of our ordinary lightning. There was unusual life and vigor; this was truly living light!

In reality, it was an infinite agglomeration of colored infusoria, of veritable globules of diaphanous jelly, provided with thread-like tentacles, and of which as many as twenty-five thousand have been counted in less than thirty cubic centimeters, or about one ounce, of water; and their light was increased by the glimmering peculiar to the jellyfish, starfish, pholades, aurelia, and other phosphorescent zoöphytes, impregnated by the grease of the organic matter decomposed by the sea, and, perhaps, the mucus secreted by the fish.

During several hours the *Nautilus* floated in these brilliant waves, and our admiration increased as we watched the marine monsters playing among themselves like salamanders. I saw there, in the midst of this fire that did not burn, the swift and elegant porpoise (the indefatigable clown of the ocean), and some swordfish, three meters long, those prophetic heralds of the hurricane, whose formidable sword would now and then strike the glass windows of the salon. Then appeared the smaller fish, the various triggerfish, the leaping mackerel, wolf-fish, and a hundred others which streaked the luminous atmosphere as they swam. This dazzling spectacle was enchanting! Perhaps some atmospheric condition increased the intensity of this phenomenon. Perhaps some storm agitated the surface of the waves. But, at this depth of some meters, the *Nautilus* was unmoved by its fury, and reposed peacefully in still water.

So we progressed, incessantly charmed by some new marvel. Conseil arranged and classed his zoöphytes, his articulata, his mollusks, his fishes. The days passed rapidly away, and I took no account of them. Ned, according to habit, tried to vary the diet on board. Like snails, we were fixed to our shells, and I declare it is easy to lead a snail's life.

Thus, this life seemed easy and natural, and we thought no longer of the life we led on land; but something happened to recall us to the strangeness of our situation.

On the 18th of January, the *Nautilus* was in 105° longitude and 15° south latitude. The weather was threatening, the sea rough and rolling. There was a strong east wind. The barometer, which had been going down for some days, foreboded a coming storm.

I went up on to the platform just as the second-in-command was taking the measure of the ship's position, and waited, according to habit, till the daily phrase was said. But, on this day, it was exchanged for another phrase not less incomprehensible. Almost immediately, I saw Captain Nemo appear, with a telescope looking towards the horizon.

For some minutes he was immovable, without taking his eye off the point enclosed within the field of the instrument. Then he lowered his telescope, and exchanged a few words with his second-in-command. The latter seemed to be a victim to some emotion that he tried in vain to repress. Captain Nemo, having more command over himself, was cool. He seemed, too, to be making some objections, to which the lieutenant replied by formal assurances. At least I concluded so by the difference of their tones and gestures. For myself, I had looked carefully in the direction indicated without seeing anything. The sky and water were lost in the clear line òf the horizon.

However, Captain Nemo paced from one end of the platform to the other, without looking at me, perhaps without even seeing me. His step was firm, but less regular than usual. He stopped sometimes, crossed his arms, and observed the sea. What could he be looking for on that immense expanse? The *Nautilus* was then some hundreds of miles from the nearest coast.

The second-in-command had taken up the telescope, and examined the horizon stead-
fastly, going and coming, stamping his foot and showing more nervous agitation than his superior officer. Besides, this mystery must necessarily be solved, and before long; for, upon an
order from Captain Nemo, the engine increased its propelling power, and the screw turned more
rapidly.

Just then, the second-in-command drew the captain's attention again. The latter stopped
walking and directed his telescope towards the place indicated. He looked for a long time. I
felt very much puzzled, and descended to the salon, and took out an excellent telescope that
I generally used. Then leaning on the cage of the watch-light, that jutted out from the front
of the platform, set myself to look over all the line of the sky and sea.

But my eye was no sooner applied to the lens, than the instrument was quickly snatched
out of my hands.

I turned round. Captain Nemo was before me, but I did not know him. His face was transfigured. His eyes shone with a somber fire; his teeth were set; his stiff body, clenched fists,
and head shrunk between his shoulders, betrayed the violent agitation that pervaded his whole
frame. He did not move. My telescope, fallen from his hands, had rolled at his feet.

Had I unwittingly provoked this fit of anger? Did this incomprehensible person imagine
that I had discovered some secret forbidden to the guests of the *Nautilus?* No; I was not the
object of this hatred, for he was not looking at me, his eye was steadily fixed upon a mysterious
point on the horizon.

At last Captain Nemo was again master of himself. His face, so profoundly altered, regained its habitual calm. He addressed some words in his strange language to his second-in-
command, then turned to me.

"Monsieur Aronnax," he said, in rather an imperious tone, "I require you to keep one
of the conditions that bind you to me."

"What is it, Captain?"

"You must be confined, with your companions, until I think fit to release you."

"You are the master," I replied, looking steadily at him. "But may I ask you one question?"

"None, sir."

There was no choice but to obey. Any resistance would have been useless.

I went down to the cabin occupied by Ned Land and Conseil, and told them the captain's
determination. You may judge how this communication was received by the Canadian. But
there was not time for explanations. Four of the crew waited at the door, and conducted us
to that cell where we had passed our first night on board the *Nautilus.*

Ned Land would have remonstrated, but the door was shut upon him.

"Will monsieur tell me what this means?" asked Conseil.

I told my companions what had passed. They were as much astonished as I, and equally
at a loss how to account for it.

Meanwhile, I was absorbed in my own reflections, and could think of nothing but the strange
fear depicted in the captain's countenance. I was incapable of putting two logical ideas together, and was losing myself in absurd hypotheses, when my cogitations were disturbed by these
words from Ned Land—

"Hallo! Lunch is ready."

And indeed the table was laid. Evidently Captain Nemo had given this order at the same
time that he had hastened the speed of the *Nautilus.*

"Will monsieur permit me to make a recommendation?" asked Conseil.

"Yes, my boy."

"Well, it is that monsieur eat his lunch. It is prudent, for we do not know what may happen."

"You are right, Conseil."

"Unfortunately," said Ned Land, "they have only given us the usual ship's fare."

"Friend Ned," asked Conseil, "what would you have said if the meal had been entirely forgotten?"

This argument cut short the harpooner's recriminations.

We sat down to table. The meal was eaten in silence. Just then, the luminous globe that lighted the cell went out, and left us in total darkness. Ned Land was soon asleep, and what astonished me was that Conseil also went off into a heavy sleep. I was thinking what could have caused this irresistible drowsiness, when I felt my brain becoming stupefied. In spite of my efforts to keep my eyes open, they would close.

I became prey to painful hallucinations. Evidently a drug had been mixed with the food we had just taken! Imprisonment was not enough to conceal Captain Nemo's projects from us, sleep was more necessary.

I then heard the hatches shut. The undulations of the sea, which caused a slight rolling motion, ceased. Had the *Nautilus* quitted the surface of the ocean? Had it gone back to the motionless beds of water?

I tried to resist sleep. It was impossible. My breathing grew weak. I felt a mortal cold freeze my stiffened and half-paralyzed limbs. My eyelids, like leaden caps, fell over my eyes. I could not raise them; a morbid sleep, full of hallucinations, took possession of my being. Then the visions disappeared, and left me in complete insensibility.

◄ CHAPTER XXIV ►
THE CORAL KINGDOM

 he next day I woke with my head singularly clear. To my great surprise I was in my own room. My companions, no doubt, had been reinstated in their cabin, without having perceived it any more than I. Of what had passed during the night they were as ignorant as I was, and to penetrate this mystery I only reckoned upon the chances of the future.

I then thought of leaving my room. Was I free again or a prisoner? Quite free. I opened the door, went along the passage, went up the central stairs. The panels, shut the evening before, were open. I went on to the platform.

Ned Land and Conseil waited there for me. I questioned them; they knew nothing. Lost in a heavy sleep in which they had been totally unconscious, they had been astonished at finding themselves in their cabin.

As for the *Nautilus,* it seemed quiet and mysterious as ever. It floated on the surface of the waves at a moderate pace. Nothing seemed changed on board.

Ned Land watched the sea with his penetrating eyes. It was deserted. The Canadian saw nothing fresh on the horizon—neither land nor sail. There was a stiff west breeze blowing, and the vessel was rolling very noticeably under the influence of long, wind-raised waves.

The *Nautilus,* after its air had been renewed, was kept at an average depth of fifteen meters, so as to rise promptly, if necessary, to the surface of the waves, an operation which, contrary to custom, was performed several times during that day of January 19th.

The second-in-command then came on to the platform, and gave the usual order, which could be heard below.

As for Captain Nemo, he did not appear. Of the people on board, I only saw the impassive steward, who served me with his usual silent regularity.

About two o'clock, I was in the salon, busied in arranging my notes, when the captain opened the door and appeared. I bowed. He made a slight inclination in return, without speaking. I resumed my work, hoping that he would perhaps give me some explanation of the events of the preceding night. He made none. I looked at him. He seemed fatigued; his reddened eyes had not been refreshed by sleep; his face showed a grief real and profound. He walked to and fro, sat down and got up again, took up a chance book, put it down, consulted his instruments without taking his habitual notes, and seemed not able to keep a moment's peace.

At last, he came up to me, and said—

"Are you a doctor, Monsieur Aronnax?"

I so little expected such a question, that I stared some time at him without answering.

"Are you a doctor?" he repeated. "Several of your colleagues have studied medicine, such as Gratiolet, Moquin-Tandon, and others."

"Well," said I, "I am a doctor and resident surgeon at the hospital. I practiced several years before entering the museum."

"Very good, sir."

My answer had evidently satisfied the captain. But not knowing what he would say next, I waited for other questions, reserving my answers according to circumstances.

"Monsieur Aronnax, will you consent to attend to one of my men?" he asked.

"Is he ill?"

"Yes."

"I am ready to follow you."

"Come then."

I admit my heart pounded, I do not know why I thought I saw a certain connection between the illness of one of the crew and the events of the day before; and this mystery interested me at least as much as the sick man.

Captain Nemo conducted me to the aft part of the *Nautilus,* and took me into a cabin situated near the sailors' quarters.

There, on a bed, lay a man about forty years of age, with an energetic face, a true type of an Anglo-Saxon.

I leaned over him. He was not only ill, he was wounded. His head, swathed in bandages covered with blood, lay on a double pillow. I undid the bandages, and the wounded man looked at me with his large eyes and gave no sign of pain as I did it.

It was a horrible wound. The skull, shattered by some deadly instrument, left the brain exposed, which was much injured. Clots of blood had formed in the bruised and broken mass, in color like the dregs of wine. There was both contusion and concussion of the brain. His breathing was slow, and some spasmodic movements of the muscles agitated his face. The cerebral phlegmasia was complete—there was paralysis of all feeling and movement.

I felt his pulse. It was intermittent. The extremities of the body were already growing cold, and I saw death inevitably approaching. After dressing the unfortunate man's wounds, I readjusted the bandages on his head, and turned to Captain Nemo.

"What caused this wound?" I asked.

"What does it matter?" he replied, evasively. "A shock has broken one of the levers of the engine, which struck this man. But your opinion as to his state?"

I hesitated before giving it.

"You may speak," said the captain. "This man does not understand French."

I gave a last look at the wounded man.

"He will be dead in two hours."

"Can nothing save him?"

"Nothing."

Captain Nemo's hand made a fist, and some tears glistened in his eyes, which I thought incapable of shedding any.

For some moments I still watched the dying man, whose life ebbed little by little. His pallor increased under the electric light that was shed over his death bed. I looked at his intelligent forehead, furrowed with premature wrinkles, which misfortune and sorrow had long ago place there. I tried to learn the secret of his life from the last words that escaped his lips. . . .

"You can go now, Monsieur Aronnax," said the captain.

I left him in the dying man's cabin, and returned to my room much affected by this scene. During the whole day I was haunted by uncomfortable suspicions, and at night I slept badly, and, between my broken dreams, I fancied I heard distant sighs like the notes of a funeral psalm. Were they the prayers of the dead, murmured in that language that I could not understand?

The next morning I went on to the platform. Captain Nemo was there before me. As soon as he perceived me he came to me.

"Professor, will it be convenient to you to make a submarine excursion today?"

"With my companions?" I asked.

"If they like."

"We obey your orders, Captain."

"Will you be so good then as to put on your diving-suits?"

There was no mention of the dying man. I rejoined Ned Land and Conseil, and told them of Captain Nemo's proposition. Conseil hastened to accept it, and this time the Canadian seemed quite willing to follow our example.

It was eight o'clock in the morning. At half past eight we were equipped for this new excursion, and provided with the two contrivances for light and breathing. The airlock door was open; and accompanied by Captain Nemo, who was followed by a dozen of the crew, we set foot, at a depth of about ten meters, on the solid bottom on which the *Nautilus* rested.

A slight slope ended in an uneven bottom, at fifteen fathoms depth. This bottom differed entirely from the one I had visited on my first excursion under the waters of the Pacific Ocean. Here, there was no fine sand, no submarine meadows, no sea-forest. I immediately recognized that marvellous region in which, on that day, the captain did the honors to us. It was the Coral Kingdom.

In the zoöphyte branch and in the alcyon class I noticed the gorgoneæ, the isidiæ, and the corollariæ.

It is to the last that coral belongs—that curious substance that was by turns classified in the mineral, vegetable and animal kingdoms. A remedy of the ancients, a jewel of modern times, it was not until 1694 that the Marseillais Peysonnel definitely placed it in the animal kingdom.

Coral is an assemblage of animalculæ, united in a polypary of a stone-like and brittle nature. These polyparies have a unique system of reproduction which produces them by budding; they possess an individual existence of their own at the same time that they participate in the communal life. It is, therefore, a sort of natural socialism. I knew the result of the last studies made on this strange zoöphyte, which petrifies at the same time that it grows, according to the very apt observation of naturalists; and nothing could be more interesting to me than to visit one of the petrified forests that Nature has planted at the bottom of the sea.

The Ruhmkorff apparatus were set going, and we followed a coral bank in the process of formation, which, helped by time, would one day close in that portion of the Indian Ocean. The route was bordered by inextricable bushes formed by the entanglement of shrubs that the little white-starred flowers covered. Sometimes, contrary to the land plants, these arborizations, rooted to the rocks, grew from top to bottom.

The light produced a thousand charming effects, playing in the midst of the branches that were so vividly colored. I seemed to see the membraneous cylindrical tubes tremble beneath the undulation of the waters. I was tempted to gather their fresh petals, ornamented with delicate tentacules, some just opened, the others budding, while small fish, swimming swiftly, touched them slightly, like flights of birds. But if my hand approached these living flowers, these animated sensitive plants, the whole colony took alarm. The white petals re-entered their red cases, the flowers faded as I looked, and the bush changed into a block of stony knobs.

Chance had thrown me into the presence of the most precious specimens of this zoöphyte. This coral was more valuable than that found in the Mediterranean, on the coasts of France, Italy, and Barbary. Its tints justified the poetical names of "Flower of Blood," and "Froth of Blood," that trade has given to its most beautiful productions. Coral is sold for five hundred francs per kilogram; and in this place, the watery beds would make the fortunes of a whole world of coral divers. This precious matter, often combined with other polyps, formed the compact and inextricable compound called "macciota," on which I noticed several beautiful specimens of pink coral.

But soon the bushes thickened, and the arborizations increased. Real petrified thickets, long spans of fantastic architecture, were disclosed before us. Captain Nemo led us under a dark gallery, where by a slight slope we reached a depth of one hundred meters. The light from our lamps produced sometimes magical effects, following the rough outlines of the natural arches, and pendants disposed like chandeliers, that were tipped with points of fire. Between the coral-line shrubs I noticed other polyps no less curious, melites, and irises with articulated ramifications, also some tufts of coral, some green, others red, like seaweed encrusted in their calcareous salts, that naturalists, after long discussion, have definitely classed in the vegetable kingdom. But according to the remark of a thinker, "this is perhaps the real point where life obscurely rises from its stony sleep, without altogether leaving its rude starting point."

At last, after walking two hours, we had attained a depth of about 300 meters, that is to say, the extreme limit on which coral begins to form. But here there was no isolated bush, nor modest thicket of low brushwood. It was an immense forest, of large mineral vegetations, enormous petrified trees, united by garlands of elegant plumarias, sea vines, all adorned with colors, and reflected light. We passed freely under their high branches, lost in the shadows of the waves, while at our feet, tubipores, meandrines, starfish, fungi, and caryophyllidæ formed a carpet of flowers sown with dazzling gems.

What an indescribable spectacle!

Ah, why could we not communicate our sensations? Why were we imprisoned under these masks of metal and glass? Why were words between us forbidden? Why did we not at least live the life of the fish that people the liquid element, or rather that of the amphibians who, during long hours, can travel as they like through the double domain of land and water?

Captain Nemo had stopped. I and my companions halted, and turning round, I saw his men were forming a semicircle round their chief. Watching attentively, I observed that four of them carried on their shoulders an object of an oblong shape.

We occupied, in this place, the center of a vast glade surrounded by the lofty foliage of the submarine forest. Our lamps threw over this place a sort of clear twilight that singularly elongated the shadows on the ground. At the end of the glade the darkness increased, and was only relieved by little sparks reflected by the points of coral.

Ned Land and Conseil were near me. We watched, and I knew that I was going to witness a strange scene. On observing the ground, I saw that it was raised in certain places by low mounds encrusted with limy deposits, and arranged with a regularity that betrayed the hand of man.

In the midst of the glade, on a pedestal of rocks roughly piled up, stood a cross of coral, that extended long arms that one might have thought were made of petrified blood.

Upon a sign from Captain Nemo, one of the men advanced; and at some feet from the cross, he began to dig a hole with a pickaxe that he took from his belt. I understood all! This glade was a cemetery, this hole a tomb, this oblong object the body of the man who had died in the night! The Captain and his men had come to bury their companion in this communal resting place, at the bottom of this inaccessible ocean!

Never before had my mind been so excited! Too many impressionable ideas crowded my brain! I could not believe what I beheld with eyes.

The grave was being dug slowly; the fish fled on all sides while their retreat was being disturbed; I heard the strokes of the pickaxe, which sparkled when it hit upon some flint lost at the bottom of the waters. The hole was soon large and deep enough to receive the body. Then the bearers approached; the body, enveloped in a tissue of white byssus, was lowered into the damp grave. Captain Nemo, with his arms crossed on his breast, and all the friends of him who had loved them, knelt in prayer . . . I and my friends also bowed our heads in respect.

The grave was then filled in with the rubbish taken from the ground, which formed a slight mound. When this was done, Captain Nemo and his men rose; then, approaching the grave, they knelt again, and all extended their hands in sign of the supreme adieu. . . .

Then the funeral procession returned to the *Nautilus,* passing under the arches of the forest, in the midst of thickets, along the coral bushes, and still on the ascent. At last the lights on board appeared, and their luminous track guided us to the *Nautilus.* At one o'clock we had returned.

As soon as I had changed my clothes, I went up on to the platform, and, a prey to conflicting emotions, I sat down near the lantern-house. Captain Nemo joined me. I rose and said to him—

"So, as I said he would, this man died in the night?"

"Yes, Monsieur Aronnax."

"And he rests now, near his companions, in the coral cemetery?"

"Yes, forgotten by all else, but not by us! We dug the grave, and the polyps undertake to seal our dead for eternity." And burying his face quickly in his hands, he tried in vain to suppress a sob. Then he added—"Our peaceful cemetery is there, some hundred feet below the surface of the waves."

"Your dead sleep quietly, at least, Captain, out of the reach of the sharks."

"Yes, sir," gravely replied the captain, "of sharks and *men.*"

PART II

◄ CHAPTER I ►

THE INDIAN OCEAN

e now come to the second part of our journey under the sea. The first ended with the moving scene in the coral cemetery, which left such a deep impression on my mind. Thus, in the midst of this great sea, Captain Nemo's life would pass even to his grave, which he had prepared in one of its most impenetrable abysses. There, not one of the ocean's monsters could trouble the last sleep of the crew of the *Nautilus,* of those friends riveted to each other in death as in life. "Nor any man either," had added the captain. Always the same fierce, implacable defiance towards human society!

I could no longer content myself with the hypothesis which satisfied Conseil. That worthy fellow persisted in seeing in the Commander of the *Nautilus* one of those unknown scientists who return mankind's contempt for indifference. For him, he was a misunderstood genius, who, tired of earth's deceptions, had taken refuge in this inaccessible medium, where he might follow his instincts freely. To my mind, this hypothesis explained but one side of Captain Nemo's character.

Indeed, the mystery of that last night, during which we had been chained in prison and asleep, and the precaution so violently taken by the captain of snatching from my eyes the telescope I had raised to sweep the horizon, the mortal wound of the man, due to some unaccountable shock to the *Nautilus*, all put me on a new track. No; Captain Nemo was not satisfied with shunning man! His formidable apparatus not only suited his instinct of freedom, but, perhaps, also the interests of some terrible reprisal.

At this moment, nothing is clear to me; I catch but a glimpse of light amidst all the darkness, and I must confine myself to writing as events shall dictate.

Nothing bound us to Captain Nemo. He knew that escape from the *Nautilus* was impossible. We were not prisoners under parole; no word of honor chained us. We were simply captives, prisoners disguised under the name of guests for the semblance of courtesy. Certainly Ned Land had not renounced hope of regaining his liberty. It was certain that he would profit by the first opportunity that chance offered. And so would I, no doubt. But it would not be without regrets, for had not Captain Nemo generously allowed us to share in the secrets of the *Nautilus?* And at the last, should we hate or admire this man? Was he a victim or a villain? And, to be frank, I did not want to abandon him forever, I would like to finish this underwater tour of the world and the revelations of all its marvels. I wanted to see all of the marvels accumulated under the seas of the globe. I wanted to witness what no man had ever seen before, and I would pay with my life, if need be! What had I learned to this date? Nothing, practically nothing, since so far we had only travelled six thousand leagues under the Pacific!

I could see that the *Nautilus* was approaching inhabited lands; if the chance were to be offered for escape, it would be cruel to sacrifice my companions to my passion for the unknown. I would have no choice but to follow them. But would this occasion present itself? As a man denied his freedom by force, deprived of his free will, I desired such an occasion; as a curious scientist, I dreaded it.

That day, the 21st of January, 1868, at noon, the second officer came to take the altitude of the sun. I mounted the platform, lit a cigar, and watched the operation. It seemed to me that the man did not understand French; for several times I made remarks in a loud voice, which must have drawn from him some involuntary sign of attention, if he had understood them; but he remained undisturbed and silent.

As he was taking observations with the sextant, one of the sailors of the *Nautilus* (the strong man who had accompanied us on our first submarine excursion to the Island of Crespo) came to clean the glass lens of the lantern. I examined the fittings of the apparatus, the power of which was increased a hundredfold by lenticular rings, placed similar to those in a lighthouse, and which projected their brilliance in a concentrated beam.[1] The electric lamp was constructed in such a way as to give its most powerful light. The light, indeed, was produced in a vacuum, which insured both its steadiness and its intensity. This vacuum economized the graphite points, between which the luminous arc was developed,—an important point of economy for Captain Nemo, who could not easily have replaced them. Under these conditions their waste was imperceptible.

When the *Nautilus* was ready to continue its submarine journey, I went down to the salon. The panels were closed, and the course marked directly west.

We were furrowing the waters of the Indian Ocean, a vast liquid plain, with a surface of 550 million hectares, and whose waters are so clear and transparent, that any one leaning over them and looking into their depths would turn giddy. The *Nautilus* usually floated between fifty and a hundred fathoms deep. We went on so for some days. To any one but myself, who had a great love for the sea, the hours would have seemed long and monotonous; but the daily walks on the platform, when I steeped myself in the reviving air of the ocean, the sight of the rich waters through the windows of the salon, reading the books in the library, the compiling of my memoirs, took up all my time, and left me not a moment of boredom or weariness.

Our health remained very satisfactory. The food on board agreed with us perfectly, and for my part, I could have passed on the variants that Ned Land, in a spirit of protest, managed to procure. Too, in this constant temperature, we were much less likely to catch colds. Besides, the madrepore *Dendrophylia,* found in Provence under the name of "sea fennel," was kept in good supply on board. The juicy flesh of its polyps furnished an excellent cough syrup.

For some days we saw a great number of aquatic birds, webfooted, sea mews or gulls. Some were cleverly killed, and, prepared in a certain way, made very acceptable water-game. Among large winged birds, carried a long distance from all lands, and resting upon the waves from the fatigue of their flight, I saw some magnificent albatrosses, uttering discordant cries like the braying of an ass, and birds belonging to the family of the longipennates. The family of the totipalmates was represented by the rapid frigate-birds, which caught fish from the surface, and by numerous phætons, or *paille-en-queue;* among others, the phæton with red stripes, as large as a pigeon, whose white plumage, tinted with pink, shows off to advantage the blackness of its wings.

The nets of the *Nautilus* captured many varieties of marine turtles, of the genus *caret,* the hawksbill, with their bulging backs and valuable shells. These reptiles, who dive easily, can remain underwater for a great length of time by closing a fleshy valve situated in the external opening of their nasal passage. Some of these *carets* were sleeping in shells, as protection against other marine animals. The flesh of these turtles is generally mediocre, but their eggs make an excellent dish.

As to the fish, they always provoked our admiration when we surprised the secrets of their aquatic life through the open panels. I saw many kinds which I never before had a chance of observing.

I shall note chiefly, the ostracions, or trunkfish, peculiar to the Red Sea, the Indian Ocean, and that part which washes the coast of America. These fish, like the tortoise, the armadillo, the sea urchin and the crustacea, are protected by a breastplate which is neither chalky nor stone, but real bone. In some it takes the form of a triangle, in others a square. Among the triangular I saw some a demi-decimeter in length, with wholesome flesh and a delicious flavor; they are

brown at the tail, and yellow at the fins, and I recommend their introduction into fresh water, to which a certain number of sea fish easily accustom themselves. I would also mention quadrangular ostracions, having on the back four large tubercles; some dotted over with white spots on the lower part of the body, and which may be tamed like birds; trigons provided with spines formed by the lengthening of their bony shell, and which, from their strange gruntings, are called "sea pigs;" also "dromedaries" with large humps in the shape of a cone, whose flesh is very tough and leathery.

I now borrow from the daily notes of Master Conseil: Certain fish of the genus Tetradon, peculiar to these seas; spenglerians, with red backs and white chests, which are distinguished by three rows of longitudinal filaments, and some electrical, seven inches long, decked in the liveliest colors. Then, some specimens of other kinds: ovoids, resembling an egg of a dark brown color, marked with white bands, and without tails; diodons, real sea porcupines, furnished with spines, and capable of swelling in such a way as to look like cushions bristling with needles; sea horses, common to every ocean; some flying pegasi, with long snouts, with their pectoral fins being much elongated and formed in the shape of wings allow, if not to fly, at least to shoot into the air; pigeon spatulæ, with tails covered with many rings of shell; macrognathi with long jaws, an excellent fish, 25 centimeters long, and brilliant with most agreeable colors; livid calliomores, with rugged heads; myriads of jumping blennies, streaked with black and with long pectoral fins, streaked across the surface of the water with prodigious speed; delicious velifera, who raise their fins like sails to catch favorable currents; splendid kurtidae, which nature has lavishly colored yellow, sky blue, silver and gold; trichoptera, with filament-like wings; *cottes,* all spotted with lemon, which produce a peculiar rustling sound; gurnards, the liver of which is considered poisonous; greenlings, which have a mobile blinker over their eyes; and finally *soufflets,* with long and tubular muzzles. These we may call the fly-catchers of the seas, armed with a gun unforeseen by Chassepot or Remington, which kill insects by shooting them with a single drop of water.

In the eighty-ninth genus of fishes, classified by Lacépède, belonging to the second sub-class of bony fish, characterized by opercules and bronchial membranes, I noticed the scorpæna, the head of which is furnished with spikes, and which has but one dorsal fin; these creatures are covered, or not, with little shells, according to the sub-class to which they belong. The second sub-class gives us specimens of didactyles three or four decimeters in length, with yellow stripes, and heads of a most fantastic appearance. As to the first sub-class, it gives several specimens of that singular-looking fish appropriately called a "sea frog," with large head, sometimes like a pot pierced with deep holes, sometimes swollen with protuberances, bristling with spikes, and covered with tubercles; it has irregular and hideous horns; its body and tail are covered with callouses; its sting makes a dangerous wound; it is both repugnant and horrible.

From the 21st to the 23rd of January the *Nautilus* went at the rate of two hundred and fifty leagues, which is five hundred and forty miles, in twenty-four hours, or twenty-two miles an hour. If we recognized so many different varieties of fish, it was because, attracted by the electric light, they tried to follow us; the greater part, however, were distanced by our speed and soon fell behind; though some kept their place in the waters by the *Nautilus* for a time.

The morning of the 24th, in 12° 5′ south latitude, and 94° 33′ longitude, we observed Keeling Island, a madrepore formation, planted with magnificent coconuts, and which had been visited by Mr. Darwin and Captain Fitzroy. The *Nautilus* skirted the shores of this desert island for a little distance. Its nets brought up numerous specimens of polyps and echinoderms, as well as curious varieties of mollusks. Some precious products of the species of delphinulæ enriched the treasures of Captain Nemo, to which I added an astræa punctifera, a kind of parasite polyp often found fixed to a shell.

Soon Keeling Island disappeared below the horizon, and our course was directed to the northwest in the direction of the Indian peninsula.

"Civilized lands!" Ned Land said to me one day, "better than those Papuan Islands, where you meet more savages than deer! In India, Professor, there are roads, trains, English, French, and Hindu towns. You couldn't go five miles without meeting a countryman. Well! Don't you think that we have worn out our Captain Nemo's hospitality?"

"No, Ned, no," I answered decisively, "let things ride, as you sailors will say. The *Nautilus* is approaching inhabited continents. It is heading toward Europe; let it take us there. When it arrives in those seas, we can consider what it is prudent to do. Besides, I cannot imagine that Captain Nemo would permit us to hunt on the coasts of Malabar or Coromandel as he did in the forests of New Guinea."

"Well, monsieur, can we not act without his permission?"

I did not answer the Canadian. I did not want an argument. Deep in my heart I wanted to take advantage of the chance that destiny had given me by casting me aboard the *Nautilus*.

From Keeling Island our course was generally slower. It was also more variable, often taking us into great depths. Several times use was made of the inclined planes, which by internal levers were placed obliquely to the waterline. In that way we went down about two or three kilometers, but without ever discovering the greatest depths of the Indian Ocean, which soundings of three thousand meters have never reached. As to the temperature of the lower strata, the thermometer invariably indicated 4° above zero (cent.). I only observed that, in the upper levels, the water was always colder in shallows than in the open sea.

On the 25th of January, the ocean was entirely deserted; the *Nautilus* passed the day on the surface, beating the waves with its powerful screw, and making them splash to a great height. Who under such circumstances would not have taken it for a gigantic cetacean? Three quarters of this day I spent on the platform. I watched the sea. Nothing on the horizon, till about four o'clock a steamer running west in the direction opposite to ours. Her masts were visible for an instant, but she could not see the *Nautilus,* it being too low in the water. I fancied this steamboat belonged to the Peninsular and Oriental Company, which runs from Ceylon to Sydney, touching at King George's Point and Melbourne.

At five o'clock in the evening, before that fleeting twilight which binds night to day in tropical zones, Conseil and I were astonished by a curious spectacle.

There is a charming animal that, according to the ancients, presages good luck if one meets it. Aristotle, Athenaeus, Pliny, and Oppian studied its habits and described it with all the poetry of Greece and Italy. The named it *nautilus* and *pompylius*. But modern science does not approve of these names, and this mollusk is now known under the name "argonaut."

If anyone had consulted Conseil, that worthy lad would have informed him that the branch of mollusk is divided into five classes. The first class, the cephlapods, which are sometimes naked and sometimes covered by a shell, is formed of two families, the dibranchiata and the tetrabranchiata, which are distinguished by the number of their gills. The family of dibranchiata is divided into three genera, the argonauts, the squids and the cuttlefish. The tetrabranchiata have only one genus, the nautilus. After hearing this classification, only a rebellious soul would confuse the argonaut, which is *acetabuliferous,* or equipped with siphons, with the nautilus, which is *tentaculiferous,* or equipped with tentacles; it would be inexcusable.

It was a shoal of argonauts travelling along on the surface of the ocean. We could count several hundreds. They belonged to the tubercle species which are peculiar to the Indian Ocean.

These graceful mollusks moved backwards by means of their locomotive tube, through which they propelled water previously drawn in. Of their eight tentacles, six were elongated and slender, and floated on the water, while the other two, rolled up flat like palm leaves, were spread to the wind like a light sail.[2] I saw their spiral-shaped and fluted shells, which Cuvier justly compares to an elegant boat. A boat indeed! It bears the creature which secretes it, but is not attached to it.

"The argonaut is free to leave its shell," I said to Conseil, "but it never does so."

"Just like Captain Nemo," responded Conseil wisely, "it would have been more appropriate if he had named his boat the *Argonaut.*"

For nearly an hour the *Nautilus* floated in the midst of this shoal of mollusks. Then I know not what sudden fright they took. But as if at a signal every sail was furled, the arms folded, the body drawn in, the shells turned over, changing their center of gravity, and the whole fleet disappeared under the waves. It was instantaneous. Never did the ships of a squadron maneuver with more unity.

At that moment night fell suddenly, and the waves, scarcely raised by the breeze, lay peaceably against the sides of the *Nautilus.*

The next day, 26th of January, we cut the equator at the eighty-second meridian, and entered the Northern Hemisphere.

During the day, a formidable troop of sharks accompanied us, terrible creatures, which multiply in these seas, and make them very dangerous. Some of them were Philipps sharks, with brown backs and whitish bellies, armed with eleven rows of teeth; and eyed sharks, their throat being marked with a large black spot surrounded with white like an eye. There were also some Isabella sharks, with rounded snouts marked with dark spots. These powerful creatures often hurled themselves at the windows of the salon with such violence as to make us feel very insecure. At such times Ned Land was possessed. He wanted to go to the surface and harpoon the monsters, particularly certain dogfish sharks, whose mouth is studded with teeth like a mosaic; and large tiger sharks nearly six meters long, the last named of which seemed to excite him most particularly. But the *Nautilus,* accelerating her speed, easily left the most rapid of them behind.

The 27th of January, at the entrance of the vast Bay of Bengal, we met repeatedly a forbidding spectacle: dead bodies floating on the surface of the water. They were the dead of the Indian villages, carried by the Ganges out to the sea, and which the vultures, the only undertakers of the country, had not been able to devour. But the sharks did not fail to help them at their funeral work.

About seven o'clock in the evening, the *Nautilus,* half submerged was sailing in a sea of milk. At first sight the ocean seemed lactified. Was it the effect of the moonlight? No; for the moon, scarcely two days old, was still lying hidden beneath the horizon in the rays of the sun. The whole sky, though bright in the starlight, seemed black by contrast with the whiteness of the waters.

Conseil could not believe his eyes, and questioned me as to the cause of this strange phenomenon. Happily I was able to answer him.

"It is called a milk sea," I explained, "a large area of white wavelets often to be seen on the coasts of Amboyna, and in these parts of the sea."

"But," said Conseil, "can monsieur tell me what causes such an effect? I suppose the water is not really turned into milk!"

"No, my boy; and the whiteness which surprises you is caused only by the presence of myriads of infusoria, a sort of little luminous worm, gelatinous and without color, of the thickness of a hair, and whose length is not more than a fifth of a millimeter. These little animals adhere to one another sometimes for several leagues."

"Several leagues!" exclaimed Conseil.

"Yes, my boy; and you need not try to compute the number of these infusoria! You will not be able; for, if I am not mistaken, ships have floated on these milk seas for more than forty miles."

I do not know if Conseil considered my advice; he was plunged in profound thought, searching no doubt for the number of fifths of a millimeter contained in forty square miles. For myself, I continued to observe the phenomenon. For several hours, the *Nautilus* cut through the white waves with its spur; I noticed that it slipped through this soapy water without a sound, as if it floated in the midst of one of those frothy eddies made in bays when currents and counter-currents sometimes converge.

Towards midnight the sea suddenly resumed its usual color; but behind us, even to the limits of the horizon, the sky reflected the whitened waves, and for a long time seemed impregnated with the vague glimmerings of an aurora borealis.

---

[1] A Fresnel lens, in other words. R.M.

[2] This was a misconception Verne shared with his contemporaries. R.M.

◄ CHAPTER II ►

A NOVEL PROPOSAL OF CAPTAIN NEMO'S

On the 28th of February, when at noon the *Nautilus* came to the surface of the sea, in 9° 4′ north latitude, there was land in sight about eight miles to westward. The first thing I noticed was a range of mountains about two thousand feet high, the shapes of which were most capricious. On taking the bearings, I knew that we were nearing the Island of Ceylon, the pearl which hangs from the lobe of the Indian Peninsula.

I searched the library for a book about this island, which is one of the most fertile in the world. I found the precise thing in a volume by H. C. Sirr, Esq., entitled *Ceylon and the Cingalese*. Returning to the salon, I noted some of the facts relative to Ceylon, known since antiquity under numerous different names. It is situated between 5° 55′ and 9° 49′ north latitude, and between 79° 42′ and 82° 4′ east longitude, using the meridian of Greenwich. In length it is 275 miles, in maximum breadth 150 miles; it is 900 miles in circumference and has an area of 24,448 square miles, which is a little less than that of Ireland.

Captain Nemo and his second-in-command appeared at this moment.

The captain glanced at the map. Then, turning to me, said—

"The Island of Ceylon is a land noted for its pearl fisheries. Would you find it agreeable to visit one of them, Monsieur Aronnax?"

"Certainly, Captain."

"Well, the thing is easy. Though if we see the fisheries, we shall not see the fishermen. The annual harvest has not yet begun. Never mind that, I will give orders to make for the Gulf of Manaar, where we shall arrive in the night."

The captain said something to his second-in-command, who immediately went out. Soon the *Nautilus* returned to her element, and the manometer showed that she was about thirty feet deep.

I searched on the map for the Gulf of Manaar. I found it near the ninth parallel, by the northwest coast of Ceylon. It is formed by the elongated line of the Island of Manaar. To get there we would have to sail up the west coast of Ceylon.

"Professor," Captain Nemo said to me, "there are pearl fisheries in the Gulf of Bengal, in the Indian Ocean, in the seas of China and Japan, in the seas of South America, the Gulf of California; but it is in Ceylon that the fishers obtain the most beautiful results. We have arrived too soon, however. The fishermen will not arrive in the Gulf of Manaar until the month of March. Then, for thirty days more than three hundred boats will take part in this lucrative exploitation of the treasures of the sea. These boats will each carry ten oarsmen and ten divers. The latter, divided into two groups, will alternately dive to depths of twelve meters, weighted with a stone tied between their feet and attached to the boat with a cord.''

"Do you mean," I asked, "that they still use such primitive methods?"

"They do," he answered, "even though these fisheries belong to the most industrialized people on the globe, the English, ceded to them by the Treaty of Amiens in 1802."

"It would seem to me that diving suits such as you employ would render great service to this operation."

"Yes, because these poor fishermen cannot stay beneath the water very long. The Englishman Percival, in his voyage to Ceylon, speaks of a Kaffir who stayed below for five minutes without coming to the surface, but I find that hard to believe. I do know of divers who can stay below for 57 seconds, and very skilful ones for 87. But these are very rare, and when they return on board, these poor men are bleeding water mixed with blood from the nose and ears. I believe that the average time for a fisherman to stay below is 30 seconds. During that time they must fill their small nets with as many pearl oysters as they can gather. But, generally, these fishermen do not live very long; their vision is enfeebled, they develop ulcers on their eyes, and sores on their bodies; sometimes they are stricken with apoplexy deep in the water."

"Yes," I said, "It is a sad occupation, and all for the satisfaction of fashion. But, tell me, Captain, how many oysters can a boat gather in one day?"

"From 40 to 50 thousand. It is said that in 1814, when the English government tried fishing on its own account, its divers gathered 76 million oysters in twenty days of work."

"At least," I asked, "these divers are sufficiently paid?"

"Scarcely, Professor. In Panama they make a dollar a week. Most often they only get a penny for each oyster that contains a pearl, and how many contain nothing?"

"A penny for those poor people who are making their masters rich! It is odious."

"Well, sir," said Captain Nemo, "you and your companions shall visit the Bank of Manaar, and if by chance some fisherman should be there, we shall see him at work."

"Agreed, Captain!"

"By the by, Monsieur Aronnax, you are not afraid of sharks?"

"Sharks!" I exclaimed.

This question I thought, at the moment, seemed useless.

"Well?" continued Captain Nemo.

"I admit, Captain, that I am not yet very familiar with that kind of fish."

"*We* are accustomed to them," replied Captain Nemo, "and in time you will be too. However, we shall be armed, and on the road we may be able to hunt some sharks. It is interesting hunting. So, till tomorrow, sir, and a great day."

This said in a careless tone, Captain Nemo left the salon.

Now, if you were invited to hunt the bear in the mountains of Switzerland, what would you say? "Very well! Tomorrow we will go and hunt the bear." It you were asked to hunt the lion in the plains of Atlas, or the tiger in the Indian jungles, what would you say? "Ha! ha! it seems we are going to hunt the tiger or the lion!" But when you are invited to hunt the shark in its natural element, you would perhaps reflect before accepting the invitation. As for myself, I passed my hand over my forehead, on which stood large drops of cold perspiration.

"Let us reflect," I said, "and take our time. Hunting otters in submarine forests, as we did in the Island of Crespo, will pass; but going around at the bottom of the sea, where one is almost certain to meet sharks, is quite another thing! I know well that in certain countries, particularly in the Andaman Islands, the Negroes never hesitate to attack them with a dagger in one hand and a running noose in the other; but I also know that few who affront those creatures ever return alive! However, I am not a Negroe, and, if I were I think a little hesitation in this case would not be ill-timed.''

And I was again daydreaming about sharks, dreaming about vast jaws armed with multiple rows of teeth, and capable of cutting a man in two. I could already feel a certain pain around my kidneys. Besides, I was disturbed by the casual manner in which the captain offered this deplorable invitation!

"Well!" I thought, "Conseil will not want to come, and that will give me an excuse not to accompany the captain."

As for Ned Land, I did not think that I could count on his behavior. Peril, the chance of a fight, these only attracted his combative nature.

I returned to reading Sirr's book, but I only leafed through it mechanically. I saw, between the lines, formidable open jaws.

At this moment, Conseil and the Canadian entered, quite composed, and even joyous. They knew not what awaited them.

"Faith, sir," said Ned Land, "your Captain Nemo—the devil take him!—has just made us a very pleasant offer."

"Ah!" said I, "you know?"

"If agreeable to monsieur," interrupted Conseil, "the Commander of the *Nautilus* has invited us to visit the magnificent Ceylon fisheries tomorrow, in monsieur's company; he did it kindly, and behaved like a real gentleman."

"He said nothing more?"

"Nothing more, sir," answered the Canadian, "except that he had already spoken to you of this little walk."

"He did," I said, "but did he not give you any details about. . . ?"

"None, Monsieur le Naturaliste. You will be coming with us, will you not?"

"Me . . . no doubt! I see that the idea is to your taste, Master Land."

"Yes! It will be curious, very curious."

"Perhaps dangerous!" I insinuated.

"Dangerous!" answered Ned, "a simple excursion to an oyster bed?"

Apparently Captain Nemo had judged it unnecessary to plant the idea of sharks in the heads of my companions. Me, I looked at them with some anxiety, as if they were already lacking a limb. Should I warn them? Yes, of course, but I didn't know how to do it.

"Please," said Conseil, "would monsieur give us some details about pearl fisheries?"

"As to the fishing itself," I asked, "or possible incidents which. . . ."

"On the fishing," replied the Canadian; "before entering upon the hunting ground, it is as well to know something about it."

"Very well; sit down, my friends, and I will teach you what I have learned from the Englishman Sirr."

Ned and Conseil seated themselves on divan, and the first thing the Canadian asked was—

"Sir, what is a pearl?"

"My worthy Ned," I answered, "to the poet, a pearl is a tear of the sea; to the Orientals, it is a dew drop solidified; to the ladies, it is a jewel of an oblong shape, of a clear brilliancy and made of a nacreous substance, which they wear on their fingers, their necks, or their ears; for the chemist, it is a mixture of phosphate and carbonate of lime, with a little gelatine; and lastly, for naturalists, it is simply an abnormal secretion of the organ that produces the mother-of-pearl among certain bivalves."

"Division of mollusks," said Conseil, "class of acephali, order of testacea."

"Precisely so, my learned Conseil; and, among these testacea, the earshell, the tridacnæ, the turbots, the pinnea marinae, in a word, all those which secrete mother-of-pearl, that is, the blue, bluish, violet, or white substance which lines the interior of their shells, are capable of producing pearls.''

''Mussels too?'' asked the Canadian.

''Yes, mussels of certain waters in Scotland, Wales, Ireland, Saxony, Bohemia, and France.''

''Good! I will remember that for the future,'' replied the Canadian.

''But,'' I continued, ''the mollusk *par excellence* which secretes the pearl is the *pearl oyster,* and *meleagrina margaritifera,* that precious pintadine. The pearl is nothing but a nacreous formation, deposited in a globular form, either adhering to the oyster shell, or buried in the folds of the creature. On the shell it is held fast; in the flesh it is loose; but it always has for a nucleus a small hard substance, which may be a barren egg, or a grain of sand, around which the pearly matter deposits itself year after year successively in thin concentric layers.''

''Are many pearls found in the same oyster?'' asked Conseil.

''Yes, my boy. Some pintadines are a perfect jewel-box. One oyster has been mentioned, though I allow myself to doubt it, as having contained no less than a hundred and fifty sharks.''

''A hundred and fifty sharks!'' exclaimed Ned Land.

''Did I say sharks?'' said I, hurriedly. ''I meant to say a hundred and fifty pearls. Sharks would not make sense.''

''Certainly not,'' said Conseil; ''but will monsieur tell us now by what means they extract these pearls?''

''They proceed in various ways. When they adhere to the shell, the fishermen often pull them off with pliers; but the most common way is to lay the pintadines on mats of the seaweed which covers the banks. Thus they die in the open air; and at the end of ten days they are in an advanced state of decomposition. They are then plunged into large reservoirs of sea water; then they are opened and washed. Now begins the double work of the sorters. First they separate the layers of pearl, known in commerce by the name of genuine silvers, bastard whites and bastard blacks, which are delivered in boxes of one hundred and twenty-five and one hundred and fifty kilograms each. Then they take the parenchyma—the flesh—of the oyster, boil it, and pass it through a sieve in order to extract the very smallest pearls.''

''The price of these pearls varies according to their size?'' asked Conseil.

''Not only according to their size,'' I answered, ''but also according to their shape, their *water* (that is, their color), and their *orient* or luster—that is, that bright and dappled sparkle which makes them so charming to the eye. The most beautiful are called virgin pearls or paragons. They are formed alone in the tissue of the mollusk, are white, often opaque, but sometimes have the transparency of an opal. They are generally round or oval. The round are made into bracelets. The oval into pendants; and, being more precious, are sold singly. Those adhering to the shell of the oyster are more irregular in shape, and are sold by weight. Lastly, in a lower order are classed those small pearls known under the name of seed pearls; they are sold by measure, and are especially used in embroidery for church ornaments.''

''But this work, separating the pearls according to their size, must be long and difficult,'' said the Canadian.

''No, my friend. The work is done with eleven sieves or screens, pierced with a number of holes. The pearls that do not pass through the sieve with 20 to 80 holes are considered first class. Those that do not pass through a screen with 100 to 800 holes are considered second class. Finally, those pearls that require the use of a strainer with 900 to 1000 holes are called seed pearls.''

''Very ingenious,'' said Conseil, ''to make these divisions, these classifications, a mechanical operation. And can monsieur now tell us how much money is made from the exploitation of the pearl oyster beds?''

"According to Sirr," I answered, "the fisheries of Ceylon are leased annually for a sum of three million sharks."

"You mean francs!" said Conseil.

"Yes, francs! Three million francs," I continued, "but I don't think that the fisheries are as profitable as they once were. It is the same with the American fisheries, which, during the reign of Charles V, produced four million francs, now reduced to two-thirds that. In short, the total value of the entire industry is about nine million francs."

"But," demanded Conseil, "have there not been famous pearls that have demanded very high prices?"

"Yes, my boy. It is said the Caesar offered Servilia a pearl valued at 120 thousand francs in today's money."

"I have heard it claimed," said the Canadian, "that a certain lady of antiquity drank pearls dissolved in vinegar."

"Cleopatra," answered Conseil.

"It must have been awful," added Ned.

"Terrible, friend Ned," replied Conseil, "but one small glass of vinegar that cost 500 thousand francs, that is quite a price."

"I regret not being able to marry the lady," said the Canadian, making an unreassuring gesture in the air.

"Ned Land marrying Cleopatra!" cried Conseil.

"But I was going to be married, Conseil," answered the Canadian, seriously, "and it was not my fault that the affair did not go through. I bought a pearl collar for Kate Tender, my fiance; then she went and married someone else. Oh well, that collar did not cost me more than a dollar and a half, even though—and the Professor will just have to take my word for this—the pearls that made it would not have passed through the twenty-hole sieve!"

"My good Ned," I answered, laughing, "those were artificial pearls, simple glass globules coated on the inside with *essence d'Orient.*"

"Huh! This *essence d'Orient,*" answered Ned, "must be very expensive stuff."

"Not very much! It is nothing more than silvery substance made from the scales of a fish called the bleak, collected in water and preserved in ammonia. It is of no value."

"Perhaps that's why Kate Tender married someone else," Master Land responded philosophically.

"But," I said, "to return to pearls of real value, I do not think that any king has possessed one superior to this one of Captain Nemo's."

"This one?" asked Conseil, pointing to a magnificent jewel enclosed behind glass.

"Yes," I said, "I would not be wrong in assigning a value to it of ten million. . . ."

"Francs!" said Conseil emphatically. "Yes, ten million francs and, no doubt, it cost the captain no more than the effort of picking it up."

"Huh!" exclaimed Ned, "who's to say that tomorrow, on our walk we might not find its equal?"

"Bah!" said Conseil. "And why not! What are those millions worth on board the *Nautilus?*"

"On board, nothing," said Ned Land, "But . . . somewhere else?"

"Oh! Somewhere else!" said Conseil, shaking his head.

"Ned is right," I said. "If we could take a pearl worth these millions to Europe or America, it would give our story great authenticity—and at the same time, would be a great price to receive for our adventures."

"I can believe that," said Ned.

"But," said Conseil, who always returned to the odd questions, "is this pearl fishing dangerous?"

"No," I answered, quickly; "particularly if certain precautions are taken."

"What does one risk in such a calling?" said Ned Land; "the swallowing of some mouthfuls of sea water!"

"As you say, Ned. By the by," said I, trying to assume Captain Nemo's careless tone, "are you afraid of sharks, brave Ned?"

"I?" replied the Canadian; "a harpooner by profession? It is my trade to make light of them!"

"But," said I, "it is not a question of fishing for them with an iron swivel, hoisting them into the vessel, cutting off their tails with a blow of a chopper, ripping them up, and throwing their entrails into the sea!"

"Then, it is a question of . . . ."

"Yes, precisely."

"In the water?"

"In the water."

"Faith; but with a good harpoon! You know, sir, these sharks are ill-made beasts. They must turn on their bellies to seize you, and in that time . . . ."

Ned Land had a way of saying "seize," which made my blood run cold.

"Well, and you, Conseil, what do you think of sharks?"

"Me!" said Conseil. "I will be frank with monsieur."

"So much the better," thought I.

"If monsieur means to face the sharks, I do not see why his faithful servant should not face them with him."

◄ **CHAPTER III** ►

A PEARL OF TEN MILLIONS

ight fell. I went to bed. I slept badly. Sharks played an important role in my dreams, and I found it both just and very injust that, entymologically speaking, the French word for shark, *requin,* should sound so much like *requiem.*

The next morning at four o'clock, I was awakened by the steward whom Captain Nemo had placed at my service. I rose hurriedly, dressed, and went into the salon.

Captain Nemo was awaiting me.

"Monsieur Aronnax," said he, "are you ready to start?"

"I am ready."

"Then, please to follow me."

"And my companions, Captain?"

"They have been told, and are waiting."

"Are we not to put on our diving suits?" asked I.

"Not yet. I have not allowed the *Nautilus* to come too near this coast, and we are some distance from the Manaar Bank; but the launch is ready, and will take us to the exact point of disembarking, which will save us a long way. It carries our diving apparatus, which we will put on when we begin our submarine journey."

Captain Nemo conducted me to the central staircase, which led on to the platform. Ned and Conseil were already there, delighted at the idea of the "pleasure party" which was preparing. Five sailors from the *Nautilus,* with their oars, waited in the launch, which had been made fast against the side.

The night was still dark. Layers of clouds covered the sky, allowing but few stars to be seen. I looked on the side where the land lay, and saw nothing but a dark line enclosing three-quarters of the horizon, from the southwest to northwest. The *Nautilus,* having returned during the night up the western coast of Ceylon, was now west of the bay, or rather gulf, formed by the mainland and the island of Manaar. There, under the dark waters, stretched the pintadine bank, an inexhaustible field of pearls, the length of which is more than twenty miles.

Captain Nemo, Ned Land, Conseil, and I, took our places in the stern of the boat. The mate went to the tiller; his four companions leaned on their oars, the painter was cast off, and we pulled away.

The boat was steered towards the south; the oarsmen did not hurry. I noticed that their strokes, strong in the water, only followed each other every ten seconds, according to the method generally adopted in the navy. While the craft was running by its own momentum, the liquid drops struck the dark depths of the waves crisply like splashes of melted lead. A little billow, spreading wide, gave a slight roll to the launch, and some wave crests splashed against the bow.

We were silent. What was Captain Nemo thinking of? Perhaps of the land he was approaching, and which he found too near to him, contrary to the Canadian's opinion, who thought it too far off. As to Conseil, he was merely there from simple curiosity.

About half past five, the first tints on the horizon showed the upper line of coast more distinctly. Flat enough in the east, it rose a little to the south. Five miles still lay between the shore and us, and it was indistinct owing to the mist on the water. Between us and the land, the sea was deserted. Not a boat, not a diver. A profound solitude reigned over this pearl fisher's rendezvous. As Captain Nemo had observed, we had arrived in the area a month too early.

At six o'clock it became suddenly daylight, with that rapidity peculiar to tropical regions, which know neither dawn nor twilight. The solar rays pierced the curtain of clouds, piled up on the eastern horizon, and the radiant orb rose rapidly. I saw land distinctly, with a few trees scattered here and there. The boat neared Manaar Island, which was rounded to the south. Captain Nemo rose from his seat and watched the sea.

At a sign from him the anchor was dropped, but the chain scarcely ran, for it was little more than a yard deep, and this spot was one of the highest points of the bank of pintadines. The boat immediately swung under the push of the current.

"Here we are, Monsieur Aronnax," said Captain Nemo. "You see that enclosed bay? Here, in a month, will be assembled the numerous fishing boats of the gatherers, and these are the waters their divers will ransack so boldly. Happily, this bay is well situated for that kind of fishing. It is sheltered from the strongest winds; the sea is never very rough here, which makes it favorable for the diver's work. We will now put on our suits, and begin our walk."

I did not answer, and while watching the suspicious waves, began with the help of the sailors to put on my heavy diving-dress. Captain Nemo and my companions were also dressing. None of the *Nautilus'* men were to accompany us on this novel excursion.

Soon we were enveloped to the throat in india-rubber clothing; the air apparatus fixed to our backs by braces. As to the Ruhmkorff apparatus, there was no necessity for it. Before putting my head into the copper helmet, I had asked a question about this of the captain.

"They would be useless," he replied. "We are going to no great depth, and the solar rays will be enough to light our walk. Besides, it would not be prudent to carry the electric light in these waters; its brilliancy might attract some of the dangerous inhabitants of the coast most inopportunely."

As Captain Nemo pronounced these words, I turned to Conseil and Ned Land. But my two friends had already encased their heads in their metal helmets, and they could neither hear nor answer.

One last question remained to ask of Captain Nemo.

"And our arms?" asked I; "our guns?"

"Guns! What for? Do not mountaineers attack the bear with a dagger in their hand, and is not steel surer than lead? Here is a strong blade; put it in your belt, and we start."

I looked at my companions; they were armed like us, and, more than that, Ned Land was brandishing an enormous harpoon, which he had placed in the launch before leaving the *Nautilus*.

Then, following the Captain's example, I allowed myself to be dressed in the heavy copper helmet, and our reservoirs of air were at once in activity. An instant later the sailors disembarked us, one after the other, in about a meter and a half of water upon an even sand. Captain Nemo made a sign with his hand, and we followed him down a gentle slope till we disappeared under the waves.

There, the fancies which had been obsessing my brain abandoned me. I became astonishingly calm. The ease of my movements filled me with confidence, and the strangeness of the spectacle captured my imagination.

The sun was already lighting up the water with great clarity. The smallest objects were visible. After ten minutes of walking, we reached a depth of five meters, and the terrain had become very flat.

Over our feet, like coveys of woodcocks in a bog, rose shoals of odd fish, of the genus monoptera, which have no other fins but their tail. I recognized the Javanese, a real serpent eight decimeters long, of a livid color underneath, and which might easily be mistaken for a conger eel if it was not for the golden stripes on its sides. In the genus stromateus, whose bodies are very flat and oval, I saw some in the most brilliant colors, carrying their dorsal fin like a scythe; an excellent eating fish, which, dried and pickled, forms an excellent dish known by the name of *Karawade;* then some tranquebars, belonging to the genus apsiphoroides, whose body is covered with a scaly cuirass of eight longitudinal plates.

The heightening sun lit the mass of waters more and more. The soil changed by degrees. To the fine sand succeeded a perfect causeway of round boulders, covered with a carpet of mollusks and zoöphytes. Among the specimens of these two branches I noticed some placenæ, with thin unequal shells, a kind of oyster peculiar to the Red Sea and the Indian Ocean; some orange lucinæ with rounded shells; auger-like *subul*ée; some of the Persian purpura that furnished the *Nautilus* with an admirable dye; horned murice five centimeters long, which raised themselves under the waves like hands ready to seize one. There were cornigerous turbinellae, all covered with spines; lingulae hyantes; and anatines, edible mollusks found in the food markets of Hindustan. There were also some marine panopyres, slightly luminous; and lastly, some admirable oculines flabelliformes, like magnificent fans, forming one of the richest vegetations of these seas.

In the midst of these living plants, and under the arbors of the hydrophytes, were layers of clumsy articulates, particularly some toothed raninæ, whose carapace formed a slightly rounded triangle; and some birgi, peculiar to these parts; and some horrible looking parthenopes with a face repugnant to look upon. Another no less hideous animal that I met several times, was an enormous crab observed by Mr. Darwin, which nature has given the instinct and necessary strength to live off coconuts. It climbs trees near the shore, throws down the nuts, which break from the fall, and works at them with its powerful pincers. Here, under these clear waves, the crab moved with unparalleled agility, while errant turtles of a species which frequents the coasts of Malabar moved slowly over the broken rocks.

At about seven o'clock we found ourselves at last surveying the oyster banks, on which the pearl oysters reproduce by millions. These precious mollusks adhere to the rocks, and are firmly attached, by the brown byssus that keeps them from moving. These oysters are inferior to the mussels, in this way, since these latter have not been denied all faculty of movement by nature.

The pearl oyster *meleagrina,* with its equal-sized valves, has a round shell, with thick walls and a very gnarled exterior. Some of these shells were spotted and streaked with green bands, that radiated down from the top. These were young oysters. The others, with rough, black surfaces, were ten years old or more, and measured five centimeters or larger.

Captain Nemo pointed with his hand to the enormous expanse of oysters; and I could well understand that this mine was inexhaustible, for Nature's creative power is far beyond man's instinct of destruction. Ned Land, faithful to this instinct, hastened to fill a net which he carried by his side with some of the finest specimens.

But we could not stop. We must follow the captain, who seemed to guide himself by paths known only to himself. The ground was sensibly rising, and sometimes on holding up my arm, it was above the surface of the sea. Then the level of the bank would sink capriciously. Often we rounded high rocks tapered into pyramids. In their dark fractures huge crustacea, perched upon their high claws like some war machines, watched us with fixed eyes; and under our feet crawled myrianidæ, glyceria, ariciæ, and various kinds of annelides, which extended their long antennas and curling tentacles.

At this moment there opened before us a large grotto, hollowed from a picturesque heap of rocks, and all carpeted with the thick warp of the submarine flora. At first it seemed very dark to me. The solar rays seemed to be extinguished by successive gradations, until its vague transparency became nothing more than drowned light.

Captain Nemo entered. We followed him. My eyes soon accustomed themselves to the relative darkness. I could distinguish the hanging and whimsical contours of the vault, supported by natural pillars, standing upon their granite base, like the heavy columns of Tuscan architecture. Why had our incomprehensible guide led us to the bottom of this submarine crypt? I was soon to know.

After descending a rather sharp slope, our feet trod the bottom of a kind of circular pit. There Captain Nemo stopped, and with his hand indicated an object I had not yet noticed.

It was an oyster of extraordinary dimensions, a gigantic tridacne, a fount which would have contained a whole lake of holy water, a basin the breadth of which was more than two meters, and consequently larger than that ornamenting the salon of the *Nautilus.*

I approached this extraordinary mollusk. It adhered by its byssus to a table of granite, and there, isolated, it developed itself in the calm waters of the grotto. I estimated the weight of this tridacne at 300 kilograms. Such an oyster would contain five kilograms of meat; and one must have the stomach of a Gargantua, to devour some dozens of them.

Captain Nemo was evidently acquainted with the existence of this bivalve. It was not the first time he had paid a visit here. I thought that he had only brought us to see this natural curiosity. I was wrong. He seemed to have a particular motive in verifying the actual state of this tridacne.

The shells were a little open; the captain came near and put his dagger between to prevent them from closing; then with his hand he raised the membrane with its fringed edges, which formed a protective cloak for the creature.

There, between the folded plaits, I saw a loose pearl, whose size equalled that of a coconut. Its globular shape, perfect clearness, and admirable lustre made it altogether a jewel of inestimable value. Carried away by my curiosity I stretched out my hand to seize it, weigh it, to touch it! But the captain stopped me, made a sign of refusal, and quickly withdrew his dagger, and the two shells closed suddenly.

I then understood Captain Nemo's intention. In leaving this pearl hidden in the mantle of the tridacne, he was allowing it to grow slowly. Each year the secretions of the mollusk would add new concentric layers. Only the captain knew of this grotto where this wonderful fruit of nature was "ripening." Only he was raising it, one might say, so that he could one day take it to his precious museum. Perhaps, following the examples of the Chinese and the Indians, he had started the growth of this pearl by introducing into the wrinkles of the mollusk a piece of glass or metal, which little by little has been covered by the nacreous material. In any case, comparing this pearl with others that I knew, and with those brilliant ones in the collection of the captain, I estimated its value at ten million francs at least. This was a superb natural curiosity, not a beautiful jewel. No feminine ear would ever be able to support it.

The visit to that opulent oyster was over. Captain Nemo left the grotto and climbed back again to the pearl oyster bed; in the midst of clear waters not yet disturbed by the work of divers.

We walked alone, like regular strollers, sometimes stopping, sometimes wandering off, according to our fancy. For my part, I no longer feared those dangers that my imagination had so ridiculously exaggerated. The sea floor was rising noticeably toward the surface of the water, and soon we were only under a meter of water and my head protruded beyond the surface of the sea. Conseil joined me and, putting his helmet next to mine, made a friendly gesture with his eyes. But the elevated plain continued for only a few fathoms and soon we were back in our own element. I felt that I now had the right to call it my own.

After ten minutes Captain Nemo stopped suddenly. I thought he had halted that we might retrace our steps. No; by a gesture he bade us crouch beside him in a deep fracture of the rock. His hand pointed to one part of the liquid mass, which I watched attentively.

About five meters from me a shadow appeared, and sank to the ground. The disquieting idea of sharks shot through my mind, but I was mistaken; and once again it was not a monster of the ocean that we had anything to do with.

It was a man, a living man, an Indian, a Black fisherman, a poor devil who, no doubt, had come to glean before the harvest. I could see the bottom of his canoe anchored some feet above his head. He dived and went up successively. A stone, cut in the shape of a sugar loaf, held between his feet, helped him to descend more rapidly, while a rope fastened him to his boat. This was all his apparatus. Reaching the bottom about five meters deep, he went on his knees and filled his bag with oysters picked up at random. Then he went up, emptied his sack, pulled up his stone, and began the operation once more, which lasted thirty seconds.

The diver did not see us. The shadow of the rock hid us from sight. And how should this poor Indian ever dream that men, beings like himself, should be there under the water watching his movements, and losing no detail of the fishing?

Several times he went up in this way, and dived again. He did not carry away more than ten at each plunge, for he was obliged to pull them from the bank to which they adhered by means of their strong byssus. And how many of those oysters for which he risked his life had no pearl in them!

I watched him closely, his maneuvers were regular, and, for the space of half an hour, no danger appeared to threaten him. I was beginning to accustom myself to the sight of this interesting fishing, when suddenly, as the Indian was on the sea floor, I saw him make a gesture of terror, rise, and make a spring to return to the surface of the sea.

I understood his terror. A gigantic shadow appeared just above the unfortunate diver. It was a shark of enormous size advancing diagonally, his eyes on fire, and his jaws open.

I was mute with horror, and unable to move. The voracious creature, with a vigorous thrust of its fins, shot towards the Indian, who threw himself on one side in order to avoid the shark's bite; but not its tail, for it struck his chest, and stretched him on the sea floor.

This scene lasted but a few seconds: the shark returned, and, turning on his back, prepared himself for cutting the Indian in two, when I saw Captain Nemo rise suddenly. Then, dagger in hand, he walked straight to the monster, ready to fight face to face with him.

The very moment the shark was going to snap up the unhappy fisherman, he perceived his new adversary, and turning over, made straight towards him.

I can still see Captain Nemo's position. Holding himself well together, he waited for the formidable shark with admirable coolness; and, when it rushed at him, threw himself on one side with wonderful quickness, avoiding the shock, and burying his dagger deep into its side. But it was not all over. A terrible combat ensued.

The shark had seemed to roar, if I might say so. The blood rushed in torrents from its wound. The sea was dyed red, and through the opaque liquid I could distinguish nothing more.

Nothing more until the moment when, like lightning, I saw the audacious captain hanging on to one of the creature's fins, struggling body to body with the monster, and dealing successive blows at his enemy, yet still unable to give a decisive one to the heart. The shark, in its struggles, churned the water with such fury that I feared it would knock me over.

I wanted to go to the captain's assistance, but, nailed to the spot with horror, I could not stir.

I watched with horror; I saw the different phases of the fight. The captain fell to the earth, upset by the enormous mass which pressed upon him. The shark's jaws opened wide, like a pair of factory shears, and it would have been all over with the captain; but, quick as thought, harpoon in hand, Ned Land rushed towards the shark and struck it with its sharp point.

The waves were impregnated with a mass of blood. They rocked under the shark's movements, which beat them with indescribable fury. Ned Land had not missed his aim. It was the monster's death rattle. Struck to the heart, it struggled in dreadful convulsions, the shock of which overthrew Conseil.

But Ned Land had disentangled the captain, who, getting up without any wound, went straight to the Indian, quickly cut the cord which held him to his stone, took him in his arms, and, with a sharp blow of his heel, mounted to the surface.

We all three followed, and in a few seconds, saved by a miracle, reached the fisherman's boat.

Captain Nemo's first care was to recall the unfortunate man to life. I did not think he could succeed. I hoped so, for the poor devil's immersion had not been long. But the blow from the shark's tail might have been his death blow.

Happily, with the captain's and Conseil's hard massaging, I saw consciousness return by degrees. He opened his eyes. What was his surprise, his terror even, at seeing four great copper heads leaning over him! And, above all, what must he have thought when Captain Nemo, drawing from the pocket of his dress a bag of pearls, placed it in his hand? This magnificent charity from the man of the seas to the poor Ceylonese Indian was accepted with a trembling hand. His wondering eyes showed that he knew not to what superhuman beings he owed both fortune and life.

At a sign from the captain we regained the oyster bank, and following the road already traversed, came in about half an hour to the anchor which held the launch of the *Nautilus* to the sea floor.

Once on board, we each, with the help of the sailors, got rid of the heavy copper helmet.

Captain Nemo's first word was to the Canadian.

"Thank you, Master Land," said he.

"It was in payment of a debt, Captain," replied Ned Land. "I owed you that."

A wan smile passed across the captain's lips, and that was all.

"To the *Nautilus*," said he.

The boat flew over the waves. Some minutes later, we met the dead shark's body floating. By the black marking of the extremity of its fins, I recognized the terrible melanopteron of the Indian Ocean, of the species of shark properly so called. It was more than twenty-five feet long; its enormous mouth occupied one-third of its body. It was an adult, as was revealed by its six rows of teeth, placed in an isosceles triangle in the upper jaw.

Conseil looked at it with scientific interest, and I am sure that he placed it, and not without reason, in the cartilaginous species, of the chondropterygian class, with fixed gills, of the selacian order, in the genus of the sharks.

While I was contemplating this inert mass, a dozen of these voracious melanopterons appeared round the boat, circling it; and, without noticing us, threw themselves upon the dead body and fought with one another for the pieces.

At half-past eight we were again on board the *Nautilus*. There I reflected on the incidents which had taken place in our excursion to the Manaar Bank. Two conclusions I must inevitably draw from it—one bearing upon the unparalleled courage of Captain Nemo, the other upon his devotion to a human being, a representative of that race from which he fled beneath the sea. Whatever he might say, this strange man had not yet succeeded in entirely killing his own heart.

When I made this observation to him, he answered in a slightly moved tone—

"That Indian, Professor, is an inhabitant of an oppressed country; and I am still, and shall be, to my last breath, one of them!"

◄ CHAPTER IV ►

THE RED SEA

 n the course of the day of the 29th of January, the Island of Ceylon disappeared beyond the horizon, and the *Nautilus,* at a speed to twenty miles an hour, slid into the labyrinth of channels which separate the Maldives from the Laccadives. It coasted even the Island of Kiltan, a land of coral originally, discovered by Vasco de Gama in 1499, and one of the nineteen principal islands of the Lacca-dive Archipelago, situated between 10° and 14° 30´ north latitude, and 69° and 50° 72´ east longitude.

We had made 16,220 miles, or 7,500 leagues, from our starting-point in Japanese waters.

The next day—30th of January—when the *Nautilus* rose to the surface of the ocean, there was no land in sight. Its course was N.N.W., in the direction of the Gulf of Oman, between Arabia and the Indian Peninsula, which serves as an outlet to the Persian Gulf.

It was evidently a block without any possible egress. Where was Captain Nemo taking us to? I could not say. This, however, did not satisfy the Canadian, who that day came to me asking where we were going.

"We are going where are captain's fancy takes us, Master Ned."

"His fancy cannot take us far, then," said the Canadian. "The Persian Gulf has no outlet: and if we do go in, it will not be long before we are out again."

"Very well, we will come out again, Master Land; and if, after the Persian Gulf, the *Nautilus* would like to visit the Red Sea, the Straits of Bab-el-Mandeb are there to give us entrance."

"I need not tell you, sir," said Ned Land, "that the Red Sea is as much closed as the Gulf, as the Isthmus of Suez is not yet cut;[1] and if it was, a boat as mysterious as ours would not risk itself in a canal with locks. So, the Red Sea is not the road to take us back to Europe."

"But I never said we were going back to Europe."

"What do you suppose, then?"

"I suppose that, after visiting the curious coasts of Arabia and Egypt, the *Nautilus* will go down the Indian Ocean again, perhaps cross the Channel of Mozambique, perhaps off the Mascarenes, so as to gain the Cape of Good Hope.''

"And once at the Cape of Good Hope?'' asked the Canadian, with insistent emphasis.

"Well, we shall penetrate into that Atlantic which we have not yet explored. Ah! friend Ned, you are getting tired of this journey under the sea? You are surfeited with the incessantly varying spectacle of submarine wonders? For my part, I shall be sorry to see the end of a voyage which it is given to so few men to make.''

"But, do you realize, Mister Aronnax,'' answered Ned, "that we have been prisoners for three months on board the *Nautilus?*''

"No, Ned, I did not realize that, nor do I want to. I have not been counting the days and hours.''

"But what of the end?''

"That will come in time. There is nothing we can do about it and this discussion is useless. If you were to say to me, my brave Ned, 'A chance to escape has offered itself,' I will discuss it with you. But that is not the case, and to speak frankly, I do not think that Captain Nemo will venture into European seas.''

By this short dialogue it can be seen that I had become a fanatic on the *Nautilus;* I was identifying myself with its captain.

Ned Land ended the conversation with these words, in the form of a monologue to himself, "All of this is well and good, but the way I see it, unless a man is free he cannot be happy.''

For four days, till the 3rd of February, the *Nautilus* cruised the Gulf of Oman, at various speeds and at various depths. It seemed to go at random, as if hesitating as to which road it should follow, but we never crossed the Tropic of Cancer.

In quitting this sea we sighted Muscat for an instant, one of the most important towns of the country of Oman. I admired its strange aspect, surrounded by black cliffs upon which its white houses and forts stood in relief. I saw the rounded domes of its mosques, the elegant points of its minarets, its fresh and verdant terraces. But it was only a passing vision, and the *Nautilus* soon sank under the somber saves of that region.

We passed along the Arabian coast of Mahrah and Hadramant, at a distance of six miles, its undulating line of mountains being occasionally relieved by some ancient ruin. The 5th of February we at last entered the Gulf of Aden, a perfect funnel introduced into the neck of Bab-el-Mandeb, through which the waters of the Indian Ocean enter the Red Sea.

The 6th of February, the *Nautilus* floated in sight of Aden, perched upon a promontory which a narrow isthmus joins to the mainland, a kind of inaccessible Gibraltar, the fortifications of which were rebuilt by the English after taking possession in 1839. I caught a glimpse of the octagon minarets of this town, which was at one time, according to the historian Edrisi, the richest commercial center on the coast.

I certainly thought that Captain Nemo arrived at this point, would back out again; but I was mistaken, for he did no such thing, much to my surprise.

The next day, the 7th of February, we entered the Straits of Bab-el-Mandeb, the name of which, in the Arab tongue, means "the Gate of Tears.'' It is twenty miles in breadth, and only fifty-two kilometers in length. For the *Nautilus,* going at full speed, the crossing was scarcely the work of an hour. But I saw nothing, not even the Island of Perim, with which the British Government has fortified the position of Aden. There were too many English or French steamers on the routes from Suez to Bombay, Calcutta, Melbourne, Bourbon, and Mauritius, furrowing this narrow passage, for the *Nautilus* to venture to show itself. So it remained prudently below.

At last, about noon, we were in the waters of the Red Sea.

The Red Sea, celebrated in Biblical tradition, is replenished rarely by rain, and not by any important river; its evaporation is so excessive that in one year its level drops a meter and a half! Singular gulf, which, enclosed and under the conditions of a lake, would entirely dry up. It is inferior in that respect to the neighboring Caspian and Dead seas, whose levels have reached a point where evaporation precisely equals the total amount of water entering them.

The Red Sea is 2,600 kilometers long and averages about 240 wide. At the time of the Ptolemies and the Roman emperors, it was the largest commercial artery in the world. The piercing of the isthmus will regain it its importance of old, which the railroads of Suez have regained in part.

I would not even seek to understand the caprice which had decided Captain Nemo upon entering the gulf. But I quite approved of the *Nautilus* entering it. Its speed was lessened: sometimes it kept on the surface, sometimes it dived to avoid a vessel, and thus I was able to observe the upper and lower parts of this curious sea.

The 8th of February, from the first hours of day, Mocha came in sight, now a ruined town, whose walls would fall at the sound of a cannon, yet which shelters here and there some verdant date trees. Once it was an important city, containing six public markets, and twenty-six mosques, and whose walls, defended by fourteen forts, formed a belt three kilometers in circumference.

The *Nautilus* then approached the African shore, where the depth of the sea was greater. There, in waters clear as crystal, through the open panels we were allowed to contemplate the beautiful bushes of brilliant coral, and large blocks of rock clothed with a splendid fur of green algæ and fuci. What an indescribable spectacle, and what variety of sites and landscapes along these reefs and volcanic islands which bound the Lybian coast! But where these shrubs appeared in all their beauty was on the eastern coast, which the *Nautilus* soon gained. It was on the coast of Tehama, for there not only did this display of zoöphytes flourish beneath the level of the sea, but they also formed picturesque interlacings which unfolded themselves about ten fathoms below the surface; more capricious but less highly colored than those whose freshness was kept up by the vital power of the waters.

What charming hours I passed thus at the window of the salon! What new specimens of submarine flora and fauna did I admire under the brightness of our electric lantern!

There were mushroom-shaped fungi; slate-colored sea anemones, among others the *thalassianthus aster;* tubipores arranged like flutes, waiting to be blown by the god Pan; shells peculiar to this sea, found in hollows in the coral, with spiral-shaped bases; and last a thousand specimens of a polypary I had not yet seen: the common sponge.

The class of sponges, first in the group of polyps, is a strange and curious product whose usefulness is incontestable. The sponge is not a plant, as some naturalists still maintain, but an animal of the last order, a polyp inferior to the coral. Its animality is undoubted, and I cannot accept the opinion of those ancients who regarded it as an intermediary between plants and animals. I must say, however, that all naturalists are not in accord as to the sponge's structure. For some it is a polyp, for others, such as Milne-Edwards, it is an individual, isolated and unique.

The class of sponges contains about three hundred species, which are found in a large number of seas. Some are found in certain rivers and have received the name *fluviatiles*. But their waters of choice are those of the Mediterranean, the Grecian archipelago, the Syrian coast and the Red Sea. There reproduce and develop the finest sponges, valued as highly as 150 francs, such as the blonde Syrian sponge and the hard Barbary sponge, etc. But I could not hope to study these zoöphytes in the seaports of the Levant, since we were separated from them by the impassable isthmus of Suez. I had to content myself with observing those in the waters of the Red Sea.

I called Conseil to my side, while the *Nautilus,* at an average depth of eight or nine meters, moved slowly past the beautiful rocks of the eastern coast.

There grew sponges of all shapes: pediculated, foliated, globular, and digital. They certainly justified perfectly names such as baskets, cups, distaffs, elk's horns, lion's feet, peacock's tails, and Neptune's gloves, which have been given to them by the fishermen, greater poets than the scientists.

From their fibrous tissue, infused with a gelatinous, semi-fluid substance, escaped an incessant little stream of water; which, after carrying life to each cell, is expulsed by a contracting movement. This substance disappears after the death of the polyp, and as it putrifies it releases ammonia. What remains are the horny and gelatinous fibers that form the domestic sponge. It is put to many uses, depending upon the degree of its elasticity, permeability and resistance to wear.

The polyparies adhere to rocks, to mollusk shells, and even to the stems of hydrophytes. They garnished the tiniest fractures, some spreading out, some growing upright and others hanging like coral excrescences. I explained to Conseil that these sponges are gathered by two methods: by a dredge or by hand. This last method, which necessitates the employment of divers, is preferable, since it does not harm the tissue of the polypary, and so they can command superior prices.

Other zoöphytes which multiply near the sponges consist principally of jellyfish of a most elegant kind. The mollusks were represented by varieties of the squid (which, according to Orbigny, are peculiar to the Red Sea); and reptiles by the *virgata* turtle, of the genus of cheloniæ, which furnish a wholesome and delicate food for our table.

As to the fish, they were abundant, and often remarkable. The following are those which the nets of the *Nautilus* brought most frequently on board:—

Rays of a brick color, with oval bodies marked with unequal blue spots, and easily recognizable by their double notched stings; arnacks with silver backs; sting rays with pointed tails; and the brockats, like large overcoats two meters long, that undulated through the water. There were aodons, completely without teeth, cartilaginous and related to the sharks; dromedary-ostracions, with a hump that terminated in a curved spine a foot and a half long; ophidians, true morays with a silver tail, bluish backs and brown pectoral fins tinted with grey, fiatoles, a species of stromatidae, striped with gold streaks and decorated with the three colors of the French flag; blennies four decimeters long; some superb caranxes, decorated with seven transverse bands of jet-black, blue and yellow fins, and gold and silver scales; centripodes; mullets with yellow heads; scares; labres; triggerfish; gobies, and a thousand other species, common to the ocean which we had just traversed.

The 9th of February, the *Nautilus* floated in the broadest part of the Red Sea, which is comprised between Souakin, on the west coast, and Kunfuda, on the east coast, one hundred and ninety miles apart.

That day at noon, after the bearings were taken, Captain Nemo mounted the platform, where I happened to be. I was determined not to let him go down again without at least pressing him regarding his future projects. As soon as he saw me he approached, and graciously offered me a cigar and said:

"Well, sir, does this Red Sea please you? Have you sufficiently observed the wonders it covers, its fishes, its zoöphytes, its gardens of sponges, and its forests of coral? Did you catch a glimpse of the towns and breakwaters on its borders?"

"Yes, Captain Nemo," I replied; "and the *Nautilus* is wonderfully fitted for such a study. Ah! It is an intelligent boat!"

"Yes, sir, intelligent, brave and invulnerable. It fears neither the terrible tempests of the Red Sea, nor its currents, nor its reefs."

"Certainly," said I, "this sea is cited as one of the worst, and in the time of the ancients, if I am not mistaken, its reputation was detestable."

"Detestable, Monsieur Aronnax. The Greek and Latin historians do not speak favorably of it, and Strabo says it was very dangerous during the time of the Etesian winds, and in the rainy season. The Arabian Edrisi portrays it under the name of the Gulf of Colzoum, and relates that vessels perished there in great numbers on the sandbanks, and that no one would risk sailing in the night. It is, he claimed, a sea subject to fearful hurricanes, strewn with inhospitable islands, and 'which offers nothing good' either on its surface or in its depths. Such, too, is the opinion of Arrian, Agatharcides, and Artemidorus."

"One may see," I replied, "that these historians never sailed on board the *Nautilus.*"

"Just so," replied the captain, smiling; "and in that respect moderns are not more advanced than the ancients. It required many ages to find out the mechanical power of steam. Who knows if, in another hundred years, we may not see a second *Nautilus?*[2] Progress is slow, Monsieur Aronnax."

"It is true," I answered; "your boat is at least a century before its time, perhaps an era. What a misfortune should the secret of such an invention die with its inventor!"

Captain Nemo did not reply. After some minutes' silence he continued—

"You were speaking of the opinions of ancient historians upon the dangerous navigation of the Red Sea."

"It is true," said I; "but were not their fears exaggerated?"

"Yes and no, Monsieur Aronnax," replied Captain Nemo, who seemed to know the Red Sea by heart. "That which is no longer dangerous for a modern vessel, well rigged, strongly built, and master of its own course, thanks to obedient steam, offered all sorts of perils to the ships of the ancients. Picture to yourself those first navigators venturing in ships made of planks sown with the cords of the palm tree, saturated with the grease of the sea dog, and covered with powdered resin! They had not even instruments wherewith to take their bearings, and they went by guess among currents of which they scarcely knew anything. Under such conditions shipwrecks were, and must have been, numerous. But in our time, steamers running between Suez and the South Seas have nothing more to fear from the fury of this gulf, in spite of contrary tradewinds. The captain and passengers do not prepare for their departure by offering propitiatory sacrifices: and, on their return, they no longer go ornamented with garlands and gold wreaths to thank the gods in the neighboring temple."

"I agree with you," said I; "and steam seems to have killed all gratitude in the hearts of sailors. But, Captain, since you seem to have especially studied this sea, can you tell me the origin of its name?"

"There exist several explanations on the subject, Monsieur Aronnax. Would you like to know the opinion of a chronicler of the fourteenth century?"

"Willingly."

"This fanciful writer pretends that its name was given to it after the passage of the Israelites, when Pharaoh perished in the waves which closed at the voice of Moses:

'To signalize that miracle, the sea became red and vermillion.'

What other name could it have, other than the Red Sea?"

"A poet's explanation, Captain Nemo," I replied; "but I cannot content myself with that. I ask you for your personal opinion."

"Here it is, Monsieur Aronnax. According to my idea, we must see in this appellation of the Red Sea a translation of the Hebrew word 'Edom;' and if the ancients gave it that name, it was on account of the particular color of its waters."

"But up to this time I have seen nothing but transparent waves and without any particular color."

"Very likely; but as we advance to the end of the gulf, you will see this singular appearance. I remember seeing the Bay of Tor entirely red, like a sea of blood."

"And you attribute this color to the presence of a microscopic seaweed?"

"Yes; it is a mucilaginous purple matter, produced by the little plants known by the name of trichodesmia, and of which it requires 40,000 to occupy the space of a square millimeter. Perhaps we shall meet some when we get to Tor."

"So, Captain Nemo, it is not the first time you have cruised the Red Sea on board the *Nautilus?*"

"No, sir."

"As you spoke a while ago of the passage of the Israelites, and of the catastrophe to the Egyptians, I will ask whether you have met with traces under the water of this great historical fact?"

"No, sir; and for a very good reason."

"What is it?"

"It is, that the spot where Moses and his people passed is now so blocked up with sand, that the camels can barely bathe their legs there. You can well understand that there would not be water enough for my *Nautilus.*"

"And that spot?" I asked.

"The spot is situated a little above the Isthmus of Suez, in the arm which formerly made a deep estuary, when the Red Sea extended to the Bitter Lake. Now, whether this passage were miraculous or not, the Israelites, nevertheless, crossed there to reach the Promised Land, and Pharaoh's army perished precisely on that spot; and I think that excavations made in the middle of the sand would bring to light a large number of arms and instruments of Egyptian origin."

"That is evident," I replied; "and for the sake of archæologists let us hope that these excavations will be made sooner or later, when new towns are established on the isthmus, after the construction of the Suez Canal; and canal, however very useless to a vessel like the *Nautilus!*"

"Very likely; but useful to the whole world," said Captain Nemo. "The ancients well understood the utility of a communication between the Red Sea and the Mediterranean for their commercial affairs: but they did not think of digging a direct canal, they took the Nile for an intermediary. Very probably the canal which united the Nile to the Red Sea was begun by Sesostris, if we may believe tradition. One thing is certain, that in the year 615 B.C., Necos undertook the works of a shipping canal to the waters of the Nile, across the plain of Egypt that faced Arabia. it took four days to go up this canal, and it was so wide that two triremes could go abreast. It was carried on by Darius, the son of Hystaspes, and probably finished by Ptolemy II. Strabo saw it navigated; but because of its slight slope from the point of entry, near Bubastes, to the Red Sea, it was only navigable for a few months in the year. This canal answered all commercial purposes to the age of Antoninus; then it was abandoned when blocked up with sand. Restored by order of the Caliph Omar, it was definitively destroyed in 761 or 762 by Caliph Al-Mansor, who wished to prevent the arrival of provisions to Mohammed ben Abdallah, who had revolted against him. During the expedition into Egypt, your General Bonaparte discovered traces of the works in the Desert of Suez; and surprised by the tide, he nearly perished before regaining Hadjaroth, at the very place where Moses had encamped three thousand and three hundred years before him."

"Well, Captain, what the ancients dared not undertake, this junction between the two seas, which will shorten the road from Cadiz to India by 9,000 kilometers, Monsieur de Lesseps has succeeded in doing; and before long he will have changed Africa into an immense island."

"Yes, Monsieur Aronnax; you have the right to be proud of your countryman. Such a man brings more honor to a nation than great captains! He began, like so many others, facing, disinterest and rebuffs; but he has triumphed, for he has the genius of will. And it is sad to think that a work like that, which ought to have been an international work, and which would have sufficed to make a reign illustrious, should have succeeded by the energy of one man. All honor to Monsieur de Lesseps!"

"Yes, honor to the great citizen!" I replied, surprised by the manner in which Captain Nemo had just spoken.

"Unfortunately," he continued, "I cannot take you through the Suez Canal; but you will be able to see the long jetty of Port Said after tomorrow, when we shall be in the Mediterranean."

"The Mediterranean!" I exclaimed.

"Yes, sir; does that astonish you?"

"What astonishes me is to think that we shall be there the day after tomorrow."

"Indeed?"

"Yes, Captain, although by this time I ought to have accustomed myself to be surprised at nothing since I have been on board your boat."

"But the cause of this surprise?"

"Well, it is the fearful speed you will have to put on the *Nautilus,* if the day after tomorrow she is to be in the Mediterranean, having made the round of Africa, and doubled the Cape of Good Hope!"

"Who told you that she would make the round of Africa, and double the Cape of Good Hope, sir?"

"Well, unless the *Nautilus* sails on dry land, and passes above the isthmus . . . ."

"Or beneath it, Monsieur Aronnax."

"Beneath it?"

"Certainly," replied Captain Nemo, quietly. "A long time ago Nature made under this tongue of land what man has this day made on its surface."

"What! Such a passage exists?"

"Yes; a subterranean passage, which I have named the Arabian Tunnel. It takes us beneath Suez, and opens into the Gulf of Pelusium."

"But isn't this isthmus composed of nothing but quicksands?"

"To a certain depth. But at fifty meters only we encounter a solid layer of rock."

"Did you discover this passage by chance?" I asked, more and more surprised.

"Chance and reasoning, sir; and by reasoning even more than by chance."

"Captain, I'm listening but my ears don't believe what they are hearing."

"Ah, Monsieur! *Autres habent et non audient*—they have ears, but hear not—an eternal truth. Not only does this passage exist, but I have often profited from it."

"Would it be indiscreet to inquire as to how you discovered this tunnel?"

"Sir," answered the captain, "there can be no secrets between men who will never part."

I ignored this insinuation, and paid attention to Captain Nemo's story.

"Professor," he said to me, "the simple reasoning of the naturalist led me to discover this passage, previously unknown. Otherwise I should not have ventured this day into the impassable Red Sea." I noticed that in the Red Sea and in the Mediterranean there existed a certain number of fishes of absolutely identical species—ophidia, fiatoles, girelles, persegae, joels, and exocoeti. Certain of that fact, I asked myself if it possible that there was a communication between the two seas. If there was, the subterranean current must necessarily run from the Red Sea to the Mediterranean, from the sole cause of difference of level. I caught a large number of fishes in the neighborhood of Suez. I passed a copper ring through their tails, and threw them back into the sea. Some months later, on the coast of Syria, I caught some of my fish ornamented with the ring. Thus the communication between the two was proved. I then sought for it with my *Nautilus;* I discovered it, ventured into it, and before long, sir, you too will have passed through my Arabian tunnel!"

---

[1]At the time Ned is talking, the Suez Canal had been under construction by Ferdinand Marie, Vicomte de Lesseps for several years. It would not be opened until 1869. R.M.

[2]The atomic submarine U.S.S. *Nautilus* was launched in 1954, less than 90 years after *20,000 Leagues* was published. R.M.

◄ CHAPTER V ►
THE ARABIAN TUNNEL

hat same day, I reported to Conseil and Ned Land the part of the conversation which most interested them. I explained that within two days we would be in the waters of the Mediterranean. Conseil clapped his hands, but the Canadian shrugged his shoulders.

"An undersea tunnel!" he cried, "a passage between two seas! Who ever heard of such a thing?"

"Friend Ned," replied Conseil, "had you ever before heard of the *Nautilus*? No! But it exists anyway. You should not shrug your shoulders so readily, or deny that something exists, on the pretext that you have never heard of it."

"Well enough!" answered Ned, shaking his head. "After all, I will ask for nothing more than this passage, through which the captain, with heaven's guidance, will carry us to the Mediterranean."

That same evening, in 21° 30′ north latitude, the *Nautilus* floated on the surface of the sea, approaching the Arabian coast. I saw Djeddah, the most important counting-house of Egypt, Syria, Turkey, and India. I distinguished clearly enough its buildings, the vessels anchored at the quays, and those whose draught of water obliged them to anchor in the roads. The sun, rather low on the horizon, struck full on the houses of the town, bringing out their whiteness. Outside, some wooden cabins, and some made of reeds, showed the quarter inhabited by the Bedouins.

Soon Djeddah was shut out from view by the shadows of night, and the *Nautilus* found herself under water slightly phosphorescent.

The next day, the 10th of February, we sighted several ships running opposite our direction. The *Nautilus* returned to its submarine navigation; but at noon, when her bearings were taken, the sea being deserted, she rose again to her waterline.

Accompanied by Ned and Conseil, I seated myself on the platform. The coast on the eastern side looked like a mass faintly printed upon a damp fog.

We were leaning on the sides of the launch, talking of one thing and another, when Ned Land, stretching out his hand towards a spot on the sea, said: "Do you see anything there, sir?"

"No, Ned," I replied, "but I have not your eyes, you know."

"Look well," said Ned, "there, on the starboard beam, about the height of the lantern! Do you not see a mass which seems to move?"

"Certainly," said I, after close attention, "I see something like a long black body on the top of the water."

"Another *Nautilus*?" asked Conseil.

"No," answered the Canadian, "but if I am not mistaken, it is a marine animal."

"A whale in the Red Sea?" demanded Conseil.

"Yes, my boy," I responded, "they are sometimes encountered here."

"It isn't a whale," said Ned Land, keeping his eyes on the object. "Whales and I, we are old acquaintances and I cannot be fooled by appearances."

"Patience," said Conseil, "the *Nautilus* is steering for the coast and before long we will know what it is for certain."

And certainly before long the black object was not more than a mile from us. It looked like a great reef deposited in the open sea. What could it be? I could not say.

"Ah! It moves! It dives!" cried Ned. "A thousand devils! What is that animal? It does not have the divided tail of the baleen whale or the cachalot and its fins look more like stumps."

"But then . . ." I began.

"Good!" exclaimed Ned, "now it is on its back, with its mammaries in the air!"

"It is a siren!" cried Conseil, "a real mermaid, if it pleases monsieur."

The word "siren" put me on the right track, and I realized that this was a creature that belonged to the order of marine animals that had inspired the fable of the mermaids, half woman and half fish.

"No," I said to Conseil, "it is not a mermaid, but rather a strange animal of which few remain in the Red Sea. It is a dugong."

"Order of sirenians, group of pisciforms, subclass of monodelphians, class of mammals, branch of vertebrates," responded Conseil.

And after Conseil had said this, there was nothing more to say.

Ned Land looked eagerly. His eyes shone with covetousness at the sight of the animal. His hand seemed ready to harpoon it. One would have thought he was awaiting the moment to throw himself into the sea, and attack it in its element.

"Oh! sir," he said, his voice trembling with emotion, "I have never killed anything like *that*!"

All the harpooner was in that last word.

At this instant Captain Nemo appeared on the platform. He saw the dugong, understood the Canadian's attitude, and addressing him, said: "If you held a harpoon just now, Master Land, would it not burn your hand?"

"Just so, sir."

"And you would not be sorry to return for one day to your trade of a fisherman, and to add this cetacean to the list of those you have already killed?"

"That would not displease me!"

"Well, you can try."

"Thank you, sir," said Ned Land, his eyes flaming.

"Only," continued the captain, "I advise you for your own sake not to miss the creature."

"Is the dugong dangerous to attack?" I asked, in spite of the Canadian's shrug of the shoulders.

"Yes," replied the captain; "sometimes the animal turns upon its assailants and overturns their boat. But for Master Land, this danger is not to be feared. His eye is prompt, his arm sure. I only recommend that he not miss this dugong, because its flesh is rightly regarded as very fine, and I do not think that Master Land would decline a morsel."

"Ah!" said the Canadian, "this beast is also considered good to eat?"

"Yes, Master Land. Its flesh is real meat and held in high esteem. In Malaysia it is reserved for the tables of princes. As a result, this excellent animal has been so relentlessly hunted that, like its cousin the manatee, it is becoming very rare."

"Then, Captain," said Conseil seriously, "if this specimen might be the last of its race, might it not be better to spare it—in the interest of science?"

"Perhaps," replied the Canadian, "but in the interest of cooking, it might be better to hunt it."

"Go ahead, Master Land," said Captain Nemo.

At this moment seven men of the crew, mute and immovable as ever, mounted the platform. One carried a harpoon and a line similar to those employed in catching whales. The launch was lifted, pulled from its socket, and let down into the sea. Six oarsmen took their seats, and the coxswain went to the tiller. Ned, Conseil, and I went to the back of the boat.

"You are not coming, Captain?" I asked.

"No, sir; but I wish you good sport."

The boat put off, and lifted by the six rowers, drew rapidly towards the dugong, which floated about two miles from the *Nautilus*.

Arrived some cables' length from the cetacean, the speed slackened, and the oars dipped noiselessly into the quiet waters. Ned Land, harpoon in hand, stood in the fore part of the boat. The harpoon used for striking a whale is generally attached to a very long cord, which runs out rapidly as the wounded creature draws it after him. But here the cord was not more than ten fathoms long, and the extremity was attached to a small barrel, which, by floating, was to show the course the dugong took under the water.

I stood and carefully watched the Canadian's adversary. This dugong, which also bears the name of the halicore, closely resembles the manatee; its oblong body terminated in a lengthened tail, and its lateral fins in perfect fingers. Its difference from the manatee consisted in its upper jaw, which was armed with two long and pointed teeth, that formed diverging tusks on each side.

This dugong, which Ned Land was preparing to attack, was of colossal dimensions; it was more than seven meters long. It did not move, and seemed to be sleeping on the waves, which circumstance made it easier to capture.

The boat approached within three fathoms of the animal. The oars rested on the rowlocks. I half rose. Ned Land, his body thrown a little back, brandished the harpoon in his experienced hand.

Suddenly, a hissing noise was heard and the dugong disappeared. The harpoon, although thrown with great force, had apparently only struck the water.

"A thousand devils!" exclaimed the Canadian, furiously. "I have missed it!"

"No," said I, "the creature is wounded—look at the blood, but your weapon has not stuck in his body."

"My harpoon! My harpoon!" cried Ned Land.

The sailors rowed on, and the coxswain made for the floating barrel. The harpoon regained, the launch followed in pursuit of the animal.

The latter came now and then to the surface to breathe. Its wound had not weakened it, for it shot onwards with great rapidity. The boat, rowed by strong arms, flew on its track. Several times it approached within some few fathoms, and the Canadian was ready to strike, but the dugong made off with a sudden plunge, and it was impossible to reach it.

Imagine the fury which overexcited impatient Ned Land! He hurled at the unfortunate creature the most energetic expletives in the English tongue. For my part, I was only vexed to see the dugong escape all our attacks.

We pursued it without relaxation for an hour, and I began to think it would prove difficult to capture, when the animal, possessed with the perverse idea of vengeance, of which he had cause to repent, turned upon the launch and assailed us in its turn.

This maneuver did not escape the Canadian.

"Look out!" he cried.

The coxswain said some words in his bizarre tongue, doubtless warning the men to keep on their guard.

The dugong came within twenty feet of the boat, stopped, sniffed the air briskly with its large nostrils (not pierced at the extremity, but in the upper part of its muzzle). Then taking a spring he threw himself upon us.

The launch could not avoid the shock, and half upset, shipped at least two tons of water, which had to be emptied; but thanks to the coxswain, we caught it sideways, not full front, so we were not quite overturned. While Ned Land, clinging to the bows, belabored the gigantic animal with blows from his harpoon, the creature's teeth were buried in the gunwale, and it lifted the whole thing out of the water, as a lion does a roebuck. We were upset over one

another, and I know not how the adventure would have ended, if the Canadian, still enraged with the beast, had not struck it to the heart.

I heard its teeth grind on the iron plate, and the dugong disappeared, carrying the harpoon with him. But the barrel soon returned to the surface, and shortly after the body of the animal, turned on its back. The boat came up to it, took it in tow, and made straight for the *Nautilus.*

It required tackle of enormous strength to hoist the dugong on to the platform. It weighed 5000 kilograms. It was cut up under the Canadian's eyes, and he oversaw every detail of the operation. That same day the steward served for dinner slices of the meat skilfully prepared by the chef. I thought it was excellent: superior to veal, to say nothing of beef.

The next day, February 11th, the larder of the *Nautilus* was enriched by some more delicate game. A flight of sea-swallows rested on the *Nautilus.* It was a species of the *Sterna nilotica,* peculiar to Egypt; its beak is black, head grey and pointed, the eye surrounded by white spots, the back, wings, and tail of a greyish color, the belly and throat white, and claws red. They also took some dozen of Nile ducks, a wild bird of high flavor, its throat and upper part of the head white with black spots.

The speed of the *Nautilus* was moderate. We went at a stroll, so to speak. I observed that the water of the Red Sea was becoming less salty, a sign that we were nearing Suez.

About five o'clock in the evening we sighted to the north the Cape of Ras Mohammed. This cape forms the extremity of Arabia Petræa, comprised between the Gulf of Suez and the Gulf of Acabah.

The *Nautilus* penetrated into the Straits of Jubal, which leads to the Gulf of Suez. I distinctly saw a high mountain, towering between the two gulfs of Ras Mohammed. It was Mount Horeb, that Sinai at the top of which Moses saw God face to face. In the imagination, this mountain is incessantly crowned with lightning.

At six o'clock the *Nautilus,* sometimes floating, sometimes immersed, passed some distance from Tor, situated at the end of the bay, the waters of which seemed tinted with red, an observation already made by Captain Nemo. Then night fell in the midst of a heavy silence, sometimes broken by the cries of the pelican and other night-birds, and the noise of the waves breaking upon the shore, chafing against the rocks, or the panting of some far-off steamer beating the waters of the Gulf with its noisy paddles.

From eight to nine o'clock the *Nautilus* remained some meters under the water. According to my calculation we must have been very near Suez. Through the panel of the salon I saw the rocky bottom brilliantly lit up by our electric lamp. The strait seemed to be growing ever more narrow.

At a quarter-past nine, the vessel having returned to the surface, I mounted the platform. Most impatient to pass through Captain Nemo's tunnel, I could not stay in one place, so came to breathe the fresh night-air.

Soon, in the shadow, I saw a pale light, half discolored by the fog, shining about a mile from us.

"A floating lighthouse," said someone near me.

I turned and saw the captain.

"It is the floating light of Suez," he continued. "It will not be long before we gain the entrance of the tunnel."

"The entrance cannot be easy?"

"No, sir, and for that reason I am accustomed to go into the steersman's cage and myself direct our course. And now if you will go down, Monsieur Aronnax, the *Nautilus* is going under the waves, and will not return to the surface until we have passed through the Arabian Tunnel."

I followed the captain. The hatches were closed, the reservoirs were filled with water and the submarine descended to twelve meters.

I was about to go back to my room, when the captain stopped me.

"Professor," he said, "would you do me the pleasure of accompanying me to the pilot house?"

"I didn't want to ask," I replied.

"Come then. You will see all that is to be seen in submarine and subterranean navigation."

Captain Nemo led me towards the central staircase; half-way down he opened a door, traversed the upper deck, and arrived in the pilot's cage, which it may be remembered rose at the extremity of the platform. It was a cabin measuring six feet square, very much like that occupied by the pilot on the steamboats of the Mississippi or Hudson. In the midst worked a wheel, placed vertically, and connected to the tiller-rope, which ran to the back of the *Nautilus*. Four light-ports with lens-shaped glasses set in grooves in the walls of the cabin, allowed the man at the wheel to see in all directions.

This cabin was dark, but soon my eyes accustomed themselves to the obscurity, and I perceived the pilot, a strong man, with his hands resting on the spokes of the wheel. Outside, the sea appeared vividly lit up by the lantern, which shed its rays from behind the cabin to the other extremity of the platform.

"Now," said Captain Nemo, "let us try to find our passage."

Electric wires connected the pilot's cage with the machinery room, enabling the captain to communicate simultaneously to his *Nautilus* the direction and the speed. He pressed a metal knob and at once the speed of the screw diminished.

I looked in silence at the high straight wall we were running by at this moment, the immovable base of a massive sandy coast. We followed it thus for an hour only some few meters off. Captain Nemo did not take his eye from the compass, suspended by two concentric circles in the cabin. By a simple gesture, the pilot modified the course of the *Nautilus* every instant.

I had placed myself at the port window and saw some magnificent substructures of coral, zoöphytes, seaweed, and large crabs, agitating their enormous claws, which they stretched out from the fissures of the rock.

At a quarter-past ten, the captain himself took the helm. A large gallery, black and deep, opened before us. The *Nautilus* went boldly into it. A strange roaring was heard round its sides. It was the waters of the Red Sea, which the incline of the tunnel precipitated violently towards the Mediterranean. The *Nautilus* went with the torrent, rapid as an arrow, in spite of the efforts of the machinery, which, in order to offer more effective resistance, beat the water with reversed screw.

On the walls of the narrow passage I could see nothing but brilliant rays, straight lines, furrows of fire, traced by the great speed, under the brilliant electric light. My heart beat fast, and I tried to repress it with my hand.

At thirty-five minutes past ten, Captain Nemo quit the helm; and, turning to me, said: "The Mediterranean!"

In less than twenty minutes, the *Nautilus*, carried along by the torrent, had passed through the Isthmus of Suez.

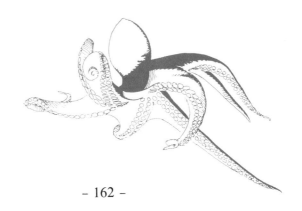

◄ **CHAPTER VI** ►

THE GRECIAN ARCHIPELAGO

 he next day, the 12th of February, at the dawn of day, the *Nautilus* rose to the surface. I hastened on to the platform. Three miles to the south the dim outline of Pelusium was to be seen. A torrent had carried us from one sea to the other. But the tunnel, easy to descend, would be impossible to return through.

About seven o'clock Ned and Conseil joined me. These inseparable friends had slept through the *Nautilus'* amazing feat, all unawares.

"Well, Sir Naturalist," said the Canadian, in a slightly joking tone, "and the Mediterranean?"

"We are floating on its surface, friend Ned."

"What!" said Conseil, "this very night?"

"Yes, this past night; in a few minutes we have passed through this impassable isthmus."

"I do not believe it," replied the Canadian.

"Then you are wrong, Master Land," I continued. "This low coast which rounds off to the south is the Egyptian coast."

"Tell someone else!" replied the headstrong Canadian.

"But since monsieur has affirmed it," said Conseil, "you must believe monsieur."

"Besides, Ned, Captain Nemo did me the honor of his tunnel, and I was in the steersman's cage while we navigated that narrow passage."

"Are you listening, Ned?" asked Conseil.

"And you, who have such good eyes, Ned, you can see the jetties of Port Said stretching into the sea."

The Canadian looked attentively.

"Certainly you are right, sir, and your captain is a first-rate man. We are in the Mediterranean. Good! Now, if you please, let us talk of our own little affair, but so that no one hears us."

I saw what the Canadian wanted, and, in any case, I thought it better to let him talk, as he wished it; so we all three went and sat down near the lantern, where we were less exposed to the wet spray of the waves.

"Now, Ned, we listen. What have you to tell us?"

"What I have to tell you is very simple. We are in Europe; and before Captain Nemo's caprices drag us once more to the bottom of the Polar Seas, or lead us into Oceania, I ask to leave the *Nautilus.*"

Ned's suggestions always troubled me. I wished in no way to shackle the liberty of my companions, but I certainly felt no desire to leave Captain Nemo. Thanks to him, and thanks to his apparatus, I was each day nearer the completion of my submarine studies; and I was re-writing my book on the submarine depths in its very element. Should I ever again have such an opportunity of observing the wonders of the ocean? No, certainly not! And I could not bring myself to the idea of abandoning the *Nautilus* before the cycle of investigation was accomplished.

"Friend Ned, answer me frankly, are you tired of being on board? Are you sorry that destiny has thrown us into Captain Nemo's hands?"

The Canadian remained some moments without answering. Then crossing his arms, he said: "Frankly, I do not regret this journey under the seas. I shall be glad to have made it; but now that it is made, let us have done with it. That is my feeling."

"It will come to an end, Ned."

"Where and when?"

"Where, I do not know—when, I cannot say; or rather, suppose it will end when these seas have nothing more to teach us. Everything that begins in this world must come to an end."

"I agree with monsieur," replied Conseil. "It is very possible that after we have toured all the oceans of the world, Captain Nemo will set us free."

"Free?" cried the Canadian, "more likely the freedom of death!"

"You exaggerate, Master Land," I said. "We have nothing to fear from the captain; but I do not agree with Conseil's ideas, either. We are now masters of the secrets of the *Nautilus,* and I do not think that its commander, in order to render us our liberty, would let us carry them to the world."

"But then, what will happen?" demanded the Canadian.

"That circumstances may occur as well six months hence as now by which we may and ought to profit."

"Oh!" said Ned Land, "and where shall we be in six months, if you please, Sir Naturalist?"

"Perhaps here, perhaps in China. You know the *Nautilus* is a rapid traveller. It goes through water as swallows through the air, or as an express train on the land. It does not fear well-travelled seas; who can say that it may not beat the coasts of France, England, or America, where escape may be attempted as advantageously as here?"

"Monsieur Aronnax," replied the Canadian, "your arguments are rotten at the foundation. You speak of the future, 'We shall be there! We shall be here!' I speak of the present, 'We are here, and we must profit by it.'"

Ned Land's logic pressed me hard, and I felt myself beaten on that ground. I knew not what argument would now tell in my favor.

"Sir," continued Ned, "let us suppose an impossibility; if Captain Nemo should today offer you your liberty, would you accept it?"

"I do not know," I answered.

"And if," he added, "this offer he made you today was never to be renewed, would you accept it?"

I could not answer.

"And what does friend Conseil think?" demanded Ned Land.

"Your friend Conseil," tranquilly responded the good lad, "your friend Conseil has nothing to say. He has no interest in the question. Unlike the master, and unlike his comrade, Ned, he is celibate. No wife, no parents, no children await his return. He is in the service of monsieur; he speaks like monsieur, he talks like monsieur and, to his great regret, he cannot be counted on to make a majority. Two persons only are present: monsieur on one side and Ned Land on the other. Friend Conseil is here to listen and keep score."

I could not help but smile at how completely Conseil had annihilated his personality. Deep within, the Canadian must have been glad not to have had to contend with him.

"Then, sir," said Ned Land, "since Conseil does not exist, the discussion is between the two of us. I have spoken, you have listened. What is your answer?"

I had to respond; hedging the issue was repugnant to me.

"Friend Ned, this is my answer. You have reasoned against me, and my arguments cannot hold up against yours. We must not rely on Captain Nemo's good-will. Common prudence forbids him to set us at liberty. On the other side, prudence bids us profit by the first opportunity to leave the *Nautilus.*"

"Well, Monsieur Aronnax, that is wisely said."

"Only one observation—just one. The occasion must be serious, and our first attempt must succeed; if it fails, we shall never find another, and Captain Nemo will never forgive us."

"All that is true," replied the Canadian. "But your observation applies equally to all attempts at flight, whether in two years' time, or in two days. But the question is still this: "If a favorable opportunity presents itself, it must be seized."

"Agreed! And now, Ned, will you tell me what you mean by a favorable opportunity?"

"It will be that which, on a dark night, will bring the *Nautilus* a short distance from some European coast."

"And you will try and save yourself by swimming?"

"Yes, if we were near enough to the shore, and if the vessel was floating at the time. Not, of course, if the shore was far away, and the boat was under the water."

"And in that case?"

"In that case, I should seek to make myself master of the launch. I know how it is worked. We must get inside, and the bolts once released, we shall come to the surface of the water, without even the pilot, who is in the bows, perceiving our flight."

"Well, Ned, watch for the opportunity; but do not forget that a hitch will ruin us."

"I will not forget, sir."

"And now, Ned, would you like to know what I think of your project?"

"Certainly, Monsieur Aronnax."

"Well, I think—I do not say I hope—I think that this favorable opportunity will never present itself."

"Why not?"

"Because Captain Nemo cannot hide from himself the fact that we have not given up all hope of regaining our liberty, and he will be on his guard, above all, in the seas, that are within sight of European coasts."

"I agree with monsieur," added Conseil.

"We shall see," replied Ned Land, shaking his head determinedly.

"And now, Ned Land," I added, "let us stop here. Not another word on the subject. The day that you are ready, come and let us know, and we will follow you. I rely entirely upon you."

Thus ended a conversation which, in the not very distant future, led to such grave results. I must say here that facts seemed to confirm my foresight, to the Canadian's great despair. Did Captain Nemo distrust us in these frequented seas? Or did he only wish to hide himself from the numerous vessels, of all nations, which ploughed the Mediterranean? I could not tell; but we were oftener beneath the water, and far from the coast. Or, if the *Nautilus* did emerge, nothing was to be seen but the pilot's cage. Sometimes it went to great depths, for, between the Grecian archipelago and Asia Minor, we could not find the bottom at even two thousand meters.

Thus, I only knew we were near the Island of Carpathos, one of the Sporades, when Captain Nemo recited these lines from Virgil—

"Est in Carpathio Neptuni gurgite vates,
    Cæruleus Proteus,"[1]

as he pointed to a spot on the planisphere.

It was indeed the ancient abode of Proteus, the old shepherd of Neptune's flocks, now the Island of Scarpanto, situated between Rhodes and Crete. I saw nothing but the island's granite base through the glass panels of the salon.

The next day, the 14th of February, I resolved to employ some hours in studying the fishes of the Archipelago; but for some reason or other, the panels remained hermetically sealed. Upon taking the course of the *Nautilus,* I found that we were going towards Candia, the ancient Isle of Crete. At the time I embarked on the *Abraham Lincoln,* the whole of this island had risen in insurrection against the despotism of the Turks. But how the insurgents had fared since that time I was absolutely ignorant, and it was not Captain Nemo, deprived of all land communications, who could tell me.[2]

I made no allusion to this event when that night I found myself alone with him in the salon. Besides, he seemed to be taciturn and preoccupied. Then, contrary to his custom, he ordered both panels to be opened, and going from one to the other, observed the mass of waters attentively. To what end I could not guess; so, on my side, I employed my time in studying the fish passing before me eyes.

Among others, I noticed some gobies aphyses, mentioned by Aristotle, and commonly known by the name of *loches de mer*, which are more particularly met with in the salt waters lying near the Nile Delta. Near them swam some sea-bream, half phosphorescent, a kind of sparus, which the Egyptians ranked among their sacred animals, whose arrival in the waters of their river announced the fertile floods, and was celebrated by religious ceremonies. I also noticed some cheilines about three decimeters long, a bony fish with transparent scales whose livid color is mixed with red spots; they are great eaters of marine vegetation, which gives them an exquisite flavor. These cheilines were much sought after by the epicures of ancient Rome; the entrails, dressed with the soft roe of the lamprey, peacocks' brains, and tongues of the flamingo, composed that divine dish of which Emperor Vitellius was so enamored.

Another inhabitant of these seas drew my attention, and led my mind back to recollections of antiquity. It was the remora, that fastens on to the shark's belly. This little fish, according to the ancients, by hooking on to the ship's bottom, could stop its movements; and one of them, by keeping back Antony's ship during the battle of Actium, helped Augustus to gain the victory. On how little hangs the destiny of nations! I observed some fine anthiæ, which belong to the order of lutjans, a fish held sacred by the Greeks, who attributed to them the power of driving sea monsters from waters they frequented. Their name means *flower,* and they justify their appellation by their shaded colors, their nuances comprising the whole gamut of reds, from the paleness of the rose to the brightness of the ruby, and the fugitive tints that clouded their dorsal fin. My eyes could not leave these wonders of the sea, when they were suddenly struck by an unexpected apparition.

In the midst of the waters a man appeared, a diver, carrying at his belt a leather purse. It was not a body abandoned to the waves; it was a living man, swimming with a strong hand, disappearing occasionally to take breath at the surface.

I turned towards Captain Nemo, and in an agitated voice exclaimed: "A man shipwrecked! He must be saved at any price!"

The captain did not answer me, but came and leaned against the panel.

The man had approached, and with his face flattened against the glass, was looking at us.

To my great amazement, Captain Nemo signed to him. The diver answered with his hand, mounted immediately to the surface of the water, and did not appear again.

"Do not be disturbed," said Captain Nemo. "It is Nicholas of Cape Matapan, nicknamed "Pesca," The Fish. He is well-known in all the Cyclades. A bold diver! Water is his element, and he lives more in it than on land, swimming continually from one island to another, even as far as Crete."

"You know him, Captain?"

"Why not, Monsieur Aronnax?"

Saying which, Captain Nemo went towards a bureau standing near the left panel of the salon. Near this piece of furniture, I saw a chest bound with iron, on the cover of which was a copper plate, bearing the monogram of the *Nautilus* with its motto: *Mobilis in Mobili.*

At that moment, the captain without noticing my presence, opened the bureau, which was a sort of strong box holding a great many ingots.

They were ingots of gold! From whence came this precious metal, which represented an

enormous sum? Where did the captain gather this gold from? And what was he going to do with it?

I did not say one word. I looked. Captain Nemo took the ingots one by one, and arranged them methodically in the chest, which he filled entirely. I estimated the contents at more than 1000 kilograms of gold, that is to say, nearly five million francs.

The chest was securely fastened, and the captain wrote an address on the lid, in characters which must have belonged to modern Greece.

This done, Captain Nemo pressed a button, the wire of which communicated with the crew's quarters. Four men appeared, and, not without some trouble, pushed the chest out of the salon. The I heard them hoisting it up the iron staircase by means of pulleys.

At that moment, Captain Nemo turned to me. "And you were saying, sir?" said he.

"I was saying nothing, Captain."

"Then, sir, if you will allow me, I will wish you good-night."

Whereupon he turned and left the salon.

I returned to my room much troubled, as one may believe. I vainly tried to sleep. I sought the connecting link between the apparition of the diver and the chest filled with gold. Soon, I felt by certain movements of pitching and tossing, that the *Nautilus* was leaving the depths and returning to the surface.

Then I heard steps upon the platform; and I knew they were unfastening the launch, and setting it upon the waves. For one instant it struck the side of the *Nautilus,* then all noise ceased.

Two hours later, the same noises, the same going and coming was renewed; the boat was hoisted on board, replaced in its socket, and the *Nautilus* again plunged under the waves.

So these millions had been transported to their address. To what point of the Continent? Who was Captain Nemo's correspondent?

The next day, I related to Conseil and the Canadian the events of the night, which had excited my curiosity to the highest degree. My companions were not less surprised than myself.

"But where does he take his millions to?" asked Ned Land.

To that there was no possible answer. I returned to the salon after having breakfast, and set to work. Till five o'clock in the evening, I employed myself in arranging my notes. At that moment—that I thought to attribute to some peculiar idiosyncrasy—I felt so great a heat that I was obliged to take off my byssus coat!

It was strange, for we were not under low latitudes; and even then, the *Nautilus,* submerged as it was, ought to experience no change of temperature. I looked at the manometer; it showed a depth of sixty feet, to which atmospheric heat could never reach.

I continued my work, but the temperature rose to such a pitch as to be intolerable.

"Could there be fire on board?" I asked myself.

I was leaving the salon, when Captain Nemo entered; he approached the thermometer, consulted it, and turning to me, said:—"Forty-two degrees centigrade."

"I have noticed it, Captain," I replied, "and if it gets much hotter we cannot bear it."

"Oh! sir, it will not get hotter if we do not wish it."

"You can reduce it as you please, then?"

"No; but I can go further from the stove which produces it."

"It is outside then?"

"Certainly; we are floating in a current of boiling water."

"Is it possible?" I exclaimed.

"Look."

The panels opened, and I saw the sea entirely white all round. A sulphurous smoke was curling amid the waves, which boiled like water in a copper pot. I placed my hand on one of the panes of glass, but the heat was so great that I quickly took it off again.

"Where are we?" I asked.

"Near the Island of Santorin,[3] sir," replied the captain, "and just in the channel which separates Nea Kameni from Palea Kameni. I wished to give you a sight of the curious spectacle of a submarine volcanic eruption."

"I thought," said I, "that the formation of these new islands was ended."

"Nothing is ever ended in the volcanic parts of the sea," replied Captain Nemo; "and the globe is always being revised by subterranean fires. Already, in 19 A.D., according to Cassiodorus and Pliny, a new island, Thera the divine, appeared in the very place where these islets have recently been formed. Then they sank under the waves, to rise again in the year 69, when they again subsided. Since that time to our day, the Plutonian work has been suspended. But, on the 3rd of February, 1866, a new island, which was named George Island, emerged from the midst of the sulphurous vapor near Nea Kameni, and settled again the 6th of the same month. Seven days after, the 13th of February, the Isle of Aphroessa appeared, leaving between Nea Kameni and itself a channel ten meters broad. I was in these seas when the phenomenon occurred, and I was able therefore to observe all the different phases. The Isle of Aphroessa, of round form, measured 300 feet in diameter, and thirty feet in height. It was composed of black vitreous lava, mixed with fragments of feldspar. And lastly, on the 10th of March, a smaller island, called Reka, showed itself near Nea Kameni, and since then, these three have joined together, forming but one and the same island."

"And the channel in which we are at this moment?" I asked.

"Here it is," replied Captain Nemo, showing me a map of the Archipelago. "You see I have marked the new islands."

"But this channel will someday be filled?"

"It is probable, Monsieur Aronnax. Since 1866 eight small islands of lava have emerged from in front of Port Saint Nicholas of Palea Kameni. It is evident that Nea and Palea will be merged in some future time. In the middle of the Pacific we have continents built by infusoria; here by the phenomenon of eruption. Look Professor, look at the work accomplished under the waves."

I returned to the window. The *Nautilus* was no longer moving, the heat was becoming unbearable. The sea, which till now had been white, was red, owing to the presence of salts of iron. In spite of the ship's being hermetically sealed, an insupportable smell of sulphur filled the salon and the brilliancy of the electric light was entirely extinguished by bright scarlet flames.

I was in a bath of perspiration, I was suffocating, I was being broiled! I was truly being cooked!

"We can remain no longer in this boiling water," said I to the captain.

"It would not be prudent," agreed the impassive Captain Nemo.

An order was given; the *Nautilus* tacked about and left the furnace, which it could not brave with impunity. A quarter of an hour later we were breathing fresh air on the surface.

The thought then struck me that, if Ned Land had chosen this part of the sea for our flight, we should never have come alive out of this sea of fire.

The next day, the 16th of February, we left the basin which, between Rhodes and Alexandria, is reckoned about 3000 meters in depth, and the *Nautilus,* passing some distance from Cerigo, quitted the Grecian archipelago, after having doubled Cape Matapan.

---

[1]"In Neptune's Carpathian Gulf there dwells a prophet/blue protéus . . ."

[2]A story recounted in Verne's novel, *The Archipelago on Fire* (1884). RM

[3]The tremendous explosion of Santorin, or Thera, in the 15th century BC may have been the inspiration for the legend of Atlantis. RM

◄ **CHAPTER VII** ►

·MACKEREL·

THE MEDITERRANEAN IN FORTY-EIGHT HOURS

he Mediterranean, the blue sea *par excellence*, the "Great Sea" of the Hebrews, "The Sea" of the Greeks, the "Mare Nostrum" of the Romans, bordered by orange-trees, aloes, cacti, and sea-pines; perfumed with the scent of the myrtle, surrounded by ragged mountains, saturated with pure and transparent air, but incessantly worked by underground fires. A perfect battlefield in which Neptune and Pluto still dispute the empire of the world! It is upon these banks, and on these waters, says Michelet, that man is renewed in one of the most powerful climates of the globe.

But, beautiful as it was, I could only take a rapid glance at the basin whose superficial area is two million square kilometers. Even Captain Nemo's knowledge was lost to me, for this enigmatic person did not appear once during our full speed passage. I estimated the length of the course which the *Nautilus* took under the waves of the sea at about six hundred leagues, and it was accomplished in forty-eight hours. Starting on the morning of the 16th of February from the shores of Greece, we had crossed the Straits of Gibraltar by sunrise on the 18th.

It was plain to me that this Mediterranean, enclosed in the midst of those countries which he wished to avoid, was distasteful to Captain Nemo. Those waves and those breezes brought back too many remembrances, if not too many regrets. Here he had no longer that independence and that liberty of movement which he had when in the open seas, and his *Nautilus* felt itself cramped between the close shores of Africa and Europe.

Our speed was now twenty-five miles an hour. It may be well understood that Ned Land, to his great disgust, was obliged to renounce his intended flight. He could not launch the boat going at the rate of twelve or thirteen meters per second. To quit the *Nautilus* under such conditions would be as bad as jumping from a train going at full speed—an imprudent thing, to say the least of it. Besides, our vessel only surfaced at night to renew its stock of air; it was steered entirely by the compass and the log.

I saw no more of the Mediterranean than a traveller by express train perceives of the landscape which flies before his eyes; that is to say, only the distant horizon, and not the nearer objects which pass like a flash of lightning.

Nevertheless, Conseil and I were able to observe some Mediterranean fish, whose powerful fins enabled them to keep up with the *Nautilus* for a few moments. We watched them carefully through the windows of the salon, and our notes permit me to describe in a few words the ichthyology of this sea.

Of the various fish that live here, I saw some clearly, others less so, without speaking of the ones that the speed of the *Nautilus* stole from my eyes. I hope that I will be permitted to use this rather whimsical classification. It is the only way I can render these rapid observations.

In the midst of the mass of waters brightly lit up by the electric light glided some of those lampreys, more than a meter long, common to almost every climate. Some of the oxyrhynchi, a kind of ray five feet broad, with white belly and ash-gray spotted back, spread out like a large shawl carried along by the current. Other rays passed so quickly that I could not see if they deserved the name of eagles which was given to them by the ancient Greeks, or the qualification of rats, toads, and bats, with which modern fishermen have named them. A few milander sharks, twelve feet long, and much feared by divers, fought rapidly among them. Sea-foxes eight feet long, endowed with a wonderful sense of smell appeared like large bluish shadows. Some dorades of the sparus genus, some of which measured 30 decimeters, showed themselves in their dress of blue and silver, encircled by small bands which contrasted sharply against the somber tints of their fins. This was a fish consecrated to Venus, the eyes of which are encased in sockets of gold; a precious species, found in all waters, fresh or salt, an inhabitant of rivers, lakes, and oceans, living in all climates, and bearing all temperatures; a race belonging to the ancient geological eras of the earth, and which has preserved all the beauty of its first days. Magnificent sturgeons, nine or ten meters long, creatures of great speed, striking the panes of glass with their strong tails, displayed their bluish backs with small brown spots; they resemble the sharks, but are not equal to them in strength, and are to be met with in all seas.

In the spring, they swim up large rivers, fighting the currents of the Volga, the Danube, the Po, the Rhine, the Loire, and the Oder, nourished by herring, mackerel, salmon, and cod. Although they belong to the class of cartilaginous fish, they are considered delicacies. They are eaten fresh, dried, pickled, or salted. In days of old it was considered fit for the table of Lucullus.

But of all the diverse inhabitants of the Mediterranean, those I observed to the greatest advantage, when the *Nautilus* approached the surface, belonged to the sixty-third genus of bony fish. They were a kind of tuna, with bluish-black backs, and silvery breastplates, whose dorsal fins threw out sparkles of gold. They are said to follow in the wake of vessels whose refreshing shade they seek from the fire of a tropical sky, and they did not belie the saying, for they accompanied the *Nautilus* as they did in former times the vessel of La Pérouse. For many a long hour they struggled to keep up with our vessel. I was never tired of admiring these creatures. They were really built for speed—their small heads, their bodies lithe and cigar-shaped, which in some were more than three meters long, their pectoral fins and forked tail endowed with remarkable strength. They swam in triangular formations, like certain flocks of birds, whose rapidity they equalled. The ancients used to say that they understood geometry and strategy. But still they do not escape the pursuit of the Provencals, who esteem them as highly as the inhabitants of the Propontis[1] and of Italy used to do; and these precious, but blind and foolhardy creatures, perish by millions in the nets of the Marseillaise fishermen.

I list, only as a reminder, those Mediterranean fish that Conseil and I saw but briefly. There were whitish gymnotes, which passed by like intangible vapors; conger eels, serpents three to four meters long, brightly colored with green, blue, and yellow; cods three feet long, whose liver is a delicate morsel; coepolae-teniae, which floated like thin seaweed; gurnards, that the poets called lyre-fish, and the fishermen whistling-fish—their noses are ornamented with two triangular, toothed plates that resemble the instrument of ancient Homer; swallow gurnards, swimming with the rapidity of the bird that gave it its name; a kind of perch, with a red head, whose dorsal fin is garnished with filaments; aloes speckled with black, gray, brown, blue, yellow, and green, and which is said to be sensitive to the silver voice of little bells; splendid turbots, pheasants of the sea, lozenge-shaped with yellowish body and fins, spotted with brown, and on the top and bottom generally marbled in brown and yellow; and finally a school of admirable red mullets, true birds of paradise of the sea, which the Romans would pay as much as 10,000 sesterces apiece to watch them die on a tabletop, watching with cruel eyes as the colors would change from deep vermilion to the pale white of death.

But I saw no miralets, trigger-fish, tetradons, sea horses, juans, bellows-fish, blennies, surmullets, wrasse, smelt, flying fish, anchovies, sea breams, boops, orphes, nor any of the principal representatives of the order of Pleuronectidae, common to both the Atlantic and Mediterranean, such as dabs, flounders, plaice and sole. All the fault of the dizzying speed which carried the *Nautilus* through these fertile waters.

As to marine mammals, I thought, in entering the Adriatic, that I saw two or three cachalots, furnished with one dorsal fin, of the genus physetera, some dolphins of the genus globicephali, peculiar to the Mediterranean, the back part of the head being marked like a zebra with small light lines; also, a dozen seals, with white bellies and black hair, known by the name of *monks*, and which really have the air of a Dominican friar; they are about three meters in length. For his part, Conseil believed he had seen a turtle six feet long, ornamented with three protruding ridges running longitudinally along its back. I regretted that I did not see this reptile, for if Conseil's description was correct, he had seen a *luth*—a very rare species. I noticed, for my part, a few caevans with elongated shells.

As to zoöphytes, for some instants I was able to admire a beautiful orange galeolaria, which had fastened itself to the port panel; it was a long filament, and was divided into an infinity of branches, terminated by the finest lace which could ever have been woven by the rivals of Arachne herself. Unfortunately, I could not take this admirable specimen; and doubtless no other Mediterranean zoöphyte would have offered itself to my observation, if, on the night of the 16th, the *Nautilus* had not, singularly enough, slackened its speed, under the following circumstances.

We were then passing between Sicily and the coast of Tunis. In the narrow space between Cape Bon and the Straits of Messina, the bottom of the sea rose suddenly. There was a perfect bank, above which there was not more than seventeen meters of water, while on either side the depth was seventy meters.

The *Nautilus* had to maneuver very carefully so as not to strike against this submarine barrier. I showed Conseil, on the map of the Mediterranean, the spot occupied by this reef.

"But if monsieur pleases," observed Conseil, "it is like a real isthmus joining Europe to Africa."

"Yes, my boy, it forms a perfect bar to the Straits of Lybia, and the soundings of Smith have proven that in former times the continents were joined between Cape Boco and Cape Furina."

"I can well believe it," said Conseil.

"I will add," I continued, "that a similar barrier exists between Gibraltar and Ceuta, which in geological times closed off the entire Mediterranean."

"What if some volcanic burst should one day raise these two barriers above the waves?"

"It is not probable, Conseil."

"Well, but if monsieur will please allow me to finish, if this phenomenon should take place, it will be troublesome for Monsieur de Lesseps, who has taken so much pains to build the Suez Canal."

"I agree with you; but I repeat, Conseil, this phenomenon will never happen. The violence of subterranean force is ever diminishing. Volcanoes, so plentiful in the first days of the world, are being extinguished by degrees; the internal heat is weakened, the temperature of the deepest strata of the earth is lowered by a perceptible quantity every century to the detriment of our globe, for its heat is its life."

"But the sun. . . ."

"The sun is not sufficient, Conseil. Can it give heat to a dead body?"

"Not that I know of."

"Well, my friend, this earth will one day be that cold corpse; it will become uninhabitable and uninhabited like the moon, which has long since lost all its vital heat."

"In how many centuries?"

"In some hundreds of thousand of years, my boy."

"Then," said Conseil, "we shall have time to finish our journey—that is, if Ned Land does not interfere with it."

And Conseil, reassured, returned to the study of the barrier, which the *Nautilus* was skirting closely at a moderate speed.

There, on the rocky and volcanic bottom, lay outspread a living flora: sponges, holothurians or sea slugs, and cydippes, ornamented with reddish curls, which emitted a slight phosphorescent light; beroes, commonly known by the name of sea-cucumbers. They were bathed in all the colors of the solar spectrum. There were walking comatulæ more than a meter wide, the purple of which completely colored the water around, tree-like euryales of great beauty; pavonaceae with long stalks; great numbers of edible urchins of various species; and green sea anemones, with grayish trunks and brown disks, almost hidden behind a hairy mass of olive tentacles.

Conseil was particularily occupied with the classification of the mollusks and articulata, and while this nomenclature may seem a little dry, it would not be fair to the brave lad to omit his personal observations.

In the branch of the mollusks, he mentions numerous scallops; spondyli stacked one upon the other; triangular wedge shells; trident-shaped hyalines, with yellow fins and transparent shells; orange pleurbranchia, like pointed eggs with green spots; aplysia, known by the name of sea-hares; dolabellae; fat acerae; umbrella shells, peculiar to the Mediterranean; sea-ears whose shells produce a mother-of-pearl very much sought after; red scallops; corrugated cockles, which the people of Languedoc prefer to oysters; clovis, dear to the natives of Marseilles; the *praires double,* white and fat, which is a species of clam abundant on the coasts of North America and eaten in considerable quantities in New York; comb shells of many colors; lithodes hiding in holes, who have a peppery taste I like; furrowed venericardiae, with bulging shells with ridged sides; cynthiae, covered with scarlet bumps; carniaria, turned up at each end so they resemble small gondolas; crowned feroles; atlantes with spiral shells; gray thetys, with white spots and covered with a fragile mantilla; aeolides, resembling little slugs; cavoliniae, crawling on their backs; auriculae—among them the auricula myosotis, an oval shell—fawn-colored scalariae, littorines, ianthinae, cinerariae, petricolae, lamellariae, cabochons, pandoras, etc.

As for the articulates, Conseil, in his notes, very justifiably divides them into six classes, three of which pertain to the marine world. These are the classes of the crustaceans, cirrhopoda and annelids.

The crustaceans are subdivided into nine orders, and the first of these include the decapods, that is to say animals with the head and thorax normally joined, with mouths composed of several pairs of jaws, and which possess four, five or six pairs of legs on the thorax. Conseil used the method of our teacher Milne-Edwards, and divided the decapods into three sections: the brachyura, macrura and anomura. These names sound barbarous, but they are correct and precise. Among the brachyura, Conseil noted the amathiae, whose head is armed with two great, diverging horns; scorpion inachidae, which—I don't know why—symbolized wisdom to the Greeks; two kinds of spider crabs, that had probably wandered into these shallows: they are usually found in deeper water; xanthi; pilumnae; rhomboides; granular calapae—very easy to digest, observed Conseil; toothless corystes; ebaliae; cymobolidae; wooly dorripi, etc. Among the macrura, subdivided into five families, were the ceriaceae; burrowers; astaci; palaemonidae and the ochyzopodes; as well as rock lobsters, of which the flesh of the female is prized. But he says nothing of the subdivision of the astaci, which includes the lobster proper, since the spiny lobster is the only one that inhabits the Mediterranean. Finally, among the anomura, he saw the drocinae, at home in any abandoned shell they can find; homolae with spiny heads; hermit crabs; porcelaines, etc.

There Conseil stopped working. He did not have time to complete his classification of the crustacea by examining the stomapods, isopods, amphipods, homopods, trilobites, branchiapods, ostracodes, and entomostracae. And to finish his study of marine articulates, he ought to have mentioned the class of cirrhopoda that included the cyclopes and the arguli, and the class of annelids which he would not have failed to divide into the tubicoles and the dorsibranchs.

The *Nautilus* having now passed the high bank in the Lybian Straits, returned to the deep waters and its accustomed speed.

From that time no more mollusks, no more articulates, no more zoöphytes; barely a few large fish passing like shadows.

During the night of the 16th and 17th February, we had entered the second Mediterranean basin, the greatest depth of which was 3000 meters. The *Nautilus,* under the impulse of its screw and inclined planes, submerged itself in the lowest depths of the sea.

There, in default of natural wonders, the sea offered to our eyes scenes both moving and terrible. We were crossing that part of the Mediterranean so fecund with tragedies. From the Algerian coast to the shores of Provence, how many ships have been lost, how many have disappeared! The Mediterranean is only a lake, compared to the vast liquid plains of the Pacific, but it is a capricious lake, with changing waves. Today it is gentle and caressing to the frail tartans that seem to float between the sea and sky, tomorrow, it rages, tormented, torn by winds, breaking the strongest ships with the incessant striking of its narrow waves.

In this rapid trip through the depths, I saw sunken ships scattered over the bottom. Some of them were already encrusted with coral, others were only coated with rust. Anchors, cannons, cannon-balls, iron fittings, propellers, pieces of machinery, broken cylinders, caved-in boilers, entire hulls floating in the water, some upright, others upside-down.

Of these lost ships, some had perished in collisions, others had struck granite reefs. Some had sunk perpendicularly, their masts still in place, their rigging stiffened by the water. They seemed to be anchored in some immense, eerie harbor, waiting for the moment to depart. As the *Nautilus* passed among them, and enveloped them in sheets of electric light, I thought that they might dip their flags in a salute. But no, there was nothing but silence and death in this field of catastrophes!

I noticed that in the depths of the Mediterranean the number of wrecks increased as we neared the Straits of Gibraltar. The coasts of Africa and Europe are closer together there, and in this narrow space, collisions are frequent. I saw a number of iron hulls, the fantastic ruins of steamers, some lying flat, other upright like formidable animals. One of these boats had a hole in its side, its funnel bent, its wheels gone except for their mountings, its rudder separated from the stern-post, but still attached by an iron chain. Its rear nameplate was corroded away by the sea. It was a terrible sight! How many lives were lost in this wreck! How many victims were drawn beneath the waves? Had some sailor survived to tell of this disaster? Or have the waves always guarded their sinister secret? I cannot explain why, but I thought that this ship, buried beneath the sea, might be the *Atlas,* vanished with all hands about twenty years before, without another word heard from her. Ah! what a grim history could be written about the depths of the Mediterranean, this vast cemetery, where so many riches have been lost, where so many victims have met their deaths.

Nevertheless, the *Nautilus* moved with rapidity and indifference, propelled by its screw through the midst of these ruins.

On the 18th of February, about three o'clock in the morning, we were at the entrance of the Straits of Gibraltar.

There are two currents: an upper one, long since recognized, which conveys the waters of the ocean into the basin of the Mediterranean; and a lower counter-current, which reasoning has now shown to exist. Indeed, the volume of water in the Mediterranean, incessantly added to by the waves of the Atlantic, and by rivers falling into it, would each year raise the level of this sea, for its evaporation is not sufficient to restore the equilibrium. As it is not so, we must necessarily admit the existence of an under-current, which empties into the basin of the Atlantic, through the Straits of Gibraltar, the surplus waters of the Mediterranean.

A fact, indeed; and it was this counter-current by which the *Nautilus* profited. It advanced rapidly through the narrow pass. For one instant I caught a glimpse of the beautiful ruins of the submarine temple of Hercules, submerged, according to Pliny and Avienus, together with the low island which supports it. A few minutes later we were floating on the Atlantic.

---

[1]The Sea of Marmara. RM

◄ CHAPTER VIII ►
VIGO BAY

he Atlantic! a vast sheet of water, whose area covers twenty-five million square miles, the length of which is nine thousand miles, with a mean breadth of two thousand seven hundred. An important sea virtually unknown to the ancients, except possibly the Carthaginians—the Dutch of Antiquity—whose commercial wanderings took them to the west coasts of Europe and Africa! An ocean whose parallel winding shores embrace an immense area, watered by the largest rivers of the world, the St. Lawerence, the Mississippi, the Amazon, the Plata, the Orinoco, the Niger, the Senegal, the Elbe, the Loire, and the Rhine, which carry water from the most civilized, as well as from the most savage countries! A magnificent plain of water, incessantly plowed by vessels of every nation, sheltered under the flags of every nation, and which terminates in those two terrible points so dreaded by mariners, Cape Horn, and the Cape of Tempests!

The *Nautilus* was piercing the water with its sharp spur, after having accomplished nearly ten thousand leagues in three and a half months, a distance greater than the equator of the earth. Where were we going now? and what was reserved for the future?

The *Nautilus,* leaving the Straits of Gibraltar, had gone far out. It returned to the surface of the waves, and our daily walks on the platform were restored to us.

I mounted at once, accompanied by Ned Land and Conseil. At a distance of about twelve miles, Cape St. Vincent was dimly to be seen, forming the southwestern point of the Spanish peninsula. A strong southerly gale was blowing. The sea was swollen and billowy; it made the *Nautilus* rock violently. It was almost impossible to keep one's footing on the platform, which the heavy rolls of the sea beat over every instant. So we descended after inhaling some breaths of fresh air.

I returned to my room, Conseil to his cabin; but the Canadian, with a preoccupied air, followed me. Our rapid passage across the Mediterranean had not allowed him to put his project into execution, and he could not help showing his disappointment.

When the door of my room was shut, he sat down and looked at me silently.

"Friend Ned," said I, "I understand how you feel; but you cannot reproach yourself. To have attempted to leave the *Nautilus* under the circumstances would have been folly!"

Ned Land did not answer; his compressed lips, and frowning brow, indicated the violent possession this fixed idea had taken of his mind.

"Let us see," I continued, "we need not despair yet. We are going up the coast of Portugal again; France and England are not far off, where we can easily find refuge. Now, if the *Nautilus,* on leaving the Straits of Gibraltar, had gone to the south, if it had carried us towards regions where there were no continents, I should share your uneasiness. But we know now that Captain Nemo does not fly from civilized seas, and in some days I think you can act with security."

Ned Land still looked at me fixedly. At length his lips parted, and he said, "It is for tonight."

I drew myself up suddenly. I was, I admit, little prepared for this communication. I wanted to answer the Canadian, but words would not come.

"We agreed to wait for an opportunity," continued Ned Land, "and the opportunity has arrived. This night we shall be but a few miles from the Spanish coast. It is cloudy. The wind blows freely. I have your word, Monsieur Aronnax, and I rely upon you."

As I was still silent, the Canadian rose and approached me.

"Tonight, at nine o'clock," said he. "I have warned Conseil. At that moment, Captain Nemo will be shut up in his room, probably in bed. Neither the engineers nor the ship's crew can see us. Conseil and I will gain the central staircase, and you, Monsieur Aronnax, will remain in the library, two steps from us, waiting my signal. The oars, the mast, and the sail, are in the launch. I have even succeeded in getting in some provisions. I have procured a wrench, to unfasten the bolts which attach it to the hull of the *Nautilus*. So all is ready, till tonight.''

"The sea is bad."

"That I allow," replied the Canadian, "but we must risk that. Liberty is worth paying for. Besides, the boat is strong, and a few miles with a fair wind to carry us, is no great thing. Who knows but by tomorrow the *Nautilus* may have carried us a hundred leagues away? Let circumstances only favor us, and by ten or eleven o'clock we shall have landed on some spot of *terra firma,* alive or dead. Therefore, by the Grace of God, until tonight.''

With these words the Canadian withdrew, leaving me almost dumb. I had imagined that, the chance gone, I should have time to reflect and discuss the matter. My obstinate companion had given me no time; and, after all, what could I have said to him? Ned Land was perfectly right. Here was an opportunity to profit by. Could I retract my word, and take upon myself the responsibility of compromising the future of my companions? Tomorrow Captain Nemo might take us far from all land.

At that moment a rather loud hissing told me that the reservoirs were filling, and that the *Nautilus* was sinking under the waves of the Atlantic.

I stayed in my cabin, avoiding the captain for fear of accidentally betraying my friends, by the emotions that must be visible on my face. A sad day I passed, between the desire of regaining my liberty of action, and of abandoning the wonderful *Nautilus,* and leaving my submarine studies incomplete. How could I leave this ocean, "my Atlantic", as it pleased me to call it, without having observed its greatest depths? Without uncovering secrets such as were revealed by the Pacific and Indian Oceans? It was like leaving a book at the first volume, or interrupting a dream at its most beautiful moment! What dreadful hours I passed thus! sometimes seeing myself and companions safely landed, sometimes wishing, in spite of myself, that some unforeseen circumstances would prevent the realization of Ned Land's project.

Twice I went to the salon. I wished to consult the compass. I wished to see if the direction the *Nautilus* was taking was bringing us nearer or taking us farther from the coast. But no, the *Nautilus* headed north, into Portuguese waters, keeping near the coast.

I must, therefore, take my part and prepare for flight. My luggage was not heavy—my notes and nothing more.

As to Captain Nemo, I asked myself what he would think of our escape; what trouble, what wrong it might cause him, and what might he do in case of our discovery or failure? Certainly I had no cause to complain of him; on the contrary, never was hospitality freer than his. In leaving him I could not be accused of ingratitude. No oath bound us to him. It was on the strength of circumstances he relied, and not upon our word, to fix us forever. Nemo's admission that he meant to keep us aboard forever justified any attempt to escape.

I had not seen the captain since our visit to the Island of Santorin. Would chance bring me to his presence before our departure? I wished it, and I feared it at the same time. I listened if I could hear him walking in the room next to mine. No sound reached my ear. His room was evidently deserted.

Then I began to wonder if this strange person was still on board. Since that night when the launch had left the *Nautilus* on its mysterious mission, I had gradually changed my ideas about him. I wondered, did Captain Nemo maintain, after all, some communication with his own species? Did he never leave the *Nautilus?* Entire weeks would go by without an encounter with him. What was he doing during these times? Under the guise of misanthropy, was he accomplishing some secret mission the purpose of which I could not imagine?

These ideas and a thousand others assailed my mind. The field for conjecture seemed infinite, in the strange situation we found ourselves in. I felt an unbearable uneasiness. This day of waiting seemed eternal. Hours struck too slowly to keep pace with my impatience.

My dinner was served in my room as usual. I ate but little, I was too preoccupied. I left the table at seven o'clock. A hundred and twenty minutes (I counted them) still separated me from the moment in which I was to join Ned Land. My agitation redoubled. My pulse beat violently. I could not remain quiet. I went and came, hoping to calm my troubled spirit by constant movement. The idea of failure in our bold enterprise was the least painful of my anxieties; but the thought of seeing our project discovered before leaving the *Nautilus,* of being brought before Captain Nemo, angry or (what was worse) saddened at my desertion, made my heart palpitate.

I wanted to see the salon for the last time. I descended the stairs, and arrived in the museum where I had passed so many useful and agreeable hours. I looked at all its riches, all its treasures, like a man on the eve of an eternal exile, who was leaving never to return. These wonders of nature, these masterpieces of art, among which, for so many days, my life had been concentrated, I was going to abandon them forever! I should like to have taken a last look through the windows of the salon into the waters of the Atlantic: but the panels were hermetically closed, and a cloak of steel separated me from that ocean which I had not yet explored.

In passing through the salon, I came near the door, let into the angle, which opened into the captain's room. To my great surprise, this door was ajar. I drew back, involuntarily. If Captain Nemo should be in his room, he could see me. But, hearing no noise, I drew nearer. The room was deserted. I pushed open the door, and took some steps forward. Still the same monk-like severity of aspect.

At that moment, I was struck by the sight of several watercolors hanging on the wall that I had not noticed during my first visit. They were portraits, portraits of those great men of history who had devoted their lives to a great human ideal: Kosciusko, the hero whose dying words were *Finis Poloniae;* Botzaris, the Leonidas of modern Greece; O'Connell, the defender of Ireland; Washington, founder of the American Union; Manin, the Italian patriot; Lincoln, killed by the bullet of a pro-slaver; and finally, the martyr to the emancipation of the black race, John Brown, hanging from a gallows, in the terrifying drawing by Victor Hugo.

What tie existed between the souls of these heroes and the soul of Captain Nemo? Would this collection of portraits help me to untangle the mystery of his existence? Was he the champion of oppressed people? the liberator of enslaved races? Had he figured in the latest social and political commotions of our century? Was he one of the heroes of the terrible American Civil War, a war as lamentable as it was glorious? . . .

Suddenly the clock struck eight. The first beat of the hammer on the bell awoke me from my dreams. I trembled as if an invisible eye had plunged into my most secret thoughts, and I hurried from the room.

There my eye fell upon the compass. Our course was still north. The log indicated moderate speed, the manometer a depth of about sixty feet. Circumstances all favored Ned's project.

I returned to my room, clothed myself warmly—sea boots, an otterskin cap, a greatcoat of byssus, lined with sealskin. I was ready, I was waiting. The vibration of the screw alone broke the deep silence which reigned on board. I listened attentively. Would no loud voice suddenly inform me that Ned Land had been surprised in his projected flight? A mortal dread hung over me, and I vainly tried to regain my coolness.

At a few minutes to nine, I put my ear to the captain's door. No noise. I left my room and returned to the salon, which was half in obscurity, but deserted.

I opened the door communicating with the library. The same insufficient light, the same solitude. I placed myself near the door leading to the central staircase, and there waited for Ned Land's signal.

At that moment the trembling of the screw sensibly diminished, then it stopped entirely.

Why had the *Nautilus* altered its speed? What would this mean to Ned's plans? I had no answer.

The silence was now only disturbed by the beatings of my own heart.

Suddenly a slight shock was felt; and I knew that the *Nautilus* had stopped at the bottom of the ocean. My uneasiness increased. The Canadian's signal did not come. I felt inclined to join Ned Land and beg of him to put off his attempt. I felt that we were not sailing under ordinary conditions.

At this moment the door of the large salon opened, and Captain Nemo appeared. He glanced at me, and, without further preamble, he said, in an amiable tone, "Ah, sir! I have been looking for you. Do you know the history of Spain?"

Now, one might know the history of one's own country by heart; but in the condition I was at the time, with troubled mind and head quite lost, I could not have said a word of it.

"Well," continued Captain Nemo, "you heard my question? Do you know the history of Spain?"

"Very slightly," I answered.

"Well, here are learned men having to learn," said the captain. "Come, sit down, and I will tell you a curious episode in that history."

The captain sat on the divan, mechanically. I sat next to him, in the shadow.

"Sir, listen well," said he; "this history will interest you particularly, for it will answer a question which doubtless you have not been able to solve."

"I listen, Captain," said I, not knowing what my interlocutor was driving at, and asking myself if this incident was bearing on our projected escape.

"Sir, if you have no objection, we will go back to 1702. You cannot be ignorant that your king, Louis XIV, thinking that a mere gesture of his was sufficient to bring the Pyrenees under his yoke, had imposed the Duke of Anjou, his grandson, on the Spaniards. This prince reigned more or less badly under the name of Philip V, and had a strong party against him abroad. Indeed, the preceding year, the royal houses of Holland, Austria, and England, had concluded a treaty of alliance at the Hague, with the intention of plucking the crown of Spain from the head of Philip V, and placing it on that of an archduke to whom they prematurely gave the title of Charles III.

"Spain had to resist this coalition; but she was almost entirely unprovided with either soldiers or sailors. However, money would not fail them, provided that their galleons, laden with gold and silver from America, once entered their ports. And about the end of 1702 they expected a rich convoy which France was escorting with a fleet of twenty-three vessels, commanded by Admiral de Château-Renault, for the ships of the coalition were already beating the Atlantic.

"This convoy was to go to Cadiz, but the Admiral, hearing that an English fleet was cruising in those waters, resolved to make for a French port.

"The Spanish commanders of the convoy objected to this decision. They wanted to be taken to a Spanish port, and if not to Cadiz, into Vigo Bay, situated on the northwest coast of Spain, which was not blocked.

"Admiral de Château-Renault had the rashness to obey this injunction, and the galleons entered Vigo Bay.

"Unfortunately, it was an open harbor which could not be defended in any way. They must therefore hasten to unload the galleons before the arrival of the combined fleet; and time would not have failed them had not a miserable question of rivalry suddenly arisen.

"You are following the chain of events?" asked Captain Nemo.

"Perfectly," said I, not knowing the end proposed by this historical lesson.

"I will continue. This is what passed. The merchants of Cadiz had a privilege by which they had the right of receiving all merchandise coming from the West Indies. Now, to unload these ingots at the port of Vigo, was depriving them of their rights. They complained at

Madrid, and obtained the consent of the weak-minded Philip that the convoy, without discharging its cargo, should remain sequestered in the roads of Vigo until the enemy had disappeared.

"But while coming to this decision, on the 22nd of October 1702, the English vessels arrived in Vigo Bay. Admiral de Château-Renault, in spite of inferior forces, fought bravely. But seeing that the treasure must fall into the enemy's hands, he burnt and scuttled every galleon, which went to the bottom with their immense riches."

Captain Nemo stopped. I admit I could not yet see why this history should interest me. "Well?" I asked.

"Well, Monsieur Aronnax," replied Captain Nemo, "we are in that Vigo Bay; and it rests with yourself whether you will penetrate its mysteries."

The captain rose, telling me to follow him. I had had time to recover. I obeyed. The salon was dark, but through the transparent glass the waves were sparkling. I looked.

For half a mile around the *Nautilus*, the waters were bathed in electric light. The sandy bottom was clean and bright. Some of the ship's crew in their diving dresses were clearing away half rotten barrels and empty cases from the midst of the blackened wrecks. From these cases and from these barrels escaped ingots of gold and silver, cascades of piastres and jewels. The sand was heaped up with them. Laden with their precious booty the men returned to the *Nautilus*, disposed of their burden, and went back to this inexhaustible fishery of gold and silver.

I understood now. This was the scene of the battle of the 22nd of October, 1702. Here on this very spot the galleons laden for the Spanish Government had sunk. Here Captain Nemo came, according to his wants, to pack up those millions with which he loaded the *Nautilus*. It was for him and him alone, America had given up her precious metals. He was the direct heir, without anyone to share, in those treasures torn from the Incas and from the people conquered of Ferdinand Cortez!

"Did you know, sir," he asked, smiling, "that the sea contained such riches?"

"I knew," I answered, "there were supposed to be two million tons of silver suspended in the water."

"Doubtless; but to salvage this money the expense would be greater than the profit. Here, on the contrary, I have but to pick up what man has lost,—and not only in Vigo Bay, but in a thousand other spots where shipwrecks have happened, and which are marked on my submarine maps. Can you understand now the source of the millions I am worth?"

"I understand, Captain. But allow me to tell you that in exploring Vigo Bay you have only been just ahead of a rival society."

"And which is that?"

"A society which has received from the Spanish Government the privilege of seeking these buried galleons. The shareholders are led on by the allurement of an enormous bounty, for these rich shipwrecks are valued at five hundred millions."

"Five hundred millions they were," answered Captain Nemo, "but they are so no longer."

"Just so," said I, "and a warning to those shareholders would be an act of charity. But who knows if it would be well received? What gamblers usually regret above all is less the loss of their money, than of their foolish hopes. After all, I pity them less than the thousands of unfortunates to whom so much riches well-distributed would have been profitable, while now they will be forever barren."

I had no sooner expressed this regret, than I felt that it must have wounded Captain Nemo.

"Barren!" he exclaimed, with animation. "Do you think then, sir, that these riches are lost because I gather them? Is it for myself alone, according to your idea, that I take the trouble to collect these treasures? Who told you that I did not make a good use of it? Do you think I am ignorant that there are suffering beings and oppressed races on this earth, miserable creatures to console, victims to avenge? Do you not understand? . . ."

Captain Nemo stopped at these last words, regretting perhaps that he had spoken so much. But I had guessed that whatever the motive which had forced him to seek independence under the sea, it had left him still a man, that his heart still beat for the sufferings of humanity, and that his immense charity was for oppressed races as well as individuals.

And I then understood for whom those millions were destined, which were forwarded by Captain Nemo when the *Nautilus* was cruising in the waters of the Cretan insurgents!

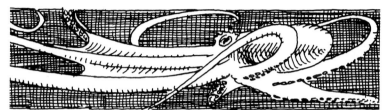

◄ CHAPTER IX ►

A VANISHED CONTINENT

he next morning, the 19th of February, I saw the Canadian enter my room. I expected this visit. He looked very disappointed.

"Well, sir?" said he.

"Well, Ned, fortune was against us yesterday."

"Yes, that damned captain had to stop exactly at the hour we intended leaving his vessel."

"Yes, Ned, he had business at his bankers."

"His bankers!"

"Or rather his banking-house. By that I mean the ocean, where his riches are safer than in the state treasury."

I then related to the Canadian the incidents of the preceding night, hoping to bring him back to the idea of not abandoning the captain; but my recital had no other result than an energetically expressed regret from Ned, that he had not been able to take a walk on the battle-field of Vigo for his own benefit.

"However," said he, "all is not ended. It is only a blow of the harpoon lost. Another time we must succeed; and tonight, if necessary. . . ."

"In what direction is the *Nautilus* going?" I asked.

"I do not know," replied Ned.

"Well, at noon we shall get our bearings."

The Canadian returned to Conseil. As soon as I was dressed, I went into the salon. The compass was not reassuring. The course of the *Nautilus* was S.S.W. We were turning our backs on Europe.

I waited with some impatience till the ship's position was marked on the chart. At about half-past eleven the reservoirs were emptied, and our vessel rose to the surface of the ocean. I rushed towards the platform. Ned Land had preceded me.

No more land in sight. Nothing but an immense sea. Some sails on the horizon, doubtless those going to Cape San Roque in search of favorable winds for doubling the Cape of Good Hope. The weather was cloudy. A gale of wind was preparing.

Ned raved, and tried to pierce the cloudy horizon. He still hoped that behind all that fog stretched the land he so longed for.

At noon the sun showed itself for an instant. The second-in-command profited by this brightness to take its height. Then the sea becoming more billowy, we descended, and the hatch closed.

An hour after, upon consulting the chart, I saw the position of the *Nautilus* was marked at 60° 17′ long, and 33° 22′ lat, at 150 leagues from the nearest coast. There was no means of flight, and I leave you to imagine the rage of the Canadian, when I informed him of our situation.

For myself, I was not particularly sorry. I felt lightened of the load which had oppressed me, and was able to return with some degree of calmness to my accustomed work.

That night, about eleven o'clock, I received a most unexpected visit from Captain Nemo. He asked me very graciously if I felt fatigued from my watch of the preceding night. I answered in the negative.

"Then, Monsieur Aronnax, I propose an interesting excursion."

"Propose, Captain?"

"You have hitherto only visited the submarine depths by daylight, under the brightness of the sun. Would it suit you to see them in the darkness of the night?"

"Most willingly."

"I warn you, the way will be tiring. We shall have far to walk, and must climb a mountain. The roads are not well kept."

"What you say, Captain, only heightens my curiosity; I am ready to follow you."

"Come then, sir, we will put on our diving suits."

Arrived at the robing-room, I saw that neither of my companions nor any of the ship's crew were to follow us on this excursion. Captain Nemo had not even proposed my taking with me either Ned or Conseil.

In a few moments we had put on our diving suits; they placed on our backs the reservoirs, abundantly filled with air, but no electric lamps were prepared. I called the captain's attention the fact.

"They will be useless," he replied.

I thought I had not heard aright, but I could not repeat my observation, for the captain's head had already disappeared in its metal sphere. I finished harnessing myself; I felt them put an iron stick into my hand, and some minutes later, after going through the usual procedure, we set foot on the bottom of the Atlantic, at a depth of 300 meters.

Midnight was approaching. The waters were profoundly dark, but Captain Nemo pointed out in the distance a reddish spot, a sort of light shining brilliantly, about two miles from the *Nautilus*. What this fire might be, what could feed it, why and how it lit up the liquid mass, I could not say. In any case, it did light our way, vaguely, it is true, but I soon accustomed myself to the peculiar darkness, and I understood, under such circumstances, the uselessness of the Ruhmkorff apparatus.

Captain Nemo and I walked beside one another, toward the glow. The sea floor rose imperceptibly. We took large strides, aided by our iron staffs, but the walk went slowly. Our feet kept sinking into a kind of soft mud mixed with algae and sown with flat rocks.

As we advanced, I heard a kind of pattering above my head. The noise increased, sometimes producing a continual crackling. I soon understood the cause. It was rain falling violently, and crisping the surface of the waves. Instinctively the thought flashed across my mind that I should be soaked through! By the water! in the midst of the water! I could not help laughing at the odd idea. But indeed, in the thick diving dress, the outside water is no longer felt, and one only seems to be in an atmosphere somewhat denser than the terrestrial atmosphere, and nothing more.

After half an hour's walk the soil became stony. Medusæ, microscopic crustacea, and pennatules lit it slightly with their phosphorescent gleam. I caught a glimpse of pieces of stone covered with millions of zoöphytes and masses of algae. My feet often slipped upon this viscous carpet of seaweed, and without my iron-tipped stick I should have fallen more than once. In turning round, I could still see the whitish lantern of the *Nautilus* which was beginning to pale in the distance.

These piles of stone that I just mentioned were arranged on the ocean floor with a regularity that was inexplicable. I noticed gigantic grooves that disappeared into the darkness, and whose length I could not guess. There were other peculiarities also, that I could not explain. I had the feeling that my heavy lead boots were crushing bones that broke with a dry crackling sound. What was this strange plain we were treading? I wanted to ask the captain, but he had not taught me that sign language used by himself and his companions on their submarine excursions—it remained incomprehensible to me.

But the rosy light which guided us increased and lit up the horizon. The presence of this fire under water puzzled me in the highest degree. Was it some electric effulgence? Was I going towards a natural phenomenon as yet unknown to the scientists of the earth? Or even (for this thought crossed my brain) had the hand of man something to do with this conflagration? Had he fanned this flame? Was I to meet in these depths companions and friends of Captain Nemo whom he was going to visit, and who, like him, led this strange existence? Should I find down there a whole colony of exiles, who, weary of the miseries of this earth, had sought and found independence in the deep ocean? All these foolish and unreasonable ideas pursued me. And in this condition of mind, over-excited by the succession of wonders continually passing before my eyes, I should not have been surprised to meet at the bottom of the sea one of those submarine towns of which Captain Nemo dreamed.

Our road grew lighter and lighter. The white glimmer came in rays from the summit of a mountain about 800 feet high. But what I saw was simply a reflection, developed by the clearness of the waters. The source of this inexplicable light was on the opposite side of the mountain.

In the midst of this stony maze, furrowing the bottom of the Atlantic, Captain Nemo advanced without hesitation. He knew this dreary road. Doubtless he had often travelled over it, and could not get lost. I followed him with unshaken confidence. He seemed to me like a genie of the sea; and, as he walked before me, I could not help admiring his stature, which was outlined in black on the luminous horizon.

It was one in the morning when we arrived at the first slopes of the mountain; but to gain access to them we must venture through the difficult paths of a vast copse.

Yes; a copse of dead trees, without leaves, without sap, trees petrified by the action of the water, and here and there overtopped by gigantic pines. It was like a coal pit, still standing, holding by the roots to the broken soil, and whose branches, like fine black paper cuttings, showed distinctly against the watery ceiling. Picture to yourself a forest in the Hartz Mountains, hanging on to the sides of the slopes, but a forest drowned. The paths were encumbered with algae and fucus, between which grovelled a whole world of crustacea. I went along, climbing the rocks, striding over extended trunks, breaking the sea-lianas, which hung from one tree to the other; and frightening the fishes, which flew from branch to branch. Pressing onward, I felt no fatigue. I followed my guide, who was never tired.

What a spectacle! how can I express it? how can I paint the aspect of those woods and rocks in writing,—their under parts dark and wild, the upper colored with red tints, by that light which the reflecting powers of the waters increased? We climbed rocks, which fell behind us with gigantic bounds and the low growling of an avalanche. To right and left ran long, dark caves, where sight was lost. Here opened vast glades which the hand of man seemed to have worked; and I asked myself if some inhabitant of these submarine regions would not suddenly appear to me.

But Captain Nemo was still climbing. I could not stay behind. I followed boldly. My stick gave me good help. A false step would have been dangerous on the narrow passes sloping down to the sides of the gulfs; but I walked with firm step, without feeling any giddiness. Now I jumped a crevice the depth of which would have made me hesitate had it been among the glaciers on the land; now I ventured on the unsteady trunk of a tree, thrown from one side of an abyss to the other, without looking under my feet, having eyes only for the wild scenery of this region. Here and there, monumental rocks, leaning on their regularly cut bases, seemed to defy all laws of equilibrium. From between their stony knees, trees sprang, like a jet under heavy pressure, and upheld others which upheld them. Natural towers, large cliffs, cut perpendicularly like curtains, or inclined at an angle which the laws of gravitation could never have tolerated in terrestrial regions.

I knew that the difference was because of the greater density of sea water. Which is how, in spite of my heavy clothing, copper helmet, and metal shoes, I was able to climb slopes of incredible steepness, surmounting them, so to speak, with all the agility of an *izard* or chamois!

This recitation of our underwater excursion must sound unbelievable! As a writer of fact, I must record what really happened, no matter how impossible it my seem. I was not dreaming; I saw and felt!

Two hours after quitting the *Nautilus,* we had ascended beyond the tree line, and a hundred feet above our heads rose the top of the mountain, which cast a shadow by the brilliant illumination from the opposite slope. Some petrified shrubs made a perilous, zigzag path. Fishes flew up under our feet like birds surprised in the long grass. The massive rocks were rent with impenetrable fractures, deep grottos, and unfathomable holes, at the bottom of which formidable creatures could be heard moving. My blood ebbed from my heart when I saw enormous antennæ blocking my road, or some frightful claw closing with a terrifying noise in the shadow of some cavity. Thousands of luminous spots shone brightly in the midst of the darkness. They were the eyes of giant crustacea crouched in their holes; giant lobsters setting themselves up like halberdiers, and moving their claws with the clicking sound of pincers; titanic crabs, pointed like guns on their carriages; and frightful looking octopi, interweaving their tentacles like a living nest of serpents.

What was this strange world I no longer knew? To what order did these articulata belong, that used a rock for a second shell? How had nature discovered the secret of their vegetative existence? How many centuries had they lived here, in the lowest depths of the sea?

We had now arrived on the first plateau, where other surprises awaited me. Before us lay some picturesque ruins, which betrayed the hand of man, and not that of the Creator. There were vast heaps of stone, among which might be traced the vague and shadowy forms of castles and temples, clothed with a world of blossoming zoöphytes, and over which, instead of ivy, algae and fucus threw a thick vegetable mantle.

But what was this portion of the globe which had been swallowed by cataclysms? Who had placed those rocks and stones like dolmen of prehistoric times? Where was I? Where had Captain Nemo's fancy taken me?

I would have liked to have asked him; but not being able to, I stopped him—I seized his arm. But shaking his head, and pointing to the highest point of the mountain, he seemed to say—"Come, come along; come higher!"

I followed, in a final dash, and in a few minutes I had climbed to the top, which commanded the whole mass of rock we had just climbed, being a dozen meters higher.

I looked down the side we had just climbed. The mountain did not rise more than seven or eight hundred feet above the level of the plain; but on the opposite side it commanded from twice that height the depths of this part of the Atlantic. My eyes ranged far over a large space lit by a violent eruption. In fact, the mountain was a volcano. At fifty feet below the peak, in the midst of a rain of stones and scoriæ, a large crater was vomiting forth torrents of lava which fell in a cascade of fire into the bosom of the water. Thus situated, this volcano lit the lower plain like an immense torch, to the limit of the horizon. I said that the submarine crater threw up lava, but no flames. Flames require the oxygen of the air to feed upon, and cannot be developed under water; but streams of lava, having in themselves the principle of their incandescence, can attain a white heat, fight vigorously against the liquid element, and turn it to vapor by contact. Rapid currents bore all these gases in diffusion, and torrents of lava, slid to the bottom of the mountain like an eruption of Vesuvius on another Torre del Greco.

There, indeed, under my eyes, ruined, destroyed, lay a town,—its roofs open to the sky, its temples fallen, its arches dislocated, its columns lying on the ground, from which one could still recognize the solid proportions of Tuscan architecture. Further on, some remains of a gigantic aqueduct; here the high base of an Acropolis, with the rough outline of a Parthenon; there traces of a quay, as if an ancient port had formerly abutted on the border of the ocean, which disappeared with its merchant vessels and its triremes of war. Further on again, long lines of sunken walls and broad deserted streets—a perfect Pompeii buried beneath the waters. Such was the sight that Captain Nemo brought before my eyes!

Where was I? Where was I? I must know, at any cost. I tried to speak, I wanted to tear off my helmet. But Captain Nemo stopped me by a gesture, and picking up a piece of chalk stone, advanced to a rock of black basalt, and traced the one word—

What a light shot through my mind! Atlantis, the ancient Meropis of Theopompus, the Atlantis of Plato, that continent denied by Origen, Porphyrus, Jamblichus, D'Anville, Malte-Brun, and Humboldt, who placed its disappearance among legendary tales, but believed by Posidonius, Pliny, Ammianus Marcellinus, Tertullian, Engel, Sherer, Tournefort, Buffon, and D'Avezac. I had it there now before my eyes, bearing upon it the undeniable testimony of its catastrophe. The region thus engulfed was beyond Europe, Asia, and Lybia, beyond the Pillars of Hercules, where those powerful people, the Atlantides, lived, against whom the first wars of ancient Greece were waged!

The historian who wrote of the great feats of these heroic times was Plato himself. His *Dialogue* between Timaeus and Critias was written, so to speak, under the inspiration of Solon, the poet and legislator.

One day, Solon had been speaking with the ancient sages of Sais, an ancient city then eight centuries old, as testified by the annals engraved on the sacred walls of its temples. One of the elders told the story of a city more ancient by a thousand years. This first Athenian city, nine hundred centuries old, had been invaded and partially destroyed by the Atlanteans. These Atlanteans, he said, occupied an immense continent, larger than Africa and Asia combined, covering an area between 12° and 40° north latitude. Their dominions even included Egypt. They had tried to conquer Greece, but had to retreat before the indomitable resistance of the Hellenes. Centuries passed. A cataclysm created floods and earthquakes. One night and one day sufficed for the destruction of Atlantis. Only its highest summits—Madeira, the Azores, the Canaries, the Cape Verde Islands—remained above the sea.

These were the historical recollections that Captain Nemo's inscription stirred in my spirit.

Thus, led by the strangest destiny, I was treading under foot the mountains of this continent, touching with my hand those ruins a thousand generations old, and contemporary with the geological epochs. I was walking on the very spot where the contemporaries of the first man

had walked. I crushed under my lead boots the skeletons of animals of fabled times, which these trees—now petrified—had shaded.

Ah! Why did I have such little time! I would have liked to have descended the steep slopes of this mountain, crossing this immense continent that undoubtedly connects Africa to America, and visit these great antedeluvian cities. Perhaps, before my eyes, I would see the war-like city Makhimos, or the pious city Eusebos, whose gigantic inhabitants lived for centuries, and who were so strong that they could build with blocks of stone that still resisted the action of the water. Some day, perhaps, another volcanic phenomenon will return to the surface of the waves these drowned ruins! A large number of underwater volcanoes are in this portion of the ocean, and many ships have felt extraordinary tremors while passing over these tormented deeps. Some have heard heavy sounds which announced a profound struggle of the elements; others have caught volcanic cinders thrown from the sea. All of this area, as far as the Equator, is continually worked by the Plutonian forces. And who knows, in some distant epoque, due to volcanic eruptions, and successive layers of lava, the summits of these igneous mountains might not reappear above the surface of the Atlantic!

While I was trying to fix in my mind every detail of this grand landscape, Captain Nemo remained motionless, leaning on a mossy stone, as if petrified in mute ecstasy. Was he dreaming of those generations long since disappeared? Was he asking them the secret of human destiny? Was it here this strange man came to steep himself in historical recollections, and live again this ancient life—he who wanted no modern one? What would I not have given to know his thoughts, to share them, to understand them!

We remained for an hour at this place, contemplating the vast plain under the brightness of the lava, which was sometimes wonderfully intense. Rapid tremblings, caused by internal bubblings, ran along the mountain. Deep noises distinctly transmitted through the liquid medium were echoed with majestic grandeur.

At this moment the moon appeared through the mass of waters, and threw her pale rays on the buried continent. It was but a gleam, but what an indescribable effect! The captain rose, cast one last look on the immense plain, and then bade me follow him.

We descended the mountain rapidly, and once past the mineral forest, I saw the lantern of the *Nautilus* shining like a star. The captain walked straight to it, and we got on board as the first rays of dawn whitened the surface of the ocean.

◀ CHAPTER X ▶
THE SUBMARINE COAL MINES

he next day, the 20th of February, I awoke very late: the fatigues of the previous night had prolonged my sleep until eleven o'clock. I dressed quickly, and hastened to find the course the *Nautilus* was taking. The instruments showed it to be still towards the south, with a speed of twenty miles an hour, and a depth of 100 meters.

Conseil entered. I told him of my nocturnal excursion, and, as the panels were open, he could see part of the submerged continent.

The *Nautilus* was cruising only ten meters above the soil of the plain of Atlantis. I felt as though I were in a balloon carried by the wind above the prairies of earth; but it would be more truthful to say that we sat in the salon as though in a car in an express train. The first objects that passed before our eyes were rocks carved fantastically, forests of trees changed from the vegetable kingdom to the mineral kingdom, their immobile silhouettes grimacing under the waves. There were also rocky masses buried beneath a tapestry of axidiae and anemones, bristling with long, vertical hydrophytes; blocks of lava with strange contours attested to the fury of the Plutonian eruptions.

While we stared at this bizarre scenery, under the electric light, I told Conseil the story of the Atlanteans, which, from a purely imaginary point of view, inspired Bailly to write so many charming pages. I spoke of the wars of these heroic people. I discussed the question of Atlantis as a man who no longer doubted its existence. But Conseil, distracted, barely listened and was indifferent to my explanations of its history.

Numerous fish swam into our view, and when fish passed by, Conseil became lost in the abyss of classification; he abandoned the world of reality. In these cases, I could do nothing but follow him into the study of ichthyology.

The species of fishes in the Atlantic did not differ much from those already noticed. There were rays of giant size, five meters long, and endowed with great muscular strength, which enabled them to shoot above the waves; sharks of many kinds, among others, a glaucus fifteen feet long, with sharp triangular teeth, and whose transparency rendered it almost invisible in the water; brown sagræ; humantins, prism-shaped, and clad with a tuberculous hide; sturgeons, resembling their cousins of the Mediterranean; brownish-yellow trumpet syngnathes, a foot and a half long, furnished with small greyish fins, without teeth or tongue, and as supple as snakes.

Among bony fish, Conseil noticed some blackish makairas, about three meters long, armed at the upper jaw with a piercing sword; other bright-colored creatures, known in the time of Aristotle by the name of the sea-dragon, which are dangerous to capture on account of the spikes on their back; also some coryphænes, with brown backs marked with little blue stripes, and surrounded with a gold border; some beautiful dorades; moonfish that looked like blue-trimmed plates, that shimmered with silver patches in the sun; and xyphias-espadons, sword-fish eight meters long, swimming in troops, fierce animals, but more herbivorous than carnivorous. Like well-behaved husbands, they obeyed the slightest whims of their mates.

But while observing the various species of marine fauna, I did not grow tired of examining the vast plains of Atlantis. Occasionally, capricious variations of the terrain would oblige the *Nautilus* to slow its speed, and it would slip with the ease of a whale through the narrow passes in the hills, If the labyrinth seemed inextricable, the submarine would rise like an airship, pass the obstacle, then regain her rapid course few meters above the sea floor. An admirable and charming way to navigate, which reminded me of travelling in a balloon, with the difference that the *Nautilus* perfectly obeyed the hand of the steersman.

About four o'clock, the soil, generally composed of a thick mud mixed with petrified wood, changed by degrees, and it became more stony, and seemed strewn with conglomerates and basaltic tuff, with a sprinkling of lava and sulphurous obsidian. I thought that a mountainous region was succeeding the long plains; and accordingly, after the *Nautilus* had travelled a few more leagues, I saw the southerly horizon blocked by a high wall which seemed to close all exit. Its summit evidently rose above the level of the ocean. It must be a continent, or at least an island,—one of the Canaries, or the Cape Verde Islands. The bearings not being yet taken, perhaps by design I was ignorant of our exact position. In any case, such a wall seemed to me to mark the limits of Atlantis, of which we had in reality passed over only the smallest part.

Nightfall did not interrupt my observations. I was alone. Conseil had gone back to his cabin. The *Nautilus*, reducing its speed, hovered above the confused masses of the seafloor, sometimes touching the bottom as if wanting to come to rest, sometimes unexpectedly returning to the surface of the waves. I could see some brilliant constellations through the crystalline water; specifically, the five or six zodiacal stars that hang on the tail of Orion.

Much longer should I have remained at the window, admiring the beauties of sea and sky, but the panels closed. At this moment the *Nautilus* arrived at the face of this high wall. What it would do now I could not guess. I returned to my room since the ship no longer moved. I laid myself down with the full intention of waking after a few hours' sleep.

But it was eight o'clock the next day when I reentered the salon. I looked at the manometer. It told me that the *Nautilus* was floating on the surface of the ocean. Besides, I heard steps on the platform. But no rolling motion betrayed the undulations of the waves.

I went to the panel. It was open; but, instead of broad daylight, as I expected, I was surrounded by profound darkness. Where were we? Was I mistaken? Was it still night? No; not a star was shining, and night has not that utter darkness.

I knew not what to think, when a voice near me said—

"Is that you, Professor?"

"Ah! Captain Nemo," I answered, "where are we?"

"Underground, sir."

"Underground!" I exclaimed. "And the *Nautilus* is still floating?"

"It always floats."

"But I do not understand."

"Wait a few minutes, our lantern will be lit, and if you like things illuminated you will be satisfied."

I went up to the platform and waited. The darkness was so complete that I could not even see Captain Nemo; but looking to the zenith, exactly above my head, I seemed to catch an undecided gleam, a kind of twilight filling a circular hole. At this instant the lantern was lit, and its vividness dispelled the faint light.

I closed my dazzled eyes for an instant, and then looked again. The *Nautilus* was stationary, floating near a promontory which formed a sort of quay. The lake in which it floated was imprisoned by a circle of walls, measuring two miles in diameter, and six in circumference. Its level (the manometer showed) could only be the same as the outside level, for there must necessarily be a communication between the lake and the sea. The high walls leaning forward on their base, grew into a vaulted roof bearing the shape of an immense funnel turned upside down, the height being about five or six hundred meters. At the summit was a circular orifice, by which I had caught the slight gleam of light, evidently daylight.

"Where are we?" I asked.

"In the very heart of an extinct volcano, the interior of which has been invaded by the sea, after some great convulsion of the earth. While you were sleeping, Professor, the *Nautilus* penetrated to this lagoon by a natural channel, which opens about ten meters beneath the surface of the ocean. This is its harbor of refuge, a sure, commodious, and mysterious one, sheltered from all gales. Show me, if you can, on the coasts of any of your continents or islands, a harbor which can give such perfect refuge from the fury of the hurricane."

"Certainly," I replied, "you are in safety here, Captain Nemo. Who could reach you in the heart of a volcano? But did I not see an opening at its summit?"

"Yes; its crater, formerly filled with lava, vapor, and flames, and which now gives entrance to the life-giving air we breathe."

"But what is this volcanic mountain?"

"It belongs to one of the numerous islands with which this sea is strewn—to vessels a simple reef—to us an immense cavern. Chance led me to discover it, and chance served me well."

Is it possible to climb through the opening that forms the crater?"

"No. For only the first hundred feet is the lower part of the inside of the mountain practicable, but above that, the walls overhang and the slope cannot be scaled."

"I see, Captain, that nature serves you everywhere and well. You are safe on the surface of this lake. No one but you can visit its waters. But of what use is this refuge, Captain? The *Nautilus* wants no port."

"No, sir; but it wants electricity to make it move, and the elements to make the electricity— sodium to feed the elements, coal from which to get the sodium, and a coal-mine to supply the coal. And exactly on this spot the sea covers entire forests embedded during the geological period, now mineralized, and transformed into coal; for me they are an inexhaustible mine."

"Your men follow the trade of miners here, then, Captain?"

"Exactly so. These mines extend under the waves like the mines of Newcastle. Here, in their diving dresses, pickaxe and shovel in hand, my men extract the coal. I do not have to ask anything from the mines of the earth. When I burn this combustible for the manufacture of sodium, the smoke, escaping from the crater of the mountain, gives it the appearance of a still active volcano."

"And we shall see your companions at work?"

"No; not this time at least; for I am in a hurry to continue our undersea tour of the world. So I shall content myself with drawing from the reserve of sodium I already possess. The time for loading is one day only, and we continue our voyage. So if you wish to go over the cavern, and make the round of the lagoon, you must take advantage of today, Monsieur Aronnax."

I thanked the captain, and went to look for my companions, who had not yet left their cabin. I invited them to follow me without saying where we were.

They mounted the platform. Conseil, who was astonished at nothing, seemed to look upon it as quite natural that he should wake under a mountain, after having fallen asleep under the waves. But Ned Land thought of nothing but finding whether the cavern had any exit. After breakfast, about ten o'clock, we went down on to the shore.

"Here we are, once more on land," said Conseil.

"I do not call this land," said the Canadian. "And besides, we are not on it, but beneath it."

Between the foot of the walls of the mountain and the waters of the lake lay a sandy shore, which, at its greatest breadth, measured five hundred feet. On this beach one might easily make the tour of the lake. But the base of the high walls was stony ground, with volcanic blocks and enormous pumice stones lying in picturesque heaps. All these detached masses, covered with polished enamel by the action of the subterranean fires, shone resplendent by the light of our electric lantern. The mica dust from the shore, rising under our feet, flew like a cloud of sparks.

The ground now rose sensibly as we drew further from the water, and we soon arrived at long circuitous slopes, steep paths, which took us higher by degrees; but we were obliged to walk carefully among these conglomerates, bound by no cement, our feet slipping on the glassy trachyte, composed of crystals of feldspar, and quartz.

The volcanic nature of this enormous excavation was confirmed on all sides, and I pointed it out to my companions.

"Picture to yourselves," said I, "what this crater must have been like when filled with boiling lava, and when the level of the incandescent liquid rose to the orifice of the mountain, as though overflowing the lips of a crucible."

"I can picture it perfectly," said Conseil. "But will monsieur tell me why the Great Architect has suspended operations, and how it is that the furnace is replaced by the quiet waters of the lake?"

"Most probably, Conseil, because some convulsion beneath the ocean produced that very opening which has served as a passage for the *Nautilus*. Then the waters of the Atlantic rushed into the interior of the mountain. There must have been a terrible struggle between the two elements, a struggle which ended in the victory of Neptune. But many ages have run out since then, and the submerged volcano is now a peaceable grotto."

"Very well," replied Ned Land, "I accept the explanation, sir; but, in our own interests, I regret that the opening of which you speak was not made above the level of the sea."

"But, friend Ned," said Conseil, "if the passage had not been under the sea, the *Nautilus* could not have gone through it."

"And I add, Master Land, that if the waters had not rushed into the mountain, this volcano would still be a volcano. So your regrets are superfluous."

We continued ascending. The grade became more and more steep and narrow. Deep rifts, which we were obliged to cross, cut our path here and there; overhanging masses had to be gotten round. We slid upon our knees and crawled on our stomachs. But Conseil's dexterity and the Canadian's strength surmounted all obstacles.

At a height of about thirty meters, the nature of the ground changed without becoming more practicable. To the conglomerate and trachyte succeeded black basalt, here spread in layers full of bubbles; there forming regular prisms, placed like a colonnade supporting the arch of the immense vault, an admirable specimen of natural architecture. Between the blocks of basalt wound long streams of lava, long since grown cold, encrusted with veins of bituminous coal; and in some places there were spread large carpets of sulphur. A more powerful light shone through the upper crater, shedding a vague glimmer over these volcanic debris forever buried in the bosom of this extinguished mountain.

But our upward march was soon stopped at a height of about two hundred and fifty feet by impassable obstacles. There was a complete vaulted arch overhanging us, and our ascent was changed to a circular walk. At last vegetable life began to struggle from the mineral. Some shrubs, and even some trees, grew from the fractures of the walls. I recognized some euphorbias, with the bitter sap coming from them; heliotropes, quite incapable of justifying their name, since the rays of the sun never touched them, sadly drooped their clusters of flowers, both their color and perfume half gone. Here and there some chrysanthemums grew timidly at the foot of an aloe with long sickly-looking leaves. But between the streams of lava, I saw some little violets still slightly perfumed, and I admit that I smelled them with delight. Perfume is the soul of the flower, and the flowers of the sea, those splendid hydrophytes, have no soul!

We had arrived at the foot of a group of sturdy dragon-trees, which had pushed aside the rocks with their muscular roots, when Ned Land exclaimed: "Ah! Monsieur, a hive! a hive!"

"A hive!" I replied, with a gesture of incredulity.

"Yes, a hive," repeated the Canadian, "and bees humming round it."

I approached, and was bound to believe my own eyes. There, at a hole bored in one of the dragon-trees, were some thousands of these ingenious insects, so common in all the Canaries, and whose produce is so much esteemed.

Naturally enough, the Canadian wished to gather the honey, and I did not have the bad grace to oppose his wish. A quantity of dry leaves, mixed with sulphur, was lit with a spark from his flint, and he began to smoke out the bees. The humming ceased by degrees, and the hive eventually yielded several pounds of the honey, with which Ned Land filled his haversack.

"When I have mixed this honey with the paste of the breadfruit," said he, "I shall be able to offer you a succulent cake."

"Upon my word," said Conseil, "it will be like spice bread!"

"Never mind the spice bread," said I; "let us continue our interesting walk."

At every turn of the path we were following, the lake appeared in all its length and breadth. The lantern lit up the whole of its peaceable surface which knew neither ripple nor wave. The *Nautilus* remained perfectly immovable. On the platform, and on the mountain, the ship's crew were working like black shadows clearly silhouetted against the bright light.

We were now going round the highest crest of the first layers of rock which upheld the roof. I then saw that bees were not the only representatives of the animal kingdom in the interior of this volcano. Birds of prey hovered here and there in the shadows, or fled from their nests

on the top of the rocks. There were sparrow-hawks with white breasts, and kestrels. Down the slopes scampered, with all the speed their long legs could make, several fine fat bustards. I leave any one to imagine the covetousness of the Canadian at the sight of this savory game, and whether he regretted having no gun. But he did his best to replace the lead by stones, and after several fruitless attempts, he succeeded in wounding a magnificent bustard. To say that he risked his life twenty times before reaching it, is but the pure truth; but he managed so well, that the creature joined the honeycombs in his bag.

We were now obliged to descend towards the shore, the crest becoming impracticable. Above us the crater seemed to gape like the mouth of a well. From this place the sky could be clearly seen, and clouds, scattered by the west wind, leaving behind them, on the summit of the mountain, their misty remnants. This was certain proof that they were only moderately high, for the volcano did not rise more than eight hundred feet above the level of the ocean.

Half an hour after the Canadian's last exploit we had regained the inner shore. Here the flora was represented by large carpets of marine crystal, a little umbrella-shaped plant very good to pickle, which also bears the name of *perce-pierre, passe-pierre,* and sea-fennel. Conseil gathered some bundles of it. As to the fauna, it might be counted by thousands of crustacea of all sorts: lobsters, crabs, *palémons mysis,* spider crabs, *galatées,* and a large number of shells, *porcelaines,* rockfish and limpets.

Then we discovered a magnificent cave. My companions and I with pleasure stretched out on its fine sand. Fire had polished its enamelled and sparkling walls, which were dusted with powdered mica. Ned Land was tapping the walls, trying to determine their thickness. I could not keep from smiling. The conversation turned as always to his eternal plans for escape, and I thought that I could give him this hope, without too much risk: that Captain Nemo had only returned to the south to renew his supply of sodium. When this was done, we would return to the coasts of Europe and America; this would permit the Canadian to have more success than his previous abortive attempts.

We had rested for an hour in this charming grotto. The conversation, which had begun lively, now grew languid. A certain drowsiness overtook us. Since there was no reason to resist sleep, I let myself fall into a deep slumber. I dreamed—and one does not choose his dreams—I dreamed that my existence had been reduced to the vegetative life of a simple mollusk. I imagined that the grotto formed the double valve of my shell. . . .

All at once, I was awakened by the voice of Conseil.

"Wake up! Wake up!" cried the good lad.

"What is it?" I asked, sitting halfway up.

"The water is rising!"

I stood up. The water was flooding in a torrent into our retreat, and, decidedly, since we were not mollusks, we had to leave.

In a few minutes we reached safety above the grotto.

"What is going on?" demanded Conseil, "some new phenomenon?"

"No, my friends," I answered, "it is the tide, just the tide, that almost took us by surprise as it did the heroes of Sir Walter Scott! The ocean is rising outside, so by the natural laws of equilibrium the level of the lake rises equally. We escaped with just a slight wetting. Let us go back to the *Nautilus* and change."

Three-quarters of an hour later, we had finished our circuitous walk, and were on board. The crew had just finished loading the sodium, and the *Nautilus* could have left that instant.

But Captain Nemo gave no order. Did he wish to wait until night, and leave the submarine passage secretly? Perhaps so. Whatever it might be, the next day, the *Nautilus,* having left its port, steered clear of all land at a few meters beneath the waves of the Atlantic.

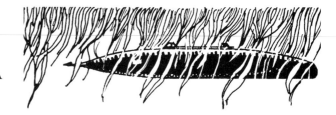

◄ CHAPTER XI ►

THE SARGASSO SEA

he direction of the *Nautilus* was not changed. All hope that we might return to European waters had to be abandoned for the moment. Captain Nemo maintained his southerly course. Where was he taking us? I dared not imagine.

That day the *Nautilus* crossed a singular part of the Atlantic Ocean. No one can be ignorant of the existence of a current of warm water, known by the name of the Gulf Stream. After leaving the Florida Channel, it goes in the direction of Spitzbergen. But before entering the Gulf of Mexico, about the forty-fourth degree of north latitude, this current divides into two arms, the principal one going towards the coast of Ireland and Norway, while the second bends to the south at about the latitude of the Azores; then, touching the African shore, and describing a lengthened oval, returns to the Antilles.

This second arm—it is rather a collar than an arm—surrounds with its circles of warm water a portion of the ocean—cold, quiet, immovable, called the Sargasso Sea. It is a perfect lake in the open Atlantic. It takes no less than three years for the great current to pass round it.

The Sargasso Sea, properly speaking, covers all the submerged region of Atlantis. Certain authors have stated that a number of the plants it contains have been uprooted from the plains of that ancient continent. It is more likely, however, that these plants, algae and seaweed are carried from the shores of Europe and America, and brought to this area by the Gulf Stream. This is one of the reasons that lead Columbus to suppose the existence of a New World. When the sailors of that hardy explorer arrived in the Sargasso Sea, they navigated with difficulty in the midst of these plants, which impeded their progress. The men were terrified, and took three long weeks to traverse it.

Such was the region the *Nautilus* was now visiting, a perfect meadow, a close carpet of algae, seaweed and tropical berries, so thick and so compact, that the stem of a vessel could hardly tear its way through. And Captain Nemo, not wishing to entangle his screw in this herbaceous mass, kept some meters beneath the surface of the waves.

The name Sargasso comes from the Spanish word "sargazzo," which means "kelp." This kelp or varech, or berry-plant, is the principal formation of this immense bank. This is the theory of the learned Maury, the author of *The Physical Geography of the Sea,* as to why these hydrophytes unite in the peaceful basin of the Atlantic.

"If bits of cork or chaff, or any floating substance, be put into a basin, and a circular motion be given to the water, all the light substances will be found crowding together near the centre of the pool, where there is the least motion. Just such a basin is the Atlantic Ocean to the Gulf Stream, and the Sargasso Sea is the centre of the whirl."

I share Maury's opinion, and I was able to study the phenomenon in its very midst, where ships rarely penetrate. Above us floated bodies of all kinds, heaped up among these brownish plants; trunks of trees torn from the Andes or the Rocky Mountains, and carried here by the Amazon or the Mississippi; numerous wrecks, remains of keels, or ships' bottoms, side planks stove in, and so weighted with shells and barnacles, that they could not again rise to the surface. And time will one day justify Maury's other opinion, that these substances, thus accumulated for centuries, will become petrified by the action of the water, and will then form inexhaustible coal mines—a precious reserve prepared by far-seeing Nature for the moment when men shall have exhausted the mines of continents.

In the midst of this inextricable mass of plants and seaweed, I noticed some charming pink star halcyons and actiniæ, with their long tails of tentacles trailing after them; jellyfish, green, red, and blue, and the great rhyzostoms of Cuvier, the large blue umbrella of which was bordered and festooned with violet.

All the day of the 22nd of February we passed in the Sargasso Sea, where such fish as are partial to marine plants and crustacea find abundant nourishment. The next day the ocean had returned to its accustomed appearance.

For nineteen days, from the 23rd of February to the 12th of March, the *Nautilus* kept in the middle of the Atlantic, carrying us at a constant speed of a hundred leagues every twenty-four hours. Captain Nemo evidently intended accomplishing his submarine program, and I imagined that he intended, after doubling Cape Horn, to return to the southern seas of the Pacific.

Ned Land had cause for fear. In these large seas, devoid of islands, we could not attempt to leave the boat. Nor had we any means of opposing Captain Nemo's will. Our only course was to submit; but what we could not gain by force or cunning, I like to think might be obtained by persuasion. This voyage ended, would he not consent to restore our liberty, under an oath never to reveal his existence?—an oath of honor which we should have religiously kept. But we must consider that delicate question with the captain. Was I free to claim this liberty? Had he not himself said from the beginning, in the firmest manner, that the secret of his life exacted from him our lasting imprisonment on board the *Nautilus?* And would not my four months' silence appear to him a tacit acceptance of our situation? And would not a return to the subject result in raising suspicions which might be hurtful to our projects, if at some future time a favorable opportunity offered to return to them? All these reasons, I thought about them, I turned them around in my head, I discussed them with Conseil, who was equally perplexed. Even though I am not easily discouraged, I realized that the chances of seeing our countrymen again were diminishing day by day. All the more so, since Captain Nemo had the temerity to be heading for the South Atlantic!

During the nineteen days mentioned above, no incident of any note happened to signalize our voyage. I saw little of the captain; he was at work. In the library I often found his books left open, especially those on natural history. My work on submarine depths, conned over by him, was covered with marginal notes, often contradicting my theories and systems. But the captain contented himself with thus purging my work; it was very rare for him to discuss it with me. Sometimes I heard the melancholy tones of his organ, played with much expression; but only at night, in the midst of the most secret darkness, when the *Nautilus* slept upon the deserted ocean. During this part of our voyage we sailed for whole days on the surface of the waves. The sea seemed abandoned. A few sailing-ships, on the road to India, were making for the Cape of Good Hope. One day we were followed by the boats of a whaler, who, no doubt, took us for some enormous whale of great price; but Captain Nemo did not wish the worthy fellows to lose their time and trouble, so ended the chase by plunging under the water. That incident greatly interested Ned Land. I do not doubt that the Canadian regretted that our iron whale had not been stricken to death by the harpoons of those whalers.

Fish that Conseil and I observed during this period differed little from ones we had studied in other latitudes. The principal ones we saw were specimens of that terrible genus of cartilaginous fish, divided into three sub-genera and no less than thirty-two species: there were striped sharks, five meters long, with flat heads larger than their bodies, rounded tails, and seven large parallel bands of black running down their backs; and ash-grey perlon sharks, with seven gill openings and only one dorsal fin placed almost in the middle of the body.

There were also some large dog-fish, a voracious fish if ever there was one. One is right to doubt the stories of fishermen, but I will recite a few. In the body of one of these animals was found the head of a buffalo and an entire calf; in another, two tunas and a sailor in uniform; in another, a soldier with his sabre; and finally, in one was a horse and rider, All these,

I must say, are only believed by fools. What is certain is that none of these animals allowed itself to be caught in the *Nautilus'* nets, so I could not verify their voracity.

Schools of elegant, playful dolphins accompanied us for entire days. they grouped in bands of five or six, hunting in packs like wolves. They are as voracious as dog-fish, if we can believe a professor of Copenhagen, who found in the stomach of one dolphin thirteen porpoises and fifteen seals. It is true that it was a grampus, the largest species known, which can exceed twenty-four feet in length. This family of dolphins includes ten genera and those that I saw were from the genus of delphini, remarkable for narrow muzzles that are four times the length of their heads. Their bodies are three meters long, black on top, pink on the bottom with occasional small spots.

I also saw, in these waters, the curious species of fish of the order acanthopterygians, of the family sciaenidae. Some authors—more poet than naturalist—believe that these fish sing melodiously, and when they unite in a choir human voices scarcely equal them. I do not dispute this, but the sciaenidae did not serenade our passage, to my regret.

Finally, Conseil classified a large number of flying fish. We were fascinated by the marvelous precision with which the dolphins chased them. No matter how far they flew, or in which direction—sometimes passing over the *Nautilus*—the unfortunate fish always found the open mouth of a dolphin waiting to receive it. There were also pirapedes, or flying gurnards, with luminous mouths, which, after nightfall, would trace rays of fire through the atmosphere, plunging into the dark sea like shooting stars.

Our navigation continued under these conditions until the 13th of March. That day the *Nautilus* was employed in taking soundings, which greatly interested me. We had then made about 13,000 leagues since our departure from the high seas of the Pacific. The bearings gave us 45° 37 ′ south latitude, and 37° 53 ′ west longitude. It was the same region in which Captain Denham of the *Herald* sounded 14,000 meters without finding the bottom. There, too, Lieutenant Parker of the American frigate *Congress,* could not touch the bottom at 15,140 meters.

Captain Nemo decided to send his *Nautilus* to the most extreme depths to check these different soundings. I prepared to take notes of the results of the experiment. The panels of the salon were opened, and the operation began of sending us to the most prodigious depths.

One can imagine that it was out of the question to dive by means of the reservoirs. They would not have sufficiently increased the *Nautilus'* specific gravity. Moreover, to resurface, we would have had to get rid of this overload of water, and the pumps would not have had the power to overcome the exterior pressure.

Captain Nemo intended seeking the bottom of the ocean by descending on a diagonal course by means of the lateral planes, set at an angle of forty-five degrees with the water-line of the *Nautilus*. Then the screw set to work at its maximum speed, its four blades beating the waves with indescribable force.

Under this powerful pressure the hull of the *Nautilus* quivered like a sonorous chord and sank smoothly under the water. The captain and I, sitting in the salon, watched the needle of the manometer deviate rapidly. Soon we passed the zone habitable to most fish. If some of the animals must live near the surface of the sea, or in rivers, others—though not many—live in the greater depths. Among the latter I noticed the hexanchus, a species of dog-fish with six gill slits; a telescope fish with huge eyes; an armored malamart with grey thoracic fins and black pectorals, and which protected its breast with pale red bony plaques. And last I saw the grenadier, which, living at a depth of 1200 meters, supported a pressure of 120 atmospheres.

I asked Captain Nemo if he had observed fish at depths greater than this.

"Fish?" he answered, "rarely. But in the present state of science, what can we presume? What do we know?"

"We know, Captain, that as we descend into the depths of the ocean, vegetable life disappears more quickly than animal life. We know that in depths where we still find animals, of vegetables there is not even a single hydrophyte. We know that scallops and oysters live at two thousand meters, and that McClintock, the hero of the polar seas, recovered a living starfish from a depth of 2500 meters. We know that the sailors on the H.M.S. *Bulldog,* brought up another starfish from 2620 fathoms—more than a league in depth. Perhaps, Captain Nemo, you can no longer say that we know nothing?"

"No, Professor," answered the captain, "I would not be that impolite. Still, I ask you for your explanation of how life can exist at these depths?"

"I can explain it on two grounds," I replied. "First, there are vertical currents, caused by differences in the salinity and the density of the water. This produces sufficient movement to sustain the rudimentary life of encrinidae and starfish."

"Precisely," said the captain.

"Second, we know that oxygen is the basis for life, and that the amount of oxygen dissolved in water increases with depth rather than decreases; the greater the pressure, the more goes into solution."

"Ah? so you know that?" replied Captain Nemo, looking a little surprised. "Well, Professor, the reasoning is good, because it is true. I will add that the swimming-bladders of fish contain more nitrogen than oxygen when the animals are caught near the surface of the water, and more oxygen than nitrogen when they are brought up from great depths. Which gives some proof to your reasoning. But continue your observations."

I looked at the manometer. The instrument indicated a depth of 6000 meters. We had been diving for one hour. The *Nautilus,* gliding on its inclined planes, was still descending. The empty waters were admirably transparent, with a diaphanous quality no painter could reproduce. An hour later, we were at 13,000 meters—about 3 1/4 leagues—and the bottom was still invisible.

At 14,000 meters I saw some blackish peaks rising from the midst of the waters; but these summits might belong to high mountains like the Himalayas or Mount Blanc, even higher; and the depth of the abyss remained incalculable.

The *Nautilus* descended still lower, in spite of the great pressure. I felt the steel plates tremble at the fastenings of the bolts; its bars bent, its walls groaned; the windows of the salon seemed to bend under the pressure of the waters. And this firm structure would doubtless have yielded, if, as its captain had said, it had not been capable of resistance like a solid block.

In skirting the slopes of these rocks, lost under the water, I still saw some shells, some serpulæ and living spinorbes, and some specimens of starfish.

But soon these last representatives of animal life disappeared; and at the depth of more than three leagues, the *Nautilus* had passed the limits of submarine life even as a balloon does when it rises above the respirable atmosphere. We had attained a depth of 16,000 meters (four leagues), and the sides of the *Nautilus* then bore a pressure of 1600 atmospheres, that is to say, 1600 kilograms—23,520 pounds—to each square centimeter of its surface.

"What a situation to be in!" I exclaimed. "To explore these deep regions where man has never trespassed! Look, captain, look at these magnificent rocks, these uninhabited grottoes, these last refuges of the globe, where life is no longer possible! What unknown sights are here! Why should we be unable to preserve a remembrance of them?"

"Would you like to carry away more than the remembrance?" said Captain Nemo.

"What do you mean by those words?"

"I mean to say that nothing is easier than to take a photographic view of this submarine region!"

I had not time to express my surprise at this new proposition, when, at Captain Nemo's call, a camera was brought into the salon![1] Through the widely opened panel, the liquid mass was bright with the electric light, which was distributed with perfect clarity. Not a shadow, not a gradation, was to be seen in our manufactured illumination. The sun itself could not have been more favorable for an operation of this kind. The *Nautilus* remained motionless, by the force of its screw, aided by the inclination of its diving planes. The instrument was aimed at its submerged subject, and in a few seconds we had obtained a perfect negative of extreme clearness.

I here give the positive, from which may be seen those primitive rocks, which have never looked upon the light of heaven; that lowest granite which forms the strong foundation of the globe; those deep grottoes, hollowed in the stony mass whose outlines were so sharp, and the border lines of which are darkly outlined, as if done by the brush of some Flemish artist. Beyond that was a horizon of mountains, an admirable undulating line forming the background of the landscape. I cannot describe the effect of these smooth, black, polished rocks, without moss, without a blemish, and of strange forms, standing solidly on the sandy carpet, which sparkled under the beams of our electric light.

But the operation being over, Captain Nemo said, "Let us go up; we must not abuse our situation, nor expose the *Nautilus* too long to such great pressure."

"Go up again!" I exclaimed.

"Hold on well."

I had not time to understand why the captain cautioned me thus, when I was thrown forward on to the carpet.

At a signal from the captain, its screw was stopped, and the diving planes raised vertically. The *Nautilus* shot upward like a balloon into the air, rising with stunning rapidity. It cut through the mass of waters with a sonorous tremor. Nothing was visible; and in four minutes it had shot through the four leagues which separated it from the ocean surface; and after emerging like a flying-fish, fell back onto the water, making the waves rebound to an enormous height.

---

[1]The first undersea photograph was taken in 1897. RM

◄ CHAPTER XII ►

CACHALOTS AND BALEEN WHALES

 uring the night of the 13th and 14th of March, the *Nautilus* returned to its southerly course. I fancied that, when at the latitude of Cape Horn, he would turn the helm westward, in order to reach the Pacific, and so complete the tour of the world. He did nothing of the kind, but continued on his way to the southern regions. Where was he going to? To the Pole? It was madness! I began to think that the captain's temerity justified Ned Land's fears.

For some time past the Canadian had not spoken to me of his projects of flight; he was less communicative, almost silent. I could see that this lengthened imprisonment was weighing upon him, and I felt that rage was burning within him. When he met the captain, his eyes lit up with a somber fire; and I feared that his natural violence would lead him into some extreme.

That day, the 14th of March, Conseil and he came to me in my room. I inquired the cause of their visit.

"A simple question to ask you, sir," replied the Canadian.

"Speak, Ned."

Nemo's secret island base
somewhere in the South Atlantic
...to extract sodium from...

2000'

GRAND OCÉAN

PACIFIQUE

13 March, 1868   Pierre Aronnax

"How many men are there on board the *Nautilus*, do you think?"

"I cannot tell, my friend."

"I should say that its working does not require a large crew."

"Certainly, under existing conditions, ten men, at the most, ought to be enough."

"Well, why should there be any more?"

"Why?" I replied, looking fixedly at Ned Land, whose meaning was easy to guess. "Because," I added, "if my surmises are correct, and if I have well understood the captain's existence, the *Nautilus* is not only a vessel: it is also a place of refuge for those who, like its commander, have broken every tie upon earth."

"Perhaps so," said Conseil, "but, in any case, the *Nautilus* can only contain a certain number of men. Could not monsieur estimate their maximum?"

"How, Conseil?"

"By calculation. Given the size of the vessel, which monsieur knows, and consequently the quantity of air it contains, knowing also how much each man requires to breathe, and comparing these results with the fact that the *Nautilus* is obliged to go to the surface every twenty-four hours . . . ."

Conseil had not finished the sentence before I saw what he was driving at.

"I understand," said I, "but that calculation, though simple enough, can give but a very uncertain result."

"Never mind," said Ned Land, insistently.

"Here it is, then," said I. "In one hour each man consumes the oxygen contained in 100 liters of air; and in twenty-four hours, that contained in 2400 liters. We must, therefore, find how many times 2400 liters of air the *Nautilus* contains."

"Just so," said Conseil.

"Now," I continued, "the displacement of the *Nautilus* being 1500 tons; and one ton holding 1000 liters, it contains 1,500,000 liters, which, divided by 2400, gives a quotient of . . ."

I made a quick calculation with pen and paper, six hundred and twenty-five. "Which means to say, strictly speaking, that the air contained in the *Nautilus* would suffice for 625 men for twenty-four hours."

"Six hundred and twenty-five!" repeated Ned.

"But remember, that all of us, passengers, sailors, and officers included, would not form a tenth part of that number."

"Still too many for three men," murmured Conseil.

"Well, my poor Ned, I can only advise patience."

"Maybe better than patience," said Conseil, "would be resignation."

Conseil has used the better word. "After all," he went on, "Captain Nemo cannot always go south! He will have to stop, he cannot pass the ice barrier, and must return to civilized waters! Then it will be time to reconsider Ned Land's plans."

The Canadian shook his head, passed his hand across his forehead, and left the room without answering.

"Will monsieur allow me to make one observation?" said Conseil. "Poor Ned is longing for everything that he cannot have. His past life is always present to him; he longs for everything that we are forbidden. His head is full of old memories and his heart aches. We must understand him. What has he to do here? Nothing; he is not learned like monsieur, and has not the same taste for the beauties of the sea that we have. He would risk everything to be able to go once more into a tavern in his own country."

Certainly the monotony on board must seem intolerable to the Canadian, accustomed as he was to a life of liberty and activity. Events were rare which could rouse him to any show of spirit; but that day an event did happen which recalled the happier days of the harpooner.

About eleven in the morning, being on the surface of the ocean, the *Nautilus* fell in with a

troop of whales—an encounter which did not astonish me, knowing that these creatures, hunted to the death, had taken refuge in high latitudes.

The role played by whales in the marine world and their influence on geographical discoveries is considerable. It was they who led, first the Basques, then the Asturians, the English and the Dutch to brave the dangers of the ocean from one end of the earth to the other. Whales frequent both northern and southern seas. Ancient legends tell us that whales led fishermen to within only seven leagues of the North Pole. That may be false, but one day it will be true, for it is probable that in chasing the whale in arctic and antarctic regions, men will finally reach those unknown points of the globe.

We were seated on the platform, with a quiet sea. The month of October in those latitudes gave us some lovely autumnal days. It was the Canadian who signalled a whale on the eastern horizon. He could not be mistaken. Looking attentively one might see its black back rise and fall with the waves five miles from the *Nautilus.*

"Ah!" exclaimed Ned Land, "if I was on board a whaler now, such a meeting would give me pleasure. It is one of large size. See with what strength its blow-holes throw up columns of air and vapor! A thousand devils! why am I bound to these steel plates?"

"What, Ned," said I, "you have not forgotten your old ideas of fishing?"

"Can a whaler ever forget his old trade, sir? Can he ever tire of the emotions caused by such a chase?"

"Have you never fished in these seas, Ned?"

"Never, sir; in the northern only; in the Bering as well as in the Davis Straits."

"Then the southern whale is still unknown to you. It is the Greenland whale you have hunted up to this time, and that would not risk passing through the warm waters of the equator."

"Ah! Professor, what are you trying to tell me?" replied the Canadian in an incredulous tone.

"Only the truth."

"Oh yes! In sixty-five, just two and a half years ago, I hauled in a whale near Greenland that had in its side a harpoon with the mark of a whaler in the Bering Sea. Now, I ask you, after being struck on the west coast of America how could the animal have appeared on the east, unless it had doubled either Cape Horn or the Cape of Good Hope, and crossed the equator?"

"I agree with friend Ned," said Conseil, "and I await monsieur's answer."

"Monsieur's answer is, my friends, whales are localized, according to their kinds, and stay in certain seas which they never leave. And if one of these creatures went from Bering to Davis Straits, it must be simply because there is a passage from one sea to the other, either on the American or the Asiatic side."

"You want me to believe that?" demanded the Canadian, winking an eye.

"We must believe monsieur," responded Conseil.

"In that case, as I have never fished in these seas, I do not know the kind of whale frequenting them."

"I have told you, Ned."

"A greater reason for making their acquaintance," said Conseil.

"Look! look!" exclaimed the Canadian in an emotional voice, "she approaches! she is right beside us! she scorns me! she knows that I cannot get at her!"

Ned stamped his feet. His hand trembled, as he grasped an imaginary harpoon.

"Are these cetacea as large as those of the northern seas?" asked he.

"Very nearly, Ned."

"Because I have seen large whales, sir, whales measuring a hundred feet! I have even been told that those of Hullamock and Umgallick, of the Aleutian Islands, are sometimes a hundred and fifty feet long."

"That seems to me exaggeration. These creatures are only balænopterons, provided with dorsal fins; and, like the cachalots, are generally much small than the Greenland whale."

"Ah!" exclaimed the Canadian, whose eyes had never left the ocean, "she is coming nearer; she is right near the *Nautilus!*"

Then returning to the conversation, he said: "You spoke of the cachalot as a small creature. I have heard of gigantic ones. They are an intelligent whale. It is said of some that they cover themselves with algae and fucus, and then are taken for islands. People encamp upon them, and settle there; light a fire . . . ."

"And build houses," said Conseil.

"Yes, joker," said Ned Land. "And one fine day the creature plunges, carrying with it all the inhabitants to the depths of the abyss."

"Something like the travels of Sinbad the Sailor," I replied, laughing. "Ah! Master Land, you are fond of tall tales! Those cachalots of yours! I hope you don't believe in them?"

"Monsieur le Naturaliste," the Canadian answered seriously, "one has to believe everything about whales!—Look how that one moves! look how it dives!—It is said that these animals can circle the globe in fifteen days."

"I think not."

"But what you don't know, Mr. Aronnax, is that at the beginning of the world the whales could swim even faster."

"Ah! truly, Ned! And why was that?"

"Because then their tails were vertical, like a fish's, and they could strike the water right to left and left to right. But the Creator, noticing that they moved too quickly, twisted their tails and from that time they beat the waves up and down to the detriment of their speed."

"Good, Ned," I said, using an expression of the Canadian's, "you want me to believe that?"

"Not too much," answered Ned, "no more than if I told you about whales existing which are three hundred feet long and weigh a hundred thousand pounds."

"That would be a lot," I said. "Nevertheless, certain whales do attain a considerable degree of development, since some, it is said, have furnished as much as 120 tons of oil."

"I have seen them," said the Canadian.

"I believe you, Ned, just as I believe that certain whales equal in weight a hundred elephants. Judge the effect produced by this mass launched at full speed!"

"Is it true, then," asked Conseil, "that they can sink ships?"

"A ship, I don't think so," I answered. "On second thought, however, in 1820, in these very same southern seas, a whale threw itself against the *Essex* and pushed her backwards at a speed of four meters a second. The waves flooded the rear and the *Essex* sank quickly."

Ned looked at me derisively. "For my part," he said, "I once received a blow from the tail of a whale—in a whaleboat, it goes without saying. My companions and I were thrown to a height of six meters. But after that whale of yours, Professor, mine seems like a baby."

"Do these animals live a long time?" asked Conseil.

"A thousand years," answered the Canadian without hesitation.

"And how do you know, Ned?"

"That's what they say."

"And why do they say this?"

"Because they know."

"No, Ned, they do not know, it is only a supposition, and this is what it is based on. Four hundred years ago, when whalers first hunted the whales, these animals grew to a size much larger than they do today. One supposes, and it's logical, that the smaller size of the whales is due to the fact that they are not allowed time to reach complete development. This is what led Bufon to say that whales could, and did, live for a thousand years. Do you understand?"

Ned Land did not understand. He wasn't even listening. The whale was again approaching. He devoured it with his eyes.

"Ah!" suddenly exclaimed Ned Land, "it is not one whale; there are ten,—there are twenty,—it is a whole school! And I not able to do anything! tied hand and foot!"

"But, friend Ned," said Conseil, "why do you not ask Captain Nemo's permission to chase them. . . ."

Conseil had not finished his sentence when Ned Land had lowered himself through the hatch to seek the captain. A few minutes afterwards the two appeared together on the platform.

Captain Nemo watched the herd of whales playing on the waters about a mile from the *Nautilus.*

"They are southern whales," said he; "there goes the fortune of the whole fleet of whalers."

"Well, sir," asked the Canadian, "can I not chase them, if only to remind me of my old trade of harpooner?"

"And to what purpose?" replied Captain Nemo; "only to destroy! We have no use for whale-oil on board."

"But, sir," continued the Canadian, "in the Red Sea you allowed us to hunt the dugong."

"Then it was to procure fresh meat for my crew. Here it would be killing for killing's sake. I know that is a privilege reserved for man, but I do not approve of such murderous pastime. In destroying the right whale and the southern whale, good and inoffensive creatures, you whalers do a criminal action, Master Land. You have already depopulated the whole of Baffin's Bay, and are annihilating a class of useful animals. Leave the unfortunate beasts alone. They have plenty of natural enemies, cachalots, swordfish, and sawfish, without *your* troubling them."

You can imagine the face of the Canadian while he listened to this lesson in morals. To try to reason with such a hunter was a waste of words. Ned Land stared at the captain and it was evident that he did not understand at all. The captain was right. The barbarous and inconsiderate greed of these fishermen will one day cause the disappearance of the last whale in the ocean.

Ned Land whistled "Yankee-doodle" between his teeth, thrust his hands into his pockets, and turned his back upon us.

Captain Nemo watched the herd of whales, and addressing me, said: "I was right in saying that whales had natural enemies enough, without counting man. These will have plenty to do before long. Do you see, Monsieur Aronnax, about eight miles to leeward, those blackish moving points?"

"Yes, Captain," I replied.

"Those are cachalots,—terrible animals, which I have sometimes met in packs of two or three hundred. As to *those,* they are cruel mischievous creatures; it would be right to exterminate them."

The Canadian turned quickly at the last words.

"Well, Captain," I said, "it is still time, in the interest of the whales."

"It is useless to expose one's self, Professor. The *Nautilus* will disperse them. It is armed with a steel spur as good as Master Land's harpoon, I imagine."

The Canadian did not put himself out enough to shrug his shoulders. Attack whales with blows of a spur! Who has ever heard of such a thing?

"Wait, Monsieur Aronnax," said Captain Nemo. "We will show you something you have never yet seen. We have no pity for these ferocious creatures. They are nothing but mouth and teeth."

Mouth and teeth! Nothing could better describe the macrocephalous cachalot, which is sometimes more than 25 meters long. Its enormous head occupies one-third of its entire body. Better armed than the whale, whose upper jaw is furnished only with whalebone, it is supplied

with twenty-five large teeth, about twenty centimeters long, cylindrical, conical at the top, each weighing two pounds. It is in the upper part of this enormous head, in great cavities divided by cartilages, that is to be found from three to four hundred kilograms of that precious oil called spermaceti. The cachalot is a clumsy creature, more tadpole than fish, according to Frédol's description. It is badly formed, the whole of its left side being (if we may say it), a "failure," and is only able to see with its right eye.

But the formidable troop was nearing us. They had seen the baleen whales and were preparing to attack them. One could judge beforehand that the cachalots would be victorious, not only because they were better built for attack than their inoffensive adversaries, but also because they could remain longer under water without coming to the surface.

There was only just time to go to the help of the whales. The *Nautilus* submerged. Conseil, Ned Land, and I took our places before the window in the salon, and Captain Nemo joined the pilot in his cage to work his ship as an engine of destruction. Soon I felt the beatings of the screw quicken, and our speed increased.

The battle between the cachalots and the baleen whales had already begun when the *Nautilus* arrived. Captain Nemo steered the submarine so that the pack of cachalots was divided in two. They did not at first show any fear at the sight of this new monster joining in the conflict. But they soon had to guard against its blows.

What a battle! Ned Land, overwhelmed by enthusiasm, kept clapping his hands. The *Nautilus* was nothing but a formidable harpoon, brandished by the hand of its captain. It hurled itself against each fleshy mass, passing through from one part to the other, leaving behind it two quivering halves of the animal. It could not feel the formidable blows from their tails upon its sides, nor the shock which it produced itself. One cachalot killed, we ran at the next, tacking on the spot that we might not miss our prey. The *Nautilus* went forwards and backwards, to the rear, answering to its helm, plunging when a cachalot dived into the deep waters, coming up with it when it returned to the surface, striking it front or sideways, cutting or tearing, in all directions and at any speed, piercing it with its terrible spur.

What carnage! What a noise on the surface of the waves! What sharp hissing, and what snorting peculiar to these enraged animals! In the midst of these waters, generally so peaceful, their tails made perfect billows.

For one hour this Homeric massacre continued, from which the cachalots could not escape. Several times ten or twelve united and tried to crush the *Nautilus* by their weight. From the window we could see their enormous mouths studded with tusks, and their formidable eyes. Ned Land could not contain himself, he threatened and swore at them. We could feel them clinging to our vessel like dogs worrying a wild boar in a copse. But the *Nautilus,* working its screw, carried them here and there, or to the upper levels of the ocean, without caring for their enormous weight, nor the powerful strain on the vessel.

At length, the mass of cachalots broke up, the waves became quiet, and I felt that we were rising to the surface. The hatch opened, and we hurried on to the platform.

The sea was covered with mutilated bodies. A formidable explosion could not have divided and torn this fleshy mass with more violence. We were floating amid gigantic bodies, bluish on the back and white underneath, covered with enormous protuberances. Some terrified cachalots were fleeing toward the horizon. The waves were dyed red for several miles, and the *Nautilus* floated in a sea of blood.

Captain Nemo joined us. "Well, Master Land?" said he.

"Well, sir," replied the Canadian, whose enthusiasm had somewhat calmed, "it is a terrible spectacle, certainly. But I am not a butcher. I am a hunter, and I call this a butchery."

"It was a massacre of vicious creatures," replied the Captain; "and the *Nautilus* is not a butcher's knife."

"I like my harpoon better," said the Canadian.

"Everyone to his own weapon," answered the Captain, looking fixedly at Ned Land.

"I feared Ned would commit some act of violence which would have deplorable consequences. But his anger was distracted by the sight of a whale which the *Nautilus* had just come up with.

The creature had not quite escaped from the cachalot's teeth. I recognized the southern baleen whale by its flat head, which is entirely black. Anatomically, it is distinguished from the white whale and the North Cape whale by the seven fused cervical vertebræ, and it has two more ribs than its cousins. The unfortunate cetacean was lying on its side, riddled with holes from bites, and quite dead. From its mutilated fin still hung a young whale which it had not been able to save from the massacre. Its open mouth let the water flow in and out, murmuring like the waves breaking on the shore.

Captain Nemo steered close to the corpse of the creature. Two of his men mounted its side, and I saw, not without surprise, that they were drawing from its breasts all the milk which they contained, that is to say, about two or three tons.

The captain offered me a cup of the milk, which was still warm. I could not help showing my repugnance to the drink; but he assured me that it was excellent, and not to be distinguished from cow's milk.

I tasted it, and was of his opinion. It was a useful reserve to us, for in the shape of salt butter or cheese it would form an agreeable variety from our ordinary food.

From that day I noticed with uneasiness that Ned Land's ill-will towards Captain Nemo increased, and I resolved to watch the Canadian's actions closely.

◄ CHAPTER XIII ►

THE ICE SHELF

 he *Nautilus* was steadily pursuing its southerly course, following the fiftieth meridian with considerable speed. Did Captain Nemo wish to reach the Pole? I did not think so, for every attempt to reach that point had hitherto failed. Also, the season was far advanced, for in the antarctic regions, the 13th of March corresponds with the 13th of September in the Northern Hemisphere, which begins the equinoctial season.

On the 14th of March I saw floating ice in latitude 55°, merely pale bits of debris from twenty to twenty-five feet long, forming banks over which the sea curled. The *Nautilus* remained on the surface of the ocean. Ned Land, who had fished in the arctic seas, was familiar with the spectacle of its icebergs; but Conseil and I admired them for the first time.

In the atmosphere towards the southern horizon stretched a white dazzling band. English whalers have given it the name of "ice blink." However thick the clouds may be, it is always visible, and announces the presence of an ice pack or bank.

Accordingly, larger blocks soon appeared, whose brilliancy changed with the caprices of the fog. Some of these masses showed green veins, as if long undulating lines had been traced with sulphate of copper; others resembled enormous amethysts with the light shining through them. Some reflected the light of day from a thousand crystal facets. Others that were shaded with vivid calcareous glints resembled a perfect town of marble.

The more we neared the south, the more these floating islands increased both in number and size. Polar birds nested by the thousands. There were petrels, damiers, puffins, and their cries were deafening. Some of them, thinking that the *Nautilus* was the carcass of a dead whale, landed on the hull and pecked at it noisily with their beaks.

During our navigation through the midst of the ice, Captain Nemo spent much time on the platform. He observed with attention the abandoned landscape. The calm expression of his face would change to one of animation. Did he believe that since these polar regions were forbidden to man, they belonged to him, the master of all impassable places? Perhaps. He did not say. He remained motionless, not moving until his instincts as a helmsman took over. He steered the *Nautilus* with consummate precision, easily evading masses of ice measuring many miles in length and in height varying from 70 to 80 meters. Sometime they entirely blocked the horizon. At the sixtieth degree of latitude, every pass had disappeared. But seeking careful-ly, Captain Nemo soon found a narrow opening, through which he boldly slipped, knowing, however, that it would close behind him.

Thus, guided by this clever hand, the *Nautilus* passed through all the ice which is classified with a precision which quite charmed Conseil. These are according to size and shape, icebergs or mountain; ice-fields or smooth plains, seeming to have no limits; drift ice or floating ice; ice-packs, or plains broken up, called *palches* when they are circular, and streams when they are in elongated pieces.

The temperature was very low; the thermometer exposed to the exterior air marked two or three degrees below zero centigrade, but we were warmly clad in fur, at the expense of the polar bears and seals. The interior of the *Nautilus,* warmed evenly by its electric apparatus, defied the most intense cold. Besides, it would only have been necessary to go a few meters beneath the waves to find a more bearable temperature.

Two months earlier we should have had perpetual daylight in these latitudes; but already we had three or four hours night, and by and by there would be six months of darkness in these circumpolar regions.

On the 15th of March we were in the latitude of the islands of New Shetland and South Orkney. The captain told me that formerly numerous tribes of seals inhabited these islands; but that English and American whalers, in their rage for destruction, massacred both adults and pregnant females alike; thus where there was once life and animation, they had left silence and death![1]

About eight o'clock on the morning of the 16th of March, the *Nautilus,* following the fifty-fifth meridian, cut the Antarctic Circle. Ice surrounded us on all sides, and hid the horizon. But Captain Nemo went from one pass to another, still going south.

"Where is he going?" I asked.

"Straight ahead," answered Conseil, "after all, when he can go no further, he will stop."

"I wouldn't swear to that!" I responded. But, to be honest, I did not look upon this new adventure with displeasure. I cannot express my astonishment at the beauties of these new regions. The ice took most superb forms. Here the grouping formed an oriental town, with innumerable mosques and minarets; there a fallen city thrown to the earth, as it were, by some convulsion of nature. The whole aspect was constantly changed by the oblique rays of the sun, or lost in the grayish fog amidst hurricanes of snow. Detonations and falls were heard on all sides, great overthrows of icebergs, which altered the whole landscape like a diorama.

Whenever the *Nautilus* submerged to avoid these cataclysms, the noise was propagated through the water with frightening intensity. When the great masses fell into the sea, they creat-ed a turmoil felt at the lowest depths. The *Nautilus* rolled and tossed like a ship abandoned to the fury of the elements.

Often seeing no exit, I thought we were definitely prisoners; but instinct guiding him at the slightest indication, Captain Nemo would discover a new pass. He was never mistaken when he saw the thin threads of bluish water trickling along the ice-fields; and I had no doubt that he had already ventured into the midst of these antarctic seas before.

On the 16th of March, however, the ice-fields absolutely blocked our road. It was not the ice cap itself, as yet, but vast fields cemented by the cold. But his obstacle could not stop Captain Nemo: he hurled himself against it with frightful violence. The *Nautilus* entered the brittle mass like a wedge, and split it with frightful crackings. It was the battering ram of the ancients hurled by infinite strength. The ice, thrown high in the air, fell like hail around us. By its own power of impulsion our machine made a channel for itself; sometimes carried away by its own impetus it lodged on the ice-field, crushing it with its weight, and sometimes buried within it, dividing the ice by a simple pitching movement, producing large rents in it.

Violent gales assailed us during these days, accompanied by thick fogs, through which we could not see from one end of the platform to the other. The wind blew brusquely from all points of the compass, and the snow lay in such hard heaps that we had to break it with blows of a pickaxe. The temperature was always at five degrees below zero centigrade; every outside part of the *Nautilus* was covered with ice. A rigged vessel could never have worked its way there, for all the rigging would have been entangled in the blocked-up pulleys. A vessel without sails, with electricity for its motive power, and wanting no coal, could alone brave such high latitudes.

In these conditions, the barometer was generally very low. It dropped as low as 73.5 centimeters. The indications of the compass could no longer be relied upon. Its needle spun in contradictory directions as we approached the south magnetic pole, which should not be confused with the geographical pole. According to Hansen, the magnetic pole is situated near 70° latitude and 130° longitude, and after the observations of Duperrey, at 135° longitude and 70° 30′ latitude. We therefore took a number of compass readings in different parts of the ship and made an average. But still, we could only estimate our route, an unsatisfactory method in the middle of these sinuous passes and incessantly changing landmarks.

At length, on the 18th of March, after twenty useless assaults, the *Nautilus* was positively blocked. It was no longer either streams, packs, or ice-fields, but an interminable and immovable barrier, formed by mountains welded together.

"The ice shelf!" said the Canadian to me.

I knew that to Ned Land, as well as to all other navigators who had preceded us, this was an impassable obstacle. The sun appearing for an instant at noon, Captain Nemo took an observation as near as possible, which gave our situation at 51° 30′ longitude and 67° 39′ south latitude. We had advanced one degree further into this antarctic region.

Of the liquid surface of the sea there was no longer a glimpse. Before the spur of the *Nautilus* lay stretched a vast plain, entangled with confused blocks. They had all the pell-mell disorder that characterizes a river before its ice breaks up, but on a gigantic scale. Here and there sharp points, and slender needles rose to a height of 200 feet; further on a steep shore, hewn as it were with an axe, and clothed with grayish tints; huge mirrors, reflecting a few rays of sunshine, half drowned in the fog. And over this desolate face of Nature a stern silence reigned, scarcely broken by the flapping of the wings of petrels and puffins. Everything was frozen— even sound.

The *Nautilus* was then obliged to stop in its adventurous course amid these fields of ice.

"Sir," said Ned Land one day, "if your captain goes any further . . . ."

"Yes?"

"He must be a superman."

"Why, Ned?"

"Because only such a person could break through the ice barrier. He is strong, your captain, but, a thousand devils! he is not stronger than nature. And when nature throws up a barrier, you had better stop, whether you like it or not!"

"Perhaps, Ned, but I for one would like to see what is on the other side of the icebank! There is nothing more irritating than to be behind a wall!"

"Monsieur is right," said Conseil. "Walls were invented to aggravate scientists. There should be no walls anywhere."

"Good!" said the Canadian, "but anyone can tell you what is behind this wall of ice."

"And what is that?" I demanded.

"Ice, and more ice!"

"You are certain of your facts, Ned," I replied, "but I am not. That is why I want to see what lies beyond."

"Well! Professor," answered the Canadian, "you must give up that idea. We have arrived at the ice barrier, that itself should be sufficient; but you can go no further. Nor your Captain Nemo, nor his *Nautilus*. Whether he wants to or not, he will have to return north, back to the country of sensible people."

I had to agree that Ned was right, and that until ships are built for navigating over fields of ice, all must halt before the great ice barrier.

In spite of our efforts, in spite of the powerful means employed to break up the ice, the *Nautilus* remained immovable. Generally, when one can proceed no further, one has a retreat still open. But here, return was as impossible as advance, for every pass had closed behind us; and for the few moments when we were stationary, we were likely to be entirely blocked. Which did, indeed, happen about two o'clock in the afternoon, the fresh ice forming around the *Nautilus'* sides with astonishing rapidity. I was obliged to admit that Captain Nemo had been more than imprudent.

I was on the platform at that moment. The captain had been observing our situation for some time past, when he said to me—

"Well, sir, what do you think of this?"

"I think that we are caught, Captain."

"Caught! What do you mean by that?"

"I mean that we cannot go either forwards or backwards, neither one or the other. That is the usual meaning of the word 'caught', at least in civilized countries."

"So, Monsieur Aronnax, you really think that the *Nautilus* cannot disengage itself?"

"With difficulty, Captain; for the season is already too far advanced for you to reckon on the breaking up of the ice."

"Ah! sir," said Captain Nemo, in an ironical tone, "you will always be the same. You see nothing but difficulties and obstacles. I affirm that not only can the *Nautilus* disengage itself, but also that it can go further still!"

"Further to the south?" I asked, looking at the captain.

"Yes, sir; it shall go to the pole."

"To the pole!" I exclaimed, unable to repress a gesture of incredulity.

"Yes," replied the captain, coldly, "to the antarctic pole—to that unknown point from whence springs every meridian of the globe. *You* know whether I can do as I please with the *Nautilus!*"

Yes, I knew that. I knew that this man was bold, even to rashness. But to conquer those obstacles which bristled round the south pole, rendering it more inaccessible than the north, which had not yet been reached by the boldest navigators—was it not a mad enterprise, one which only a maniac would have conceived?

It then came into my head to ask Captain Nemo if he had already discovered that pole which had never yet been trodden by a human creature.

"No, sir," he replied; "but we will discover it together. Where others have failed, *I* will not fail. I have never yet led my *Nautilus* so far into southern seas; but, I repeat, it shall go further yet.''

''I can well believe you, captain,'' said I, and continuing in a slightly ironical tone: ''I believe you! Let us go ahead! There are no obstacles for us! Let us smash this iceberg! Let us blow it up; and if it resists, let us give the *Nautilus* wings to fly over it!''

''Over it, sir!'' said Captain Nemo, quietly; ''no, not *over* it, but *under* it!''

''Under it!'' I exclaimed. A sudden idea of the captain's projects flashed upon my mind. I understood; the wonderful qualities of the *Nautilus* were going to serve us in this superhuman enterprise!

''I see we are beginning to understand one another, sir,'' said the captain, half smiling. ''You begin to see the possibility—I should say the success—of this attempt. That which is impossible for an ordinary vessel, is easy to the *Nautilus*. If a continent surrounds the pole, we must stop before it; but if, on the contrary, the pole is washed by open sea, it will go to the pole.''

''Certainly,'' said I, carried away by the captain's reasoning; ''if the surface of the sea is solidified by the ice, the lower depths are still fluid by the providential law which has placed the maximum density of the waters of the ocean one degree higher than the freezing point. And, if I am not mistaken, the portion of this ice shelf which is above the water, is as four to one to that which is below. Am I not correct?''

''Very nearly, sir; for one foot of iceberg above the sea there are three below it. If these ice mountains are not more than 100 meters above the surface, they do not extend more than 300 beneath. And what are 300 meters to the *Nautilus?*''

''Nothing, sir.''

''It could even seek at greater depths that uniform temperature of sea-water, and there brave with impunity the thirty or forty degrees of surface cold.''

''Just so, sir—just so,'' I replied, getting animated.

''The only difficulty,'' continued Captain Nemo, ''is that of remaining several days without renewing our provision of air.''

''Is that all? The *Nautilus* has vast reservoirs; we can fill them, and they will supply us with all the oxygen we want.''

''Well thought of, Monsieur Aronnax,'' replied the captain, smiling. ''But not wishing you to accuse me of recklessness, I will first give you all my objections.''

''Have you any more to make?''

''Only one. It is possible, if an open sea exists at the south pole, that it may be covered with ice; and, consequently, we shall be unable to come to the surface!''

''Good, sir, but do you forget that the *Nautilus* is armed with a powerful spur, and could we not send it diagonally against these fields of ice, which would open at the shock?''

''Ah! sir, you are full of ideas today!''

''Besides, Captain,'' I added, enthusiastically, ''why should we not find the sea open at the South Pole as well as at the north? The poles of cold and the poles of the earth's axis do not coincide, either in the southern or in the northern regions; and, until it is proved to the contrary, we may suppose that there exists either a continent or an ocean free from ice at these two points of the globe.''

''I think so too, Monsieur Aronnax,'' replied Captain Nemo. ''I only wish you to observe that, after having made so many objections to my project, you are now crushing me with arguments in its favor!''

Captain Nemo spoke the truth. I was exceeding his own audacity! It was now I who was urging him on to the pole! I was the leader, I was the pacesetter . . . But no! poor fool. Captain Nemo had known better than you the pros and cons of the question. It had amused him to see me carried away by impossible dreams!

Meanwhile, not a moment was being lost. At a signal the second-in-command appeared.

The two men conversed rapidly in their incomprehensible language, and because either the second-in-command had been notified beforehand, or he considered the project practicable, he showed no surprise.

But as impassive as he was, he did not exceed the impassibility of Conseil, when I told that good lad of our intention to press on to the South Pole. A "whatever please monsieur" greeted my communication, and I had to be content with that. As for Ned Land, he shrugged his shoulders higher than ever.

"You," he said to me, "you and your captain, I pity you both!"

"But we will reach the pole, Master Ned."

"It is possible, but you won't be returning!"

And Ned Land returned to his cabin, "to keep himself from doing anything desperate," he said as he left.

The preparations for this audacious attempt now began. The powerful pumps of the *Nautilus* were forcing air into the reservoirs and storing it at high pressure. About four o'clock, Captain Nemo announced the closing of the hatches on the platform. I threw one last look at the massive ice shelf which we were going to cross. The weather was fine, the atmosphere clear enough, the cold very great, being twelve degrees below zero centigrade; but the wind having gone down, this temperature was not so unbearable.

About ten men mounted the sides of the *Nautilus*, armed with pickaxes to break the ice around the vessel, which was soon free. The operation was quickly performed, for the fresh ice was still very thin. We all went below. The ballast tanks were filled with the newly liberated water, and the *Nautilus* soon descended.

I had taken my place with Conseil in the salon; through the open window we could see the lower depths of the southern ocean. The thermometer went up, and the needle of the manometer deviated on the dial.

At about 300 meters, as Captain Nemo had foreseen, we were floating beneath the undulating bottom of the iceberg. But the *Nautilus* went lower still—it went to the depth of 800 meters. The temperature of the water at the surface showed twelve degrees below zero centigrade, it was now only eleven; we had gained two. I need not say the temperature inside the *Nautilus* was raised by its heating apparatus to a much higher degree. Every maneuver was accomplished with wonderful precision.

"We shall get through, if monsieur pleases," said Conseil.

"I believe we shall!" I said, in a tone of firm conviction.

In this open sea, the *Nautilus* had taken its course direct to the pole, without leaving the fifty-second meridian. From 67° 30′ to 90°, twenty-two and a half degrees of latitude remained to travel; that is, about five hundred leagues—more than a thousand miles. The *Nautilus* kept up a mean speed of twenty-six miles an hour—the speed of an express train. If that was kept up, in forty hours we should reach the pole.

For a part of the night the novelty of the situation kept us, Conseil and myself, at the window. The sea was lit with the electric lantern. But it was deserted. Fish did not sojourn in these imprisoned waters: they only found there a passage to take them from the Antarctic Ocean to the open polar sea. Our pace was rapid; we could feel it by the quivering of the long steel body.

About two in the morning, I took some hours' repose, and Conseil did the same. In passing down the corridor I did not meet Captain Nemo: I supposed him to be in the pilot's cage.

The next morning, the 19th of March, at five o'clock, I took my post once more in the salon. The electric log told me that the speed of the *Nautilus* had been slackened. It was then going towards the surface; but prudently emptying its reservoirs very slowly.

My heart beat fast. Were we going to emerge and regain the open polar atmosphere? No! A shock told me that the *Nautilus* had struck the bottom of the iceberg, still very thick, judging from the deadened sound. We had indeed "grounded," to use a marine expression, but in an inverse sense, and at a depth of three thousand feet. This would give four thousand feet of ice above us; one thousand emerging above the water line. The ice shelf was then higher here than at its borders—not a very reassuring fact.

Several times that day the *Nautilus* tried again, and every time it struck the ice which lay like a ceiling above it. Sometimes it met with the ice at 900 meters, which meant a total thickness of 1200 meters, only 300 of which rose above the surface. It was twice the height it was when the *Nautilus* had gone under the waves.

I carefully noted the different depths, and thus obtained a submarine profile of the range as it was revealed under the water.

That night no change had taken place in our situation. Still ice between four and five hundred meters in depth! It was evidently diminishing, but still what a thickness between us and the surface of the ocean!

It was then eight. According to the daily custom on board the *Nautilus,* its air should have been renewed four hours ago; but I did not suffer much, even though Captain Nemo had not yet made any demand upon his reserve of oxygen.

My sleep was painful that night; hope and fear besieged me by turns: I rose several times. The groping of the *Nautilus* continued. About three in the morning, I noticed that the lower surface of the iceberg was only about fifty yards deep. One hundred and fifty feet now separated us from the surface of the water. The ice shelf was by degrees becoming an ice-field, the mountain a plain.

My eyes never left the manometer. We were still rising diagonally to the surface, which sparkled under the electric rays. The iceberg was stretching both above and beneath into lengthening slopes; mile after mile it was getting thinner.

At length, at six in the morning of that memorable day, the 19th of March, the door of the salon opened, and Captain Nemo appeared.

"The sea is open!" was all he said.[2]

---

[1]In these and many other passages, Jules Verne was one of the very first writers to decry the savaging of our natural resources. RM

[2]In 1955 the atomic submarine U.S.S. *Nautilus* reached the North Pole by sailing beneath the ice cap that covers the Arctic Ocean. RM

◄ CHAPTER XIV ►
THE SOUTH POLE

rushed on to the platform. Yes! the open sea, with but a few scattered pieces of ice and moving icebergs; a long stretch of sea; a world of birds in the air, and myriads of fishes under those waters, which varied from intense blue to olive green, according to the depth. The thermometer marked three degrees centigrade above zero. It felt like spring, shut up as we had been beneath the ice shelf, whose lengthened mass was dimly seen on our northern horizon.

"Are we at the pole?" I asked the captain, with a beating heart.

"I do not know," he replied. "At noon I will take our bearings."

"But will the sun show himself through this fog?" said I, looking at the leaden sky.

"However little it shows, it will be enough," replied the captain.

About ten miles south, a solitary island rose to a height of 200 meters. We made for it, but carefully, for the sea might be strewn with reefs.

One hour later we had reached it, in two hours we had made the round of it. It measured four or five miles in circumference. A narrow channel separated it from a considerable stretch of land, perhaps a continent, for we could not see its limits. The existence of this land seemed to give some credence to Maury's hypothesis. The ingenious American has remarked, that between the South Pole and the sixtieth parallel, the sea is covered with floating ice of enormous size, which is never met with in the North Atlantic. From this fact he has drawn the conclusion that the Antarctic Circle encloses a considerable continent, as icebergs cannot form in open sea, but only on the coasts. According to these calculations, the mass of ice surrounding the southern pole forms a vast cap, the circumference of which must be, at least, 4000 kilometers. But the *Nautilus*, for fear of running aground, had stopped about three cables' length from a strand over which reared a superb heap of rocks. The boat was launched; the captain, two of his men bearing instruments, Conseil, and myself, were in it. It was ten in the morning. I had not seen Ned Land. Doubtless the Canadian did not wish to admit the presence of the South Pole.

A few strokes of the oar brought us to the sand, where we ran ashore. Conseil was going to jump on to the land, when I held him back.

"Sir," said I to Captain Nemo, "to you belongs the honor of first setting foot on this land."

"Yes, sir," said the captain; "and if I do not hesitate to tread this South Pole, it is because, up to this time, no human being has left a trace there."

Saying this, he jumped lightly on to the sand. His heart must have beat with emotion. He climbed a rock which sloped to a little promontory; and there, with his arms crossed, mute and motionless, and with an ardent look, he seemed to take possession of these southern regions. After five minutes passed in this ecstasy, he turned to us.

"When you like, sir."

I landed, followed by Conseil, leaving the two men in the boat.

For a long way the soil was composed of a reddish tuff, something like crushed brick; covered by scoriæ, streams of lava, and pumice stones. One could not mistake its volcanic origin. In some parts, slight curls of smoke emitted a sulphurous smell, proving that the internal fires had lost nothing of their expansive powers. Though, having climbed a high cliff, I could see no volcano for a radius of several miles. We know that in these Antarctic countries, James Ross found two craters, Erebus and Terror,[1] in full activity, on the 167th meridian, latitude 77° 32'.

The vegetation of this desolate continent seemed to me much restricted. Some lichens of the species *Unsnea melanoxantha* lay upon the black rocks. Some microscopic plants, rudimentary diatoms, a kind of cell between two quartz shells; long purple and scarlet fucus, supported on little air-filled bladders, which the breaking of the waves brought to the shore. These constituted the meagre flora of this region.

The shore was strewn with mollusks, little mussels, limpets, smooth bucards in the shape of a heart, and particularly some clios, with oblong membraneous bodies, the head of which was formed of two rounded lobes. I also saw myriads of arctic clios, three centimeters long, of which a whale would swallow a whole world at a mouthful; and some charming pteropods, perfect sea-butterflies, animating the waters on the skirts of the shore.

Among other zoöphytes, there appeared in the deep water some coral shrubs, of that kind which, according to James Ross, live in the Antarctic seas to the depth of more than 1000 meters. Then there were little alcyons, belonging to the species *Procellaria pelagica,* as well as a large number of asteriads, peculiar to these climates, which included starfish studding the soil.

But where life abounded most was in the air. There thousands of birds of all kinds fluttered and flew, deafening us with their cries. Others crowded the rocks, looking at us without fear as we passed by, and pressing familiarly under our feet. There were penguins, so agile in the water, that they have been taken for the rapid bonitos, but heavy and awkward on the ground. They were uttering harsh cries, a large assembly, sober in gesture, but extravagant in clamor.

Among the birds I noticed the chionis, of the long-legged family, as large as pigeons, white, with a short conical beak, and the eye framed in a red circle. Conseil laid in a stock of them, for these winged creatures, properly prepared, make an agreeable meat. Sooty albatrosses passed in the air (the expanse of their wings being at least four meters) and justly called the vultures of the ocean; some gigantic petrels, including a species called *quebrantehuesos,* with arched wings and who are great eaters of seals, and some damiers, a kind of small duck, the under part of whose body is black and white; then there were a whole series of petrels, some whitish, with brown-bordered wings, others blue, peculiar to the antarctic seas, and so oily, as I told Conseil, that the inhabitants of the Faroe Islands had nothing to do before lighting them but to put a wick in.

"A little more," said Conseil, "and they would be perfect lamps! But then, we cannot expect Nature to have previously furnished them with wicks!"

About half a mile further on, the soil was riddled with penguins' nests, a sort of laying ground out of which many birds were issuing. Captain Nemo had some hundreds hunted. Their flesh is very good to eat. They uttered a cry like the braying of an ass, were about the size of a goose, slate color on the body, white beneath, with a yellow line round their throats; they allowed themselves to be killed with a stone, never trying to escape.

The fog did not lift, and at eleven the sun had not yet shown itself. Its absence made me uneasy. Without it no observations were possible. How then could we decide whether we had reached the pole?

When I rejoined Captain Nemo, I found him leaning on a piece of rock, silently watching the sky. He seemed impatient and vexed. But what was to be done? This rash and powerful man could not command the sun as he did the sea.

Noon arrived without the orb of day showing itself for an instant. We could not even tell its position behind the curtain of fog. Soon the fog turned to snow.

"Till tomorrow," said the captain, quietly, and we returned to the *Nautilus* amid these atmospheric disturbances.

During our absence, the nets had been cast and I observed with interest the fish that were hauled on board. The antarctic seas serve as a refuge to a great number of migratory species, who flee the storms of higher zones only to fall, it is true, under the teeth of porpoises and seals. I noticed some southern sea-scorpions about a decimeter long; a species of cartilaginous fish, whitish with livid transverse stripes, and armed with spikes; antarctic chimerae, three feet long, with very long bodies, smooth, silvery-white skin, round heads, three fins on their backs, and the muzzle ending in a kind of trunk that curved toward the mouth. I tasted its flesh, but found it very insipid; this was not the opinion of Conseil, who liked it very much.

The tempest of snow continued till the next day. It was impossible to remain on the platform. From the salon, where I was taking notes of incidents happening during this excursion to the polar continent, I could hear the cries of petrels and albatrosses sporting in the midst of this violent storm. The *Nautilus* did not remain motionless, but followed the coast, advancing ten miles more to the south in the half light left by the sun as it skirted the edge of the horizon.

The next day, the 20th of March, the snow had ceased. The cold was a little greater, the thermometer showing two degrees below zero centigrade. The fog was rising, and I hoped that that day our observations might be taken.

Captain Nemo not having yet appeared, the boat took Conseil and myself to shore. The soil was still of the same volcanic nature. Everywhere were traces of lava, scoriæ, and basalt; but the crater which had vomited them I could not see. Here, as lower down, this polar continent was alive with myriads of birds. But their dominion was now shared with large troops of sea mammals, looking at us with their soft eyes. There were several kinds of seals, some stretched on the earth, some on rafts of ice, many going in and out of the sea. They did not flee at our approach, never having had anything to do with man; and I reckoned that there were provisions there for hundred of vessels.

"We're lucky," said Conseil, "that Ned Land did not accompany us!"

"Why it that, Conseil?"

"Because that mad hunter would have killed everything."

"All might be too much to say, but I agree, I doubt that we could have prevented our Canadian friend from harpooning many of these magnificent cetaceans. That would not have pleased Captain Nemo, since he is opposed to spilling the blood of inoffensive creatures."

"He is right."

"Of course, Conseil. But, I say, are you not going to classify these superb specimens of marine fauna?"

"Monsieur knows well," answered Conseil, "that I am not very good in practice. Will monsieur tell me the names of these creatures?" asked Conseil.

"They are seals and walruses."

"Two genera, that belong to the family of pinnipeds," my learned Conseil hastened to add, "order of carnivores, group of unguiculates, subclass of monodelphians, class of mammals, branch of vertebrates."

"Good, Conseil," I answered, "but the two genera, seals and walruses, are divided into species, and if I am not mistaken, here is our chance to observe them. Let's move on."

It was now eight in the morning. Four hours remained to us before the sun could be observed with advantage. I directed our steps towards a vast bay cut in the steep granite shore.

There, I can aver that earth and ice were lost to sight by the numbers of sea-mammals covering them, and I involuntarily sought for old Proteus, the mythological shepherd who watched these immense flocks of Neptune. There were more seals than anything else, forming distinct groups, male and female, the father watching over his family, the mother suckling her little ones, some of whom already were strong enough to go a few steps. When they wished to move, they took little jumps, made by the contraction of their bodies, and helped awkwardly enough by their clumsy fins, which as with the lamantin, their cousin, forms a perfect forearm. I should say that, in the water, which is their element par excellence, these creatures, whose spine is flexible, with smooth and close skin, narrow pelvis, and webbed feet, swim admirably. In resting on the earth they take the most graceful attitudes. Thus the ancients, observing their soft and expressive looks, which cannot be surpassed by the most beautiful look a woman can give, their limpid, voluptuous eyes, their charming positions, and the poetry of their manners, metamorphosed them: the male into the triton and the female into the mermaid.

I made Conseil notice the considerable development of the lobes of the brain in these intelligent cetaceans. No mammal, except man, has such a quantity of cerebral matter; they are also capable of receiving a certain amount of education, are easily domesticated, and I think, with other naturalists, that, if properly taught, they would be of great service as fishing-dogs.

The greater part of them slept on the rocks or on the sand. Among these seals, properly so called, which have no external ears (in which they differ from the otter, whose ears are prominent), I noticed several varieties of stenorhynchae about three meters long, with a white coat, bulldog heads, armed with teeth in both jaws, four incisors at the top and four at the bottom, and two large canine teeth in the shape of a *'fleur-de-lis.'* Among them glided sea-elephants, a kind of seal, with short flexible trunks. The giants of this species measured twenty feet round, and ten meters in length. They did not move as we approached.

"These creatures are not dangerous?" asked Conseil.

"No; not unless you attack them. When seals have to defend their young, their rage is terrible, and it is not uncommon for them to break fishing-boats to pieces."

"They are quite right," said Conseil.

"I do not say they are not."

Two miles further on we were stopped by the promontory which sheltered the bay from the southerly winds. Beyond it we heard loud bellowings such as a herd of cattle would produce.

"Well!" said Conseil; "a concert of bulls!"

"No; a concert of walruses."

"They are fighting?"

"They are either fighting or playing."

"If monsieur has no objection, I would like to see them."

"Of course, Conseil."

We now began to climb the blackish rocks, amid unforeseen landslides, and over stones which the ice made slippery. More than once I rolled over at the expense of my kidneys. Conseil, more prudent or more steady, did not stumble, and helped me up, saying—

"If monsieur would have the kindness to take wider steps, monsieur would preserve his equilibrium better."

Arrived at the upper ridge of the promontory, I saw a vast white plain covered with walruses. They were playing among themselves, and what we heard were bellowings of pleasure, not of anger.

Walruses resemble seals in the form of their bodies, and the arrangement of their limbs. But they have no canine teeth or incisors in their lower jaws, and the canines in their upper jaws are two defensive tusks, eighty centimeters long and measuring thirty-three centimeters in circumference at the root. These teeth, made of a compact, unstriated ivory, are harder even than an elephant's, do not yellow, and are much sought after. As a result, the walrus is the subject of a hunt that will continue until the last one is dead. The hunters massacre indiscriminately both pregnant females and young, at a rate of 4000 a year.

As I passed near these curious animals, I could examine them leisurely, for they did not move. Their skins were thick and rugged, of a yellowish tint, approaching to red; their hair was short and scant. Some of them were four meters long. Quieter, and less timid than their cousins of the north, they did not, like them, place sentinels round the outskirts of their encampment.

After examining this city of walruses, I began to think of returning. It was eleven o'clock, and if Captain Nemo found the conditions favorable for observations, I wished to be present at the operation. However, there did not seem much hope that the sun would appear this day. There were heavy clouds on the horizon, that blocked our view. It seemed as if the sun were jealous, and did not want to reveal to humans this unapproachable point of the globe.

Therefore, we were obliged to return to the *Nautilus*. We followed a narrow pathway running along the summit of the bluff.

At half-past eleven we had reached the place where we landed. The boat had run aground bringing the captain. I saw him standing on a block of basalt, his instruments near him, his eyes fixed on the northern horizon, near which the sun was then describing a lengthened curve.

I took my place beside him, and waited without speaking. Noon arrived, and, as before, the sun did not appear. It was unfortunate. Observations were still wanting. If not accomplished tomorrow, we must give up all idea of finding our position.

We were indeed exactly at the 20th of March. Tomorrow, the 21st, would be the equinox; not allowing for refraction, the sun would disappear behind the horizon for six months, and with its disappearance the long polar night would begin. Since the September equinox it had been above the northern horizon, rising by lengthened spirals up to the 21st of December. After this period, the summer solstice of the northern regions, it had begun to descend; and tomorrow was to shed its last rays upon this place.

I communicated my fears and observations to Captain Nemo.

"You are right, Monsieur Aronnax," said he. "If tomorrow I cannot take the altitude of the sun, I shall not be able to do it for six months. But precisely because chance has led me into these seas on the 21st of March, my bearings will be easy to take, if at twelve we can see the sun."

"Why, captain?"

"Because when the sun describes such lengthened curves, it is difficult to measure exactly its height above the horizon, and grave error may be made with instruments."

"What will you do, then?"

"I shall only need my chronometer," replied Captain Nemo. "If tomorrow, the 21st of March, the disc of the sun, allowing for refraction, is exactly cut in half by the northern horizon, it will show that I am at the South Pole."

"Just so," said I. "But this statement is not mathematically correct, because the equinox does not necessarily begin at noon."

"Very likely, sir; but the error will not be more than a hundred meters and we do not want more. Till tomorrow then!"

Captain Nemo returned on board. Conseil and I remained to survey the shore, observing and studying until five o'clock. I recovered no unusual objects, except a penguin egg, remarkable for its size, for which a collector would pay more than a thousand francs. It was cream-colored, with rays and markings that ornamented it like hieroglyphics. A rare bauble. I entrusted it to the hands of Conseil, that careful lad with sure feet, who carried it as though it were precious Chinese porcelain, and delivered it intact to the *Nautilus.* Then I went to bed, not, however, without invoking, like the Indian, the favor of the radiant star.

The next day, the 21st of March, at five in the morning, I mounted the platform. I found Captain Nemo there.

"The weather is lightening a little," said he. "I have some hope. After breakfast we will go on shore, and choose a post for observation."

That point settled, I sought Ned Land. I wanted to take him with me. But the obstinate Canadian refused, and I saw that his taciturnity and his bad humor grew day by day. After all I was not sorry for his obstinacy under the circumstances. Indeed, there were too many seals on shore, and we ought not to lay such temptation in this unthinking fisherman's way.

Breakfast over, we went on shore. The *Nautilus* had gone some miles further south in the night. It was a whole league from the coast, above which dominated in a sharp peak about four or five hundred meters high. The boat took with me Captain Nemo, two men of the crew, and the instruments, which consisted of a chronometer, a telescope, and a barometer.

While crossing, I saw numerous whales belonging to the three kinds peculiar to the southern seas; the true baleen whale, or in English, "right whale," which has no dorsal fin; the "humpback," or balænopteron, with grooved chest, and large whitish fins, which in spite of its name, do not resemble wings; and the fin-back, of a yellowish-brown, the liveliest of all the cetacea. This powerful creature is heard a long way off when he throws to a great height columns of air and vapor, which look like whirlwinds of smoke. These different mammals were disporting themselves in herds in the quiet waters; and I could see that this basin of the antarctic pole served as a place of refuge to those cetacea too closely hunted by the whalers.

I also noticed long whitish rows of salpae, a kind of gregarious mollusk, and large medusæ floating on the agitated waves.

At nine we landed; the sky was brightening, the clouds were flying to the south, and the fog seemed to be leaving the cold surface of the waters. Captain Nemo went towards the peak, which he doubtless meant to be his observatory. It was a painful ascent over the sharp lava and the pumice stones, in an atmosphere often impregnated with a sulphurous smell from the fumaroles. For a man unaccustomed to walk on land, the captain climbed the steep slopes with an agility I never saw equalled, and which a hunter of chamois would have envied.

We were two hours getting to the summit of this peak, which was half porphyry and half basalt. From thence we looked upon a vast sea, which, towards the north, distinctly traced its boundary line against the depths of the sky. At our feet lay fields of dazzling whiteness. Over our heads a pale azure, free from fog. To the north the disc of the sun seemed like a ball of fire, already cut into a crescent by the horizon. From whales playing on the bosom of the water rose sheaves of liquid jets by hundreds. In the distance lay the *Nautilus* like a whale asleep on the water. Behind us, to the south and east, an immense country, and a chaotic heap of rocks and ice, the limits of which were not visible.

On arriving at the summit, Captain Nemo carefully took the mean altitude with the barometer, for he would have to consider that in taking his observations.

At a quarter to twelve, the sun, then seen only by refraction, looked like a golden disc shedding its last rays upon this deserted continent, and seas which man has not yet ploughed.

Captain Nemo, furnished with a telescope fitted with a reticule which, by means of a mirror, corrected the refraction, watched the star sinking by degrees, below the horizon following a lengthened diagonal. I held the chronometer. My heart beat fast. If the disappearance of the half-disc of the sun coincided with twelve o'clock on the chronometer, we were at the pole itself.

"Twelve!" I exclaimed.

"The South Pole!" replied Captain Nemo, in a grave voice, handing me the glass, which showed the sun cut in exactly equal parts by the horizon.

I looked at the last rays crowning the peak, and the shadows mounting by degrees up its slopes. At that moment Captain Nemo, resting with his hand on my shoulder, said:

"Sir, in 1600 the Hollander Gheritk, driven by currents and storms, reached 64° south latitude and discovered New Shetland. In 1773, on the 17th of January, the illustrious Cook, following the 38th meridian, arrived at 67° 30 ' south latitude, and in 1774, on the 30th of January, on the 109th meridian, he reached 71° 15 ' south latitude. In 1819, the Russian Bellinghausen reached the 69th parallel, and in 1821, he reached the 76th at 111° west longitude. In 1820, the Englishman Brunsfield was stopped at the 65th degree. In that same year, the American Morrel, whose records are doubtful, followed the 42nd meridian and discovered open sea at 70° 14 ' south latitude. In 1825, the Englishman Powell could not get past the 62nd degree. That same year, a simple English seal fisherman, Weddell, got as far as 72° 14 ' on the 35th meridian, and to 74° 15 ' on the 36th. In 1829, the Englishman Forester, commander of the *Chanticleer,* took possession of the antarctic continent at 63° 26 ' south latitude and 66° 26 ' longitude. In 1831, the Englishman Briscoe, on the first of February, discovered Enderby Land at 68° 50 ' south latitude. In 1832, on the fifth of February, he discovered Adelaide Land at 67°, and on the 21st Graham Land at 64° 45 '. In 1838, the Frenchman Dumont d'Urville, stopped by the icebank at 62° 57 ', discovered Louis-Phillipe Land. Two years later, on a new trip to the south, he found Adelie Land at 66° 30 ', on the 21st of January. Eight days later, at 64° 40 ', he found the Claire Coast. In 1838, the Englishman Wilkes advanced as far as the 69th parallel on the hundredth meridian. In 1839, the Englishman Balleny discovered Sabrina Land at the edge of the antarctic circle. Finally, in 1842, Englishman James Ross, in charge of the *Erebus* and *Terror,* on January 12 at 76° 56 ' south latitude and 171° 7 ' east longitude discovered Victoria Land. On the 23rd of the same month, he reached the 74th parallel, the highest latitude yet attained. On the 27th, he reached 76° 8 ', on the 28th 77° 32 ', on February 2 he had reached 78° 4 ', but later in 1842 he could not get past the 71st degree. And now! I,

Captain Nemo, on this 21st day of March 1868, at latitude 90°, have reached the South Pole; and I take possession of this part of the globe, equal to one-sixth of the known continents."

"In whose name, Captain?"

"In my own, sir!"

Saying which, Captain Nemo unfurled a black banner, bearing an N in gold embroidered on its bunting. Then turning towards the day star, whose last rays lapped the horizon of the sea, he exclaimed: "Adieu, sun! Disappear, radiant star! rest beneath this open sea, and let a night of six months spread its shadows over my new domains!"

---

[1]Named for the ships of his expedition, in 1841. RM

◄ CHAPTER XV ►
ACCIDENT OR INCIDENT?

he next day, the 22nd of March, at six in the morning, preparations for departure were begun. The last gleams of twilight were melting into night. The cold was great; the constellations shone with wonderful intensity. In the zenith glittered that wondrous Southern Cross—the polar star of antarctic regions.

The thermometer showed twelve degrees below zero centigrade, and when the wind freshened, it was most biting. Patches of ice increased on the open water. The sea was freezing everywhere. Numerous blackish patches spread on the surface, showing the formation of fresh ice. Evidently this southern basin froze during the six winter months and was then absolutely inaccessible. What became of the whales in that time? Doubtless they went beneath the ice shelf, seeking more practicable seas. As to the seals and walruses, accustomed to live in a hard climate, they remained on these icy shores. These creatures instinctively know to break holes in the ice fields, and to keep them open. To these holes they come for air; when the birds, driven away by the cold, have migrated to the north, these sea mammals remain sole masters of the polar continent.

The reservoirs were filling with water, and the *Nautilus* was slowly descending. At 1000 feet deep it stopped; its screw beat the water, and it advanced straight towards the north, at a speed of fifteen miles an hour. Towards night it was already cruising under the immense body of the ice shelf.

The panels of the salon were closed as a precaution, since the hull of the *Nautilus* could strike a submerged block of ice. So I passed the day putting my notes in order. My mind was filled with memories of the pole. We had reached that inaccessible point without fatigue, without danger, as if our floating wagon glided on rails like a train. And now we began the return. Were there surprises reserved for us? I thought so, since this series of underwater marvels seemed inexhaustible! During the five and a half months since chance brought us on board, we had travelled 14,000 leagues, longer than the equator of the earth. How many incidents, curious or terrible, made our voyage fascinating: the hunt in the forests of Crespo, running aground in the Torres Straits, the coral cemetery, the pearl-fisheries of Ceylon, the Arabian Tunnel, the

fires of Santorin, the millions in Vigo Bay, Atlantis, the South Pole! During that night, all these memories passed in dream after dream, not allowing my brain to rest for an instant.

At three in the morning I was awakened by a violent shock. I sat up in my bed and listened in the darkness, when suddenly I was thrown into the middle of the room. The *Nautilus,* after having grounded, had listed considerably.

I groped along the wall, and by the staircase to the salon, which was lit by the luminous ceiling. The furniture was upset. Fortunately, the display cases, whose legs were firmly set, had held fast. The pictures on the starboard-side were no longer hanging, but were flat against the wall, while those of the port-side were hanging at least a foot from the wall. The *Nautilus* was lying on its starboard side perfectly motionless.

I heard footsteps, and a confusion of voices; but Captain Nemo did not appear. As I was leaving the salon, Ned Land and Conseil entered.

"What is the matter?" said I, at once.

"I came to ask monsieur," replied Conseil.

"A thousand devils!" exclaimed the Canadian, "I know well enough! The *Nautilus* has grounded; and judging by the way she lies, I do not think she will right herself as she did the first time in the Torres Straits."

"But," I asked, "has she at least come to the surface of the sea?"

"We do not know," said Conseil.

"It is easy to decide," I answered. I consulted the manometer. To my great surprise it showed a depth of more than 360 meters. "What does that mean?" I exclaimed.

"We must ask Captain Nemo," said Conseil.

"But where shall we find him?" said Ned Land.

"Follow me," said I, to my companions.

We left the salon. There was no one in the library. No one was at the central staircase, nor by the berths of the ship's crew. I thought that Captain Nemo must be in the pilot's cage. It was best to wait. We all returned to the salon.

I will pass over the Canadian's recriminations with silence. I let his temper cool, and he vented his foul humor without comment from me.

For twenty minutes we remained thus, trying to hear the slightest noise which might be made on board the *Nautilus,* when Captain Nemo entered. He seemed not to see us; his face, generally so impassive, showed signs of uneasiness. He watched the compass silently, then the manometer; and going to the planisphere, placed his finger on a spot representing the southern seas.

I would not interrupt him; but, some minutes later, when he turned towards me, I said, using an expression he had employed in the Torres Straits—

"An incident, Captain?"

"No, sir; an accident this time."

"Serious?"

"Perhaps."

"Is the danger immediate?"

"No."

"The *Nautilus* has stranded?"

"Yes."

"And this stranding has happened—how?"

"From a caprice of nature, not from the incompetence of man. No mistake has been made in our maneuvers. But we cannot prevent equilibrium from producing its effects. We may brave human laws, but we cannot resist natural ones."

Captain Nemo had chosen a strange moment for uttering this philosophical reflection. On the whole, his answer helped me not at all.

"May I ask, sir, the cause of this accident?"

"An enormous block of ice, a whole mountain, has turned over," he replied. "When icebergs are undermined at their base by warmer water or repeated shock, their center of gravity rises, and the whole thing turns over, it somersaults. This is what has happened; one of these blocks, as it fell, struck the *Nautilus,* then, gliding under its hull, raised it with irresistible force, raising it to a higher level, where it is lying on its side."

"But can we not get the *Nautilus* off by emptying its reservoirs, that it may regain its balance?"

"That, sir, is being done at this moment. You can hear the pumps working. Look at the needle of the manometer; it shows that the *Nautilus* is rising, but the block of ice is rising with it; and, until some obstacle stops its ascending motion, our position cannot be altered."

Indeed, the *Nautilus* still held the same position to starboard; doubtless it would right itself when the block of ice stopped. But at this moment who knows if we may not strike the upper part of the iceberg, and if we may not be frightfully crushed between the two glassy surfaces?

I reflected on all the consequences of our position. Captain Nemo never took his eyes off the manometer. Since the fall of the iceberg, the *Nautilus* had risen about a hundred and fifty feet, but it still made the same angle with the perpendicular.

Suddenly a slight movement was felt in the hull. Evidently it was righting a little. Things hanging in the salon were noticeably returning to their normal position. The walls were nearing the upright. No one spoke. With beating hearts we watched, we felt the straightening. The floor became horizontal under our feet. Ten minutes passed.

"At last we have righted!" I exclaimed.

"Yes," said Captain Nemo, going to the door of the salon.

"But are we floating?" I asked.

"Certainly," he replied; "since the reservoirs are not empty; and, when empty, the *Nautilus* must rise to the surface of the sea."

The captain left, and I understood that, on his orders, the ascension of the *Nautilus* was halted. In fact, we had nearly struck the underside of the icebank, and it was better to stay between the upper and lower levels.

"We had a narrow escape!" sighed Conseil.

"Yes. We might have been crushed between the blocks of ice, or forever imprisoned within them. Then, with no way to renew our air . . . Yes! It was a narrow escape!"

"If it is over!" murmured Ned Land.

I did not want to enter into a useless discussion with the Canadian, so I did not respond. The panels opened at that moment, and the exterior illumination poured in through the glass.

We were suspended in open water; but at a distance of about ten meters, on either side of the *Nautilus,* rose a dazzling wall of ice. Above and beneath was the same wall. Above, because the lower surface of the iceberg stretched over us like an immense ceiling. Beneath, because the overturned block, having slid by degrees, had found a resting-place against the lateral walls at two points, which kept it in that position. The *Nautilus* was really imprisoned in a perfect tunnel of ice more than twenty meters in breadth, filled with quiet water. It would be easy to get out of it by going either forward or backward, and then make a free passage under the ice shelf, some hundreds of meters deeper.

The luminous ceiling had been extinguished, but the salon was still resplendent with intense light. It was the powerful reflection of the electric lantern's beams from the glassy walls of ice. I cannot describe the effect of the voltaic rays upon the great blocks so capriciously cut; upon every angle, every ridge, every facet was thrown a different light, according to the nature of the veins running through the ice. A dazzling mine of gems, particularly of sapphires, their blue rays mixing with the green of the emerald. Here and there were opal shades of infinite softness, running through bright spots like fiery diamonds, the brilliancy of which the eye

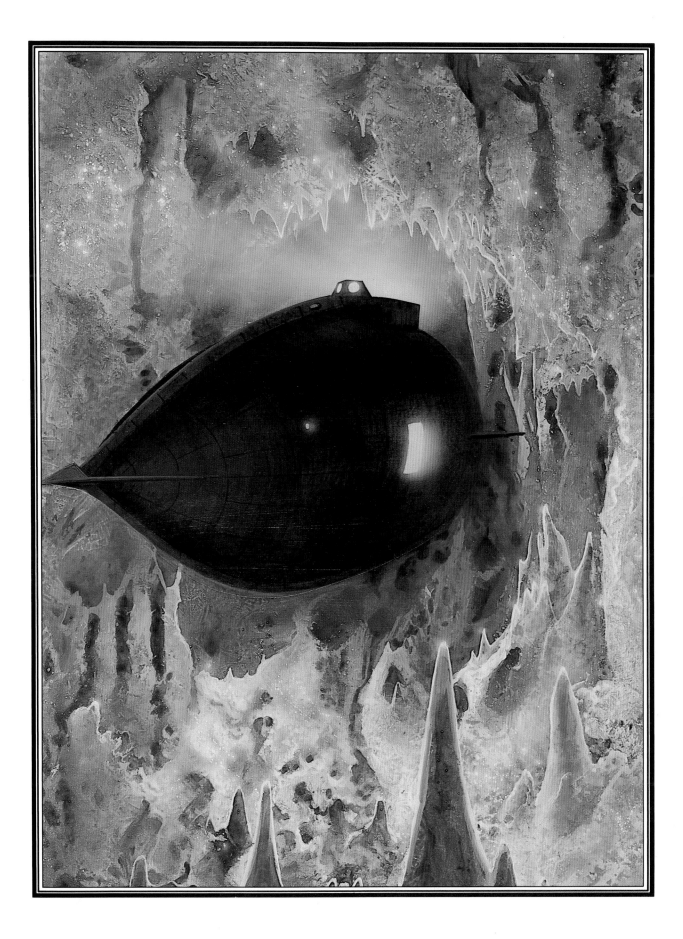

could not bear. The power of the lantern seemed increased a hundredfold, like a lamp through the ridged lenses of a first-class lighthouse.

"How beautiful! How beautiful!" cried Conseil.

"Yes," I said, "it is a wonderful sight. Is it not, Ned?"

"Eh! A thousand devils! Yes," answered Ned Land, "it is superb! I am mad at being obliged to admit it. No one has ever seen anything like it; but the sight may cost us dear. And if I must say all, I think we are seeing here things which God never intended man to see!"

Ned was right, it was too beautiful. Suddenly a cry from Conseil made me turn.

"What is it?" I asked

"Monsieur must close his eyes! Monsieur must not look!" Saying which, Conseil clapped his hands over his eyes.

"But what is the matter, my boy?"

"I am dazzled, blinded!"

My eyes turned involuntarily towards the glass, but I could not stand the fire which seemed to devour them.

I understood what had happened. The *Nautilus* had put on full speed. All the quiet luster of the ice-walls was at once changed into flashes of sheet-lightning. The fire from these myriads of diamonds was blurred together. The *Nautilus,* sent speeding by its propeller, voyaged through sheets of fire.

The panels of the salon were closed. We held our hands in front of our eyes, imprinted with concentric lights that floated before our retinas, caused by the sunlike rays that had struck them. It took some time for our troubled eyes to recover.

At last we could remove our hands.

"Faith, I should never have believed it," said Conseil.

"As for me, I don't believe it yet!" retorted the Canadian.

"When we get back to land," continued Conseil, "we will be so blase after all these marvels of nature, what will we think of the miserable continents and petty works of the hand of man? No! The inhabited world will no longer be worthy of us!"

Such words from the mouth of an imperturbable Fleming showed the degree of excitement to which our enthusiasm had risen. But the Canadian threw cold water on it.

"The inhabited world! don't let that worry your head. Keep calm, friend Conseil, you'll not see that world again!"

It was then five in the morning; and at that moment a shock was felt at the bow of the *Nautilus.* I knew that its spur had struck a block of ice. It must have been a false maneuver, for this submarine tunnel, obstructed by blocks, did not offer very easy navigation. I thought that Captain Nemo, by changing his course, would either go around these obstacles, or else follow the windings of the tunnel. In any case, the road before us could not be entirely blocked. But, contrary to my expectations, the *Nautilus* took a decided retrograde motion.

"We are going backwards?" said Conseil.

"Yes," I replied. "This end of the tunnel can have no exit."

"And then?"

"Then," said I, "the maneuver is very simple. We must go back again, and go out at the southern opening. That is all."

In speaking thus, I wished to appear more confident than I really was. But the retrograde motion of the *Nautilus* was increasing; and, powered by the reversed screw, it carried us at great speed.

"It will be a delay," said Ned.

"What does it matter, some hours more or less, provided we get out at last?"

"Yes," repeated Ned Land, "provided we do get out at last!"

A short time later I walked from the salon to the library. My companions were silent. I soon threw myself on an ottoman, and took a book which my eyes overran mechanically. A quarter of an hour later, Conseil, approaching me, said, "Is what monsieur reading very interesting?"

"Very interesting," I replied.

"I should think so. It is monsieur's own book monsieur is reading."

"My book?"

And indeed I was holding in my hand the work on the *Great Submarine Depths*. I did not even notice it. I closed the book, and returned to my pacing. Ned and Conseil rose to go.

"Stay here, my friends," said I, detaining them. "Let us remain together until we are out of this trap."

"As monsieur pleases," Conseil replied.

Some hours passed. I often looked at the instruments hanging from the wall. The manometer showed that the *Nautilus* kept at a constant depth of more than three hundred meters; the compass still pointed to the south; the log indicated a speed of twenty miles an hour, which, in such a cramped space, was excessive. But Captain Nemo knew that he could not hasten too much, and that minutes were worth centuries to us.

At twenty-five minutes past eight a second shock took place, this time from behind. I turned pale. My companions were close by my side. I seized Conseil's hand. We looked questioningly at one another, betraying our thoughts more eloquently than any words.

At this moment the captain entered the salon. I went up to him.

"Our course is barred southward?" I asked.

"Yes, sir. The iceberg has shifted, and closed every outlet."

"We are blocked up, then?"

"Yes."

◄ CHAPTER XVI ►
WANT OF AIR

hus, around the *Nautilus,* above and below, was an impenetrable wall of ice. We were prisoners of the ice shelf! The Canadian struck the table with his formidable fist. Conseil was quiet. I watched the captain. His countenance had resumed its habitual imperturbability. His arms were crossed. He was deep in thought. The *Nautilus* did not move. The captain then spoke:

"Gentlemen," he said, calmly, "there are two ways of dying in the circumstances in which we are placed." (This inexplicable person had the air of a mathematics professor lecturing to his pupils.) "The first is to be crushed; the second is to die of suffocation. I do not speak of the possibility of dying of hunger, for the supply of provisions in the *Nautilus* will certainly last longer than we shall. Let us then calculate our chances at crushing and asphyxiation."

"As to suffocation, Captain," I replied, "that is not to be feared, because our reservoirs are full."

"Just so; but they will only yield two days' supply of air. Now, for thirty-six hours we have been hidden under the water, and already the stale atmosphere of the *Nautilus* requires renewal. In forty-eight hours our reserve will be exhausted.''

"Well, Captain, we will escape before forty-eight hours!''

"We will attempt it, at least, by piercing the wall that surrounds us.''

"On which side?''

"A sounding will tell us. I am going to run the *Nautilus* aground on the lower ice, and my men will attack the iceberg on the side that is least thick.''

"Can the salon windows be opened?''

"It will not be inconvenient, since we are not moving.''

Captain Nemo went out. Soon I discovered by a hissing noise that the water was entering the reservoirs. The *Nautilus* sank slowly, and rested on the ice at a depth of 350 meters, the depth at which the lower ice bank was immersed.

"My friends,'' I said, "our situation is serious, but I rely on your courage and energy.''

"Sir,'' replied the Canadian, "this is no longer the time to burden you with my complaints. I am ready to do anything for the general safety.''

"Good, Ned,'' and I held out my hand to the Canadian.

"I will add,'' he continued, "that being as handy with the pickaxe as with the harpoon, if I can be useful to the captain, he can command my services.''

"He will not refuse your help. Come, Ned!''

I led him to the room where the crew of the *Nautilus* were putting on their diving-suits. I told the captain of Ned's proposal, which he accepted. The Canadian put on his sea-costume, and was ready as soon as his working-companions.

Each carried on his back the Rouquayrol apparatus, with tanks filled with a large quantity of pure air. This was a considerable, but necessary, drain on the *Nautilus'* reserves. They did not take the Ruhmkorff lamps, which would have been useless in the midst of water illuminated by the electric light.

When Ned was dressed, I re-entered the salon, where the windows were uncovered and, posted near Conseil, I examined the surrounding beds that supported the *Nautilus*.

Some moments later, we saw a dozen of the crew set foot on the bank of ice, among them Ned Land, easily recognized by his stature. Captain Nemo was with them.

Before proceeding to break through the walls, he took soundings, to be sure of working in the right direction. Long soundings were bored in the side walls, but after fifteen meters they still found only solid ice. It was useless to attack it on the ceiling-like surface since the iceberg itself measured more than 400 meters in thickness. Captain Nemo then sounded the lower surface. There ten meters of ice separated us from the outside water. Such was the thickness of the ice-field. It was necessary, therefore, to cut from it a piece equal in area to the waterline of the *Nautilus*. There were about 6500 cubic meters to remove so as to dig a hole through which we could descend below the field of ice.

The work was begun immediately, and carried on with indefatigable energy. Instead of digging round the *Nautilus,* which would have involved great difficulty, Captain Nemo had an immense trench outlined eight meters from the port quarter. Then the men set to work simultaneously with their tools at several points on that line. Presently their pickaxes attacked this compact matter vigorously, and large blocks were detached from the mass. By a curious effect of specific gravity, these blocks, lighter than water, fled, so to speak, to the vault of the tunnel, that increased in thickness at the top in proportion as it diminished at the base. But that mattered little, so long as the lower part grew thinner.

After two hours' hard work, Ned Land came in exhausted. He and his comrades were replaced by new workers, whom Conseil and I joined. The second-in-command on the *Nautilus* superintended us.

The water seemed singularly cold, but I soon got warm handling the pickaxe. My move-

ments were free enough, although they were made under a pressure of thirty atmospheres.

When I re-entered, after working two hours, to take some food and rest, I found a perceptible difference between the pure air with which the Rouquayrol apparatus supplied me, and the atmosphere of the *Nautilus,* already changed with carbon dioxide. The air had not been renewed for forty-eight hours, and its vivifying qualities were considerably enfeebled. However, after a lapse of twelve hours, we had only removed a layer of ice one meter thick from the marked surface, which was only about 600 cubic meters! Reckoning that it took twelve hours to accomplish this much, it would take five nights and four days to bring this enterprise to a satisfactory conclusion.

"Five nights and four days! And we have only air enough for two days in the reservoirs!"

"Without taking into account," said Ned, "that, even if we get out of this damned prison, we shall still be imprisoned under the ice shelf, shut out from all possible communication with the atmosphere."

True enough! We could then foresee the minimum time necessary for our deliverance? Might we be suffocated before the *Nautilus* could regain the surface of the waves? Was it destined to perish in this icetomb, with all those it enclosed? The situation was terrible. But everyone had looked the danger in the face, and each was determined to do his duty to the last.

As I expected, during the night a second layer a meter thick was removed enlarging the immense hollow. But in the morning when, dressed in my diving-suit, I traversed the slushy mass at a temperature of six or seven degrees below zero, I noticed that the side walls were gradually closing in. The water farthest from the trench, that was not warmed by the men's work, showed a tendency to freeze. In the presence of this new and imminent danger, what would become of our chances of safety? How hinder the solidification of the water, that eventually would burst the sides of the *Nautilus* like glass?

I did not tell my companions of this new danger. What was the good of damping the energy they displayed in the painful work of escape? But when I went on board again, I told Captain Nemo of this grave complication.

"I know it," he said, in that calm tone which could ease the most terrible apprehensions. "It is one danger more; but I see no way of escaping it; the only chance of safety is to go more quickly than the freezing. We must keep ahead of it, that is all."

Keep ahead of it! But then, I should have been accustomed to his manner of speaking!

For several hours on this day I used my pickaxe vigorously. The work kept my spirits up. Besides, to work was to leave the *Nautilus,* and breathe directly the pure air drawn from the reservoirs, and supplied by our apparatus, and to escape the impoverished and lifeless atmosphere of the ship.

Towards evening the trench was dug one meter deeper. When I returned on board, I was nearly suffocated by the carbon dioxide with which the air was saturated—ah! if we had only the chemical means to drive away this deleterious gas! We had plenty of oxygen. All this water contained a considerable quantity, and by breaking it down with our powerful batteries, it would restore the life-giving gas. I had thought over it well; but of what good was that, since the carbon dioxide produced by our respiration had invaded every part of the vessel? To absorb it, it was necessary to fill some jars with caustic potash, and to shake them incessantly. Now this substance was wanting on board, and nothing could produce it.

On that evening, Captain Nemo had to open the taps of his reservoirs, and let some pure air into the interior of the *Nautilus;* without this precaution, we should never have awakened from our sleep.

The next day, March 26, I resumed my miner's work in beginning the fifth meter. The side walls and the lower surface of the iceberg had thickened visibly. It was evident that they would meet before the *Nautilus* was able to disengage itself. Despair seized me for an instant and my pickaxe nearly fell from my hands. What was the good of digging if I must be suffocated, crushed by the water that was turning into stone?—a punishment that the ferocity of savages would not have invented!

Just then Captain Nemo, who had been directing the work, and working hard himself, passed near me. I touched his hand and showed him the walls of our prison. The wall to starboard had advanced to at least four meters from the hull of the *Nautilus.*

The captain understood me, and signalled to me to follow him. We went on board. I took off my diving-suit, and accompanied him into the salon.

"Monsieur Aronnax, we must attempt some desperate means, or we shall be sealed up in this solidified water as in cement."

"Yes; but what is to be done?"

"Ah! if only my *Nautilus* were strong enough to bear this pressure without being crushed!"

"Well?" I asked, not catching the captain's idea.

"Do you not understand," he replied, "that this congelation of the water could help us? Do you not see that, by its solidification, it would burst through this field of ice that imprisons us, as, when water freezes, it bursts the hardest stones? Do you not perceive that it would be an agent of safety instead of destruction?"

"Yes, Captain, perhaps. But whatever resistance to crushing the *Nautilus* possesses, it could not support that terrible pressure, and would be flattened into an iron plate."

"I know it, sir. Therefore we must not reckon on the aid of nature, but on our own exertions. We must stop this solidification. We must stop it. Not only are the side walls pressing together; but there is not ten feet of water before or behind the *Nautilus.* The congelation gains on us on all sides."

"How long will the air in the reservoirs last for us to breathe on board?"

The captain looked in my face. "After tomorrow they will be empty!"

A cold sweat came over me. However, ought I to have been astonished at the answer? On March 22, the *Nautilus* had been in the open polar seas. We were now at the 26th of March. For five days we had lived on the reserve on board. And what was left of the respirable air must be kept for the workers. Even now, as I write, my recollection is still so vivid, that an involuntary terror seizes me, and my lungs seem to be without air!

Meanwhile, Captain Nemo reflected silently, and evidently an idea had struck him; but he seemed to reject it answering himself in the negative. At last, these words escaped his lips: "Boiling water!" he muttered.

"Boiling water?" I cried.

"Yes, sir. We are enclosed in a space that is relatively confined. Would not jets of boiling water, constantly injected by the pumps, raise the temperature in this area, and slow the freezing?"

"Let us try it," I said, resolutely.

"Let us try, Professor."

The thermometer then stood at minus seven degrees centigrade outside. Captain Nemo took me to the galleys, where the vast distillatory machines stood that furnished by evaporation the drinkable water. They filled these with water, and all the electric heat from the batteries was thrown through the coils that were submerged in the liquid. In a few minutes this water reached a hundred degrees centigrade, the boiling point. It was directed towards the pumps, while fresh water replaced it in proportion. The heat developed by the batteries was such that the cold water, drawn up from the sea, after having gone through the machines, came boiling into the body of the pump.

The pumping was begun, and three hours later the thermometer marked minus six degrees below zero outside. One degree had been gained. Two hours later, the thermometer only marked four degrees centigrade.

"We shall succeed," I said to the captain, after having anxiously watched the result of the operation.

"I think," he answered, "that we shall not be crushed. We have only suffocation to fear."

During the night the temperature of the water rose to one degree below zero centigrade. The pumping of hot water could not carry it to a higher point. But as the freezing of sea-water occurs at about two degrees, I was at last reassured against the dangers of freezing solid.

The next day, March 27, six meters of ice had been cleared from the hole. Four meters only remained to be cleared away. There was yet forty-eight hours' work. The air could not be renewed in the interior of the *Nautilus*. And this day would make it worse.

An intolerable weight oppressed me. Towards three o'clock in the evening, this feeling rose to a violent degree. Yawns dislocated my jaws. My lungs panted as they inhaled this burning gas, which became more and more rarified. A mental torpor took hold of me. I was powerless, almost unconscious. My brave Conseil, though exhibiting the same symptoms and suffering in the same manner, never left me. He took my hand and encouraged me, and I heard him murmur, "Oh! if I could only not breathe, so as to leave more air for monsieur!"

Tears came into my eyes on hearing him speak thus.

If our situation was intolerable in the interior, with what haste and gladness would we put on our diving-suits to work in our turn! Pickaxes resonated on the frozen ice-beds. Our arms ached, the skin was torn off our hands. But what were these fatigues, what did the wounds matter? Vital air came to the lungs! we breathed! we breathed!

Yet this time, no one prolonged his voluntary task beyond the prescribed time. His task accomplished, each one handed in turn to his panting companions the apparatus that supplied him with life. Captain Nemo set the example, and submitted first to this severe discipline. When the time came, he gave up his apparatus to another, and returned to the lifeless air on board, calm, unflinching, unmurmuring.

On that day the ordinary work was accomplished with unusual vigor. Only two meters remained to be raised from the surface. Two meters only separated us from the open sea. But the reservoirs were nearly emptied of air. The little that remained ought to be kept for the workers; not an atom for the *Nautilus!*

When I went back on board, I was half suffocated. What a night! I know not how to describe it. The next day my breathing was oppressed. Dizziness accompanied the paid in my head, and made me like a drunken man. My companions showed the same symptoms. Some of the crew had a rattling in the throat.

On that day, the sixth of our imprisonment, Captain Nemo, finding the pickaxes worked too slowly, resolved to crush the ice-bed that still separated us from the open water. This man's coolness and energy never forsook him. He subdued his physical pains by moral force. He never quit thinking, scheming and acting.

By his orders the vessel was lightened, that is to say, raised from the ice-bed by a change of specific gravity. When it floated the crew towed it so as to bring it above the immense trench we had made in the shape of the water-line. Then filling the reservoirs of water, we descended until the *Nautilus* filled the hole.

Then all the crew came on board, and the airlock doors were shut. The *Nautilus* then rested on the bed of ice, which was not one meter thick, and which the sounding leads had perforated in a thousand places.

The taps of the reservoirs were then opened, and a hundred cubic meters of water was let in, increasing the weight of the *Nautilus* by 100,000 kilograms.

We waited, we listened, forgetting our sufferings in renewed hope. Our safety depended on this last chance.

Notwithstanding the buzzing in my head, I soon heard a vibrating sound under the hull of the *Nautilus*. The ice cracked with a singular crash, like tearing paper, and the *Nautilus* sank.

"We are out!" murmured Conseil in my ear.

I could not answer him. I seized his hand, and pressed it with an involuntary convulsion.

All at once, carried away by its frightful excess of weight the *Nautilus* sank like a bullet under the waters; that is to say, it fell as if it was in a vacuum!

Then all the electric force was put on the pumps, that soon began to force the water out of the reservoirs. After some minutes, our fall was stopped. Soon, the manometer indicated an ascending movement. The screw, going at full speed, made the iron hull tremble to its very bolts, and drew us towards the north.

But, how long is this navigation under the iceberg to last before we reach the open sea? Another day? I shall be dead first!

Half stretched upon a divan in the library, I was suffocating. My face was purple, my lips blue, my faculties suspended. I neither saw nor heard. All notion of time had gone from my mind. My muscles could not contract.

I do not know how many hours passed thus, but I was conscious of the agony that was coming over me. I felt as if I was going to die . . . .

Suddenly I came to. Some breaths of air penetrated my lungs. Had we risen to the surface of the waves? Were we free of the iceberg?

No; Ned and Conseil, my two brave friends, were sacrificing themselves to save me. Some atoms of air still remained at the bottom of one Rouquayrol apparatus. Instead of using it, they had kept it for me, and while they were being suffocated, they gave me life drop by drop. I wanted to push back the thing; they held my hands, and for some moments I breathed freely.

I looked at the clock; it was eleven in the morning. It ought to be the 28th of March. The *Nautilus* went at the frightful pace of forty miles per hour. It literally tore through the water.

Where was Captain Nemo? Had he succumbed? Were his companions dead with him?

At the moment, the manometer indicated that we were not more than twenty feet from the surface. A mere plate of ice separated us from the atmosphere. Could we not break it?

Perhaps! In any case the *Nautilus* was going to attempt it. I felt it take an oblique position, lowering the stern, and raising the spur. The introduction of water had been the means of disturbing its equilibrium. Then, impelled by its powerful screw, it attacked the ice field from beneath like a formidable battering-ram. It broke it little by little by backing and then rushing forward with full speed against the field, which gradually gave way; and at last, with one supreme effort, it shot forwards on to the icy field, that was crushed beneath its weight.

The hatch was opened—one might say torn off—and the pure air flooded in abundance to all parts of the *Nautilus*.

◄ **CHAPTER XVII** ►

FROM CAPE HORN TO THE AMAZON

ow I got on to the platform, I have no idea; perhaps the Canadian had carried me there. But I breathed, I inhaled the revivifying sea air. My two companions were getting drunk with the fresh molecules. Unlike unhappy men who had been too long without eating, so they could not with impunity indulge in the simplest foods that were given them, we, on the contrary, had no need to restrain ourselves; we could draw this air freely into our lungs, and it was the breeze, the breeze alone, that filled us with this voluptuous enjoyment!

"Ah!" said Conseil, "how delightful this oxygen is! Monsieur need not fear to breathe it. There is enough for all the world."

Ned Land did not speak, but he opened his jaws wide enough to frighten a shark. And what powerful inhalations! The Canadian drew in breaths like a furnace at full blast.

Our strength soon returned, and when I looked round me, I saw we were alone on the platform. There were none of the crew. Neither was there Captain Nemo. The strange seamen in the *Nautilus* were contented with the air that circulated in the interior; none of them had come to drink in the open air!

The first words I spoke were words of gratitude and thankfulness to my two companions. Ned and Conseil had prolonged my life during the last hours of this long agony. No gratitude could repay such devotion.

"Well! Professor," answered Ned Land, "do not speak of it! Why give us any credit? It was merely a matter of arithmetic. Your life is worth more than ours. We had to save it."

"No, Ned," I replied, "it is not worth more. No one is better than a good and generous man, such as you are!"

"All right! All right!" repeated the Canadian, embarrassed.

"And you, my brave Conseil, you must have suffered."

"Not too much, if monsieur will permit me to say so. I was short a few mouthfuls of air, but think I would have gotten used to it. Besides, when I saw monsieur faint, it took away my desire to breathe. It took, so to speak, the wind—" Conseil, embarrassed by the banality he was about to utter, stopped speaking.

"My friends," said I, moved by emotion, "we are bound one to the other forever, and with me you have the right . . . ."

"Which I shall take advantage of," exclaimed the Canadian.

"What do you mean?" said Conseil.

"I mean the right to take you with me when I leave this infernal *Nautilus.*"

"Well," said Conseil, "and after all this, are we going in the right direction?"

"Yes," I replied, "for we are going the way of the sun, and here the sun is in the north."

"No doubt," said Ned Land; "but it remains to be seen whether he will bring the ship into the Pacific or the Atlantic Ocean, that is, into frequented or deserted seas."

I could not answer that question, and I feared that Captain Nemo would rather take us to that vast ocean that touches both the coasts of Asia and America. He would thus complete the tour round the submarine world, and return to those waters in which the *Nautilus* could sail freely. But if we returned to the Pacific, away from all inhabited lands, what then of Ned Land's plans?

We ought, before long, to settle this important point. The *Nautilus* went at a rapid pace.

The polar circle was soon passed, and the course shaped for Cape Horn. We were off the tip of the American continent on March 31, at seven o'clock in the evening.

Then all our past sufferings were forgotten. The remembrance of that imprisonment in the ice was effaced from our minds. We only thought of the future. Captain Nemo did not appear again either in the drawing room or on the platform. The point shown each day on the planisphere, and marked by the second-in-command, showed me the exact position and direction of the *Nautilus*. Now, on that evening, it was evident, to my great satisfaction, that we were going back to the north by way of the Atlantic.

I told the Canadian and Conseil of the result of my observations.

"Good news," answered the Canadian, "but where is the *Nautilus* going?"

"I cannot say, Ned."

"Maybe after the South Pole, the captain plans to assault the North Pole, and return to the Pacific by the famous Northwest Passage?"

"I would not dare him," responded Conseil.

"Well!" said the Canadian, "we will have left his company long before then."

"In any case," added Conseil, "this masterful man who is Captain Nemo, we will not have regretted knowing him."

"Especially after we have left him!" retorted Ned Land.

The next day, April 1, when the *Nautilus* ascended to the surface, some minutes before noon, we sighted land to the west. It was Tierra del Fuego, which the first navigators named thus, the "Land of Fire," from seeing the quantity of smoke that rose from the natives' huts. This land of fire is a large collection of islands which extend 30 leagues long and 80 leagues wide, between 53° and 56° south latitude and 67° 50′ and 77° 15′ west longitude. The coast seemed low to me, but in the distance rose high mountains. I even thought I had a glimpse of Mount Sarmiento, that rises 2070 meters above the level of the sea. It is a pyramidal mountain of schist, with a very pointed summit, which, according as it is misty or clear, "is a sign of fine or of wet weather", I told Ned.

"A famous barometer, then, my friend."

"Yes, sir, a natural barometer, which served me well when navigating the passages of the Straits of Magellan."

At that moment the peak appeared clearly against the deep sky. It was a sign of good weather. And it was correct.

The *Nautilus*, diving again under the water, approached the coast, which was only some few miles off. From the glass windows in the salon, I saw long seaweeds, and gigantic fuci—that varech, of which the open polar sea contains so many specimens, with their sharp polished filaments; they measured about 300 meters in length—real cables, thicker than one's thumb; and having great tenacity, they are often used as ropes for vessels. Another weed known as velp, with leaves four feet long, rooted in the coral concretions, grew at the bottom. It served as nest and food for myriads of crustacea and mollusks, crabs and cuttlefish. There seals and otters had splendid repasts, eating the flesh of fish with sea vegetables, according to English custom.

Over these fertile and luxuriant depths the *Nautilus* passed with great rapidity. Towards evening, it approached the Falkland group, the rough summits of which I recognized the following day. The depth of the sea was moderate. I believed, not without reason, that these two islands, surrounded by a great number of islets, were once part of Patagonia. The Falklands were probably discovered by the celebrated John Davis, who gave them the name South Davis Islands. Later, Richard Hawkins called them the Maiden Islands, the islands of the Virgin. They were after that called the Malouines, at the beginning of the 18th century, by fishermen from Saint Malo, and finally the Falklands by the English, to whom they belong today.

Near the shores, our nets brought in beautiful specimens of algae, and particularly a certain fucus, the roots of which were covered with the best mussels in the world. Geese and ducks landed by dozens on the platform, and soon took their places in the pantry on board. With regard to fish, I observed specimens of the goby species, especially and boulerots, some two decimeters long, spangled all over with white and yellow spots.

I also admired numerous medusæ, and the finest of the sort, the crysaora, peculiar to the sea around the Falkland Islands. Sometimes they were shaped like very smooth, hemispherical umbrellas, with reddish brown stripes, and ending in a dozen symmetrical tentacles; sometimes they were inverted baskets, from which gracefully hung large leaves on long red branches. They swam by agitating four leaf-shaped arms, and letting drift their opulent headdress of tentacles. I should have liked to preserve some specimens of these delicate zoöphytes: but they are like clouds, shadowy apparitions, that dissolve and evaporate, when out of their native element.

When the last heights of the Falklands had disappeared below the horizon, the *Nautilus* sank to between twenty and twenty-five meters, and followed the American coast. Captain Nemo still did not show himself.

Until the 3rd of April we did not quit the shores of Patagonia, cruising sometimes under the ocean, sometimes at the surface. The *Nautilus* passed beyond the large estuary formed by the mouth of the Plata, and was, on the 4th of April, fifty miles off the coast of Uruguay. Its direction was northwards, and followed the long windings of the coast of South America. We had then made 16,000 leagues since our embarkation in the seas of Japan.

About eleven o'clock in the morning, the Tropic of Capricorn was crossed at the thirty-seventh meridian, and we passed Cape Frio. Captain Nemo, to Ned Land's great displeasure, did not like the neighborhood of the inhabited coasts of Brazil, for we went past it at a giddy speed. Not a fish, not a bird of the swiftest kind could follow us, and the natural curiosities of these seas escaped all observation.

This speed was kept up for several days, and in the evening of the 9th of April we sighted the most easterly point of South America: Cape San Roque. But then the *Nautilus* turned again, and sought the depths of a submarine valley which is between this cape and Sierra Leone on the African coast. This valley splits at the latitude of the Antilles, and terminates in the north at an enormous depression 9000 meters deep. In this place, the geological basin of the ocean forms, as far as the Lesser Antilles, a cliff six kilometers in height, sharp and steep; and at the latitude of the Cape Verde Islands, is another cliff not less considerable, that completes the enclosure of all the sunken continent of Atlantis. The bottom of this immense valley is scattered with some mountains, that give to these submarine places a picturesque aspect. I speak, moreover, from the manuscript charts that were in the library of the *Nautilus*—charts evidently done by Captain Nemo's own hand, and made after his personal observations.

For two days the deserted and deep waters were visited by the *Nautilus*. The submarine was furnished with long diagonal sideplanes which carried it to all depths. But, on the 11th of April, it surfaced suddenly, and appeared at the mouth of the Amazon River. This is a vast estuary, the outflow of which is so considerable that it freshens the sea-water for a distance of several leagues into the Atlantic.[1]

The equator was crossed. Twenty miles to the west were the Guianas, a French territory, on which we could have found an easy refuge; but a stiff breeze was blowing, and the furious waves would not have allowed a small boat to face them. Ned Land understood that, no doubt, for he spoke not a word about it. For my part, I made no allusion to his schemes of flight, for I would not urge him to make an attempt that must inevitably fail.

I made the time pass pleasantly by interesting studies. During the days of April 11th and 12th, the *Nautilus* did not leave the surface of the sea, and the net brought in a marvellous haul of zoöphytes, fish and reptiles.

Some zoöphytes had been fished up by the chain of the nets; they were for the most part beautiful phyctallines, belonging to the actinidian family, and among other species the

Phyctalis protexta, peculiar to that part of the ocean, with a little cylindrical body, ornamented with vertical lines, speckled with red dots, crowning a marvellous blossoming of tentacles. As to the mollusks, they consisted of some I had already observed—turritellas, olive porphyry shells, with regular intercrossed lines, and red spots standing out plainly against the flesh; fantastic pteroceras, like petrified scorpions; translucent hyaleas, argonauts, cuttlefish (excellent eating), and certain species of squid that naturalists of antiquity had classed among the flying-fish, and that serve principally for bait for cod-fishing.

There were several species of fish along these shores that I had little opportunity to study. Among the cartilaginous ones: petromyzons-pricka, a sort of eel, fifteen inches long, with a greenish head, violet fins, grey-blue back, brown belly, silvered and sown with bright spots, the pupil of the eye encircled with gold—a curious animal, that the current of the Amazon had carried to the sea, for they inhabit fresh waters; tuberculated rays, with pointed snouts, and a long loose tail, armed with a long jagged sting; little sharks, a meter long, with grey and whitish skin, and several rows of teeth, bent back, that are generally known by the name of *pantoufliers;* vespertilios, a kind of red isosceles triangle, half a meter long, whose pectorals are fleshy prolongations that make them look like bats. However, a horny appendage, situated near the nostrils, has given them the name of sea-unicorns; lastly, some species of triggerfish, the curassavian, whose spotted flanks were of a brilliant gold color; and the capriscus of clear violet, with varying shades like a pigeon's throat.

I end here this catalogue, which is somewhat dry perhaps, but very exact, with a series of bony fish that I observed: passans, belonging to the apteronotes, whose snout is very obtuse and white as snow, the body a beautiful black, marked with a very long loose fleshy strip; odontognathes, armed with spikes; sardines, three decimeters long, glittering with a bright silver light; a species of mackerel provided with two anal fins; centronotes of a blackish tint, that are fished for with torches, long fish, two meters in length, with fat flesh, white and firm, which, when they are fresh, taste like eel, and when dry, like smoked salmon; labres, half red, covered with scales only at the bottom of the dorsal and anal fins; chrysoptera, on which gold and silver blend their brightness with that of ruby and topaz; golden-tailed spares, the flesh of which is extremely delicate, and whose phosphorescent properties betray them in the midst of the waters; orange-colored giltheads with a long tongue; sciaena, with gold caudal fins; acanthopterans; anableps from Surinam, etc.

Notwithstanding this "etcetera," I must not omit to mention fish that Conseil will long remember, and with good reason.

One of our nets had hauled up a sort of very flat rayfish, which, with the tail cut off, formed a perfect disc, and weighed twenty kilograms. It was white underneath, red above, with large round spots of dark blue encircled with black. It had very glossy skin, terminating in a bilobed fin. Laid out on the platform, it struggled, tried to turn itself by convulsive movements, and made so many efforts, that one last somersault had nearly sent it into the sea. But Conseil, not wishing to let the fish go, rushed to it, and, before I could prevent him, had seized it with both hands.

In a moment he was overthrown, his legs in the air, and half his body paralyzed, crying: "Oh! master, master! come to me!"

It was the first time the poor boy had not spoken to me in the third person!

The Canadian and I took him up, and rubbed his contracted arms till he became sensible. Then that eternal classifier murmured in a halting voice: "Class of cartilaginous fish, order of chondropterygians, with fixed gills, suborder of selacians, family of rays, genus of torpedoes!"

"Yes, my friend," I answered, "it was a torpedo which has left you in such a deplorable state."

"Ah! Monsieur, may believe me," answered Conseil, "but I will get my revenge on the animal."

"How?"

"I will eat it."

And that is what he did, but it was purely for spite, for frankly, it was as tough as leather. The unfortunate Conseil had attacked an electric ray of the most dangerous kind, the cumana. This odd animal, in an excellent conductor like water, strikes fish at several meters distance, so great is the power of its electric organ, the two principal surfaces of which do not measure less than twenty-seven square feet.

The next day, April 12, the *Nautilus* approached the Dutch coast, near the mouth of the Maroni. There several groups of sea-cows herded together; they were manatees, that, like the dugong and the stellera, belong to the sirenian order. These beautiful animals, peaceable and inoffensive, from six to seven meters in length, weigh at least four thousand kilograms. I told Ned Land and Conseil that provident nature had assigned an important role to these mammals. Indeed, they, like the seals, are designed to graze on the submarine prairies, and thus destroy the accumulation of weed that obstructs the tropical rivers.

"And do you know," I added, "what has been the result since men have almost entirely annihilated this useful race? That the putrified weeds have poisoned the air, and the poisoned air causes the yellow fever, that desolates these beautiful countries. Poisonous vegetations have multiplied under the torrid seas, and illness has irresistibly spread from the mouth of the Rio de la Plata to Florida!

"If we are to believe Toussenel, this plague is nothing to what it would be if the seas were cleared of whales and seals. Then, infested with poulps, jellyfish, and cuttlefish, they would become immense centers of infection, since their waves would not possess 'these vast stomachs that God had charged to scour the surface of the seas.'"

However, without disputing these theories, the crew of the *Nautilus* took possession of half a dozen manatees. They provisioned the larders with excellent flesh, superior to beef and veal. This sport was not interesting. The manatees allowed themselves to be hit without defending themselves. Several thousand kilos of meat were stored up on board destined to be dried.

On this day, a singular method of fishing was used, and the stores of the *Nautilus* were increased, since these seas were so full of game. The nets caught in their meshes a number of fish whose heads terminated in an oval plaque with fleshy edges. They were echeneides belonging to the third family of sub-brachian malacopterygiens; their flattened discs where composed of transverse movable cartilaginous plates, by which the animal was able to create a vacuum, and so to adhere to any object like a cupping-glass or leech.

The remora that I had observed in the Mediterranean belongs to this species. But the one of which we are speaking was the *Echeneis osteochera,* peculiar to this sea. As they were caught, they were placed in vats of water.

The fishing over, the *Nautilus* neared the coast. Here a number of sea-turtles were sleeping on the surface of the water. It would have been difficult to capture these precious reptiles, for the least noise awakens them, and their solid shell is proof against the harpoon. But the echeneis effects their capture with extraordinary precision and certainty. This animal is, indeed, a living fishhook, which would make the fortune of an inexperienced fisherman. The crew of the *Nautilus* tied a ring to the tail of these fish, so large as not to encumber their movements, and to this ring a long cord, lashed to the ship's side by the other end. The echeneids, thrown into the sea, directly began their game, and fixed themselves to the breastplate of the turtles. Their tenacity was such, that they were torn apart rather than let go their hold. The men hauled them on board, and with them the turtles to which they adhered.

They took also several cacouannes a meter long, which weighed 200 kilos. Their carapace, covered with large horny plates, thin, transparent, brown, with white and yellow spots, fetch a good price in the market. Besides, they were excellent from an edible point of view, as well as the fresh turtles, which have an exquisite flavor.

This day's fishing brought to a close our stay on the shores of the Amazon, and by nightfall the *Nautilus* had regained the high seas.

---

[1]A fact that Verne employed in the surprise ending of his novel, *The Chancellor* (1875). RM

◄ CHAPTER XVIII ►

THE SQUIDS

or several days the *Nautilus* kept well off from the American coast. Evidently it did not wish to risk the waters of the Gulf of Mexico, or of the Caribbean. It was not that there was insufficient water under the keel, since the average depth in these seas is 1800 meters, but, probably, that this region, with so many islands and so frequented by ships, was inconvenient for Captain Nemo.

April 16th, we sighted Martinique and Guadaloupe from a distance of about thirty miles. I saw their tall peaks for an instant.

The Canadian, who counted on carrying out his projects in the Gulf, by either landing, or hailing one of the numerous boats that coast from one island to another, was quite disheartened. Flight would have been quite practicable, if Ned Land had been able to take possession of the boat without the captain's knowledge. But in the open sea it could not be thought of.

The Canadian, Conseil, and I, had a long conversation on this subject. For six months we had been prisoners on board the *Nautilus.* We had travelled 17,000 leagues; and, as Ned Land said, there was no reason why it should not come to an end. He made an unexpected proposal. He suggested that I put this question to Captain Nemo point-blank: Did the captain plan to keep us on board indefinitely?

The idea seemed unwise; to me, it seemed doomed to failure. We could hope nothing from the Captain of the *Nautilus,* but only from ourselves. Besides, for some time past he had become graver, more retired, less sociable. He seemed to shun me. I met him rarely. Formerly, he was pleased to explain the submarine marvels to me; now, he left me to my studies, and came no more to the salon.

What change had come over him? For what cause? I had done nothing for him to reproach me for. Perhaps our presence on board had begun to disturb him? Even then, I had no reason to hope that the man would set us free.

I asked Ned to let me think things over. If this plan did not succeed, it would arouse his suspicions, make our situation difficult, and hinder the Canadian's plans. I must add that I could not use our physical condition as an argument. Except for the ordeal beneath the ice shelf at the South Pole, we had never been in better health, neither Ned, Conseil nor I. The healthy food, the salubrious atmosphere, the regularity of our lives, and the uniformity of temperature, kept all maladies away. And for a man who had forsaken all memories of the earth, for Captain Nemo, whose home this was, who could come and go as he pleased, who took his own mysterious paths, I could understand such an existence. But we—we had not broken with humanity. For my part, I did not wish to bury with me my curious and novel studies.

I had now the right to write the true book of the sea; and this book, sooner or later, I wished to see daylight.

Meanwhile, in the waters of the Antilles, ten meters below the surface, by the open panels, what interesting things I had to enter on my daily notes! There were, among other zoöphytes, "galleys" or Portuguese men-of-war—known under the name of *Physalis pelagica,* a sort of large oblong bladder, with mother-of-pearl tints, holding out their membranes to the wind, and letting their blue tentacles float like threads of silk; charming jellyfish to the eye, real nettles to the touch, that distil a corrosive fluid. Among the articulata there were annelides, sea-worms, a meter and a half long, furnished with a pink horn, and with 1700 locomotive organs, that writhe through the waters, and throw out in passing all the colors of the solar spectrum. There were, in the fish category, some Malabar rays, enormous gristly things, ten feet long, weighing 600 pounds, the pectoral fin triangular in the middle of a slightly humped back, the eyes fixed in the extremities of the face, at the back of the head. They floated like wreckage and sometimes covered our window like an opaque shutter. There were American triggerfish, which nature has dressed in black and white; long, fleshy gobies, with yellow fins and prominent jaws; mackerel six decimeters long, with short, pointed teeth, covered with small scales, belonging to the albacore species. Then, in swarms, appeared grey mullet, covered with stripes of gold from the head to the tail, beating their resplendent fins, like masterpieces of jewellery. Consecrated formerly to Diana, these mullet were particularly sought after by rich Romans, and of which the proverb says, "Whoever takes them does not eat them." Lastly, pomacanthe dorees, ornamented with emerald bands, dressed in velvet and silk, passed before our eyes like Veronese lords; spurred spari passed with a stroke of their powerful thoracic fins; clupanodons fifteen inches long, enveloped in their phosphorescent light; ordinary mullet beat the sea with their large, fat tails; red coregoni seemed to cut the waves with their sharp pectoral fins; and silvery selenes, worthy of the name, rose on the horizon of the waters like so many moons with whitish rays.

What other marvellous and new specimens might I have observed if the *Nautilus* had not been sinking little by little into deeper water! The inclined planes drew it to depths of 2000 and 3500 meters. Animal life was represented only by sea lilies, starfish, charming pentacrines with medusa heads, with a straight stalk supporting a little chalice, trochi, some "bleeding teeth," and fissurellas, a coastal mollusk of huge size.

April 20th, we had risen to a mean depth of 1500 meters. The land nearest us then was the archipelago of the Bahamas. They were set before us like cobblestones. There rose high submarine cliffs, walls formed of worn blocks arranged like bricks, between which were black holes which the rays from our electric light could not illuminate.

These rocks were covered with large weeds, giant laminariæ and enormous fuci, a perfect tangle of hydrophytes worthy of a world of Titans.

As we talked about these colossal plants, Conseil, Ned and I were led naturally into the subject of gigantic sea animals. One was evidently destined to nourish the other. Nevertheless, as I looked through the window of the nearly motionless *Nautilus,* I saw among the long filaments only the principal articulata of the division of branchipodes, violet sea spiders with long legs, and clios peculiar to the seas of the Antilles.

It was about eleven o'clock when Ned Land drew my attention to a formidable swarming, which was being produced within the large seaweeds.

"Well," I said, "these are proper caverns for octopi, and I should not be astonished to see some of these monsters."

"What!" said Conseil; "squids, real squids, of the cephalopod class?"

"No," I said; "octopi of huge dimensions. But Ned Land is wrong, no doubt; I can see nothing."

"Too bad," replied Conseil, "I would like to come face-to-face with one of the squids

I have heard so much of, and which can drag ships to the bottom of the abyss. The beasts are called krak—"

"Crack is right," said the Canadian ironically.

"Krakens," continued Conseil, finishing his word without noticing the pleasantries of his companion.

"I will never believe that such animals exist," said Ned.

"Why not?" asked Conseil. "We believed in monsieur's narwhal!"

"And we were wrong, Conseil."

"No doubt! but there are others who still believe in it."

"That's probable, Conseil, but for my own part, I've decided not to admit to the existence of these monsters until I have dissected one with my own hands."

"Doesn't monsieur," demanded Conseil, "believe in giant squids?"

"Who the devil does believe in them?" cried the Canadian.

"Many people, friend Ned."

"Not fishermen; scientists, perhaps!"

"Excuse me, Ned, but both fishermen and scientists!" said Conseil, with the most serious air in the world; "I remember perfectly having seen a large vessel drawn under the waves by a cephalopod's arm.

"You saw that?" said the Canadian.

"Yes, Ned."

"With your own eyes?"

"With my own eyes."

"Where, pray, might that be?"

"At St Malo," answered Conseil, imperturbably.

"In the port?" said Ned, ironically.

"No; in a church," replied Conseil.

"In a church!" cried the Canadian.

"Yes; friend Ned. In a picture representing the octopus in questions."

"Good!" said Ned Land, bursting out laughing, "Friend Conseil has been making a joke!"

"He is quite right," I said. "I have heard of this picture; but the subject represented is taken from a legend, and you know what to think of legends in the matter of natural history! Besides, when it is a question of monsters, the imagination is apt to run wild. Not only is it supposed that the octopi can draw down vessels, but a certain Olaüs Magnus speaks of a cephalopod a mile long, that was more like an island than an animal. It is also said that the Bishop of Nidros was building an altar on an immense rock. Mass finished, the rock began to walk, and returned to the sea. The rock was a giant squid."

"Is that all?" asked Ned.

"No, another bishop, Pontoppidan of Bergham, also speaks of an octopus on which a regiment of cavalry could maneuver."

"Those ancient clergymen could tell good stories!" said Ned.

"Lastly, the ancient naturalists speak of monsters whose mouths were like gulfs, and which were too large to pass through the Straits of Gibraltar."

"I don't believe it!" exclaimed Ned.

"But how much of these stories is true?" asked Conseil.

"Nothing, my friends; at least of that which passes the limit of truth and becomes fable or legend. Nevertheless, there must be some ground for the imagination of the story-tellers. One cannot deny that there exists a large species of octopi and squid, smaller, however, than the whales. Aristotle has stated the dimensions of a squid as five cubits, or 3.10 meters. Our fishermen frequently see some that are more than 1.80 meters long. Some skeletons of squids are preserved in the museums of Trieste and Montpelier, that measure two meters in length.

Besides, according to the calculations of some naturalists, one of these animals, only six feet long, would have tentacles twenty-seven feet long. That would suffice to make a formidable monster.''

"Do they fish for them in these days?" asked Ned.

"If they do not fish for them, sailors see them at least. One of my friends, Captain Paul Bos of Havre, has often affirmed that he met one of these monsters, of colossal dimensions, in the Indian Ocean. But the most astonishing fact, and which does not permit of the denial of the existence of these gigantic animals, happened some years ago, in 1861.

"What is the fact?" asked Ned Land.

"This is it. In 1861, to the north-east of Teneriffe, very nearly in the same latitude we are in now, the crew of the despatch-boat *Alecton* perceived a monstrous squid swimming in the water. Captain Bouguer went near to the animal, and attacked it with harpoons and guns, without much success, for balls and harpoons simply passed through the soft flesh as though through a jelly. After several fruitless attempts, the crew tried to pass a slip-knot round the body of the mollusk. The noose slipped as far as the caudal fins, and there stopped. They tried then to haul it on board, but its weight was so considerable that the tightness of the cord separated the tail from the body, and, deprived of this ornament, he disappeared under the water.''

"Indeed! is that a fact?"

"An indisputable fact, my good Ned. They proposed to name this poulp 'Bouguer's squid.'''

"What length was it?" asked the Canadian.

"Did it not measure about six meters?" said Conseil, who posted at the window, was examining anew the irregular windings of the cliff.

"Precisely," I replied.

"Its head," rejoined conseil, "was it not crowned with eight tentacles, that beat the water like a nest of serpents?"

"Precisely."

"Had not its eyes, placed at the back of its head, considerable development?"

"Yes, Conseil."

"And was not its mouth like a parrot's beak, but one of formidable size?"

"Exactly, Conseil."

"Very well! no offense to monsieur," he replied, quietly, "if this is not Bouguer's squid, it is, at least, one of its brothers."

I looked at Conseil. Ned Land hurried to the window.

"What a horrible beast!" he cried.

I looked in my turn, and could not repress a gesture of disgust. Before my eyes was a horrible monster, worthy to figure in the legends of the monstrous.

It was a giant squid of enormous dimensions, being eight meters long. It swam backwards in the direction of the *Nautilus* with great speed, watching us with its enormous staring blue-green eyes. Its eight arms, or rather feet, fixed to its head, that have given the name of cephalopod to these animals, were twice as long as its body, and were twisted like the Furies' hair. One could distinctly see the 250 suckers on the inner side of the tentacles. They were shaped like hollow hemispheres. some of them were sticking to the window, like suction-cups. The monster's mouth, a horned beak like a parrot's, opened and shut vertically. Its tongue was horny and furnished with several rows of pointed teeth. It came out quivering from a veritable pair of shears. What a freak of nature, a bird's beak on a mollusk! Its spindle-like body formed a fleshy mass that might weigh 20,000 to 25,000 kilograms. The color changed with great rapidity, according to the irritation of the animal, it passed successively from livid grey to reddish brown.

What irritated this mollusk? No doubt the presence of the *Nautilus*, more formidable than itself, and on which its suckers or its jaws had no hold. Yet, what monsters these squids are!

what vitality the Creator has given them! what vigor in their movements, seeing that they possess three hearts!

Chance had brought us in presence of this squid, and I did not wish to lose the opportunity of carefully studying this specimen of the cephalopods. I overcame the horror that inspired me; and, taking a pencil, began to draw it.

"Perhaps this is the same which the *Alecton* saw," said Conseil.

"No," replied the Canadian; "for this is whole, and the other had lost its tail!"

"That is no reason," I replied. "The arms and tails of these animals are regenerated; and, in seven years, the tail of Bouguer's squid has no doubt had time to grow."

"Well," answered Ned, "if this isn't the one, maybe it's one of those over there!"

By this time other poulps appeared at the starboard window. I counted seven. They formed a procession after the *Nautilus,* and I heard their beaks gnashing against the iron hull.

I continued my work. These monsters kept pace with such precision, that they seemed unmoving.

I could have traced their outline on the window. Of course, our speed was not great.

Suddenly the *Nautilus* stopped. A shock made it tremble in every member.

"Have we struck anything?" I asked.

"In any case," replied the Canadian, "we shall be free, for we are still floating."

The *Nautilus* was floating, no doubt, but it did not move. The blades of the screw no longer beat the water. A minute passed, Captain Nemo followed by his second-in-command, entered the salon.

I had not seen him for some time. He seemed somber. Without noticing or speaking to us, he went to the panel, looked at the squids and said something to his second-in-command.

The latter went out. Soon the panels were shut. The ceiling was lighted.

I went towards the captain.

"A curious collection of poulps?" I said, feeling like an amateur standing in front of an aquarium.

"Yes, indeed, Mr. Naturalist," he replied; "and we are going to fight them, man to beast."

I looked at him. I thought I had not heard aright.

"Man to beast?" I repeated.

"Yes, sir. The screw is stopped. I think that the horny jaws of one of the squids is entangled in the blades. That is what prevents our moving."

"What are you going to do?"

"Rise to the surface, and slaughter all of this vermin."

"A difficult enterprise."

"Yes, indeed. The electric bullets are powerless against the soft flesh, where they do not find resistance enough to go off. But we shall attack them with the hatchet."

"And the harpoon, sir," said the Canadian, "if you do not refuse my help."

"I will accept it, Master Land."

"We will follow you," I said, and following Captain Nemo, we went towards the central staircase.

There, about ten or twelve men with boarding hatchets were ready for the attack. Conseil and I took two hatchets; Ned Land seized a harpoon.

The *Nautilus* had then risen to the surface. One of the sailors, posted on the top ladder-step, unscrewed the bolts of the hatch. But hardly were the screws loosed, when the hatch rose with great violence, evidently pulled by the suckers of a squid's arm.

Immediately one of these arms slid like a serpent down the opening, while twenty others waved above. With one blow of the axe, Captain Nemo cut this formidable tentacle, that slid wriggling down the ladder.

Just as we were pressing one on the other to reach the platform two other arms, lashing

the air, came down on the seaman placed before Captain Nemo, and lifted him up with irresistible power.

Captain Nemo uttered a cry, and rushed out. We hurried after him.

What a scene! The unhappy man, seized by the tentacle, and fixed to the suckers, was balanced in the air at the caprice of this enormous trunk. He rattled in his throat, he was stifled, he cried, "Help! help!" These words, *spoken in French,* startled me profoundly! I had a fellow-countryman on board, perhaps several! That heartrending cry! I shall hear it all my life.

The unfortunate man was lost. Who could rescue him from that powerful embrace? However, Captain Nemo had rushed to the squid, and with one blow of the axe had cut through one arm. His second-in-command struggled furiously against other monsters that crept up the flanks of the *Nautilus.* The crew fought with their axes. The Canadian, Conseil, and I, buried our weapons in the fleshy masses; a strong smell of musk penetrated the atmosphere. It was horrible!

For one instant, I thought the unhappy man, entangled with the squid, would be torn from its powerful suction. Seven of the eight arms had been cut off. One only wriggled in the air, brandishing the victim like a feather. But just as Captain Nemo and his lieutenant threw themselves on it, the animal ejected a stream of black liquid which was secreted by a sac in the abdomen. We were blinded with it. When the cloud dispersed, the squid had disappeared, and with it my unfortunate countryman!

With what rage we attacked these monsters! Ten or twelve squids now invaded the platform and sides of the *Nautilus.* We rolled pell-mell into the midst of this nest of serpents, that wriggled on the platform in the waves of blood and black ink. It seemed as though these slimy tentacles sprang up like the Hydra's heads, growing back as fast as we cut them off. Ned Land's harpoon, at each stroke, was plunged into the staring green eyes of the squid. But my bold companion was suddenly overturned by the tentacles of a monster he had not been able to avoid.

Ah! how my heart beat with emotion and horror! The formidable beak of the squid was open over Ned Land. The unhappy man would be cut in two. I rushed to his aid. But Captain Nemo was before me; his axe disappeared between the two enormous jaws, and miraculously saved the Canadian; then rising, plunged his harpoon deep into the triple heart of the squid.

"I owed you that!" said the captain to the Canadian.

Ned bowed without replying.

The combat had lasted a quarter of an hour. The monsters, vanquished, mutilated, beaten to death, left us at last, and disappeared under the waves.

Captain Nemo, red with blood, nearly exhausted stood without moving beside the lantern and gazed upon the sea that had swallowed up one of his companions, and great tears gathered in his eyes.

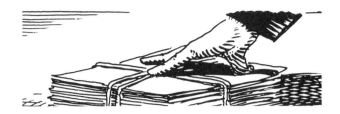

◄ CHAPTER XIX ►

THE GULF STREAM

his terrible scene of the 20th of April none of us can ever forget. I have written it under the influence of violent emotion. Since then I have tried to revise the recital. I have read it to Conseil and to the Canadian. They found it exact as to facts, but insufficient as to effect. To paint such pictures, one must have the pen of the most illustrious of our poets, the author of *The Toilers of the Sea,* Victor Hugo.

I have said that Captain Nemo wept while watching the waves; his grief was great. It was the second companion he had lost since our arrival on board. And what a death! That friend, crushed, stifled, bruised by a formidable arms of a squid, pounded by its iron jaws, would not rest with his comrades in the peaceful coral cemetery!

In the midst of the struggle, it was the despairing cry uttered by the unfortunate man that had torn my heart. The poor Frenchman, forgetting his artificial language, had taken to his own mother tongue, to utter a last appeal. Among the crew of the *Nautilus,* associated with the body and soul of the Captain, recoiling like him from all contact with men, I had a fellow countryman. Did he alone represent France in this mysterious association, evidently composed of individuals of various nationalities? It was one of those insoluble problems that rose up unceasingly before my mind.

Captain Nemo entered his room, and I saw him no more for some time. But that he was sad, despairing and irresolute I could see by the vessel, of which he was the soul, and which reflected all his impressions. The *Nautilus* did not keep on in its settled course; it floated about like a corpse at the will of the waves. Although the screw had been repaired, it was seldom used. The submarine went at random. The captain could not tear himself away from the scene of the last struggle, from this sea that had devoured one of his men.

Ten days passed thus. It was not till the 1st of May that the *Nautilus* resumed its northerly course, after having sighted the Bahamas at the mouth of the Bahama Channel. We were then following the largest current of the sea, a real river that has its own banks, its own fish, and its own temperatures. I mean the Gulf Stream.

It is really a river, that flows freely to the middle of the Atlantic, and whose waters do not mix with the ocean waters. It is a salt river, salter than the surrounding sea. Its mean depth is 3000 feet, its mean breadth 70 miles. In certain places the current flows with the speed of four kilometers an hour. The volume of its waters is more considerable than that of all the rivers of the globe combined. The true source of the Gulf Stream, discovered by Commander Maury, its point of departure, if you will, is situated in the Bay of Biscay. There, its waters, still without temperature or color, begin to form. It descends to the south, as far as equatorial Africa, warming its waves in the rays of the torrid zone, crosses the Atlantic, reaches Cape San Roque on the Brazilian coast, and splits into two branches. One is bathed again by the warm molecules of the Caribbean. There, the Gulf Stream, charged with maintaining a temperature equilibrium and with mixing the waters of tropical and northern seas, takes on its role of stabilizer. Brought to a white heat in the Gulf of Mexico, it moves north along the coast of America, as far as Newfoundland, where it is deflected by the pressure of the cold current from the Davis Straits. It resumes its oceanic route, following one of the Great Circles of the globe on a loxodromic, or rhumb line, dividing into two arms at the 43rd parallel. One, aided by the northeast trade winds, returns to the Bay of Biscay and the Azores;

the other, after warming the shores of Ireland and Norway, goes beyond Spitzbergen, where its temperature drops to 4° Centigrade (40 Fahrenheit) and it empties into the open sea at the pole. It was on this ocean river that the *Nautilus* then sailed. Upon leaving the Bahama Channel, 40 leagues wide and 350 meters deep, the Gulf Stream moves at a rate of eight kilometers an hour. This speed slows gradually as it moves north, a regularity we hope persists, since, as has been remarked, if its speed or direction were modified, the climate of Europe would be perturbed with incalculable consequences.

Towards noon, I was on the platform with Conseil. I told him all the particulars relative to the Gulf Stream. When my explanations were finished, I invited him to plunge his hand into the current.

Conseil obeyed, and was astonished to discover a sensation of neither hot nor cold.

"The reason," I told him, "is that the temperature of the water of the Gulf Stream, when it leaves the Gulf of Mexico, is little different than that of blood. The Gulf Stream is a vast heater that permits the coasts of Europe to be eternally robed in green. And, if we are to believe Maury, the heat of this current, if totally used, would release enough calories to keep molten a river of iron the size of the Amazon or Missouri."

At that moment, the speed of the Gulf Stream was 2.25 meters per second. The current is so distinct from the surrounding sea, that its waters are compressed and rise a little higher than the cold water. Its waters are darker and richer in marine salts, the pure indigo of its waves can be distinguished from the green of its environment. The line of demarcation is so clear, that the *Nautilus,* as far north as the Carolinas, had its spur in the waves of the Gulf Stream, while its propeller still beat the water of the ocean.

This current carried with it all kinds of living things. Argonauts, so common in the Mediterranean, were there in quantities. The most remarkable of the cartilaginous variety were the rays, whose slender tails form nearly the third part of the body, and that looked like large lozenges twenty-five feet long; also, small sharks a meter long, with large heads, short rounded muzzles, pointed teeth in several rows, and whose bodies seemed covered with scales.

Among the bony fish I noticed some grey wrasse, peculiar to these waters; black giltheads, whose eye shone like fire; sciaenidae, or croakers, a meter long, with large snouts thickly set with little teeth, that uttered little cries; black centronotes, which I have mentioned before; blue coryphænes, in gold and silver; parrotfish, like the rainbows of the ocean, that could rival in color the most beautiful tropical birds; blennies with triangular heads; bluish rhombs, or garfish, destitute of scales; batrachoides, or toadfish, covered with yellow transversal bands in the shape of a Greek τ; masses of little gobies spotted with brown; dipterodons with silvery heads and yellow tails; several specimens of salmon; mugilomores, or mullets, slender in shape, shining with a soft light that Lacépède dedicated to his amiable wife; and lastly, a beautiful fish, the American seahorse, that, decorated with all the orders and ribbons, frequents the shores of this great nation, that esteems orders and ribbons so little.

I must add that, during the night, the phosphorescent waters of the Gulf Stream rivalled the electric power of our lantern, especially in the stormy weather that threatened us so frequently.

May 8th, we were passing Cape Hatteras, at the parallel of North Carolina. The width of the Gulf Stream there is seventy-five miles, and its depth 210 meters. The *Nautilus* still went at random; all supervision seemed banished from on board. I thought that, under these circumstances, escape would be possible. Indeed, the inhabited shores offered everywhere an easy refuge. The sea was incessantly ploughed by the numerous steamers that ply between New York or Boston and the Gulf of Mexico, and overrun day and night by the little schooners coasting about the various parts of the American shore.

We could hope to be picked up. It was a favorable opportunity, notwithstanding the thirty miles that separated the *Nautilus* from the coasts of the Union.

But an unfortunate circumstance thwarted the Canadian's plans: the weather was very bad. We were nearing those shores where tempests are frequent, that country of waterspouts and cyclones actually created by the current of the Gulf Stream. To tempt the sea in a fragile boat was begging certain destruction. Ned was forced to agree. He fretted, seized with a nostalgia that only flight could cure.

"Sir," he said that day to me, "this must come to an end. I must make a clean breast of it. This Nemo is leaving land behind and is going up to the north. But I declare to you, I have had enough of the South Pole, and I will not follow him to the North."

"What is to be done, Ned, since flight is impracticable just now?"

"We must speak to the captain," said he, "you said nothing when we were in your native seas. I will speak, now that we are in mine. When I think that before long the *Nautilus* will be near Nova Scotia, and that near Newfoundland is a large bay, and into that bay the St. Lawrence empties itself, and that the St. Lawrence is my river, the river that flows by Quebec my native town—when I think of this, I feel furious, it makes my hair stand on end. Sir, I would rather throw myself into the sea! I will not stay here! I am stifled!"

The Canadian was evidently losing all patience. His vigorous nature could not stand this prolonged imprisonment. His face altered daily; his temper became more surly. I knew what he must suffer, for I was seized with nostalgia myself. Nearly seven months had passed without our having had any news from land; Captain Nemo's isolation, his altered spirits, especially since the fight with the squids, his taciturnity, all made me view things in a different light. I no longer had the enthusiasm of the early days. One had to be Flemish like Conseil to accept this situation, to live in surroundings reserved for whales and other inhabitants of the sea. Truly, this brave lad, if in place of lungs he would take gills, would make a very handsome fish!

"Well, sir?" said Ned, seeing I did not reply.

"Well, Ned! do you wish me to ask Captain Nemo his intentions concerning us?"

"Yes, sir."

"Although he has already made them known?"

"Yes, I wish it settled finally. Speak for me, and in my name alone, if you like."

"But I so seldom meet him. He avoids me."

"That is one more reason to see him."

"I'll ask him, Ned."

"When?" demanded the Canadian, insistently.

"When I see him."

"Mr. Aronnax, should I go find him myself?"

"No, let me do it. Tomorrow . . . ."

"Today," said Ned Land.

"All right. Today, I'll see him," I answered the Canadian, who, left to his own devices, would certainly have compromised us all.

I remained alone. Now that it had been decided, I resolved to finish it quickly. I like to get things done immediately.

I went to my room. From thence I meant to go to Captain Nemo's. It would not do to let this opportunity of meeting him slip. I knocked at the door. No answer. I knocked again, then turned the handle. The door opened.

I went in.

The captain was there. Bending over his worktable, he had not heard me. Resolved not the leave without having spoken, I approached him. He raised his head quickly, frowned, and said roughly, "You here? What do you want?"

"To speak to you, Captain."

"But I am busy, sir; I am working. I leave you at liberty to shut yourself up. Cannot I be allowed the same?"

This reception was not encouraging; but I was determined to see things through.

"Sir," I said coldly, "I have to speak to you on a matter that admits of no delay."

"What is that, sir?" he replied, ironically. "Have you discovered something that has escaped me, or has the sea delivered up any new secrets?"

We were at cross-purposes. But before I could reply, he showed me an open manuscript on his table, and said, in a more serious tone, "Here, Monsieur Aronnax, is a manuscript written in several languages. It contains the sum of my studies of the sea; and, if it please God, it shall not perish with me. This manuscript, signed with my name, completed with the history of my life,[1] will be shut up in a little insubmersible case. The last survivor of all of us on board the *Nautilus* will throw this case into the sea, and it will go wherever it is borne by the waves."

This man's name! his history written by himself! His mystery would then be revealed some day. But, at this moment, I saw a way of steering the conversation toward the matter at hand.

"Captain," I said, "I can only approve of this idea that makes you act thus. The result of your studies must not be lost. But the means you employ seem to me to be primitive. Who knows where the winds will carry this case, and in whose hands it will fall? Could you not use some other means? Could not you, or one of your men. . . ."

"Never, sir!" he said, hastily interrupting me.

"But I and my companions are ready to keep this manuscript in store; and, if you will put us at liberty. . . ."

"At liberty!" said the captain, rising.

"Yes, sir; that is the subject on which I wish to question you. For seven months we have been here on board, and I ask you today, in the name of my companions, and in my own, if your intention is to keep us here always?"

"Monsieur Aronnax, I will answer you today as I did seven months ago: Whoever enters the *Nautilus* must never quit it."

"You impose actual slavery on us!"

"Give it whatever name you please."

"But everywhere the slave has the right to regain his liberty. And by any means necessary!"

"Who denies you this right? Have I ever tried to chain you with an oath?"

He looked at me with his arms crossed.

"Sir," I said, "to return a second time to this subject will be neither to your nor to my taste; but, as we have entered upon it, let us go through with it. I repeat, it is not only myself whom it concerns. Study is to me a relief, a diversion, a passion that could make me forget everything. Like you, I am willing to live in obscurity, in the frail hope of bequeathing one day, to future time, the result of my labors, inside a hypothetical container consigned to the hazards of the waves and winds. In a word, I admire you, and could without displeasure follow you in a life of which I only understand certain points. But it is the other aspects of your life which are surrounded by complications and mysteries of which I and my companions are not part. But the, when our hearts could go out to you, touched by your sorrows or inspired by acts of genius or courage, we were forced to suppress even the smallest tokens of sympathy and admiration which is natural in the presence of something beautiful and good, whether it be in a friend or an enemy. Well then! it is the feeling that we are strangers to everything that touches you, that makes our position unacceptable, impossible, not only for me, but impossible for Ned Land most of all.

But it is otherwise with Ned Land. Every man, worthy of the name, deserves some consideration. Have you thought that love of liberty, hatred of slavery, can give rise to schemes of revenge in a nature like the Canadian's? That he could think, attempt, and try. . . ."

I was silenced; Captain Nemo rose.

"Whatever Ned Land thinks of, attempts, or tries, what does it matter to me? I did not seek him! It is not for my pleasure that I keep him on board! As for you, Monsieur Aronnax, you are one of those who can understand everything, even silence. I have nothing more to say to you. Let this first time you have come to talk of this subject be the last; the next time I will not listen to you."

I retired. Our situation was critical. I related my conversation to my two companions.

"We know now," said Ned, "that we can expect nothing from this man. The *Nautilus* is nearing Long Island. We will escape, whatever the weather may be."

But the sky became more and more threatening. Symptoms of a hurricane became manifest. The atmosphere was becoming white and misty. On the horizon fine streaks of cirrus clouds were succeeded on the horizon by masses of nimbocumulus. Other low clouds passed swiftly by. The swollen sea rose in huge billows. The birds disappeared, with the exception of the petrels, those friends of the storm. The barometer fell noticeably, and indicated the extreme tension of the atmosphere. The mixture of the storm glass was decomposed under the influence of the electricity that pervaded the atmosphere. At struggle of the elements was approaching.

The tempest burst on the 18th of May, just as the *Nautilus* was floating off Long Island, some miles from the harbor of New York. I can describe this strife of the elements for, instead of fleeing to the depths of the sea, Captain Nemo, by an unaccountable caprice, decided to brave it at the surface.

The wind blew from the south-west at first, blowing freshly. It began at about five meters a second, and by three o'clock it was blowing at 25 meters a second.

Captain Nemo, unshakable during the squalls, had taken his place on the platform. He had made himself fast, to prevent being washed overboard by the monstrous waves that broke over the deck. I had hoisted myself up, and made myself fast also, dividing my admiration between the tempest and this extraordinary man who was defying it.

The raging sea was swept by huge cloud-drifts, which were actually saturated with the waves. I no longer saw the small intermediary waves that form in the hollows between the larger crests. Nothing but long, murky undulations, so compact that their crests never broke. Their height was increasing. They urged each other on. The *Nautilus,* sometimes lying on its side, sometimes standing up like a mast, rolled and pitched terribly.

About five o'clock a torrent of rain fell, that lulled neither sea nor wind. The hurricane blew nearly forty-five meters a second. It is under these conditions that it overturns houses, breaks iron gates, and displaces twenty-four pound guns. However, the *Nautilus,* in the midst of the tempest, confirmed the words of a clever engineer, "There is no well-constructed hull that cannot defy the sea!" This was not a resisting rock, which the storm could destroy, it was a steel spindle, obedient and movable, without rigging or masts, that braved its fury with impunity.

However, I watched these raging waves carefully. They measured five meters in height, and 150 to 175 meters long, and their speed of propagation was five meters in height, fifteen meters per second, half the speed of the wind. Their bulk and power increased with the depth of the water. I understood the role waves play, imprisoning air in their sides and forcing it into the depths of the sea, where life is nurtured by the oxygen. Their extreme force of pressure—it has been calculated—is more than 3000 kilograms per square foot against whatever surface they strike. Such waves as these at the Hebrides, have displaced masses weighing 84,000 lbs. They are those which, caused by the earthquake of December 23, 1864, after destroying the town of Tokyo, in Japan, crossed the Pacific at 700 kilometers an hour and broke the same day on the shores of America.

The intensity of the tempest increased with the night. The barometer, as in 1860 at Reunion during a cyclone, fell to 710 millimeters. At the close of day, I saw a large vessel pass along the horizon struggling painfully. She was trying to lie to under half steam, to keep up above the waves. It was probably one of the steamers of the line from New York to Liverpool, or Le Havre. It soon disappeared in the gloom.

At ten o'clock in the evening the sky was on fire. The atmosphere was streaked with vivid lightning. I could not bear the brightness of it; while the captain, looking at it, seemed to envy

the spirit of the tempest. A terrible noise filled the air, a complex noise, made up of the howls of the crushed waves, the roaring of the wind, and the claps of thunder. The wind veered suddenly to all points of the horizon; and the cyclone, rising in the east, returned after passing by the north, west, and south, in the counterclockwise course pursued by the circular storms of the southern hemisphere.

Ah, that Gulf Stream! It deserves its name of the King of Tempests! It is that which causes those formidable cyclones, by the difference of temperature between its air and its currents.

A shower of flame had succeeded the rain. The drops of water were changed to sharp spikes of fire. One would have thought that Captain Nemo was courting a death worthy of himself, a death by lightning. As the *Nautilus,* pitching fearfully, raised its steel spur in the air, it seemed to act as a conductor, and I saw long sparks burst from it.

Crushed and without strength, I crawled to the hatch, opened it, and descended to the salon. The storm was then at its height. It was impossible to stand upright in the interior of the *Nautilus.* Captain Nemo came down about midnight. I heard the reservoirs filling by degrees, and the *Nautilus* sank slowly beneath the waves.

Through the open windows in the salon I saw large terrified fish, passing like phantoms in the fiery water. Some were struck before my eyes!

The *Nautilus* was still descending. I thought that at about fifteen meters deep we should find calm. But no! the upper levels were too violently agitated for that. We had to seek repose at more than fifty meters in the bowels of the deep.

But there, what quiet, what silence, what peace! Who could have told that such a hurricane had been let loose on the surface of that ocean?

---

[1]The secret of Captain Nemo's life was finally revealed in the *The Mysterious Island* (1875). R.M.

◄ CHAPTER XX ►
AT LATITUDE 47° 24ʹ AND LONGITUDE 17° 28ʹ

In consequence of the storm, we had been driven eastward once more. All hope of escape on the shores of New York or the St. Lawrence had faded away; and poor Ned, in despair, had isolated himself like Captain Nemo. Conseil and I, however, never left each other.

I said that the *Nautilus* had gone toward the east. I should have said (to be more exact), the northeast. For some days, it wandered first on the surface, and then beneath it, amid those fogs so dreaded by sailors. These are due principally to melting ice, which fills the air with humidity. How many ships have been lost on these shores, while seeking the uncertain lights of the coast! What accidents are due to these thick fogs! What shocks upon these reefs when the wind drowns the breaking of the waves! What collisions between vessels, in spite of their warning lights, whistles, and alarm bells!

The bottoms of these seas look like a field of battle, where still lie all the conquered of the ocean; some old and already encrusted, others fresh and reflecting from their iron bands and copperplates the brilliancy of our lantern.

Many of these had gone down with all hands, including immigrants, at these points all indicated as statistically dangerous: Cape Race, Saint Paul Island, the Strait of Belle Isle, the estuary of the Saint Lawrence! And in the last few years only, how many victims have been listed in the funeral annals of the lines of the Royal Mail, Inman, and Montreal: the *Solway, Isis, Paramatta, Hungarian, Canadian, Anglo-Saxon, Humboldt,* and the *United States,* all run aground; the *Arctic,* and the *Lyonnais,* sunk in collisions; the *President, Pacific,* and the *City of Glasgow,* vanished for unknown reasons; somber debris in the middle of which cruised the *Nautilus,* as though passing in review of the dead!

On the 15th of May we were at the extreme south of the Grand Bank of Newfoundland. This bank consists of alluvia, or large mounds of organic matter, brought either from the Equator by the Gulf Stream, or from the North Pole by the counter current of cold water which skirts the American coast. There also are heaped up those erratic blocks which are carried along by the broken ice. Close by, a vast charnel-house of fish, mollusks, and zoöphytes, which perish here by millions.

The depth of the sea is not great at Newfoundland—not more than some hundreds of fathoms; but towards the south is a depression of 3000 meters. There the Gulf Stream widens. It is a blossoming of its waters. It loses some of its speed and some of its temperature, and it becomes a sea.

Among the fish frightened by the passage of the *Nautilus,* I noticed a cyclopterus a meter long, with a blackish back and orange stomach, which sets for its cousins a very poor example of marital fidelity; an unernack of great size, a kind of emerald moray, that makes an excellent dish; big-eyed karraks, with heads that resemble dogs; blennies, oviparous like snakes; gobies *boulerots* or black gudgeons two decimeters long; grenadiers with long tails, brilliant with a silver sheen, a fast fish that had ventured far from its arctic waters.

The nets caught a fish hardy, audacious, vigorous, well-muscled, and armed with spikes on the head and needles on the fins, a veritable scorpion two or three meters long; the arch enemy of blennies, cod and salmon. It was the bull-head of the northern seas, with lumpy brown body and red fins. The fishermen of the *Nautilus* had trouble with this animal, which, thanks to its gill-covers, can preserve its respiratory organs from drying in contact with the air, and can live several hours out of the water.

I list here—for the record—the bosquians, little fish that accompany ships in the arctic seas; sharp-snouted bleaks, peculiar to the northern Atlantic; hog-fish; and finally the gadidae, whose principal species is the cod, which we discovered in their preferred waters, the inexhaustible Grand Bank of Newfoundland.

One might call cod mountain-fish, since Newfoundland is but the top of an undersea mountain. As the *Nautilus* opened their close-pressed ranks, Conseil made this observation:

"These are cod?" he said, "but I believed that cod were flat, like flounders or sole."

"Naive boy!" I cried, "cod are only flat in a grocery store, where they are opened and spread out. In the water, they are spindle-shaped fish like the mullet, perfectly formed for swimming."

"I will believe monsieur," answered Conseil. "What swarms, what masses!"

"Yes, my friend, and there would be many more if not for their enemies, the hog-fish and man! Do you know how many eggs have been counted in only one female?"

"I will pick a good number," answered Conseil: "five hundred thousand."

"Eleven million, my friend."

"Eleven million! Before I will accept such a number, I will count them myself."

"Go ahead and count, Conseil. But it would be easier to believe me. The French, Americans, English, Danish, and Norwegians all hunt cod by the thousands. They consume prodigious quantities, and without the astonishing fecundity of this fish, the seas would soon be depopulated of it. In England and America alone, five thousand ships with 75 thousand seamen are employed in cod-fishing. Each ship returns with an average 40 thousand fish, or 25 million altogether. On the coasts of Norway, the results are similar."

"Well," answered Conseil, "I will trust monsieur. I will not count them."

"What?"

"The eleven million eggs. But may I make one remark?"

"What's that?"

"If all these eggs were to hatch, only four codfish would suffice to feed England, America and Norway."

While we were skimming the bottom of the Newfoundland bank, I saw perfectly the long lines, armed with two hundred hooks, which each boat sends down by the dozens. Each line was held down at one end by a small anchor, and held at the surface by a string attached to a cork buoy. The *Nautilus* maneuvered adroitly in the midst of that undersea network.

We did not stay long in those frequented regions. We continued up to 42° north latitude. This is the latitude of Saint John, in Newfoundland, and Heart's Content, where the transatlantic cable ends.

The *Nautilus,* instead of continuing north, changed its direction to the east, as if to follow the telegraphic plateau on which rested the cable, and where multiple soundings have measured with extreme exactness the relief of the seafloor.

It was on the 17th of May, about 500 miles from Heart's Content, at a depth of more than 2800 meters, that I saw the electric cable lying on the bottom. Conseil, to whom I had not mentioned it, thought at first that it was a gigantic sea-serpent and was about to classify it, as usual. But I undeceived the worthy fellow, and by way of consolation related several particulars in the laying of this cable.

The first one was laid in the years 1857 and 1858; but, after transmitting about 400 telegrams, would not act any longer. In 1863, the engineers constructed another one, measuring 3400 kilometers in length, and weighing 4500 tons, which was carried on the *Great Eastern.* This attempt also failed.

On the 25th of May the *Nautilus,* being at a depth of more than 3836 meters, was on the precise spot where the rupture occurred which ruined the earlier enterprise. It was within 638 miles of the coast of Ireland. At half-past two in the afternoon, they discovered that communication with Europe had ceased. The electricians on board resolved to cut the cable before fishing it up, and at eleven o'clock at night they had recovered the damaged part. They spliced it, and it was once more submerged. But some days later it broke again, and could not be recovered from the depths.

The Americans, however, were not discouraged. Cyrus Field, the bold promoter of the enterprise, at the risk of all his own fortune, set a new subscription afoot, which was at once purchased, and another cable was constructed on better principles. The bundles of conducting wires were each enveloped in gutta-percha, and protected by a wadding of various textiles, contained in a metallic covering. The *Great Eastern* sailed on the 13th of July 1866.

The operation worked well. Still, one incident occurred. Several times in unrolling the cable they observed that nails had been recently forced into it, evidently with the motive of destroying it. Captain Anderson, the officers, and engineers, consulted together, and had it posted up that if the offender was surprised on board, he would be thrown without further trail into the sea. From that time the criminal attempt was never repeated.

On the 23rd of July the *Great Eastern* was not more than 500 miles from Newfoundland, when they telegraphed from Ireland news of the armistice concluded between Prussia and Austria after the battle of Sadowa. On the 27th, in the midst of heavy fogs, they reached the port of Heart's Content. The enterprise was successfully terminated; and for its first dispatch, young America addressed old Europe in these words of wisdom so rarely understood— "Glory to God in the highest, and on earth peace, goodwill towards men."[1]

I did not expect to find the electric cable in its pristine state, such as it was on leaving the manufactory. The long serpent, covered with the remains of shells, bristling with foraminiferæ, was encrusted with a kind of rocky coating which served as a protection against all boring mollusks. It lay quietly sheltered from the motions of the sea, and under a favorable pressure for the transmission of the electric spark which passes from Europe to America in .32 or thirty-two hundredths of a second. Doubtless this cable will last for a great length of time, for they find that the gutta-percha covering is improved by the sea-water.

Besides, on this level, so well chosen, the cable is never so deeply submerged as to cause it to break. The *Nautilus* followed it to the lowest depth, which was more than 4431 meters, and there it lay without any anchorage. And then we reached the spot where the accident had taken place in 1863.

The bottom of the ocean there formed a valley about 120 kilometers broad, in which Mont-Blanc might have been placed without its summit appearing above the waves. This valley is closed at the east by a perpendicular wall more than 2000 meters high. We arrived there on the 28th of May, and the *Nautilus* was then not more than 150 kilometers from Ireland.

Was Captain Nemo going to continue north toward the British Isles? No. To my great surprise he made for the south, once more coming back towards European seas. In rounding the Emerald Isle, I caught a brief sight of Cape Clear, and the light at Fastenet which guides the thousands of vessels leaving Glasgow or Liverpool.

An important question then arose in my mind. Did the *Nautilus* dare venture into the English Channel? Ned Land, who had reappeared since we had been nearing land, did not cease to question me. How could I answer? Captain Nemo remained invisible. After having shown the Canadian a glimpse of American shores, was he going to show me the coast of France?

But the *Nautilus* was still going southward. On the 30th of May, it passed in sight of the Land's End, between the extreme point of England and the Scilly Isles, which were left to starboard.

If he wished to enter the Channel he must go straight to the east. He did not do so.

During the whole of the 31st of May, the *Nautilus* described a series of circles on the water, which greatly interested me. It seemed to be seeking a spot it had some trouble in finding. At noon, Captain Nemo himself came to check the ship's log. He spoke no word to me, but seemed gloomier than ever. What could sadden him thus? Was it his proximity to European shores? Had he some recollections of his abandoned country? If not, what did he feel? Remorse or regret? For a long while this thought haunted my mind, and I had a kind of presentiment that before long chance would betray the Captain's secrets.

The next day, the 31st of June, the *Nautilus* continued the same process. It was evidently seeking some particular spot in the ocean. Captain Nemo took the sun's altitude as he had done the day before. The sea was beautiful, the sky clear. About eight miles to the east, a large steam vessel could be discerned on the horizon. No flag fluttered from its mast, and I could not discover its nationality.

Some minutes before the sun passed the meridian, Captain Nemo took his sextant, and watched with great attention. The perfect rest of the water greatly helped the operation. The *Nautilus* was motionless; it neither rolled nor pitched.

I was on the platform when the altitude was taken, and the Captain pronounced these words: "It is here."

He turned and went below. Had he seen the vessel which was changing its course and seemed to be nearing us? I could not tell.

I returned to the salon. The panels closed, I heard the hissing of the water in the reservoirs. The *Nautilus* began to sink, vertically, for its screw communicated no motion to it.

Some minutes later it stopped at a depth of more than 833 meters, resting on the seafloor.

The luminous ceiling was darkened, then the panels were opened, and through the glass I saw the sea brilliantly illuminated by the rays of our lanterns for at least half a mile round us.

I looked to the port side, and saw nothing but an immensity of quiet waters.

But to starboard, on the bottom appeared a large protuberance, which at once attracted my attention. One would have thought it a ruin buried under a coating of white shells, much resembling a covering of snow. Upon examining the mass attentively, I could recognize the thick form of a vessel bare of its masts, which must have sunk. It certainly belonged to past times. This wreck, to be thus encrusted with lime, must already be able to count many years passed at the bottom of the ocean.

What was this vessel? Why did the *Nautilus* visit its tomb? Could it have been anything but a shipwreck which had drawn it under the water? I knew not what to think, when near me in a slow voice I heard Captain Nemo say: "At one time this ship was called the *Marseillais.* It carried seventy-four guns, and was launched in 1762. In 1778, the 13th of August, commanded by La Poype-Vertrieux, it fought boldly against the *Preston.* In 1779, on the 4th of July, with Admiral d'Estaing's squadron, it assisted at the taking of Grenada. In 1781, on the 5th of September, it took part in the battle of Comte de Grasse, in Chesapeake Bay. In 1794, the French Republic changed its name. On the 16th of April, in the same year, it joined the squadron of Villaret-Joyeuse, at Brest, being entrusted with the escort of a cargo of wheat coming from America, under the command of Admiral Van Stabel. On the 11th and 12th *Prairial* of Year II, this squadron fell in with an English vessel. Sir, today is the 13th *Prairial,* the 1st of June 1868.[2] Seventy-four years ago, to the day, on this very spot, in latitude 47° 24′, longitude 17° 28′, this vessel, after fighting heroically, losing its three masts, with water in its hold, and a third of its crew disabled, preferred sinking with its 356 sailors to surrendering. Its flag nailed to the poop, it disappeared under the waves to the cry of 'Long live the Republic!'"

"The *Avenger!*" I exclaimed.

"Yes, sir, the *Avenger!* A good name!" muttered Captain Nemo, crossing his arms.

---

[1] Jules Verne himself made a trip to America on the *Great Eastern* in 1867. On the trip he gathered material for *20,000 Leagues.* He was even able to interview Cyrus Field in person. Verne, while in New York, stayed at the same Fifth Avenue Hotel Aronnax did. R.M.

[2] These strange calendar terms are from the Revolutionary Calendar, used in France for a short time following the French Revolution. R.M.

◄ CHAPTER XXI ►

A HECATOMB

aptain Nemo's way of describing this unlooked-for scene, the history of the patriot ship, told at first so coldly, and the emotion with which this strange man pronounced the last words, the name of the *Avenger,* the significance of which could not escape me, all impressed itself deeply on my mind. My eyes did not leave the captain; who, with his hand stretched out to sea, was watching with glowing eyes the glorious wreck. Perhaps I was never to know who he was, from whence he came, or where he was going to, but I saw the *man* moved, as distinct from the scientist. It was no common misanthropy which had shut Captain Nemo and his companions within the *Nautilus,* but a hatred, either monstrous or sublime, which time could never weaken.

Did this hatred still seek for vengeance? The future would soon teach me that.

But the *Nautilus* was rising slowly to the surface of the sea, and the form of the *Avenger* disappeared by degrees from my sight. Soon a slight rolling told me that we were in the open air. At that moment a dull boom was heard. I looked at the captain. He did not move.

"Captain?" said I.

He did not answer. I left him and mounted the platform. Conseil and the Canadian were already there.

"What was that explosion?" I asked.

"It was a gunshot," replied Ned Land.

I looked in the direction of the flagless vessel I had seen earlier. It was nearing the *Nautilus,* and we could see that it was putting on steam. It was within six miles of us.

"What is that ship, Ned?"

"By its rigging, and the height of its lower masts," said the Canadian, "I bet she is a man-of-war. May it reach us; and, if necessary, sink this damned *Nautilus!*"

"Friend Ned," replied Conseil, "what harm can it do to the *Nautilus?* Can it attack it beneath the waves? Can it cannonade us at the bottom of the sea?"

"Tell me, Ned," said I, "can you recognize what country she belongs to?"

The Canadian knitted his eyebrows, dropped his eyelids, and screwed up the corners of his eyes, and for a few moments fixed a piercing look upon the vessel.

"No, sir," he replied; "I cannot tell what nation she belongs to, for she shows no colors. But I can declare she is a man-of-war, for a long pennant flutters from her main-mast."

For a quarter of an hour we watched the ship which was steaming towards us. I could not, however, believe that she could see the *Nautilus* from that distance; and still less, that she could know what this submarine engine was.

Soon the Canadian informed me that she was a large armored two-decker ram. A thick black smoke was pouring from her two funnels. Her sails were so tightly furled, they merged with the outlines of the yards. She showed no flag at her mizzen-peak. The distance prevented us from distinguishing the colors of her pennant, which floated like a thin ribbon.

She advanced rapidly. If Captain Nemo allowed her to approach, there was a chance of salvation for us.

"Sir," said Ned Land, "if that vessel passes within a mile of us I shall throw myself into the sea, and I should advise you to do the same."

I did not reply to the Canadian's suggestion, but continued watching the ship. Whether English, French, American, or Russian, she would be sure to take us in if we could only reach her.

"Monsieur might well recall," said Conseil, "that we have had some experience in swimming. Monsieur can rely upon me to help him, if he decides to follow friend Ned."

Presently white smoke burst from the fore part of the warship; some seconds later the falling shell, splashed at the stern of the *Nautilus*. Shortly afterwards the loud explosion of the gun struck my ear.

"What! They are firing at us!" I exclaimed.

"Brave men!" murmured Ned.

"They do not recognize us as shipwrecked sailors, hanging onto the wreck!"

"If it pleases monsieur . . . Well!" exclaimed Conseil, drying off the water splashed onto him by a second shell, "if it pleases monsieur, they have recognized the narwhal and they are firing at the narwhal."

"But," I exclaimed, "surely they can see that there are men here?"

"It is, perhaps, because of that!" replied Ned Land, looking at me.

A whole flood of light burst upon my mind. Doubtless they knew now how to believe the stories of the pretended monster. No doubt, on board the *Abraham Lincoln,* when the Canadian struck it with the harpoon, Commander Farragut had recognized in the supposed narwhal a submarine vessel, more dangerous than a supernatural cetacean?

Yes, it must have been so; and on every sea they were now seeking this terrible engine of destruction!

Terrible indeed! if, as we supposed, Captain Nemo employed the *Nautilus* in works of vengeance! On the night when we were imprisoned in that cell, in the midst of the Indian Ocean, had he not attacked some vessel? The man buried in the coral cemetery, had he not been a victim of the shock caused by the *Nautilus?* Yes, I repeat, it must be so. One part of the mysterious existence of Captain Nemo had been unveiled; and, if his identity had not been recognized, at least, the nations united against him were no longer hunting a chimerical creature, but a man who had vowed an implacable hatred against them.

All the terrible past rose before me. Instead of meeting friends on board the approaching ship, we could only expect pitiless enemies.

The number of shells falling around us multiplied. Some of them struck the sea and ricochetted, losing themselves in the distance. But none touched the *Nautilus*.

The warship was not more than three miles from us. In spite of the violent cannonade, Captain Nemo did not appear on the platform; but if one of the conical projectiles had struck the hull of the *Nautilus* it would have been fatal.

The Canadian then said, "Sir, we must do all we can to get out of this dilemma. Make a signal! A thousand devils! They will then, perhaps, understand that we are honest folks."

Ned Land took his handkerchief to wave in the air; but he had scarcely displayed it, when he was struck down by an iron hand, and fell, in spite of his great strength, upon the deck.

"Fool!" exclaimed the Captain, "do you wish to be pierced by the spur of the *Nautilus* before it is hurled at this vessel?"

If Captain Nemo was terrible to hear, he was still more terrible to see. His face was deadly pale, under the spasms of his heart, which for an instant it must have ceased to beat. His pupils were fearfully contracted. He did not *speak,* he *roared,* as, with his body thrown forward, he wrung the Canadian's shoulders.

Then, leaving him, and turning to the warship, whose shot was still raining around him, he exclaimed, "Ah, ship of an accursed nation, you know who I am! I do not need your flag to know you! Look! and I will show you mine!"

And on the fore part of the platform Captain Nemo unfurled a black flag, similar to the one he had placed at the South Pole. At that moment, a shot struck the hull of the *Nautilus* obliquely, without piercing it; and, ricocheting past the captain, was lost in the sea.

He shrugged his shoulders; and addressing me, said, "Get below," he said shortly, "you and your companions get below!"

"Sir," I exclaimed, "are you going to attack this vessel?"

"Sir, I am going to sink it."

"You will not do that!"

"I *shall* do it," he replied, coldly. "And I advise you not to judge me, sir. Fate has shown you what you ought not have seen. The attack has begun, my reply will be terrible; go down."

"What is that vessel?"

"You do not know? Very well! so much the better! its nationality to you, at least, will be a secret. Go down!"

We could but obey. About fifteen of the sailors surrounded the captain, looking with implacable hatred at the vessel nearing them. One could feel that the same desire of vengeance animated every soul.

I went down at the moment another projectile struck the hull of the *Nautilus,* and I heard the captain exclaim: "Strike, mad vessel! Shower your useless shot! You will not escape the spur of the *Nautilus!* But it is not here that you shall perish! I would not have your ruins mingle with those of the *Avenger!*"

I reached my room. The captain and his second-in-command had remained on the platform. The screw was set in motion, and the *Nautilus,* moving with great speed, was soon beyond the reach of the ship's guns. But the pursuit continued, and Captain Nemo contented himself with merely keeping his distance.

About four in the afternoon, being no longer able to contain my impatience, I went to the central staircase. The hatch was open, and I ventured on to the platform. The captain was still walking up and down with nervous step. He was looking at the ship, which was five or six miles to leeward. He was going round it like a wild beast, and drawing it eastward, allowing them to pursue. But he did not attack. Perhaps he still hesitated?

I wished to intervene once more. But I had scarcely spoken, when Captain Nemo imposed silence, saying: "I am the law, and I am the judge! I am the oppressed, and there is the oppressor! Through him I have lost all that I loved, cherished, and venerated—country, wife, children, father, and mother. I saw all perish! All that I hate is there! Say no more!"

I cast a last look at the man-of-war, which was putting on steam, and rejoined Ned and Conseil.

"We must escape!" I exclaimed.

"Good!" said Ned. "What is that ship?"

"I do not know, but whatever it is, it will be sunk before night. In any case, it is better to perish with it, than be made accomplices in a retaliation, the justice of which we cannot judge."

"That is my opinion too," said Ned land, coolly. "Let us wait for night."

Night arrived. Deep silence reigned on board. The compass showed that the *Nautilus* had not altered its course. The beating of the screw churned the waves with regularity. It was on the surface, rolling slightly, first to one side, then the other.

My companions and I resolved to fly when the vessel should be near enough either to hear us or to see us; for the moon, which would be full in two or three days, shone brightly. Once on board the ship, if we could not prevent the blow which threatened it, we could, at least, do all that circumstances would allow. Several times I thought the *Nautilus* was preparing for attack; but Captain Nemo contented himself with allowing his adversary to approach, and then fled once more before it.

The first part of the night passed without any incident. We watched for an opportunity for action. We spoke little, for we were too much moved. Ned Land would have thrown himself into the sea, but I forced him to wait. According to my idea, the *Nautilus* would attack the ship at her waterline. To do which she would not need to submerge, and then it would not only be possible, but easy to fly.

At three in the morning, full of uneasiness, I mounted the platform. Captain Nemo had not left it. He was standing at the forepart near his flag, which a slight breeze displayed above his head. He did not take his eyes from the vessel. The intensity of his look seemed to attract, and fascinate, and draw the warship onward more surely than if he had been towing it.

The moon was then passing the meridian. Jupiter was rising in the east. Amid this peaceful scene, sky and ocean rivalled each other in tranquillity, the sea offering to the orbs of night the finest mirror they could ever have in which to reflect their image.

As I thought of the deep calm of these elements, compared with all those passions brooding imperceptibly within the *Nautilus,* I shuddered.

The vessel was within two miles of us. It was ever nearing that phosphorescent light which showed the presence of the *Nautilus.* I could see its green and red lights, and its white lantern hanging from the large mizzenmast. An indistinct glow shone through its rigging, showing that the furnaces were heated to the uttermost. Sheaves of sparks and red ashes flew from the funnels, shining in the atmosphere like stars.

I remained thus until six in the morning, without Captain Nemo noticing me. The ship stood about a mile and a half from us, and with the first light of day the firing began afresh. The moment could not be far off when, the *Nautilus* attacking its adversary, my companions and myself should forever leave this man whom I dared not judge.

I was preparing to go down to remind them, when the second-in-command mounted the platform, accompanied by several sailors. Captain Nemo either did not, or would not, see them. Some steps were taken which might be called "the call to battle stations." They were very simple. The iron railing around the platform was lowered, and the lantern and pilot cages were pushed within the hull until they were flush with the deck. The long surface of the steel cigar no longer offered a single point to hinder its maneuvers.

I returned to the salon. The *Nautilus* still floated; some rays of light were filtering through the liquid enlivened by the red streaks of the rising sun. This dreadful day of the 2nd of June had dawned.

At five o'clock, the log showed that the speed of the *Nautilus* was slackening, and I knew that it was allowing the enemy to draw nearer. Besides, the gunshots were heard more distinctly, and the projectiles, hitting the water, were extinguished with a strange hissing noise.

"My friends," said I, "the moment is come. One grasp of the hand, and may God protect us!"

Ned Land was resolute, Conseil calm, myself so nervous that I knew not how to contain myself.

We all passed into the library; but the moment I pushed the door opening on to the central staircase, I heard the upper hatch close sharply.

The Canadian rushed on to the stairs, but I stopped him. A well-known hissing noise told me that the water was running into the reservoirs, and in a few minutes the *Nautilus* was some meters beneath the surface of the waves.

I understood the maneuver. It was too late to act. The *Nautilus* did not wish to strike at the impenetrable armor-plating, but below the waterline, where the metallic covering no longer protected the ship.

We were again imprisoned, unwilling witnesses of the dreadful drama that was preparing. We had scarcely time to reflect. Taking refuge in my room, we looked at each other without speaking a word. A deep stupor had taken hold of my mind: thought seemed to stand still. I was in that painful state of expectation preceding a dreadful explosion. I waited, I listened, every sense was merged into that of hearing!

The speed of the *Nautilus* was accelerated. It was preparing to ram. The whole ship trembled.

Suddenly I screamed. I felt the shock, but comparatively light. I felt the penetrating power of the steel spur. I heard rattlings and scrapings. But the *Nautilus,* carried along by its powerful propulsion, passed through the mass of the vessel like a needle through sailcloth!

I could stand it no longer. Mad, out of my mind, I rushed from my room into the salon. Captain Nemo was there, mute, gloomy, implacable; he was looking through the port panel. A large mass cast a shadow on the water; and that it might lose nothing of her agony, the *Nautilus* was going down into the abyss with her. Ten meters from me I saw the open hull through which the water was rushing with the noise of thunder, then the double line of guns and the netting. The bridge was covered with black writhing shadows.

The water was rising. The poor creatures were crowding the ratlines, clinging to the masts, struggling under the water. It was a human ant heap overtaken by the sea!

Paralyzed, stiffened with anguish, my hair standing on end, with eyes wide open, panting, without breath, and without voice, I too was watching! An irresistible attraction glued me to the glass!

The enormous vessel sank slowly. The *Nautilus* followed, watching every movement: Suddenly an explosion took place. The air compressed within the hull blew up her decks, as if the magazines had caught fire. The force of the explosion rocked the *Nautilus.*

Then the unfortunate vessel sunk more rapidly. Her topmast, laden with victims, now appeared; then her spars, bending under the weight of men; and last of all, the top of her mainmast. Then the dark mass disappeared, and with it the dead crew, drawn down by the powerful vortex. . . .

I turned to Captain Nemo. That terrible avenger, a perfect archangel of hatred, was still looking. When all was over, he turned to his room, opened the door, and entered. I followed him with my eyes. On the end wall beneath his heroes, I saw the portrait of a woman still young, and two little children. Captain Nemo looked at them for some moments, stretched his arms towards them, and kneeling down burst into deep sobs.

◄ CHAPTER XXII ►

THE LAST WORDS OF CAPTAIN NEMO

he panels had closed on this dreadful vision, but light had not returned to the salon: all was silence and darkness within the *Nautilus.* It was leaving this scene of desolation, a hundred feet beneath the water, with great speed. Whither was it going? To the north or south? Where was the man flying to after such a horrible reprisal?

I had returned to my room, where Ned and Conseil remained silent enough. I felt an insurmountable horror for Captain Nemo. Whatever he had suffered at the hands of these men, he had no right to punish thus. He had made me, if not an accomplice, at least an eyewitness of his vengeance. It was too much.

At eleven the electric light reappeared. I passed into the salon. It was deserted. I consulted the different instruments. The *Nautilus* was flying northward at the rate of twenty-five miles an hour, now on the surface, and now thirty feet below it.

On taking the bearings by the chart, I saw that we were passing the mouth of the Channel, and that our course was hurrying us towards the northern seas at an incomparable speed.

We were travelling so rapidly that I scarcely saw the long-nosed sharks; the hammerheads; the spotted dogfish that frequent these seas; the great sea-eagles; the swarms of seahorses, that resemble knights in a game of chess; eels that writhed like firework serpents; armies of crabs fleeing sideways with their pincers crossed over their carapaces; and finally troops of porpoises struggling to match the speed of the *Nautilus*. But observing, studying and classifying were now out of the question. That night we had crossed two hundred leagues of the Atlantic. The shadows fell, and the sea was covered with darkness until the rising of the moon.

I went to my room, but could not sleep. I was troubled with dreadful nightmare. The horrible scene of destruction was continually before my eyes.

From that day, who could tell into what part of the North Atlantic basin the *Nautilus* would take us? Always with unaccountable speed; always in the midst of these northern fogs. Would it touch at Spitzbergen, or on the shores of Novaga Zemlya? Should we explore those unknown seas, the White Sea, the Sea of Kara, the Gulf of Ob, the Archipelago of Lyakhov, and the unknown coasts of Asia? I could not say. I could no longer judge of the time that was passing. The clocks on board had been stopped. It seemed, as in polar countries, that night and day no longer followed their regular course. I felt myself being drawn into that strange region where the fevered imagination of Edgar Allan Poe roamed. Like the fabulous Arthur Gordon Pym,[1] at every moment I expected to see that "shrouded human figure, very far larger in its proportions than any dweller among men."

I estimated (though, perhaps, I may be mistaken), I estimated this adventurous course of the *Nautilus* to have lasted fifteen or twenty days. And I know not how much longer it might have lasted, had it not been for the catastrophe which ended this voyage. Of Captain Nemo I saw nothing whatever now, nor of his second-in-command. Not a man of the crew was visible even for an instant. The *Nautilus* was almost incessantly under water. When we came to the surface to renew the air, the hatches opened and shut automatically. There were no more marks on the planisphere. I knew not where we were.

And the Canadian, too, his strength and patience at an end, appeared no more. Conseil could not draw a word from him; and fearing that, in a dreadful fit of madness, he might kill himself, watched him with constant devotion every moment. One can see given the conditions, that our situation was untenable.

One morning (what date it was I could not say), I had fallen into a heavy sleep towards the early hours, a sleep both painful and unhealthy, when I suddenly awoke. Ned Land was leaning over me, saying, in a low voice, "We are going to flee!"

I sat up.

"When shall we go?" I asked.

"Tonight. All supervision on board the *Nautilus* seems to have ceased. A stupor seems to reign on board. You will be ready, sir?"

"Yes; where are we?"

"In sight of land that I made out this morning through the fog,—twenty miles to the east."

"What country is it?"

"I do not know; but whatever it is, we will take refuge there."

"Yes, Ned, yes. We will flee tonight, even if the sea should swallow us up!"

"The sea is bad, the wind violent, but twenty miles in that light boat of the *Nautilus* does not frighten me. Unknown to the crew, I have been able to procure food and some bottles of water."

"I will follow you."

"But," continued the Canadian, "if I am surprised, I will defend myself; I will force them to kill me."

"We will die together, friend Ned."

I had made up my mind. The Canadian left me. I reached the platform, on which I could with difficulty support myself against the shock of the waves. They sky was threatening; but, as land was in those thick fogs, we must flee. Not a day nor an hour must be lost.

I returned to the salon, fearing and yet hoping to see Captain Nemo, wishing and yet not wishing to see him. What could I have said to him? Could I hide the involuntary horror with which he inspired me? No. It was better that I should not meet him face to face; better to forget him. And yet. . . .

How long seemed that day, the last that I should pass in the *Nautilus.* I remained alone. Ned Land and Conseil avoided speaking, for fear of betraying themselves.

At six I dined, but I was not hungry; I forced myself to eat in spite of my disgust, that I might not weaken myself.

At half-past six Ned Land came to my room, saying, "We shall not see each other again before our departure. At ten the moon will not be risen. We will profit by the darkness. Come to the boat; Conseil and I will wait for you."

The Canadian went out without giving me time to answer.

Wishing to verify the course of the *Nautilus,* I went to the salon. We were running N.N.E. at frightful speed, and more than fifty meters deep.

I cast a last look on these wonders of nature, on the riches of art heaped up in this museum, upon the unrivalled collection destined to perish at the bottom of the sea, with him who had formed it. I wished to fix a final impression of it in my mind. I remained an hour thus, bathed in the light of that luminous ceiling, and passing in review those treasures shining under their glass. Then I returned to my room.

I dressed myself in strong sea clothing. I collected my notes, placing them carefully about me. My heart beat forcefully. I could not slow its pulsations. Certainly my trouble and agitation would have betrayed me to Captain Nemo's eyes.

What was he doing at this moment? I listened at the door of his room. I heard the sound of steps. Captain Nemo was there. He had not gone to rest. At every moment I expected to see him appear, and ask me why I wished to flee. I was constantly on the alert. My imagination magnified everything. This frame of mind became at last so poignant, that I asked myself if it would not be better to go to the captain's room, see him face to face, and brave him with look and gesture.

It was the inspiration of a madman; fortunately I resisted the desire, and stretched myself on my bed to quiet my bodily agitation. My nerves were a little calmer, but in my excited brain I saw over again all my existence on board the *Nautilus;* every incident, either happy or unfortunate, which had happened since my disappearance from the *Abraham Lincoln*—the submarine hunt, the Torres Straits, the savages of Papua, the running aground, the coral cemetery, the passage of Suez, the island of Santorin, the Cretan diver, Vigo Bay, Atlantis, the icebank, the South Pole, the imprisonment in the ice, the fight among the squids, the storm in the Gulf Stream, the *Avenger,* and the horrible scene of the vessel sunk with all her crew. . . . All these events passed before my eyes like a moving backdrop unrolling. Then Captain Nemo seemed to grow enormously, his features to assume superhuman proportions. He was no longer my equal, but a man of the waters, the genie of the sea!

I was then half-past nine. I held my head between my hands to keep it from bursting. I closed my eyes, I would not think any longer. There was another half hour to wait, another half hour of a nightmare, which might drive me mad.

At that moment I heard the distant strains of the organ, a sad harmony to an undefinable chant, the wail of a soul longing to break these earthly bonds. I listened with every sense, scarcely breathing; plunged, like Captain Nemo, into that musical ecstasy, which was drawing him to the limits of the world.

Then a sudden thought terrified me. Captain Nemo had left his room. He was in the salon, which I must cross to escape. There I should meet him for the last time. He would see me, perhaps speak to me! A gesture of his might destroy me, a single word chain me on board!

But ten was about to strike. The moment had come for me to leave my room, and join my companions.

I must not hesitate, even if Captain Nemo himself should rise before me. I opened my door carefully; and even then, as it turned on its hinges, it seemed to me to make a dreadful noise. Perhaps the sound only existed in my own imagination.

I crept along the dark stairs of the *Nautilus,* stopping at each step to slow the pounding of my heart.

I reached the door in the angle of salon, and opened it gently. The salon was plunged in profound darkness. The strains of the organ sounded faintly. Captain Nemo was there. He did not see me. Even if the lights had been full on I do not think he would have noticed me, so entirely was he absorbed in the ecstasy.

I crept along the carpet, avoiding the slightest sound which might betray my presence. I was at least five minutes reaching the door, at the opposite side, opening into the library.

I was going to open it, when a sigh from Captain Nemo nailed me to the spot. I knew that he was rising. I could even see him, for the light from the library came through to the salon. He came towards me silently, with him arms crossed, gliding like a spectre rather than walking. His breast was swelling with sobs; and I heard him murmur these words (the last which ever struck my ear): "Almighty God! enough! enough!"

Was it a confession of remorse which thus escaped from this man's conscience? . . .

In desperation I rushed through the library, mounted the central staircase, and following the upper passage reached the boat. I crept through the opening, which had already admitted my two companions.

"Let us go! Let us go!" I exclaimed.

"At once!" replied the Canadian.

The orifice in the plates of the *Nautilus* was first closed, and fastened down by means of a wrench, with which Ned Land had provided himself; the opening in the boat was also closed. The Canadian began to loosen the bolts which still held us to the submarine boat.

Suddenly a noise within was heard. Voices were answering each other loudly. What was the matter? Had they discovered our flight? I felt Ned Land slipping a dagger into my hand.

"Yes," I murmured, "we know how to die!"

The Canadian had stopped in his work. But one word many times repeated, a dreadful word, revealed the cause of the agitation spreading on board the *Nautilus.* It was not we the crew were excited about!

"The maëlstrom! The maëlstrom!" I exclaimed.

The maëlstrom![2] Could a more dreadful word in a more dreadful situation have sounded in our ears? Were we then upon the dangerous coast of Norway? Was the *Nautilus* being drawn into this gulf at the moment our boat was going to leave its sides?

We knew that at the tide the pent-up waters between the islands of Faroe and Lofoten rush with irresistible violence, forming a whirlpool from which no vessel ever escapes. From every point of the horizon enormous waves were meeting, forming a gulf justly called the "Navel of the Ocean," whose power of attraction extends to a distance of fifteen kilometers. It, not only draws in ships, but whales are sacrificed, as well as white bears from the northern regions. It was there that the *Nautilus,* voluntarily or involuntarily, had been run by the Captain. The *Nautilus* was describing a spiral, the radius of which was lessening by degrees. The boat, which was still fastened to its side, was carried along with giddy speed. I felt that sickly

giddiness which arises from long-continued whirling round. We were in terror. Our horror was at its height, the circulation of our blood had stopped, our nerves were annihilated and we were covered with cold sweat, like a sweat of agony! And what noise around our frail boat! What roarings repeated by an echo miles away! What an uproar was that of the waters broken on the sharp rocks at the bottom, where the hardest bodies are crushed, and trees worn away, "with all the fur rubbed off," according to a Norwegian phrase!

What a situation to be in! We rocked frightfully. The *Nautilus* defended itself like a human being. Its steel muscles cracked. Sometimes it seemed to stand upright, and we with it!

"We must hold on," said Ned, "and look after the bolts! We may still be saved if we stick to the *Nautilus.* He had not finished the words, when we heard a cracking noise, the bolts gave way, and the boat, torn from its socket, was hurled like a stone from a sling into the midst of the whirlpool.

My head struck on an iron rib, and with the violent shock I lost all consciousness.

---

[1]The hero of Poe's antarctic adventure, *The Narrative of Arthur Gordon Pym* (1838). Poe had left the work unfinished, so in 1895 Verne completed the tale in his *Sphinx of the Icefields.* R.M.

[2]Verne's favorite American author, Edgar Allan Poe, also wrote a story about this famous whirlpool, *"A MS Found in a Bottle."*

◄ CHAPTER XXIII ►

CONCLUSION

hus ends the voyage under the seas. What passed during that night—how the boat escaped from the eddies of the maëlstrom—how Ned Land, Conseil, and myself ever came out of the gulf, I cannot tell. But when I returned to consciousness, I was lying in a fisherman's hut, on the Lofoten Isles. My two companions, safe and sound, were near me pressing my hands. We embraced each other heartily.

At that moment we could not think of returning to France. The means of communication between the north of Norway and the south are rare. And I am therefore obliged to wait for the steamboat running twice monthly from Cape North.

And among the worthy people who have so kindly received us, I revise my record of these adventures once more. It is exact. Not a fact has been omitted, not a detail exaggerated. It is a faithful narrative of this incredible expedition in an element inaccessible to man, but to which Progress will one day open a road.

Shall I be believed? I do not know. And it matters little, after all. What I now affirm is this: that I have a right to speak of these seas, under which, in less than ten months, I have crossed 20,000 leagues, in that submarine tour of the world, which has revealed so many wonders in the Pacific and Indian Oceans, the Red Sea, the Mediterranean, the North and South Polar Seas, and the Atlantic.

But what has become of the *Nautilus?* Did it resist the grasp of the maëlstrom? Does Captain Nemo still live? And does he still pursue under the ocean those terrible reprisals? Or, did he stop after that last hecatomb?

Will the waves one day carry to us the manuscript containing the history of his life? Shall I ever know the name of this man? Will the missing vessel tell us by its nationality that of Captain Nemo?

I hope so. And I also hope that his powerful vessel has conquered the sea at its most terrible gulf, and that the *Nautilus* has survived where so many other vessels have been lost! If it be so—if Captain Nemo still inhabits the ocean, his adopted country, may hatred be appeased in that savage heart! May the contemplation of so many wonders extinguish for ever the spirit of vengeance! May the judge disappear, and the philosopher continue the peaceful exploration of the sea! If his destiny be strange, it is also sublime. Have I not understood it myself? Have I not lived ten months of this extra-natural life? And to the question asked by Ecclesiastes 6,000 years ago, "Who has ever fathomed the depths of the abyss?" two men, among all men, have the right to give an answer—

CAPTAIN NEMO AND MYSELF.

AFTERWORD

About Jules Verne

Born in Nantes, France on February 8, 1828, Jules Verne grew up in this seaport town on Ile Feydeau, an island in the Loire River. His father, a maritime lawyer, was said to have the "soul of a classical poet" because he did some translations and read aloud the books of Sir Walter Scott and Fenimore Cooper. Jules' mother was descended from merchants and in her attic were sea chests packed with West Indies bills of lading. The maternal grandfather would periodically disappear to whereabouts unknown.

Verne's favorite books were *Robinson Crusoe* and *Swiss Family Robinson.* When the Loire flooded each March, he and his brother, Paul, imagined that their ship-shaped island was a vessel being swept out to sea. About town, were fishermen drying their nets and the day's catch of cod while tanned sailors told stories of exotic places. When Jules was eleven, he signed on as a cabin boy, but his father intercepted the ship downriver. His mother made Jules promise to "henceforth, travel only in my imagination."

Jules was to follow his father and grandfather into law and was sent to Paris to study. A handsome man with red-gold hair and magnetic eyes, Verne soon began writing and forming literary friendships, among the latter, Alexander Dumas. He joined a society that promoted heavier-than-air flight. Although he passed his law exams, his brother-in-law found Jules a seat on the Bourse (Stock Exchange) in 1857.

When he sold *Five Weeks in a Balloon* to Jules Hetzel in 1863, the result was a best-seller and a twenty-year, two-books-a-year contract with Hetzel. Verne quit the stock exchange with the comment: "I have written a novel in a new genre, one all my own." By 1905, he had written 65 volumes in the collection called *Voyages Extraordinaires,* which sent readers to the diamond fields of Africa, gold mining in the Yukon, through India on a steam elephant, down the Amazon, around the world in a flying machine, and into the space. More than 300 films have been made from his books.

Verne worked on *20,000 Leagues* from 1865 to 1868, writing on board his yacht, the *Saint-Michel.* He researched and talked with sailors and scientists; he took a trip across the Atlantic and talked with Cyrus Field, who was onboard, about things experienced in the recent laying of the transatlantic cable. In 1870, *20,000 Leagues* was published.

Verne's grave in Amiens shows the figure of Verne thrusting aside the lid of his tomb and reaching for the sky with an outstretched hand. The inscription reads: "Toward Immortality and Eternal Youth."

About Captain Nemo

When Verne styled his first draft of Captain Nemo, the captain was a Polish patriot who hated the Russians because they had killed his family in the rebellion of 1863. Jules Hetzel, the publisher, vetoed this idea since the political climate between France and Russia was touchy and there was no need to antagonize the Russians.

Thus, Nemo appears without a firm nationality. His handwriting is "Germanic," his dark complexion suggests to Aronnax a Mediterranean birthplace, he supports the Greek rebels and claims a brotherhood with the Indian pearl fisherman. His monogram "N" recalls that of the French emperor, Napoleon Bonaparte. Finally, in *The Mysterious Island,* Verne reveals Nemo's birthplace—but that is a secret for you to read there.

Was Nemo modeled after a real person? Robert Fulton, the inventor of the original *Nautilus* in 1800, has been suggested as have Colonel Charras, who opposed Napoleon III and Albert I of Monaco, a great oceanographer. The Russians have linked Nemo with Gustave Flourens, supporter of the Greek revolt. Even Sherlock Holmes' nemesis, Professor Moriarty, has been mentioned. Perhaps, Nemo is a composite of all these people, plus Verne himself, who shared the Captain's great passion for "music, freedom and the sea."

About the *Nautilus*

Undoubtedly, next to Captain Nemo, the *Nautilus* is the most important character of the book. Many submarines had been tried in the twenty-five years before Verne began working on *20,000 Leagues.* One of these, *Le Plongeur,* was at the Paris Exhibition in 1867 and from it, Verne may have captured the unique idea of a lifeboat riding piggy-back on the hull from this sub.

Nevertheless, there are many things about Verne's *Nautilus* that were unprecedented. Its use of electricity did not occur in a real submarine until 1881. Its airlock inspired designer Simon Lake in the 1890s. The diving suits were based on one actually invented and used by Benoit Rouquayrol and August Denayrouze in 1865; an improved suit similar to Nemo's was introduced by Denayrouze in 1875. Truly, the *Nautilus* was a magnificent scientific, imaginative invention and force for Captin Nemo's political perspective.

ABOUT THE ILLUSTRATOR

Ron Miller was born in Minneapolis, Minnesota in 1947. His illustrations have appeared in numerous publications, including *Space World, Science Digest, Washington Post Magazine*, and *Omni*, as well as on many book covers and jackets. One of today's foremost science fiction illustrators, he has works in the permanent collection of NASA, the Smithsonian Institution, and Pushkin Museum in Moscow. He has authored and co-authored several books on science fiction art, was the art director of the Albert Einstein Planetarium in the Smithsonian National Air and Space Museum, and has contributed his talents to several space exploration committees. *Twenty Thousand Leagues Under the Seas* is Ron's first book for the Unicorn Heirloom Collection. He first became interested in Jules Verne after watching the Disney version of *Twenty Thousand Leagues Under the Seas*. Later, he supplied artwork based on Jules Verne's work to the Discoveryland section of the European Disneyland. He owns a large collection of Verne's works— nearly 300 volumes. Ron lives with his wife and six cats in Virginia, and is continuing his work in science fiction.

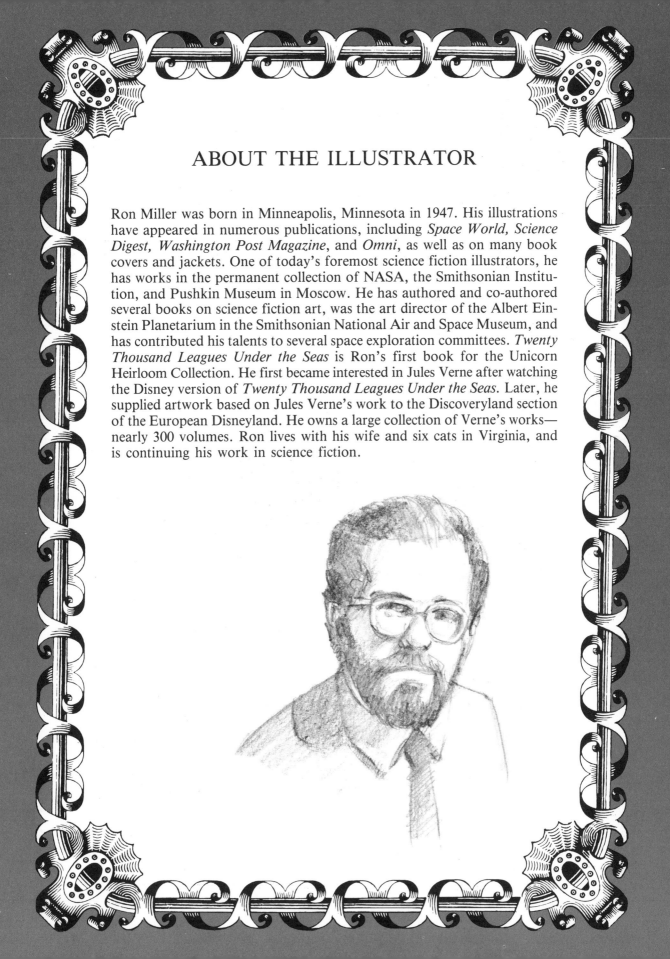

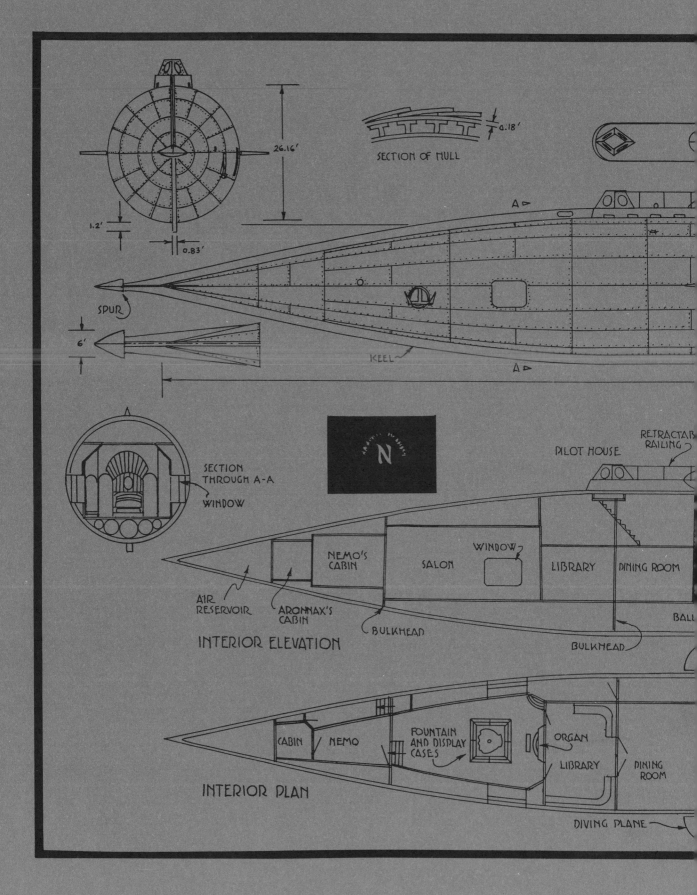

26.16'

1.2'

0.83'

SECTION OF HULL

0.18'

SPUR

6'

KEEL

A

A

SECTION
THROUGH A-A

WINDOW

N

PILOT HOUSE

RETRACTAB
RAILING

AIR
RESERVOIR

ARONNAX'S
CABIN

NEMO'S
CABIN

SALON

WINDOW

LIBRARY

DINING ROOM

BALL

BULKHEAD

BULKHEAD

INTERIOR ELEVATION

INTERIOR PLAN

CABIN

NEMO

FOUNTAIN
AND DISPLAY
CASES

ORGAN

LIBRARY

DINING
ROOM

DIVING PLANE